## Praise for *London Belongs to Me*

Featured by the *Huffington Post*, *Elle.com*, *USA TODAY*, *Cosmopolitan.com*, *Buzzfeed*, *MSN*, *PopSugar*, *Redbook*.com, *Reader's Digest Canada*, *Today's Parent*, *Yahoo! Beauty*, *Parade*, *Brit+Co*, and *Culturalist*

"Middleton's novel is a love letter to London … even the most skeptical or cynical readers will surrender to the many delights of this compelling narrative. Prepare to be seduced by engaging characters, irresistible in their own quirky way, and transported by keen descriptions of the sights, sounds, and tastes of London."

—*Kirkus Reviews*

"Middleton's novel is everything a chick-lit story should be. The heroine is so well-developed—with her quirks, nuances, and relatability … and Middleton's writing style helps the story flow beautifully and freely … This novel comes with our highest recommendations because it truly makes for a perfect read by the fireplace on a cold winter day. Top pick! 4.5/5 stars."

—*RT Book Reviews*

"The lovers of Bridget [Jones's] single girl, younger days in London are going to adore *London Belongs to Me*, the coming-of-age story of a girl (who could be Bridget's younger American cousin!) coming to London to find love and adventure."

—*Redbook*

"Pack your bags and wave hello to the Queen with this page-turning journey across the pond!"

—*Buzzfeed*

“Wow, folks, this new London-based novel will send your heart swooning. A stunning portrait of modern London life, with unput-downable prose, this [debut novel] belongs on every Anglophile’s bookshelf.”

—*PopSugar*

“*London Belongs to Me* is a delight. A sweet, nostalgic debut that will transport readers to those first heady days of being on one’s own in the great wide world.”

—Andrea Dunlop, author of *Losing the Light*

“Any Anglophile will relate to heroine Alex’s love of the Big Smoke—even when it’s not so kind to her. But while navigating the city and the theatre district, Alex is also navigating her first foray into new adulthood, and with that we get an emotive love letter to London that you’ll never want to end.”

—Nicole Trilivas, author of *Girls Who Travel*

“If you’ve ever had a dream and struggled to break into your field (especially the arts) you can relate to Alex trying to make it as a playwright. Middleton also explores Alex’s struggles with anxiety attacks, which I appreciated as I think addressing mental health issues in fiction is so important, not just portraying people with ‘perfect lives.’ And my geeky side loved the references to *Sherlock*, *Harry Potter*, and other fandoms. I’m looking forward to the sequel!”

—Kristin Contino, author of *The Legacy of Us*

Jacquelyn Middleton is an award-winning freelance writer. She previously worked in television broadcasting, and lives in Toronto with her husband and Schipperke. She's addicted to Bookstagram, loves London far too much, and has a thing for red Vespas.

*London, Can You Wait?* is her second novel.

Follow Jacquelyn:
Instagram @JaxMiddleton_Author, Twitter @JaxMiddleton,
Facebook @JacquelynMiddletonAuthor, or visit her webpage at
www.JacquelynMiddleton.com

**Also by Jacquelyn Middleton**

*London Belongs to Me*

A NOVEL

JACQUELYN MIDDLETON

KIRKWALL
BOOKS

**KIRKWALL BOOKS**

**USA – CANADA - UK**

This book is a work of fiction. Names, characters, places and incidents either are the product of the author's imagination or are used fictitiously. Any resemblance to actual persons, living or dead, business establishments, events or locales is entirely coincidental.

***London, Can You Wait?***

ISBN: 978-0-9952117-5-9

First Paperback Edition, October 2017

For my husband—my best friend, my biggest cheerleader, and my reason to believe that long-distance relationships are worth fighting for. xoxo

DEAR READERS,

The story of Alex and Mark in *London, Can You Wait?* can be read as a standalone; however, you will get more out of the characters, their backstory, and their world if you read *London Belongs to Me* first.

*London, Can You Wait?* takes place just over a year after *London Belongs to Me* concluded.

Enjoy!

P.S. I've included a glossary at the back of the book to explain a few terms (hello, mitching!) that might not be familiar to all readers.

# ONE

"Nothing makes us so lonely as our secrets."
– Paul Tournier

*Dublin suburbs, Sunday, August 6, 2017*

Mark would *never* forgive her.

Alex dove onto the duvet, violently shaking her purse upside down, scattering its contents across the pristine single bed. Wide-eyed and manic, her jittery hands scrambled across the soft material, tossing her American passport, a vial of prescription pills, and a football magazine onto a pile of serene white pillows, wrinkle-free and welcoming. Her heart lurched. *Come on, come on, Sinclair!* It had to be there somewhere…

Hiding in her makeup bag? Nope. Her wallet? The twenty-four-year-old wheezed and sputtered, her fingers flicking through shop loyalty cards and stabbing into the bill compartment. She flung British pounds on the bed, revealing…nothing. *Wait*—underneath her cracked, old-school iPod? An earbud cord ensnared her fingers, halting her feverish hunt. "Shit!" With a frustrated flick, she escaped the tangled web. *Damn. Where the hell is it?*

"Lex! Come see this." Mark's voice, buoyed with excitement,

echoed downstairs.

*Nooo.* Mark couldn't see *this*. A sour taste rose in her mouth. With open arms, she scooped up the mess from the bed, dumping it all into the purse with one exception—a small silver rectangular box, its lid slightly askew. Just two minutes earlier, Alex had whipped it open to find only the whiteness of its cardboard walls staring back at her. She peeked inside again, half hoping for a magically different result. Nope. *Empty, empty, empty!*

Mark's all-important gift used to call the pretty presentation box home. On her trip from London, the box had been stowed safely at the bottom of her purse. Mark needed it to be easily accessible, and Alex—being Alex—had refused to allow history to repeat. Nope. This little box had been kept close, spared a trip in her checked luggage so if her case went missing, Mark's amazing birthday surprise would still go ahead as planned.

And boy, had he planned. Alex had never seen him so driven or committed, not even with acting roles. It was like the twenty-five-year-old's life depended on the timely completion of this task. For eight months, he was like a man possessed: complicated phone calls during breaks on set, entire paycheques eaten up getting everything just so. He had even flown into Dublin five times on the sly from Aberdeen, San Francisco, and Bangkok to oversee the final details in person. Mark had joked that this present for his mother was the gift that kept on giving—it had given him his first grey hair, thousands of frequent flyer points, and plenty of sleepless nights.

By contrast, Alex's role in the whole production couldn't have been simpler: carry the gift through security at Gatwick and keep it safe during the hour-long flight to Dublin. *Easy peasy*, as British school kids say—and yet, sure enough, she had screwed everything up.

Alex fell to her knees, her flouncy sundress pooling around her hips as she peeked under the bed, searching for a hint of curly red ribbon or a sliver of nickel brass. *Dammit.* Only a few dust bunnies cowered in the darkness. How could she explain that the computerized key Mark had coddled for weeks had vanished? The key was the only one in their possession, the only one that would open the front door to the newly renovated dream home Mark had purchased for his mother. Without it, Mark's big reveal was ruined, and he would be crushed. *Great!* Nausea rolled in her stomach. Unlike previous goofy mistakes, Mark wouldn't find this cute. He would never forgive her.

The dulcet tones of the von Trapp children blared downstairs from the living room. What was Mark doing, blasting *The Sound of Music* on his mother's old television? Whatever. As long as it kept him down there…

Her blue eyes darted once more around Mark's boxy childhood bedroom, her glance ignoring sun-faded football ribbons, a long-abandoned PlayStation, their luggage piled in the corner…*wait a minute*. Mark's backpack…was missing. He'd had it earlier, hadn't he? The morning's packing had been a cartoonish blur. Mark's train down from Aberdeen had arrived late, leaving him with just minutes to grab some clothes and necessities. She had pitched in, hurriedly making space in their carry-on bags, swapping belongings in the process. *Maybe*... Could the key have ended up in Mark's backpack?

The TV's volume downstairs crept up slightly with an added vocalist. "…*So long, farewell, auf Wiedersehen*...Lex, where *are* you?"

Her guy—who would only release his inner songbird after a few pints—was giving Julie Andrews a run for her money stone-cold sober. Someone was definitely in high spirits—for now.

*The backpack. It has to be in Mark's backpack!*

"Yeah, coming!" Alex sprung to her feet, a flood of pins and needles attacking her calves.

She hobbled out of the bedroom and paused atop the staircase, its drop rivaling the steepest of London Underground's escalators. *Be careful.* A neck-breaking tumble down this threadbare death trap was one misstep away. She clutched the handrail, but it wobbled, about to give way. There wasn't any need to fix it; Mark's mother no longer ventured upstairs. Alex's hand flew to the wall for safety as her bare feet met the first step, then the next. Her fingers skirted a collection of family memories, lovingly embraced by dusty mismatched frames hanging from the faded wallpaper.

One photo, a professionally snapped black and white shot from a wedding, slowed her pace. You didn't have to be Sherlock to deduce from the picture that Mark and his older sister Grace were related. The Keegan siblings shared fair complexions, jet-black hair, perfectly arched black eyebrows, and most notably, doe eyes the colour of dark chocolate. With one glance, they could melt your heart, persuade you to rob a bank—probably both at the same time. Grace and her husband, Rhys, the tall curly-haired fellow embracing her in the photograph, had recently moved back from Wales and were in on Mark's carefully choreographed surprise, too. Like Alex, they had a simple task: bring their mother home from their family holiday in Cornwall and arrive at her semi-detached house at three o'clock.

Alex always felt awkward and self-conscious when meeting new people, but these three driving from the Dublin airport weren't just *any* people, they were Mark's nearest and dearest. During the twenty months she had been dating Mark, Alex had never met his mother, his sister, or his brother-in-law, but she had heard plenty of heartwarming stories, and here was the photographic proof. Picture after picture showcased idyllic moments: seaside picnics, Christmases complete with the obligatory paper crowns, and baby photos—*so many* baby photos.

Her eyes landed on a giggly infant, toothless with chipmunk cheeks and Michelin Man arms. *Is that Mark?* Once when he was drunk, Mark let it slip that his sister called him 'Fappy'—a combo of fat and happy—and this photo proved why. Alex's sexy beau, a favourite of fangirls everywhere, had been a chubby cherub of a baby.

Several other photos shared pride of place along the stairway wall, but Alex hadn't been in Mark's orbit long enough to know whom all the cheeky children and dashing adults were—and if she didn't find that key, she might never find out. Botching Mark's surprise would destroy that desperately desired good first impression with his mother, and maybe even shatter Alex's relationship with her son. More than anything, Alex wanted to *be* on this wall, *one day*, to have a future with Mark, a proper commitment, but those hopes were fading with each passing minute. Two weeks had passed since her last panic attack, but she was currently swimming dangerously close to the rocks.

"Wish me luck," she whispered to the photos and raced off the bottom step, leaving the Keegans' picture-perfect life behind.

Entering the living room, she inhaled slowly, deeply. *Don't show panic. Be breezy.* Mark didn't need to know about the butterfly battle raging within her stomach. A wide smile crept across her face, just missing her eyes as they skimmed the floor for his backpack. "Hey babe." She fussed with her blonde hair tied in a high ponytail.

"Hello stranger." Mark's thumb was getting a workout, flipping through TV channel after TV channel. "Were you in my old bedroom, discovering my teenage secrets?" He dropped the remote on the sofa and stood up, his hands claiming her waist. Leaning in, his mouth didn't hesitate, meeting hers with gentle but needy kisses as he pressed against her.

Alex parted her lips and slid her hands up Mark's arms and into his thick hair, worry and loneliness letting go as their kisses grew deeper and more urgent. *Finally.* For four weeks, she had craved his touch, this private moment. *Thank God, he tastes the same.* A dizzying surge of warmth and happiness flooded her body, all the way down to her toes, curling into the carpet.

Mark's hands skimmed upwards from her waist, prompting every nerve ending in their path to scream, *Don't stop!* It was amazing how kissing him could still make her forget the simplest things: her name, where she was...how to stand. She grabbed his denim-covered ass, steadying herself as breaths grew fast and shallow and his hands cupped her breasts.

His lips pulled away. "Lex?"

Her eyes fluttered open, catching a streak of light by the front door…a sunbeam, stretching across a backpack—THE backpack. Her stare bounced back to Mark.

He pressed his lips against hers again, a soft, lingering peck promising so much more. Alex's heart raced, as much for her boyfriend as what she hoped to find loose in that bag.

He pulled away with a smile. "This weekend's going to be awesome."

"One to remember." Alex ducked under his chin, hiding her face.

Mark wrapped his arms around her. "I can't wait to show Mum the kitchen—it's completely wheelchair accessible, and the walk-in tub…it's amazing." His eyes swept the cosy room where he spent many an evening as a child. "I made a promise to Dad that I'd look after Mum. I just want to feel like I've done him proud, you know? Not be a disappointment…"

"Mark, you are *not* a disappointment…believe me."

"I've always wanted to buy Mum a new house. Lex, I can't believe I've actually gone and done it."

She lifted her head. "When are they arriving?"

"Soon. Gracie just texted her ten-minute warning from the car."

Alex's stomach fell. *Great. And the award for 'Worst Girlfriend Ever' goes to…*

The TV bellowed with a familiar voice tinged with a bang-on Scottish accent.

"Oh, God…" Mark let go of Alex and lunged for the remote, turning the TV off. "Nothing worse than seeing this ugly mug on screen."

Alex edged towards the backpack, her tight lips dissolving into a proud smile; it was Mark's breakthrough BBC role in *Lairds and Liars*. "Freddie said they're running the first two seasons back to back for the long weekend. You should be flattered."

"With all my new projects, people will be sick of me."

"Fat chance of that. Those fans from the airport tailed us most of the way here. Didn't you notice?"

"Seriously? Were you ever that devoted to Ben Whishaw?"

"You mean *stalky*? God, no."

A shrill car horn trumpeted from the driveway and Mark jumped. "Christ, that was ten minutes?"

Alex twitched, pointing at the backpack. "I'll toss that in your room, so your mum won't have to steer her wheelchair around it."

"Good idea." He peeked through the front window's net curtains. "Rhys might need a hand." With bare feet and a cheek-busting grin, he rushed out the front door.

Alex grabbed his backpack and scurried up the stairs. Just steps into his bedroom, she dumped the bag's contents onto the bed. She separated each item on the duvet: Mark's iPad, his headphones, a dog-eared script, her *Glamour* magazine, a yellow Matchbox car, some new fan letters, his Vespa key…but no *house* key tied with a red ribbon. A burst of summer warmth sailed up the stairs, carrying laughter and happy voices into the bedroom. The front door banged shut, sending Alex's heart crashing into her stomach.

"*Fuuuck*," she mumbled under her breath. Reality couldn't be avoided now—she must have dropped the key in the rush at their London flat. It was official: she had ruined Niamh's birthday, and that desperately desired good first impression? *So long, farewell, auf Wiedersehen, good-night...*

She punched the backpack. Mark was usually pretty easy-going, but this…*this* might crack him in half.

"Hey!"

She jumped, her heart nearly bursting from her chest. "You scared the crap out of me." She shoved the backpack on top of the mess.

Mark snickered naughtily around the doorjamb. "What are you like? Come, meet my family."

Alex's eyes welled up. "Mark, I'm so sorry…"

"About what?" He glanced over his shoulder, down the stairs where excited Irish accents stepped all over one another.

"I've lost your mum's present." Chasing breaths, she blurted out the words. "I've lost the key—"

"No, you haven't." A grin lit up his face as he walked into the room.

"What—"

"I took it from your purse." His hand disappeared into his back pocket, pulling out a key dangling from a small pewter disk. "I grabbed it after we came in, when you dashed to the loo."

Her jaw dropped.

"Sorry babe, forgot to tell you. I put it on a special keychain."

Alex breathed a huge sigh of relief. "I was turning myself inside out with worry!" She pouted, playfully slapping him on the chest.

"Aw, Mouse!"

Mouse—small in stature and addicted to cheese sandwiches; Mark's nickname for her was a perfect fit. Just hearing it in his adorable Irish brogue was enough to release the vice gripping her chest.

"Dad loved this old keychain, ya know…" He laid the jumble of nickel and pewter, engraved with a treble clef, face up in the palm of her hand and cleared his throat. "Sure, it's old and banged up, but Mum will love it. It…" His voice trembled. "It tells our story."

"Aw, babe. It's lovely." A smile tugged the corners of her mouth. She flipped the keychain over, her fingers tracing over a faint engraving: *Niamh Grace Mark Kieran* inside the outline of a Celtic heart. "Who's Kieran?"

"Oh, one of my middle names. Keegan boys get them; the girls don't. It's a sore point with Gracie." He clutched Alex's hand and slowly scooped up the birthday surprise from her palm. "Is the box around?"

Alex grabbed the silver gift box from the bed and lunged at Mark, desperate for a hug.

He squeezed her butt, his eyebrows furrowing. "You okay?"

"Marmalade…" Alex whispered.

Mark kissed her forehead. Marmalade was their private SOS, a code word signaling that one of them needed a reassuring *I'm here, babe, you'll be all right* during a difficult or anxious moment.

"You've got this, Mouse."

She pressed her lips to his neck. "I want today to be perfect for you, and I really want your family to like me…"

He pulled back, nudging her bangs from her eyes. "Mum will love you."

"God, I hope so." She handed over the box.

"She will. She can't wait to meet you—and call me crazy, but I can't wait to meet *your* mum. It's about time."

Alex winced. "Ooh, too much excitement. I need another pee. Give me three minutes?"

"I'll give you two, tops." Mark kissed her on the nose and glanced at the gift in his grip. "I can't wait to see Mum's face! We'll give it to her at dinner." He tossed the box up in the air and snatched it, his grin growing as he bounded out of the room.

Alex quickly scooped up Mark's scattered belongings, dropping them in his backpack. One item was stuck in the crevice between the bed and the wall: a small square black box with *Brown Thomas* barely visible on its lid. Its bashed-in corners and scuffed silver lettering drew her curiosity. She shook it and something rolled around inside. *Cufflinks?* Mark was like a magpie—always carting around various family heirlooms.

A sharp tug removed the stubborn lid. Another box lay nestled inside, this one gunmetal grey with rounded corners and a hinged lid. Her thumb pulled upwards, the box's tight hinge whining, hesitant to budge. Finally, the lid popped open, revealing its secret.

Lost for breath…lost for words…Alex snapped the box closed.

# TWO

"D'ya see this sword, Mackintosh?" Mark pointed a small plastic knife at Alex, lying on her stomach across a tartan blanket. "It once belonged to the Clan Dhònnchaidh, but my ancestors claimed it in a great battle." He snarled in a Scottish burr, his eyes darkening beneath the brim of his baseball cap. "If I find out yer lyin', I swear on the graves of my forefathers, I'll slice yer from ear to ear, leaving ya to rot in a ditch outside Dalnaspidal where even the ravens—" His face froze. "Fuck it! I got that wrong, didn't I? What's that line again?"

Alex inhaled deeply, enjoying the fragrance of blooming hyacinth and fresh-cut grass wafting through St. Stephen's Green, a popular oasis in the heart of Dublin. Her finger traced along Mark's *Lairds and Liars* script. "It's '*...a ditch outside Dunalstar...*'" She stumbled. "I mean, *Dunalasteer*...no, '*Dunalastair where even the ravens wouldn't pick your carcass clean.*' Jeez!" She laughed. "This is hard!"

"I know, right—these Gaelic names!" Mark scrunched his eyes. "They're going to revoke my Irish card if I can't get them right!"

Alex laughed harder. A goldcrest's high-pitched *zi-zi-zee* chirped from a nearby tree overlooking their sunny patch of grass.

"At this rate, I'll still be muttering lines to myself on the train back to Aberdeen. People will think I'm certifiable."

"Try again?" Alex plucked a strawberry from the takeout container sat between them.

Mark dipped the plastic knife into a small pot of Nutella, his easy smile spreading through his three-day stubble. "Actually, can we back up? I've been toying with whispering the lines *before* that, about his wife's disappearance." The knife reappeared, covered in gooey, chocolatey, hazelnut happiness, and he smoothed it over a croissant, recently baked and still warm. "Whatcha think?"

She chewed the sweet strawberry, contemplating. "Well, a subtle delivery will definitely make the words more shocking, more…visceral." Her eyes fell back to the page as she swallowed. "And maybe, *pause* before you mention the laird's drowning, *then* launch into the rant about the sword, forefathers, ravens…it will hit the audience harder, for sure."

"That's my girl! You always know the best way to deliver lines."

"Writer's intuition, babe!" She grinned, pushing herself up from the blanket. She leaned over his script and their Monday afternoon picnic of fruit, baked goods, and cider, kissing him.

He held her kiss then let go, his eyes lost in hers. "Well, sexy playwright lady, there's no one else I'd rather practice lines with." He smiled and bit into his croissant coated in nutty sweetness. A smudge of chocolate remained on his upper lip.

"There's no one else I'd rather have as my dramaturg." Her thumb lovingly swept the Nutella from his lip. "That idea you had this morning, I think it'll fix that scene I'm struggling with." She sucked her thumb. "Changing the thirtysomething to a pregnant teen…it raises the stakes."

"See, we're a team, Sinclair!" Mark offered his croissant for a bite. "Mum thinks so, too."

Alex bit off a small piece and sat beside him, savouring the creamy chocolate and basking in the gentle, warm breeze flirting with her hair. “Yesterday was so lovely. Your mum…her tears when she held your dad’s keychain…” Alex laid her head on Mark’s shoulder. “She kept whispering, ‘*Mark, you shouldn’t have.*’ It made me love you so much, I could burst.”

“Aw, Mouse.” He swapped his lunch for his Ray-Bans. “It did my heart good to see her so happy.” He nodded, staring at the blanket. “But…”

“But what?”

Shielded by his sunglasses, his eyes washed over her. “Nothing.”

Alex lifted her head. “I know you miss your dad even more at times like this, but he would be so proud of you. We all are. Grace couldn’t stop gushing about her baby brother—it was so cute!”

A wistful smile briefly raised his cheeks. He cradled Alex’s face in his hands and kissed her softly on the lips. “I’m glad you got on so well with her—and Mum. They’ve both been bugging me to meet you for ages. Prepare yourself, though—you’re in for lots of Facebook comments, texts, and random calls. When they like someone, they *really* like them! You’ll be wishing you never met them—or me!”

“Fat chance of that, Keegan!” Alex kissed him. “They couldn’t have been more welcoming. Gracie and I got on like a house on fire.”

“Yeah, about that…what *were* you conspiring about with her? Don’t deny it—you two went quiet when I walked back into the room.”

“Girl stuff!” Alex theatrically zipped her lips.

“Oh, really? Well, that’s me put in my place.” He chuckled. “Honestly, yesterday couldn’t have gone better.”

Alex furrowed her brow. “I hope I can say the same when we

visit Florida in December."

Mark sipped his can of cider. "Robbie and I get along great over FaceTime..."

"My *brother* isn't the problem."

"I'll charm your mom and sister, you'll see." He took another swig.

"Mom and Kathryn are an acquired taste, and with you being an actor..."

Mark grinned. "They'll see how suited we are for each other."

She shook her head. "They're nothing like Dad, Mark. He's supportive of the whole writing/acting thing—Mom isn't."

"It'll be okay, really." He kissed her temple. "It's not the end of the world if she doesn't like me, and anyway, those ten days will fly by. We'll be in New York, snapping selfies by that massive Christmas tree before you know it. Just you and me, yeah?"

Her frown turned into a big smile. "Yeah! New York will be so romantic!" She snatched a strawberry. "Hard to believe, though. I haven't been back to the States in over two years. You've been to five countries since January! Crazy!"

Mark took a deep breath. "That country count might creep up to six, Mouse...the PR guy at the BBC sent me a text this morning—four of the *Lairds* cast are going to the comic con in Toronto..."

"Yeah...?" She chewed, swallowing quickly.

"They kinda want me to join them. You could come too!"

"Ooh, yeah! I've never been to Canada...!" She picked up her phone from the blanket and opened her calendar app. "When is it?"

"Three days after *Lairds* wraps...we'd have to fly out on August 31$^{st}$. The con runs Friday through Sunday. Truth be told, I could really use the cash. Mum's house emptied my savings, and the con would be a quick payday."

Alex squinted. "Shit, my attachment starts on the 30$^{th}$..."

"Aw, really? Christ, you can't bail on the National." Mark bit his lip. "It's just a con…I don't have to go…"

"Don't skip it because I can't go. With all the *Lairds* gang, you'll have a great time. I bet the organizers will do Q&A panels and group photo ops, and the fans will love it. Really, Mark, you should go."

"Are you sure? It means I'll only see you for, like, two days before I'm off again."

"I know, but you'll be back down the weekend *before* that—"

"What's the weekend before that?" He pulled out his phone.

Alex glanced at her calendar. "That industry BBQ thingy in Greenwich."

"Ah, right. Yeah, I totally forgot to put that in my schedule. God, I feel like a yo-yo…up and down between Aberdeen and London."

Alex scrolled through a list of industry events in her phone, and one caught her eye. As much as she'd prefer to have Mark home with her, she didn't want him to miss out. "You know, maybe you should stick around for your movie at the Toronto International Film Festival? It starts after the con."

"I already told the director no, but…" He looked up from his screen. "I guess I *could* do TIFF. I've never done a film fest before…"

"That South Africa shoot was almost a year ago. It'll be fun seeing your castmates again—"

"Yeah…yeah, *it would*." Mark added the con and TIFF to his phone's calendar.

"And you'd still be home for a few days before you leave for country number seven…"

"Austria? Yeah, that shoot's gonna be a tough one."

Alex left her phone on the blanket and twisted a grape from its bunch. "Hey, remember that clip? The one of Whishy at TIFF for

*Cloud Atlas*? So many fans!"

"Yeah, it was fandemonium! I'll have to stock up on Sharpies."

She popped the grape in her mouth. "Aw, I really wish I could go, but…I'm excited about my attachment."

He pulled her close into a hug. "As you should be, Mouse. They don't just invite anyone."

Alex sank into his chest. "That's why I have to stay, give it my all."

"Someone's gonna be writing up a storm while I'm fighting off fangirls and schmoozing at TIFF! You'll be too busy to miss me."

"Yeah, won't even notice you're gone!" She sat up and returned to his *Lairds* script. "So, that ditch in Dunalastair? Start at the top?" Alex smiled longingly at Mark and snatched his half-eaten croissant.

***MARK***
***Thirteen years earlier***
***Dublin, October 2004***

"Mark Keegan! What the hell?" Fifteen-year-old Grace snatched her brother by the ear.

"Ow! Christ, Gracie!" Mark dropped a half-empty bottle of cider onto the grass and his eyes flew to his recently acquired friends, a group of boys known for drinking, skipping class, and talking back at teachers.

"Swigging booze in the park during lunch? *Jesus*, Mark, you're only twelve!"

"Let *go* of me—"

Mark's friends laughed and taunted him. "Oooh, Keegan, gettin' beat up by your sister? Ya big wuss!"

"Gracie! Let go!"

"Embarrassed are you, Fappy? *Tough*!" She yanked his ear and marched him out of the park, their feet crunching and kicking through piles of crumpled brown leaves.

"Where are we going?"

"Home for a bollocking, you little wanker."

"But class starts in ten minutes—"

"Like you care! No wonder your grades have sucked lately." Grace exchanged his ear for the arm of his jacket and dug in her fingers. "Shut up and be thankful you're dealing with me and not Mum. She's doing a double shift at the dry cleaners, so your arse is mine."

"You can't do this." He tried to shake his sister off. "You're not in charge of me!" Mark tugged his arm away, sending a packet of cigarettes to the ground.

"Jesus!" Grace snapped up the evidence. "Smoking, too? What *else* have you been doing? Have you been getting *high* with those idiots? Because I know *all* about them, Mark. They're losers. They spend most afternoons in detention—"

"Lay off, Gracie. You don't understand."

"Oh, I understand all right." She waved the cigarette package in his face. "Every night last week? You weren't at footy practice, were you? You were in detention, *admit it*!"

Mark swiped at her hand but missed. "Gracie, give them back. Please don't tell Mum. Come on! Give 'em, *back*!"

She stashed the cigarettes in her bag. "Was it for leaving school grounds during lunch like today? Or mitching class…or drinking? Is that what you do these days? Sneak off on the way back from gym class? Meet your new eejit friends in the park, smoke some fucking weed?! Tell me, or I'm marching you straight to Mum right now!"

Mark had never seen his sister so angry with him and knew she wasn't bluffing. "I've only tried it a few times…"

"Once is too bloody many!" She shoved him towards their semi-detached house. "Get your arse inside before someone sees you."

Grace slammed the front door behind them. "Mark, what the FUCK! Are you really this *thick*? Don't you see that you're throwing your life away? What's Mum gonna say? Do you have *any* idea what this will do to her?"

"Don't *tell* her then. Christ, Gracie, just…leave me the fuck alone!"

"Listen, you have to stop this shit, NOW! Dad's been dead for nine weeks, and you going off the rails like this, becoming a bad lad—that's just not *you*, Mark."

He rolled his eyes. "Okay, I'll stop—*I promise*."

"A promise? From you? That's worth NOTHING, and you know it. All you do lately is lie." She shook her head furiously. "I can only hide so much of your crap from Mum. Are you hell-bent on hurting her? Didn't you learn *anything* two weeks ago?"

"I didn't do that on purpose—"

"Oh, come on. That was a *dirty* tackle. You almost broke that poor kid's leg, and everyone saw it. Do you think your coach suspended you for nothing? Look, I know your heart is broken with everything that's happened, Mark—*mine is too*! But you can't take out your anger on the football pitch or hang around with those louts, trying to blot out your feelings with drugs and booze."

Mark's cheeks grew pink with anger. "So, what? You want me to smile? Pretend everything is great? Act like happy little Mark, the way I was before he..." Mark swallowed heavily. "Sorry, Gracie, I can't. No, I won't! I *like* hanging out with Cathal and his mates. It's not hurting anyone, so mind your own business."

"Jesus, are you *serious*? After everything you've put this family through *already*—" Grace bit her tongue, but it was too late.

"I *knew* it!" Mark's eyes filled with tears. "You blame *me*, don't you? You *and* Mum, you blame ME—"

"Oh, God, no—Mark, I didn't mean it like that. I'm sorry—"

"No, *go on*, I wanna hear you say it, Gracie! Don't stop. SAY IT! It's ALL my fault—all of it. If it wasn't for *me*—"

"Don't do this to yourself...not again." Grace began to cry. She leaned over and pulled her brother to her chest. "Nobody blames you, Mark."

In her embrace, Mark's expression turned from fury to anguish and a flood of hot tears overwhelmed his cheeks. The Keegan siblings crumpled to the living room floor, sobbing in each other's arms, their loss still raw.

After a few minutes, Grace broke through their tears.

"It wasn't anybody's fault, Fappy. It was God's will or fate or something."

Mark wiped his nose with his sleeve. "What do you know…you're only fifteen."

"I know more than you do." She handed him a tissue. "So, you better listen to me, or I'll box your ears again, you little eejit."

They sat in silence for a minute.

"Gracie, do you ever wish you were someone else?"

She snickered. "Sure, Britney bloody Spears."

"Not popstars, just a normal everyday person…but with a happier life."

"No, not really. I wish I could've swapped places with *you*, though, just for five minutes…"

"Me? *Why*?"

"I would give anything to have talked to Dad like you did, one last time. You were so lucky, being awake that morning. What did he say *exactly*? Tell me again, Mark."

"Gracie, you know what he said. You've asked me a hundred times, and I've told you a hundred times."

"But tell me *again*."

Mark told her for the one hundred and first time.

Grace smiled. "There you go. You made a sacred promise, and Keegans *never* break their promises, right? *Please*, Mark, promise you'll keep your word to Dad, from today onwards?"

Mark nodded solemnly. "I promise."

# THREE

*London, Saturday, November 4, 2017*

A congregation of uninvited guests—a dozen teenage girls—loitered across from All Saints Church, a quaint Victorian building draped by mature trees in Hackney, East London. Fuelled by coffee and hormones, they giggled and fidgeted, ready to pounce. A pack of parka-cloaked paparazzi kept them company, yawning beneath their long-lensed cameras.

"Hey guys!" Alex zigzagged through a slow-moving parade of shiny SUVs on Livermere Road and caught up to her friends on the church's doorstep. "Mark just texted!" she whispered to Lucy, Freddie, and Simon as she eyed the crowd across the street. "He's landed. He's on his way!"

"Lovely jubbly!" Freddie tossed his wavy fringe out of his eyes and hugged Alex. "I've all but forgotten what my bezzie mate looks like."

"Bride or groom?" An usher foisted a cluster of wedding programs under their noses.

"We're friends with both," said Simon, his Canadian accent

standing out. "The groom's side, I guess—"

"No, bride. Definitely bride," Alex interrupted. "Let's sit on her side…just in case." She looked past the usher and smiled at the clusters of tall glass vases that held burning white candles at the end of each pew. The amber glow danced along the wood floor, creating a romantic, fairy-tale setting.

The usher swept his hand towards the centre aisle of the Gothic church.

Freddie put on his glasses and glanced over the program. He hunched his shoulders, shrinking his six-foot frame to whisper in Alex's ear. "It's criminal! I mean, who doesn't have bridesmaids?" The twenty-five-year-old barely paused to catch his breath, pulling Lucy into the conversation. "Do you reckon it's some weird tradition…not being British? Weddings shouldn't be messed with. Go full-on traditional or don't bother."

"Is that what you're gonna do, you big girl?" teased Lucy.

"Steady on! I won't become Mr. Desjardins anytime soon." He raised his voice, ensuring that his fiancé could hear. "We can't plan anything until Simon tells his parents he's gay."

Looking up from his program, Simon gave Alex a tight-lipped smile.

The four friends surveyed the left side of the church. Eager aunties wrapped in autumn hues sat beside fidgety uncles. Accents from around the United Kingdom and abroad echoed against the old walls, and the scent of hairspray and aftershave hung in the damp air.

"I think this is the best we can get and still sit together." Freddie pointed at two back-to-back rows. "Four seats here, two seats there."

"You guys take that row." Lex nodded, glancing at her phone. "I'll sit behind you, save a place for Mark."

Simon scooted along the bench. "*If* he shows," the thirty-five-year-old whispered to his fiancé. The old wooden pew groaned under their weight despite Simon's yoga-toned physique and Freddie's tall, waif-like figure.

"I bagsie the aisle." Lucy sat down beside Freddie and slipped out of her cape, showing off the silk tiers of her aqua dress and a twisted silver bracelet cuff, a family heirloom from Jamaica.

Freddie looked over at Lucy and squinted. "What's *that*?"

Lucy hunched her shoulders, looking at her program. Her dark curls tumbled over her neck. "What's what?"

"You *know*. Stop hiding it. Move your hair."

"It's nothing."

Freddie smiled wildly. "Oh, no, it's definitely *something*." He glanced up at Alex for support, but she was still in the aisle, texting.

Simon twisted around Freddie, desperate for a peek.

"It's a *burn* from three days ago." Lucy's nose dove deeper into her program. "Never straighten your hair in a rush."

"No, it's not. I *know* a love bite when I see one, lady!" Freddie licked his lips. "Lucy Hardy, *who* did you shag—"

"Crap!" Alex brushed her bangs out of her eyes. "Mark had to ditch his cab…traffic's a nightmare. He's walking here!" She ducked into the pew behind her friends and shrugged off her wool coat. Her hands smoothed the skirt of her tea-length plum dress.

Simon turned around. "Pretty dress, Lex." The up-and-coming womenswear designer nodded his approval.

"Thanks!"

Freddie joined in with a grin. "I *love* the subtle sparkle, but the Lady of the Forest thing you've got going on is a bit too… Galadriel."

"Forest, what?" Alex ran her fingers along the band of chiffon that nipped in at her waist.

Lucy pivoted to face her friend. "There's an oak leaf stuck in your fascinator."

"You're kidding?"

Freddie leaned over, plucking the crunchy leaf from her hair.

A flush reddened Alex's face. "Ergh, thanks." She patted her updo for any additional accoutrements courtesy of Mother Nature.

Freddie twirled the leaf in his fingers and playfully tucked it in Simon's jacket pocket.

A new arrival invaded Alex's peripheral vision. "Harry!" She leapt to her feet.

"Hi!" He happily kissed her on both cheeks and bent down to do the same with Lucy. "Hello, you!"

Harry Manville looked immaculate, every inch of his navy suit tailored exquisitely, like he had stepped out of a Tom Ford advert in *GQ*. "Can I squeeze in beside you, Lex?"

"Sorry, I'm saving a spot for Mark."

"We've got room." Simon shifted to his left and motioned for Freddie to follow, freeing up space on Lucy's left.

"Where's your plus one, then?" Lucy asked as Harry slipped past her knees.

"Stood me up. A friend needed her today more than I did. You?"

"Chickened out—didn't ask him." The twenty-four-year-old rolled her eyes.

"You? Chicken?" Harry smirked.

"Aw, there he is." Alex leaned onto Lucy's bench. "Tom looks like he belongs on a wedding cake."

The groom took his place at the front of the church, snapping his knuckles under the cuffs of his morning suit while he chatted with the vicar. Even on his wedding day, Tom Chadwick-Smythe looked raffish and chic, like he had just rolled out of bed. He raked a hand through his tousled brown hair. Alex caught his eye and matched the thespian's crooked grin with a soppy smile.

Freddie's right hand crept into the inside pocket of his jacket.

"Why so fidgety?" Simon scratched his neatly trimmed beard. "Cut it out."

*Crinkle.* Freddie ducked his head. *Crinkle.* "But…I'm *staaarving.*"

Lucy chuckled into her hand. "You didn't?!"

Simon's eyes shifted from his fiancé to Lucy and back again. "Didn't what?"

"He's packing snacks," said Lucy.

Harry and Alex laughed.

"Cheese and onion crisps." Freddie revealed the package with a flourish, winking over his shoulder at Alex. "Want one?"

"Freddie Ryan, bloody hell. How old are you—five?" Simon looked around, making sure no one had noticed. "Put them away."

Freddie frowned, his hand landing heavily in his lap. "Yes, Dad."

"Are we're cramping your style, Si?" Lucy shifted in her seat, giving her butt a break from the rock-hard oak bench. "I'd hate to be blamed for damaging your reputation as London Field's most stylish shopkeeper." Being snarky to Simon was becoming Lucy's favourite pastime.

Simon sneered, staring at the colourful Cyberman tattoo on Lucy's bicep. "Shopkeeper? I'm so much more than *that.*"

Harry ignored their snippy exchange and twisted around, resting his right arm on the back of the bench. Alex was looking at the weathered leather Bibles slotted in front of her knees, and he flicked one of the bowing purple feathers in her fascinator. "I can't believe you're wearing that thing."

"I'm channeling Kate Middleton." Alex snuck a peek at the right side of the church. She swallowed heavily and widened her eyes.

Freddie turned to eavesdrop.

"No need to worry, Lex." Harry scratched a dark blond eyebrow. "Their cousin told me at the door—Olivia's a definite no-show."

Alex's shoulders relaxed. "Really?"

"Whoo, Lex!" Freddie raised a fist in triumph. "You've scared that play-stealing clothes horse away for good!"

Harry nodded. "Up until this morning, Tom didn't know if his sister was flying over. Apparently, she just started a theatre arts program for at-risk youth in the Bronx."

Lucy snorted. "Poor kids have had a tough life already—why make them suffer more, dealing with that stuck-up bitch?"

Harry shrugged.

Alex raised her eyebrows. "Thank God you didn't marry her."

"Lucky escape, mate, lucky escape." Freddie nodded.

Harry sighed. "Tell me about it."

A parade of wealth and excess filled up the pews behind Tom. Trust-fund supported Chadwick-Smythe cousins, plastic surgery mavens, and men of bloated self-importance were joined by a clique of twenty-something women, all angular shoulders and protruding hip bones, draped in the latest designer creations. They perched delicately among the groom's former school chums from Harrow.

Freddie laughed. "I bet when the vicar says 'speak now or forever hold your peace' most of Hackney and half of Chelsea will stand up. It's funny how chlamydia brings people back together. Tom never did shy away from a casual shag." He leaned over Harry. "Lucy, speaking of shags—"

"Check *her* out," Lucy interrupted. "That blonde over there, the loud one with…" Lucy rounded her fingers into two large cups in front of her chest.

"The fake tan?" Alex stretched to look past Harry and Lucy. "That's Caprice, Olivia's friend. She used to be one of Tom's regular booty calls."

Harry nodded in agreement.

"Yikes. Is she *drunk*? In church?" Lucy narrowed her eyes. "Oh, Tom, your former fuck buddy is nasty. Her skin is *orange*."

"It's fighting with her tangerine frock," Freddie joined in. "Orange is the new *blechhh*."

Laughing, Lucy turned around, her attention drifting over Alex's head. A smirk tightened her lips. "Well, well, well! Cutting it close, Mr. Keegan."

Alex broke out into a grin worthy of a lottery win.

"Hey guys…*Lex*." Mark paused, his eyes savouring every inch of the girlfriend he had been away from in Austria for the past six weeks. He swept his unruly hair off his forehead and slipped into the pew beside Alex, his hands reaching instinctively for her face. "God, I've missed you."

His lips joined hers, breathing her in and delivering a firm kiss, his dark stubble—still damp with perspiration from his rush from the airport—tickling her skin.

*Not as much as I've missed you!* Alex was torn between discretion and the ache in her heart to kiss Mark's face off. Her hands brushed down his neck, landing on his shoulders and pulling him closer. If only they were anywhere *but* there—their flat, his *Lairds* dressing room, even a restaurant bathroom—but she would have to wait. They both would; this kiss was just a restrained preview of what was to come later.

Freddie cleared his throat, hesitant to interrupt his friends' clinch. "Any later, Keegs, and you'd have been walking Naomi down the aisle."

Mark eased back from Alex's lips and smiled, shrugging off his backpack and wrapping his left arm around her waist. "I almost didn't make it. My flight left Salzburg an hour late, and then my Uber got stuck in traffic just south of London Fields. I walked the rest of the way here." His eyes returned to Alex. "C'mere, gorgeous." He held her cheek and kissed her softly, keeping their contact respectful and PG-rated.

"Is that the guy from that show?"

"It IS true—Tom and Naomi are friends with Mark Keegan."

Whispers rose from across the aisle, the soon-to-be-wed groom no longer the main attraction.

"Psst, guys." Lucy winced, catching a woman on the groom's side holding up a phone, pointed in their direction. "You've got an audience."

Mark grinned against Alex's lips and pulled away. "What else is new?"

Hesitant to look away from her boyfriend, Alex glanced across the church. Several people pointed, a few uttered "Oh, my God" too loudly, but Alex didn't care. The love of her life was *here*, clutching her tightly, his fingers playing with an escaped tendril of her hair. She turned back to Mark and straightened his purple tie. "I can't believe you made it!"

"Neither can his fan club outside." Simon rolled his eyes. "Or the paparazzi. Who invited *them*?"

Mark shrugged. "Sorry it took me so long. I had to sign for the girls, otherwise they'd freeze waiting out there."

"Nice ego boost, though." Harry smiled. "Fans wherever you go."

"It's fun, but they were a bit freaked. Two of the girls looked like they were gonna throw up, and one had an asthma attack. She had to dig out her puffer."

Alex slipped her hand into Mark's. "Being a Keeganite should come with a health warning."

"You've always had a magical touch with the ladies." Freddie laughed.

"But only one counts." Mark tugged Alex closer.

The gentle strains of Ed Sheeran's "Kiss Me" filled the room. The guests rose to their feet as one and looked to the church's entrance where statuesque Naomi, dressed in a stunning silk gown, appeared with her father. Mr. Khan held her arm tightly, proud to walk his youngest daughter down the aisle. An excited giggle escaped her lips as she took her first step towards her groom.

Alex stole a peek at Tom. His blue-green eyes sparkled and his lips parted, breathless at the sight of his beautiful bride. Just two years earlier, he had been sleeping with a different woman most nights of the week, but here he was, committed to Naomi, starting a future together, 'forsaking all others.' Alex had never seen him so happy or entirely focused. She glanced tearily at Mark, and his eyes were already locked on her. He squeezed Alex's hand and mouthed, "I love you."

# FOUR

A privately booked double-decker bus rumbled through East London, carrying twenty-two of Tom and Naomi's wedding guests to their reception three miles away in Clerkenwell. Missing from the bus were most of Tom's posh friends and family, who deemed riding on the Routemaster slumming it.

Laughing and holding plastic flutes of complimentary champagne, Alex and Mark surfed each bone-shaking bump from the front seat of the half-full upper deck, careful not to slop fizz on their wedding finery. Lucy slurped her glass in the seat immediately behind them while Harry, Freddie, and Simon were out of sight, satisfied with holding court on the bus's lower level.

Lucy leaned forward, resting an arm on the back of Alex and Mark's seat. "I'm pissed. Naomi stole my wedding."

Confused, Alex finished her champagne and glanced at Mark, her eyes watering.

"Ah-*choo*! Ah-*chooooo.*" Relief—*finally.* Alex's nose had been twitching for the past five minutes, the dust spit out by the bus's cranked-up heating system probably to blame.

"Allergic to weddings, much?" Mark's thumb gently brushed a

lost eyelash from Alex's cheek.

"This double-decker bus…I've always wanted a totally London-centric wedding," said Lucy. "I told Naomi months ago. Remember last spring at the Cat and Mutton when her stupid royal wedding answer cost us the pub quiz?"

Alex wasn't sure she did remember, but she nodded anyway, her affirmation punctuated with a slight grimace. The fascinator's headband was digging into her scalp with its prickly claws. *Jeez, how does Kate Middleton wear these things?* She stashed her empty plastic flute behind her on the seat.

"And then I said my ideal reception would be in a funky pub…and guess where we're headed. Coincidence? *Yeah, right.*"

Alex shifted her headband, her suffering roots given a slight reprieve. "Everything they've done so far has surprised me. Naomi was so hush-hush about her plans. I figured we'd be bored stiff in the country in a drafty castle with more bathrooms than guests." Lucy puffed out her cheeks. "You should be happy, Lucy. You can chill, drink pints, dance barefoot…if I had a pub reception, I'd have mini fish and chips." Alex barely drew a breath. "And chocolate cupcakes!"

Mark smiled and watched the red and blue doors of the two-storey terrace houses on Shepherdess Walk pass by. He downed his champagne in one go and yawned.

Lucy frowned. "You didn't mention *cupcakes* to her, did you?"

"Maybe. Probably? You know Naomi—don't get her started on baking or cooking. She can talk for hours about recipes."

"And sex." Lucy winked.

"I know, right? She makes Rihanna look like a nun!" Alex was on a roll, riffing with Lucy in the way only best friends can. Laughing, she turned to Mark—his eyes were now closed, his head against the window, trying to catch a quick nap.

She twirled a stray piece of hair around her finger. It had been two years ago, just before Alex started dating Mark, that she'd found out about his steamy, short-lived relationship with Naomi. Freddie had called it a "bonk-a-thon", joking that for four months the two actors had barely come up for air, but Mark wasn't emotionally invested, and Naomi, on the heels of accepting a lead role in the American touring production of *Kinky Boots*, ended it. Mark had a few dates but nothing steady until Alex came along several months later, and Naomi continued to bed Britain's top male talent until one evening…

"It's crazy." Lucy's eyebrow peaked. "If Tom hadn't met up with you and Harry at the National, if Naomi wasn't working the Long Bar…we wouldn't be here. That must have been some pint Naomi pulled that night."

"I think Naomi pulled more than just his pint."

Lucy snickered. "The head must have been *perfect*."

Alex tried to stifle a snort of laughter. She didn't want to wake Mark or bring him into this conversation.

"It says a lot that you two were able to become friends, to cast her in your play…" Lucy glanced at Mark.

"That's ancient history. Anyway, she's been a good friend." Alex skirted Lucy's gaze and looked at her dozing boyfriend.

There were still moments when Naomi's breezy, open-book approach to her carnal exploits made Alex feel…awkward. No amount of female friendliness would ever erase the fact that Naomi's lips and hands had intimate knowledge of her boyfriend's body and how to please him. Being friends with a woman who had seen your partner naked, who had slept with him before you were on the scene, was difficult to swallow sometimes. The only way Alex could deal with it was to remind herself that the past was just that—gone, faded away—and Mark's present, and hopefully his future, belonged to her.

Lucy stared at the bubbles floating halfway up her champagne flute. “Well, I’m telling you now, if she calls me *Luce* again or steals my baby names, our friendship is over.”

“You’ve chosen baby names? Lucy, you don’t even have a boyfriend.” Alex shook her head. *Ow.* The headband bit farther into her scalp. If the stupid hat was going to see the cutting of the cake, head shaking would have to be kept to a minimum.

“I’ve had names picked out since I was a kid, after reading *Charlotte’s Web*.”

“Lucy! Seriously? You like the name *Wilbur*?”

“No! Charlotte. It’s so pretty—actually, Charlotte reminds me of you.”

“I remind you of a *spider*? Cheers—”

“No, Lex, the last line of the book—you know, the one about the best friend who’s also a good writer? It’s *you*, it is!”

“Aw, Lucy—”

“Oh, hold this?” Lucy handed Alex her champagne and pushed back some curls to adjust a sparkly rhinestone earring.

Alex blinked, catching a shadow on her friend’s neck. “Lucy, what’s that purple mark? Looks like a bruise…or a hick—”

“Oh, that.” Lucy cleared her throat and snatched back her flute. “I burned my neck. Bloody flat iron. It looked worse three days ago.”

“Looks sore. For a minute, I thought *maybe*, you and Charlie finally—”

“Yeah, right!”

Mark’s eyes crept open.

Alex stroked his thigh. “You okay, babe?”

He rubbed his eyelids which hovered at half-mast. “I’m fine, yeah.” His Irish lilt sounded deflated and unconvincing. “All this rushing about is catching up with me. This shoot has been a killer.”

They swayed back and forth in their seats as the bus careened around an army of orange pylons. Seeking stability as much as intimacy, Alex wrapped her arms around Mark's neck, pulling him closer. "Well, that's because *you*, my talented boyfriend, give everything to your roles. No wonder you're exhausted. But, in three weeks, it's holiday time! New York City in December is *so* beautiful, and I'll finally get to show you Florida. I know meeting my mom won't be a highlight, but we'll make the best of it."

Mark glanced at Lucy and hunched farther into his girlfriend. "Mouse, there's been a slight change in plans." He murmured so only she could hear.

"A slight change?"

He drooped his head, evading her eyes. "It's my *next* job, *A Promise Unspoken*, the movie in Newfoundland...*Canada*..." Mark winced. "It's been moved up...to this year."

Alex scrunched up her eyebrows. "This year?" The smile abandoned her face. "But you already told your agent and the director—we're spending December in the States."

"I *did*, but they've had to move up the start date to save the production. Some funding fell through. The producers tapped into tax credits that are only available now. We start filming this month—"

"Instead of March?" Her sharp tone, punctuated by a loud metallic squeak from the bus caught Lucy's attention. "How long have you known?"

Mark's eyes wandered. "For a bit."

"How long is *a bit*?" Alex's arms retreated from his shoulders.

"Four weeks—"

"*Four weeks*!"

"I wanted to tell you *in person*." Mark swallowed heavily. "Production will go through to mid-February...with two days off at Christmas."

With his mother's house finished, Alex had thought she would see more of Mark now, not less. "So, just like that, our holiday is cancelled?"

"Not cancelled, babe, postponed. We can go straight after the movie wraps. I still want to meet your mum—and your sister and brother."

Alex sagged in her seat and looked out the front window, the landmarks rushing past dissolving into watery blobs. Mark breathed in deeply. Noticing the tears collecting in her eyes, he clasped her hand.

"Think of it this way, Mouse: the postponement might be a *good* thing. It gives you time to start smoothing things over with your mom. You don't want to go all that way and end up fighting the entire time. That would be such a waste—"

"No, you know what's a waste?" Alex's throat pinched tight. She pulled her hand away from his, crossing her arms. "Cancelling again…especially after last April. I can't believe this, Mark. You said we'd go for *sure* this time. You said work wouldn't interfere with another holiday…*and* now we won't be together at Christmas either."

"I know, but it's out of my control. I can't say no to the producers, can I? Not if I'm already signed on."

"Actually, you can, Mark. You just won't."

"Come on, Lex." His fingers wrestled with his shirt collar. "There was nothing I could do. It's not my fault."

The bus drove through an obstacle course of fluorescent construction signs and uneven pavement, bouncing and jarring its upper deck passengers. Alex and Mark both reached for the metal handle that crossed the back of their seat, bracing themselves.

"It's never your fault." Her eyes widened as she rocked with the bus's momentum. "It's always your agent, the producer, the director. They ask for a re-shoot, you drop everything. A castmate wants to run lines after hours, so you bail on Lucy's party. We were celebrating her promotion, and you didn't show up…"

Lucy bit her cheek, her wide eyes flying down to a new Snapchat image from Freddie on her phone.

"You even missed most of my birthday dinner because of a costume fitting. A *costume fitting*, Mark—like *that* couldn't have waited? If you don't speak up once in a while, it *is* your fault." She yanked the scratchy headpiece from her hair, ripping out several strands in the process. "Ow! Great! Fucking great."

Naomi's family members, visiting from France and India, stopped talking and stared.

Mark tilted his head, seeking privacy in the crook of his girlfriend's neck. "Alex, I already apologized about the birthday thing and Lucy's party."

She tugged at the knotted hair stuck in the fascinator's teeth.

Their silence drew Lucy's gaze. Naomi's relatives politely looked away.

Mark kissed her on the forehead and drew her in. "Please don't be upset," he whispered. "Look, I'll try harder to protect our time together, okay? Work's been mental. It's just taking me a while to figure out how to balance everything, but I will. You and I are in this together. Everything I do is for us, to make a better life for you and me."

*You and me*. Alex exhaled deeply. She knew they were on the same side, but his job and everything that came with it—the lengthy separations, demanding directors, intrusive fans—often felt like her enemy. She had waited six long weeks to be reunited with Mark, and the dread of him leaving again so soon weighed heavily. In twenty-one hours, he'd be halfway across Europe again, gone for three more weeks, followed by the film in Newfoundland with an ocean creating another unwelcome separation. She shouldn't be spending these precious hours arguing with him.

"And I appreciate that." Alex softened her tone and lowered

her voice so Mark was her only audience. "You *know* I do, but you don't see how the workaholic in you blindly takes over. Life shouldn't be all work. It makes me worry, Mark. You're running yourself into the ground. It's not healthy."

"I know, Mouse, but like Wink says, I have to strike while the iron's hot."

Alex rolled her eyes. *Wink.* His agent had such a stupid name.

"I know, it's a cliché, but he's got a point. This job is all about the immediate future. Right now, casting agents and directors want me, but that won't always be the case. Slacking off just when things are going well could damage my career. Wink says, '*Blow the next chance and you're yesterday's news.*'"

The bus pounded through a patch of potholes.

"But you should make *your* demands known, too. Stand up for yourself. Just because your agent thinks something is a great idea doesn't mean it is."

"I know, I know. I get carried away. I still can't believe they want me. I'm flattered."

"You're like a puppy sometimes, Mark, so eager to please everyone—"

"We'll figure it out. Other actors balance their careers and personal lives without any problems, it's just new to us."

Alex twirled a lock of Mark's hair that had fallen onto his forehead. "Your job frustrates me sometimes, but I love you, so…"

"I *will* make it up to you. Promise."

"Yeah, well *sexy time* on FaceTime won't cut it, mister…"

"Ah, the ol' look, but don't touch? Kill me now!" He lifted his chin. "I've got a better idea. How 'bout I get some flights sorted? Fly you over to Newfoundland for a visit, and once the movie's done in February, we'll go to Miami for a month, live near the beach, and ignore all our calls. It'll be fantastic, right?"

A slight smile nudged her cheeks. Visiting Florida during

Spring Break wasn't her idea of fun, *but* if it meant more time with Mark… She had missed him so much, she would agree to pretty much anything he asked. "Right."

A tire hit another pothole, shaking the bus with a teeth-chattering rattle. Alex hugged Mark tightly, desperate to keep him close, to feel safe again.

Over her shoulder, Mark caught the St. John Street sign sailing past. "Hey, we're here." He kissed her quickly and leaned back with a loved-up grin. "Let's find you some chocolate cupcakes."

The bus swayed to the left and halted along the curb, allowing guests to pour onto the sidewalk in front of The Peasant pub. Simon, Freddie, and Harry stood underneath the green awnings, waiting for their friends to join them. On the upper deck, Alex, Mark, and Lucy hung back, politely offering Naomi's relatives first dibs on the steep steps down to the bus's main floor.

While Mark adjusted his suit jacket, Alex abandoned the fascinator on her seat. She raised her eyebrows at Lucy as she stood atop the stairs.

Lucy nodded at the discarded hat. "Giving in?"

"Yeah, it hurts a bit too much," said Alex.

# FIVE

After satisfying their appetites with juicy roast beef, Yorkshire puddings, pakoras, and chicken tikka masala, disco divas and smooth movers headed back downstairs to the pub's main floor for the evening's festivities.

Sat in a corner, Alex laid her head on her boyfriend's shoulder, a champagne-fueled buzz pushing their earlier argument to the back of her mind. She nibbled the chocolate icing curls on her second cupcake. A third cupcake, a peace offering from Mark, tempted from a plate balancing on her lap. His arm rested happily along her shoulder, the two of them captivated by Freddie's superhuman efforts on the dance floor.

Brimming with more energy than a double-shot Americano, Freddie was giving two of Naomi's sari-wearing aunties a dance clinic, showing off his fluid moves during The Jacksons' "Shake Your Body (Down to the Ground)". To his left, Simon unapologetically thrashed about, but his lack of rhythm and punchy movements repelled fellow revelers, concerned for their safety.

Lucy squeezed through the crowd, carrying a pudgy baby dressed in a lavishly beaded white dress.

"Wow, wedding favours sure have changed." Mark gave the sprog a wide berth.

Lucy bounced the little one in her arms. "Ha! Meet Jasmine, Naomi's niece. Isn't she *adorable*?" She thrust the baby in Alex's face. "Smell her. I could just eat her up!"

"Erm, thanks, but I'll stick to the cupcakes." Alex didn't budge.

"Well, at least hold her. See what it might be like for you and Mark to play happy families."

Alex scrunched up her nose and popped a piece of the third cupcake into her mouth. Lucy stared back at her, a wriggly Jasmine dangling over Alex's lap. "You'll never know unless you get some practice in. Go on, she won't bite…"

The DJ segued from the King of Pop into "Let Go for Tonight" by Foxes. Alex perked up, her foot tapping anxiously to the beat. "No, but she'll probably puke on me." She handed her crumb-sprinkled plate to a passing server and dabbed her lips with a napkin.

Mark laughed and snaked his hand around his girlfriend's waist. "Lucy, you know better. If it's not furry and meowing, Lex isn't interested."

"We should dance before the DJ switches to ABBA again." Alex's eyes darted past Lucy, blinking rapidly at the guests flailing about and throwing shapes behind her friend's back. Several pairs of abandoned Jimmy Choos and studded Valentino pumps littered the perimeter of the dance floor.

Lucy's shoulders fell. "I know, it's your favourite song. Go. I'll return Jazzy to her mum and meet you there."

Mark barely had time to loosen his tie before Alex kicked off her heels, grabbed his hand, and pulled him into the pack of gyrating bodies. No surprise, Freddie and Simon were bouncing around in the centre.

"About time, ya wallflowers." Freddie yanked Alex away from Mark, twirling her into his chest. "Hey, Sparkly Girl! To quote that glitter pixie, Kylie Minogue, '*Your disco needs you*!'"

He smooched her cheek and released her back to Mark, the three of them joining Simon's pogoing spree, jumping up and down and singing the lyrics at the top of their lungs. Lucy, now free of Jazzy, invaded their huddle. Even the bride and groom joined in, dragging Harry in their wake.

Alex beamed at her friends—everyone who mattered was here. She threw her arms around Mark's neck, her hips rocking in time with his. She would've been perfectly happy for the moment to go on with no end in sight, all her fears and worries temporarily lost to the music. If only you could *live* within a song, a perfect little bubble where love ruled and the lyrics sang out your most heartfelt feelings, a musical haven where work commitments couldn't steal away your boyfriend, leaving loneliness and frustration in his place.

The DJ mixed into a slower tune, perfect for a romantic clinch on the dance floor. Parched from their marathon dance-off, Freddie and Simon dashed to the bar while Harry snatched Lucy's hand before she could slip away. Alex stepped back into her heels.

"Ooh, this one's an oldie. Must be for the parents." Mark pulled Alex close as they swayed together on the dance floor. He kissed her tenderly as if he had all the time in the world.

Taking a breath, Alex explained, "It's the Cars, 'Drive'..."

Mark smirked. "You and your ol' musical cheese. Good thing you're cute with it."

"This song's not cheesy, it's beautiful." She smiled, feeling safe in his arms. "So, what do you think?"

"About what, this song?"

"Not the song, silly." She licked her lips and played with the hair at the nape of his neck.

"Oh, you minx!" Mark's eyes fell to the plunging v-neck of

her dress. "Maybe I should disappear for weeks on end more often."

"Don't you dare."

"Is this a hint? Time to sneak away…" His whisper gave in to his lips kissing their way down her neck as his fingers dug into her waist, pulling her closer.

"Tempting—" Alex gasped as his tongue slipped along the nape of her neck. Warmth surged through her body, flushing her cheeks. "But Naomi would kill us." Her fingers disappeared into his thick hair.

"No, she wouldn't. She'd understand." His mouth claimed hers again, his tongue daring her to leave everyone behind.

Alex welcomed his challenge, losing herself in the moment and erasing all thoughts of Naomi and cheesy love songs from her mind.

Mark broke free first, quick breaths leaving his lips. His eyes, full of need and want and impatience, didn't stray. With an impish grin, his hand swept over her bottom as he pushed his hips into hers.

*Woah.* Mark was ready—*now.* "You don't waste any time, Mr. Keegan." Alex's eyes danced around the pub. "Okay."

"Really?"

"Yeah, but you haven't answered my question."

"The answer's always yes." He blinked slowly, his eyelids heavy with anticipation.

Alex laughed. "No, Mark, I meant…what do you think about all *this*?"

"Lovely ceremony. Smashing party. Bit too much ABBA." His mouth returned to her neck. "Can we go now?"

"That's not what I was asking…"

He tilted his head to the side, searching her face for clues.

Alex chewed the corner of her bottom lip. "What do you think about *us*…getting married one day?"

His eyes popped open, twice their size. "Ah, *okay.* That's not what I expected. Where's this coming from? The first of your friends gets hitched and you're overcome with fuzzy feels?"

"No." She scrunched up her nose. "It's been on my mind for a while now…"

"Really? You've never mentioned it, although I did overhear you and Lucy, ages ago, something about marriage after thirty? So, what's that—six more years of dirty, unwed sex in our future?" He gently nibbled her earlobe as he pressed hard against her again. "I say, bring it…starting *now*."

"Mark!"

"What?" He laughed. "Don't play all innocent with me, Sinclair. I know better."

She tugged on his shoulders. "Be serious for a minute. We love each other, right?"

"Right."

"Well, don't you want to be committed—officially? It's the obvious next step."

"Yeah, but it's a step that people rush into for the wrong reasons. I think a lot of couples do it because things 'get stale', but that's not us, is it? We're *happy*. We keep each other on our toes, and the sex is amazing." He nuzzled her neck, breathing her in and delivering soft kisses towards her décolletage. "If it ain't broke…"

Her eyebrows squished together. "If it ain't broke, then…why wait?"

Mark lifted his head, his eyes scanning the small dance floor. "Well, for one thing, we're both crazy busy. Can you imagine? Organizing a wedding while working your attachment?"

"My attachment ends next week."

"Already? Christ, this year's been a blur. Who's to say the National won't pick up that play? Wouldn't it make more sense to establish our careers first, while we're young and everything's happening, and *then* get married?"

*While everything's happening? For you, maybe.* Alex stifled a frown as Tom and Naomi danced slowly past. "We can do both. If it's important, you find a way."

"Lex, does this have anything to do with our argument earlier?"

"No..." Alex pulled back with a squint.

"Because me being away for long stretches won't magically be fixed by a wedding ring."

"It's just...we're so busy looking after our professional lives, our private lives could use some TLC, too. You said it yourself on the bus—we need to find a balance between the two."

"That's true..." Mark sighed heavily. "But to be honest, Mouse, I'm not ready to get hitched. I mean, I will be, *one day*. Marriage is great, and my parents had such a happy one." He smirked, and drew her closer. "In the meantime, Vespa rules, right? Hop on, hold tight, and remember to enjoy the ride."

The ride, the never-ending ride towards...what? Where *were* they headed? *One day* was a destination impossible to navigate, off the edge of the map, and how could she plan for *one day* when this past year she never knew if he was coming or going...or staying? Panic rose in her throat as tears threatened her makeup. She lowered her head to Mark's chest, glancing sideways at Harry and Lucy nearby, engaged in friendly conversation while locked in a dance floor embrace.

Mark lifted her chin with his hand and looked into her eyes. Alex blinked several times, unable to erase the weepy evidence. "Mouse, I know my news today threw you for a loop, and it seems like we're never together, but things *will* get better." His hand tightened around her waist. "Don't worry. I'll sort out flights for Newfoundland, and you can come visit, okay?"

Those large brown eyes beckoned, so hopeful, so persuasive—impossible to resist.

The twinge in Alex's chest didn't budge. As she nodded, a grin nudging her freckles betrayed the unwavering quiver in her stomach.

"That's my girl." He smiled.

The DJ picked up the pace with "Happy" by Pharrell Williams and Mark squeezed Alex's arm. "Yes! My request—*finally.*" Freddie and Simon showed up out of nowhere, bouncing beside Mark in a display of giddy solidarity. Alex stepped away, raising an imaginary glass to her lips. Mark nodded and dove into the abyss of sweaty revellers, the music engaging his body fully. Squeezing through the crowd alone and skirting the grabby hands of Tom's drunken uncle, the smile fell from Alex's face.

# Six

Passing a pair of rumpled teenagers kissing like the end of the world was looming, Alex spied Lucy leaning against a magenta wall, a framed Depeche Mode "Master and Servant" poster keeping her company. "You and Harry looked cosy."

"Nah, we're just taking pity on each other." Lucy adjusted the slipping shoulder strap on Alex's dress. "He's so hospitable, making sure I've got a drink. No wonder Bespoke is such a success."

Right on cue, the twenty-five-year-old appeared at Lucy's elbow with two flutes of champagne. "Here you go, ladies. Tom's parents bailed, so he's asked me to circulate. I'll catch you in a bit…"

Alex waited to speak until the club owner was out of reach. "Two glasses?" Her lips hovered over the flute's rim. "I bet this one was Harry's until I hijacked you." She gulped a mouthful, followed by another.

"Nice try, Ms. Matchmaker. Dating Harry would be like dating your brother. Anyway, I'm still stuck on that *other* blond."

"Why don't you just tell Charlie you like him? Why torture yourself, wondering if he feels the same way? It's better to know."

"Never say never. With a little Dutch courage, anything's possible. Maybe I'll pounce on him at New Year's."

Lucy exhaled slowly and walked with Alex towards the wooden stairwell leading upstairs. Their new vantage point would keep them safe from flailing arms but still offer a view of their friends' dancing shenanigans. "I don't want to make it awkward. I think he sees me as *just* his flatmate, nothing more." Lucy sighed. "Always the bridesmaid, never the bride, eh?"

Pharrell Williams gave way abruptly for ABBA's "Voulez-Vous." Lucy bobbed her head to the music and laughed, catching sight of the guys pulling disco moves with Naomi that would make John Travolta cringe. "Simon's rat-arsed. He'd never crease up his suit like that if he was sober." She squealed and leaned into Alex. "Check out Mark! He's learned a thing or two from Freddie, all those nights at Zippers before he met you. Fuck, he's got moves—look at those hip thrusts. It's almost pornographic. All the better for you, eh, babe?"

Lucy's words evaporated into the music. Alex was lost in her champagne's bubbles, her mind elsewhere.

"And speaking of pornographic, my jaw aches! It's hard work, blowing the Harrow rugby team behind the bar, and then Tom strolled up and asked, '*Where's mine?*' And I said, '*Piss off. I'm not one of your old tarts looking for a final fling.*'" She poked Alex with her elbow.

"Sorry…you what?"

"God, if the blowjob line didn't pull you back, I feared where I'd be headed next…"

Alex lowered her brows. "Blowjob?"

"*Never mind.* You were off on another planet just then, probably picturing what the two of you will get up to later—not that I blame you."

"Right…"

Lucy playfully placed her hand on Alex's forehead. "You okay? Your man's been away for six weeks and a shag isn't top of mind? If I were you, I'd say screw the reception and get busy with him in the loos."

"No, it *is* top of mind, it's just—"

"It's just what? What are you waiting for? Mark's crazy for you—sickeningly so." She pointed to the dance floor. "Just look at him, he keeps spinning around, waving you over...*voulez-vous*. Ha! Why the fuck are *vous* still here with *me*? Get in!"

Alex ignored Lucy's orders, her thoughts wandering again. "If we're crazy for each other and hate being apart, we should...get married."

Lucy spluttered on a mouthful of champagne. "M-M-Married?" She bent forward, her hand flying to her mouth. *Cough, cough, cough.* "B-But you're"—*cough cough*—"only twenty-f-f-four."

"You okay?" Alex rubbed her friend's back.

"Are *you*?" Lucy straightened up, her eyes watering. *Cough.* "That went down"—*cough*— "wrong way."

Alex watched her boyfriend whooping it up with Freddie and Simon on the dance floor, a hint of wistfulness in her eyes.

Lucy swallowed again and again, the burning in her throat refusing to fade. "You haven't even hit your two-year anniversary and you're thinking *marriage*?"

"It's in less than two months."

Lucy glanced at the boys and then at her friend. "Lex, seriously? You've never been one to doodle *Mrs. Mark Keegan* in the margins of your plays. Why are you suddenly all wedding obsessed?"

"Keep your voice down." Alex clenched her jaw. "I'm NOT obsessed."

Lucy threw a hand up in the air defensively. "Okay, if you say you're not, you're not. Don't get shirty—I'm just trying to understand where you're coming from." She blew out her cheeks.

Alex scowled, dropping the duo into silence. A minute felt like an hour. She had to tell her best friend…

"I found a ring in Mark's backpack."

Lucy look startled. "A RING? *When*?"

"August, in Dublin, the day we showed his mum the new house. Mark doesn't know—I put it straight back."

"And *now* you're telling me? Three months later—"

Alex kept her volume low. "I didn't say anything because I knew you'd tease me for being *that* girl."

"That's true, I would've. So, c'mon then, how big was it? Did you need sunnies?"

"Lovely little diamond, white gold band, understated but pretty—*really* pretty."

"What the fuck? Did he buy it *before* he became a household name? It sounds like a Kinder Egg toy." Lucy frowned. "He can do better than that."

"Actually, it's a family heirloom. Grace told me."

"You asked Grace—in front of Mark?"

"No! He was in the kitchen with his mum, saying hi to someone on the phone. Rhys was in the bathroom. Grace and I were at the dinner table, talking about the family photos along the stairs. There's a gorgeous shot of her and Rhys' wedding where she's holding up this blinding square-cut diamond ring—"

"Sounds like Grace's bloke has better taste in rings."

Alex glared. "You sound more like *that* girl than I do. Who cares if it's large, square, yellow—it's not about the *actual* ring. It's about what it symbolizes."

"Yeah, that your man is minted." Lucy sniffed. "So, how did you two get talking about the blink-and-you'll-miss-it hand-me-down?"

"Grace talked about the night she got engaged and said that

when Mark was ready to propose, he would have their mum's ring. She described it, and it sounded just like the one in his backpack."

Lucy's eyes widened. "Fuck…"

"I know, right?"

"So *that's* why you've been so weird!" Lucy sipped her champagne.

"Don't blame me, Mark started it—he's the one with the engagement ring." Alex peered into her glass. "I was never all about marriage, but now that I've actually *seen* it…and with Christmas coming up, our anniversary, I keep thinking he's gonna ask! I've gotten all obsessed since finding that ring. Lucy, who have I *become*?"

"You've become Gollum, but, you know, without the body odour and bulging eyes. *My precioussssss*—"

"Shut up." Alex swatted at her friend.

"Well! You do have big feet like him."

"Stop! I thought it might happen next month in New York but with that trip cancelled—"

"I thought you were gonna kill him on the bus."

"I brought it up while we were dancing, just now."

"What? The ring?"

"No! Marriage…"

"Shit, Lex. Sometimes you don't know when to leave well enough alone."

"He wants to wait. What the fuck, Lucy? Is he *acting*, trying to throw me off the scent? Or maybe he's changed his mind…"

"Lex, *come on*. Fess up. What's really bothering you?"

Alex's eyes sought out Mark, but she could no longer find him in the crush. "He's never here."

"Babe, you knew when you started dating an actor that work would take him away."

"Yeah, to do a play up in Sheffield or a TV series in Scotland, but South Africa, Thailand, California, *Newfoundland* for weeks—*months* on end? That's completely different, and it's happened *so* quickly."

"Go with him."

"And ignore my own work?"

"You're no longer giving tours at the National, so what's the problem? You can write anywhere."

"No, I can't. I had that writing group at the Royal Court. Then, the Donmar commission started, and there was no way I'd bail on the attachment. Anyway, I can't afford to follow Mark around."

"You'd be alone a lot, too, in strange places with strange foods." Lucy chuckled. "You'd bloody starve, Miss Picky Pants."

"It sucks. We haven't spent *five days* in a row together since April. I'm thrilled he's getting bigger roles and great reviews, honestly, I am—he deserves all that success and more, but…"

"But what?"

"I'm afraid he's working himself too hard. I'm afraid…I'm afraid he'll start to go off me, forget about me."

Lucy chuckled as a teen stole a half-full champagne flute left on the stairs. "As if! I've heard all about your FaceTime sex sessions."

Alex's jaw dropped. "What?"

"Blame Freddie. You know he's terrible at keeping secrets."

"Ergh, I can't *believe* Mark told him."

"I can't believe Mark still hasn't realized that Freddie's got loose lips."

"Lucy, Mark's fame and all the upheaval it's caused makes our lives feel out of control, unpredictable, and I *hate* unpredictable. How can we plan for our future when our present is just a turbulent long-distance relationship with no end in sight? He says he loves me, wants to be with me, but that's just words—"

"Says the playwright."

"His actions don't back them up. *I'm* the one making all the sacrifices, compromising everything. After lunch tomorrow, he'll be gone again, and it makes me super anxious. I need some kind of stability, some security, and *that's* what that ring symbolizes to me. That's why I want to get married. It's not about the party, the dress—"

"But you already moved in together. That's not stable enough?"

"No. If anything, it feels worse sometimes, like I've got more to lose now—"

"I knew it." Lucy sipped her champagne.

"Knew what?"

"Your anxiety is flaring again. You've been having panic attacks, haven't you?"

"No…"

"Now it all makes sense." Lucy stared at her. "The quick exits, the last-minute excuses. You didn't have food poisoning. That's why you skipped Naomi's hen weekend, wasn't it? Oh, babe, when did they start again?"

Alex raised her glass to her lips.

"Lex, answer me."

"Seven months ago. My doctor gave me some pills, but I haven't tried them yet."

"What happened seven mo—" Lucy widened her eyes. "Oh, *right*."

"Lucy, *don't* tell Mark."

"Never mind Mark, why didn't you tell *me*? I could've helped!"

"Because I catch a sniffle and you drop everything. Your concern would make Freddie curious, and if Freddie found out…"

"He would tell Mark." Lucy nodded. "But wouldn't it be good if Mark knew? I bet he'd try to be home more, and I thought that was what you wanted?"

"It is, but I don't want him turning down jobs because of my panic attacks. He's living his dream, Lucy—I'd never take that away from him or ask him to choose between me or work. If we got married, I bet I wouldn't feel so anxious. Life would be more secure…I just think I'd feel more settled, knowing where we were headed. Maybe I wouldn't sweat his absences as much? With a ring on his finger, he'd never forget me, either…"

Lucy smiled sympathetically. "Oh, Lex. Marriage won't guarantee that you two will stay together. Just look at my parents—fuck, look at *yours*!"

"I know all that, but why should having divorced parents and a dysfunctional childhood automatically make me a commitment-phobe? If anything, the opposite is true—I know what NOT to do. I don't want to lose him, Lucy."

"Don't be daft. Look, he's got this engagement ring, yeah? And now he knows you *want* to get married. So, you're dealing with when, not if, *right*? You just need to be patient, let him get there in his own time, babe. I wouldn't be surprised if he proposes with the ring inside a snapdragon, the old romantic."

"Or a big bag of chocolate Buttons." A shy smile returned to Alex's face.

"You've got a good thing with Mark. Don't spoil it by fixating on the future or dwelling on what *could* go wrong. You're with him *now*—that's what matters. He's totally committed to you, and any idiot can see you two were made for each other. And hey, the next time you're feeling anxious, *please* talk to me, okay?"

Alex nodded.

Another ABBA tune blasted from the speakers—"Dancing Queen" this time—and Naomi took centre stage on the dance floor. Lucy screwed up her face. "Fuuuuuck, the queen of shameless self-promotion strikes again." She turned her back. "I guess it's my job to remind Naomi that she's a swing in *Mamma Mia!*, not the lead. She's taking the piss."

"Didn't she tell you?" Alex shouted over the music as a sweaty Freddie bounded over. "After the honeymoon, she becomes an ensemble member *and* the understudy for the role of Sophie. She found out this morning."

"Now we'll *have* to go see it." Freddie stuck out his tongue. "Bloody musicals. Better pack an EpiPen. I may keel over in my ice cream from anaphylactic shock."

Looking past Freddie and Lucy, Alex's face lit up.

"You're only excited because you like cheesy tunes and jazz hands," said Freddie.

Mark swooped in and laid a sweaty arm over Alex's shoulder. "Hey stranger." His lips didn't hold back, reclaiming her mouth and ignoring all the distractions that lurked only an elbow away: their friends, the reception—the world—could wait.

Her free hand slipped through Mark's hair, its messy chaos impossible to resist.

He broke away with a smile, helping himself to Alex's champagne. "That Caprice grabbed Si's butt. She's so drunk, she can't even tell he's gay."

"Excuse me, Mark?"

Mark, Alex, Freddie, and Lucy turned towards the posh voice. A thirty-something brunette with gravity defying breasts bursting from a low-cut designer dress hovered with a cocktail napkin in her hand. "Can I have your autograph? I'm a huge fan."

Alex gave the woman a smile, but the fan ignored her like she was invisible.

"Abso-bloody-lutely." Mark disentangled himself from his girlfriend and handed back her glass, empty. "Bride or groom?"

"Wha—*oh*, ha! You're so adorable." The fan grasped Mark's forearm. "Groom, I'm Tom's cousin." She thrust her bulging chest towards him and chatted incessantly in his ear while pressing a pen and the napkin into his hands.

Alex felt like a third wheel. She drummed her fingers on the champagne flute. "Bar?" She snatched Lucy's free hand.

They weaved through the partiers, leaving Mark with Freddie and the woman.

"Talk about boob-a-palooza," Lucy sniped over her shoulder.

"She's out of luck if she thinks Mark will be impressed. He's more of an ass man."

"TMI, Alex!"

She glanced down at her A-cup chest. "Well, he must be, right? If he's with me?"

"Doesn't that woman have any class? He's at a private party—leave him be. Tom should've had a word with his creepy relatives."

"It's his wedding day, he's got more important things to worry about than being Mark's bodyguard. Anyway, that's my job."

Lucy laughed, watching Freddie leave Mark's side. "And you suck at it." She stared, not afraid to be obvious with her stink eye. "You should've told her to back off. She's taking loads of selfies. Even Freddie's had enough."

"It doesn't matter what I say. Mark won't stop until she walks away."

Absorbed in their conversation, Mark took his time, signing three more autographs for the woman, his kind eyes making her feel like the most important person in the room. Alex always joked that her boyfriend's superpower was charisma. Funny or not, it was true—people were drawn to Mark and loved talking to him.

"Keegs is impressive," said Lucy. "He asks questions—and actually *listens*. If I were in his shoes, I'd scribble my initials and be off."

"You and me both." Alex turned back to the bar.

"This must piss you off to no end, though."

"It was cool in the beginning and didn't happen too often, but now..." She smiled, trying to get the bartender's attention. "Our time together is so rare. We'll be having a private moment and suddenly get interrupted. It's unsettling and scary. These people feel like they *know* Mark, but they're strangers. I guess for a guy it's not frightening, but it freaks me out a bit. This one's Tom's cousin, so..."

"God, she's practically drooling. Mark should've worn wellies."

Alex looked over her shoulder. "Yeah, women like her, they don't rein it in when I'm standing *right there*. Imagine what they're like when I'm not in the room." She didn't elaborate—she didn't have to. Alex had learned to trust Mark; women hit on him all the time, but he never took the bait.

"She's called her friends over now." Lucy crossed her arms as Alex turned around.

The Kensington squad draped their Pilate-toned arms over Mark's shoulders and around his waist, desperately clinging to him for photo after photo. He chatted, posed patiently, and accepted more napkins to autograph.

A short brunette, no older than fifteen, eased into the scrum and asked Mark a question. He leaned forward, his undivided attention all hers. The booming bass on the dance floor made it difficult to think, let alone hold an easy conversation. He shook his head and encouraged the teen to repeat her query in his ear.

A smile rose from Alex's lips. This fan, polite and respectful, wasn't like the others, grabbing at him, looking for their pound of famous flesh. Moments like this one made Alex proud to be a fan and even prouder to be Mark's girlfriend. She relaxed against the bar. Mark grinned warmly, answering the teenager's question while signing her paper.

The thumping music faded as Naomi stepped forward. "It's

time, ladies!" She waved her bouquet. "Before I pass the torch to the next bride-to-be, Tommy and I would like to thank everyone for celebrating with us."

Naomi's new husband snuck up behind her, an unlit celebratory cigar in his mouth and a finger pointing at the shiny platinum band on his left hand. The guests howled with laughter, the notion of Tom *married* unthinkable just a few months ago. Naomi jutted out her chin and smiled. He was hers, and she was his, their vows and wedding rings, like Kryptonite repelling anyone who deemed otherwise.

"We couldn't have asked for a more beautiful sendoff. We wish we could spend more time with you, but the beaches of Bora Bora beckon."

The crowd *oohed* with mock envy.

Tom yanked the cigar from his mouth, snaked his arms around Naomi's waist, and kissed her neck like no one was watching.

"Maybe that will be me and Mark soon, eh?" Alex's eyes met her boyfriend's in the crowd of glowing faces. He winked and resumed signing an autograph.

Lucy held Alex's hand, giving it a squeeze.

"Now would all the single ladies—"

"And *poofs*, darling!" Freddie shouted from the far side of the bar. He handed his camera to Simon with instructions to video the flower fight for his fledgling YouTube channel.

"And poofs." Naomi laughed. "Gather here now, please." She raised her eyebrows not so subtly at Alex and Lucy.

"Come on!" Alex dragged Lucy by the hand. "It'll be a laugh!" She looked over at Mark, who was now free of female company and deep in conversation with Harry.

Alex and Lucy lurked behind Freddie, who was jockeying with the competition—a gaggle of late-arriving *Mamma Mia!* castmates fresh from their curtain call, the pack of Kensington heiresses post

Mark assault, and a hiccupping Caprice, tangerine arms outstretched, ready to pounce on the prize and the marital promise held within its petals.

Tom stepped aside as Naomi turned her back for the toss. "Un…deux…trois!"

The bouquet shot over her shoulder, barely clearing the festive bunting strung below the pub's ceiling. Squealing women reached out with impatient hands, clawing and scratching for position, their feral efforts jostling Alex aside. Caprice swatted in desperation, but her booze-addled balance sealed her fate. She careened sideways into Lucy with such force that the bouquet of posies catapulted off her head and landed safely in the arms of Freddie.

# SEVEN

By two a.m., Alex was feeling no pain. Chattering non-stop and sliding around the back seat of the Uber SUV, her spaghetti arms kept slipping off Mark's shoulders, his pleas for her to hang on lost in another fit of uncontrollable giggles. She clutched a cookie wedding favour in one hand while unsuccessfully fumbling with Mark's belt buckle with the other.

Five minutes later, he delicately carried his tired girlfriend up the three flights of stairs to their flat in London Fields and closed the door on the night's excitement. Setting her down atop wobbly legs, he tossed his keychain on the black chair by the door, dropped his backpack on the floor, and removed her coat and his suit jacket, laying both over the nearby armrest of the sofa. He pulled Alex in and held her there, murmuring in her ear. "Sorry, Mouse, but your floppy bunny routine is cancelling any action tonight. I'm willing and able, but you're—"

"Gagging for it!" She dropped the cookie and lunged, wrapping her arms around his shoulders.

Mark laughed and shook his head. "It's not gonna happen."

Alex loved a challenge. She perked up as if she had been magically infused with three large cups of black coffee. "OH, YES IT IS."

Her eager hands woke up along with the rest of her body, her fingers sliding down his chest and stomach. She clicked open his belt buckle, popped the button on his trousers, and forcefully shoved them towards the floor as her lips hungrily reached for his mouth. She slipped a hand under his shirt, following the dark hair trailing downwards from his belly button and underneath the band of his boxer briefs, her fingers exploring, teasing.

Mark left Alex's lips ever so briefly, gasping, his body responding to her touch. "Lex…it's so good to be *home*."

Alex didn't waste any time, reclaiming his mouth while unbuttoning his shirt with her free hand. If Mark was only there for ten more hours, she had to make the most of it.

He abandoned his trousers in the living room and grabbed her by the waist, tossing her over his shoulder for the few steps to the bedroom. Within seconds, Mark's tie, shirt, underwear, and socks mingled on the blond hardwood with Alex's dress and panties. Entangled between the sheets, Mark traced his fingers over Alex's warm skin, relearning all her curves, all her secrets, the distance between them vanishing with each deep kiss and breathless moan.

A sliver of golden sunlight snuck through a small gap in the bedroom curtains and crept across the clothes-strewn floor. Alex and Mark snoozed soundly, oblivious to the earnest chorus of robins chirping outside the window. The wall-mounted radiator hummed in unison, its seasonal tune overtaken by the sharp buzz of a smartphone. Alex jolted awake, her mind too cloudy to recall if it was Friday, Sunday…Monday?

A clumsy hand landed on the bedside table, just missing

Mark's surprise gift of fresh snapdragons—his preemptive apology two days earlier in case work kept him from the wedding—and her alarm clock. The long plastic arms of Benedict Cumberbatch clicked through each passing second, his knowing smirk taunting Alex with a dose of attitude. Back in July, Freddie's birthday gift of a homemade *Sherlock* alarm clock seemed hilarious, but right now, waking up to a judgmental 'Batch so early in the morning didn't tickle her funny bone one bit. *Shoot, it's already twenty past eleven? Only one hour and forty minutes left…*

She jerked up onto an elbow, snatching her phone from the table, only to catch a text from Lucy—something about the *National Mail*—fading from the screen. The room spun like an overwound top. *Ergh.* She fell back into the comfy nest of pillows, her stomach off kilter and her temples throbbing from—so—much—exertion. Her tongue stuck to the roof of her mouth; no toothbrush or paste had passed her lips before she fell asleep. She swallowed twice, but the stale taste of champagne wouldn't fade, punishing her for the excesses of the night before.

Text unread, she abandoned her phone in the sheets and shifted her head cautiously. *Damn.* Smudges of last night's mascara and eyeshadow decorated the edge of the top sheet, and a torn condom wrapper surfed the comforter. Across the pillows, Mark dozed deeply, his long, dark eyelashes flickering every few seconds, keeping him locked into whatever adventure he was running through in his sleep. Alex smiled and cuddled into him, her bare breasts riding the rise and fall of his chest. She inhaled. *Mmmm.* A faint trace of his cologne remained, mixed with his natural scent. If only she could bottle the heavenly smell. It was the first thing she had noticed about him when they locked eyes on one another that fateful May afternoon in the Royal Court's lobby almost two and a half years ago.

Looking back now, that serendipitous meeting felt like a fairy tale, and in just eight weeks' time, their two-year anniversary would arrive along with a New Year's Eve countdown, popping champagne corks, and "Auld Lang Syne". *Two years*. Alex smiled at Mark, lost in memories that still made her swoon. When they'd first gotten together, the fledging playwright and not-yet-famous Irish actor had always been attached at either the hip or the lips. Countless hours were spent sharing their dreams, working under the same roof at the National Theatre, and exploring London, their loved-up dates taking them to plays, music festivals, karaoke in Chinatown, and so much more. Alex's hobbies began to blur into Mark's pastimes and vice versa, causing Freddie and Lucy to refer to their smitten friends as *Marlex*.

"*Are Marlex dragging us to Ultimate Frisbee tomorrow?*"

"*Fucking ace, Marlex got us tickets to watch* The Lost Boys *in Regent's Park!*"

Five months into their relationship, Mark's television debut in *Lairds and Liars* arrived. Once the first episode of the six-part drama series aired, Alex and Mark's quiet, under-the-radar life evaporated. Mark's raw portrayal of Callum McKenna, a twenty-two-year-old former soldier striving to avenge his young wife's death in $18^{th}$-century Scotland, stole the nation's hearts. Forget Ross Poldark; so long, Jon Snow; bye-bye, Jamie Fraser—dashing Callum relegated all such competitors for fangirl affection to the back of the line.

Mark quickly left his National bartending job to dive into acting full-time. Gone were Alex and Mark's shared breaks, late-night cinema dates, and lazy weekends intertwined in bed. Without warning, it seemed like Mark no longer belonged to just Alex. Everyone wanted a piece of the show's breakout star—casting agents, directors, fans—and the job offers flew into his agent's inbox faster than they could be considered.

For the next seventeen months, his skyrocketing popularity

meant stints back in bonnie Scotland, slaying enemies on muddy fields and kissing dairymaids, as well as trading punches with tough guys on film in far-flung locations such as South Africa and California. Sharing her boyfriend had become the new normal, like it or not.

Alex softly kissed Mark's neck, his heart beating strongly beneath her chest. She snuggled deeper into him, wishing she could pin him down, stop the clock, and make him stay. Their reunions were becoming shorter and less frequent. Although they talked most days, they were lucky if they shared a meal or bed once every four weeks. Alex had adopted, with a touch of irony, Amy Pond's nickname from *Doctor Who*, The Girl Who Waited. Alex's deep-seated fears of abandonment, nudged to the dark corners of her mind since they had started dating, were tapping her on the shoulder once again.

She took a deep breath, her glance flitting around their bedroom. Had they really been living together for seven months now? Well, seven months *on paper*. The reality was actually thirty-nine days out of two hundred and eighteen—she had counted.

Their one-bedroom open-plan flat on Martello Street in London Fields, just down the road from Harry's old place, still needed a paint job. The bedroom was home to a bed, two hastily built IKEA nightstands and a dresser (the construction of which had almost killed their relationship), and a shared closet so overstuffed it needed an *enter at risk of death* sign. Stacks of books sprouted towards the ceiling, and a vintage bar cart held Mark's turntable and the vinyl collection that used to belong to his dad. Maybe in the new year they could both put work aside for a week or two and decorate properly, not just adding a candle here or a throw there. *Yeah, right.* When Mark returned home, the last thing they wanted to do was traipse around John Lewis or Debenhams.

Alex loved their London Fields neighbourhood and longed for

Mark to grow fond of it, too. He lived out of a suitcase most of the year, so Alex wanted him to feel settled and truly at home in their little love nest overlooking the park. If only he didn't have to rush away in an hour's time, she would take him for a relaxing swim in the heated London Fields lido, and then for a delicious Sunday roast at the Cat and Mutton pub down the road. If his free time stretched into Monday, she could picture him now—playing footy in the park with the local kids after school, showing off his goal-scoring prowess before heading to the pub's weekly quiz night with their friends. She snickered. Freddie's quiz meltdowns were legendary. He would always dispute wrong answers and descend into a prickly mood if their team didn't win, and—much to Simon's annoyance—only Mark could coax him out of it.

Alex exhaled quietly, her smile wavering. In less than two years, their lives had shifted so dramatically. She was writing but spinning her wheels, having had no luck getting a second play produced after *Thirteen*, while the bartending, jobbing actor she'd fallen in love with was now appearing on TV weekly. She couldn't walk along the street without spotting her boyfriend's face, his eyebrows furrowed with determination, staring down from a *Lairds* ad on a double-decker bus. Her heart threatened to burst with pride, but a growing hollowness in her stomach hinted that their time was running out.

Mark stirred. His eyelashes fluttered several times before his eyes focused, first on the comedy and tragedy masks tattoo on Alex's shoulder and then on the tumbleweed of blonde hair nestled below his chin. His left arm lay trapped underneath her body.

"Ah, Mouse…"

His raspy salutation lifted the corners of her mouth. He wriggled his arm, only freeing it when Alex shifted her shoulder.

Licking his lips, he broke into a wide smile. "It *is* a good morning, pinned to the bed by my girl." He extended his half-asleep arm and claimed her once again, enveloping her naked body and pulling her on top of him. His hand stroked the soft curve of her waist.

"Mmm, morning stranger." Alex raised her head, kissing him. The bedroom shifted, thanks to her hangover, and she cuddled into the nook of his neck. "Babe, just lie here. Don't move." Her hand crept across his smooth chest, desperate to pull him closer, desperate to feel the comfort of his beating heart again. "I need *gentle* this morning."

Mark smirked. "Hmmm, that's not what you growled in my ear a few hours ago, tiger!"

"You're kidding, right?" Alex whispered into his neck.

"Nope. You ambushed me. I feared for my safety."

"It's all so fuzzy…" She glanced up at him, careful not to move too quickly.

"It was…" Mark playfully rolled his eyes back into his head. "…ravenous, but the second time…" He bit his bottom lip, his finger skimming her hip. "I couldn't string together a coherent sentence afterwards, it was so off-the-charts *ah-may-zing*—it's almost like you were trying to convince me to miss my flight."

*Spinning room be damned.* She lifted her head, a beaming smile rising. "Did I? Convince you, I mean?"

"Almost." Mark frowned. "You know I would if I could."

Alex's heart sank along with her cheeks. Tears stung her eyes, so she hid her face in his chest. Mark was leaving again, and there was nothing she could do to prevent it, but she could avoid saying good-bye. Good-bye always reminded her of their first fight, before they were lovers, on the stairs of the National. It was the first and last time she had said good-bye and walked away from him. She had made a promise to herself that she would never say it to him again, and she had noticed that Mark never said it to her, either. He parted with 'see ya soon', but never 'good-bye.' She hated the foreverness of it, and maybe Mark did, too.

"I wish you could come with me, see Lake Altaussee. The mountains are bloody breathtaking." A loud yawn escaped his mouth. "And you could watch me doing my thing, hanging upside down from a horse."

"Like that makes me feel better," she mumbled into his chest. "I wish you would go back to doing theatre. Movie stunts *terrify* me."

"They only let me do the easy ones, the bastards. My stunt double earns his wage, believe me, but never mind that. Tell me more about your attachment. How do you feel about it coming to an end?"

"I'd kill for a few more weeks. I love being back at the National. It still feels like *our* place." She pressed her lips to his neck. "It's been hard work, but worth it. I've cried and pulled my hair out over *Upton Park*, but it's definitely better for it. They've really pushed me."

"Yeah, I've heard they're tough. I'm proud of you, Mouse. A hundred quid says they'll add your script to their development roster."

"Even if they don't, I should be able to shape it into something another theatre might want."

"Exactly. This experience will lead to other attachments, meetings, creative relationships…"

"And I have that meeting next week at the Garrick about developing something, too. I would love to work with them."

"It's all happening!" Mark smiled. "Next thing you know, Whishy will be performing your words. I can see it now…"

Alex grinned. Always her biggest cheerleader, Mark really did think Ben Whishaw would star in one of her plays one day.

"Well, if that's not inspiration to keep writing, I don't know what is." Her finger traced heart shapes on his chest. "I need to keep busy so I won't miss your pale Irish ass so much."

"I'll be back in three weeks." He hugged her tightly, burying his nose in her messy hair. "And we'll have time together before I leave for Newfoundland."

"Yeah, two days." Alex sniffed beneath her bangs.

"We'll make the most of them." Mark glanced over at Sherlock chipping away the seconds, the minutes, like the hands on a doomsday clock. Each click of his arms ticked closer to their own personal midnight when they would be ripped from each other yet again.

Mark's fingers tenderly moved the hair from her face. "I've got an hour before I head to Gatwick." His eyes bore into hers. "How about a repeat performance?"

"I wish. There's a jackhammer in my head. I don't think I can sit up, let alone…"

"I know what might help." Mark rolled Alex onto her back and lowered himself on top, carefully holding up his weight with his left hand while his right hand stroked her cheek.

She wrapped her arms around his neck and pulled, forcing Mark's arm to give way and his full weight to drop on top of her. They both groaned and laughed breathlessly, their smiles mirroring each other.

Mark brushed his lips against her mouth. "And here I thought you needed *gentle*."

She inhaled his breath and held it, feeling every inch of his body pressed against her skin. "I love you, Mark, always."

He tilted his head, kissing her softly until Alex let him in, opening her lips and showing him how much he would be missed. She drew him closer, each deepening kiss masking the ache in her heart. He was still there and yet the dread and loneliness of living day-to-day without him was there, too, back again, tarnishing their final hour together. She spread her legs and kissed him faster, harder, desperate to feel the moment and nothing else, but a breathless sob broke through her lips.

"Lex?" Mark panted, his lips soft against hers. His right hand left her ass and trailed over her hip, across her thigh and between her legs, his fingers caressing, circling. "It's okay," he whispered. "It's okay."

Alex trembled and kissed him, her damp eyes afraid to blink, afraid to lose him—every minute, every *second* had to count.

"I love you, Lex, always."

He kissed her ear, neck, and breasts, sending shivers along her spine. Each press of his lips on her skin, each flick of his tongue…Alex hoped it helped him memorize every freckle, every hollow. Her nails dug into his back as his hand continued to tease.

He looked up and smiled, hovering over her mouth again. "Didn't I say this would help?" He lowered himself to her lips, parting them quickly with his tongue. The kiss was urgent but caring, needy yet gentle, expressing how he felt when words wouldn't do. He pulled away and shrugged off the bed covers.

Patient kisses down her stomach gave way to his warm tongue flirting lower and lower, continuing what his fingers had started. Alex shuddered, her breath catching in her throat. She bit her lip, lost in dizziness.

"Mark—oh, *God…*"

She gasped and arched her back, pressing her head into the pillows. Her eyelashes fluttered closed as she moaned and clutched fistfuls of Mark's mussed-up hair like she was holding on for dear life.

# EIGHT

*Nine days later*

Alex squeezed through the noisy patrons of the Marquis Cornwallis. The Bloomsbury pub offered little breathing space; tourists fresh from the British Library and University of London students seeking a boozy distraction from coursework hogged the tables and most of its floor space. She grabbed a stool at the bar. A sickly knot, an unwanted souvenir from thirty minutes before, wouldn't budge from her throat.

She called Mark.

"*Hello. Sorry, I'm not here right now…*" Her heart sunk. Truer words were never spoken. "*…please leave a message. Promise, we will speak soon.*" *BEEP*.

"Hey, it's me. Everything okay? I…haven't heard from you in three days. I had that meeting this morning, so…call me when you can? Love you."

Her finger jabbed the disconnect button then she typed a quick text to him: *Marmalade*.

Five minutes passed—nothing. She blinked, holding back the

rising tears that threatened to breach her eyelashes.

Instagram would have to do. She flicked through #MarkKeegan, desperate to feel close to him, even if it was one-sided and two-dimensional. Despite pleas from his BBC publicist, Mark had never buckled, holding firm on his pre-fame decision to steer clear of all social media platforms. He still had his rarely used Facebook page, but it was locked down to a handful of friends and family, and two months before he had said no to an official website.

Scrolling along, several funny Mark-inspired memes appeared along with fan selfies from his film shoot in Thailand the previous April. Mark smiled back at her through the photos, his sunny expression reassuring, like he was telling her, "Don't worry, Mouse." Travelling deeper into the hashtag, a series of sneaky photos from their picnic in St. Stephen's Green and Tom and Naomi's wedding crept up the screen, blurry and crooked, snapped on the sly without permission.

"Hey babe, sorry I'm late. Did you order me a pint?"

Alex wiped her nose and slapped her phone down on the bar. "Yep."

Lucy dropped her satchel on the floor and whipped off her puffer jacket, barely stopping for breath. The glasses she didn't need but wore for work still sat on her nose. "Today's been a total pisser. There's this anti-kale movement spreading on Twitter and Pret's trying to fend it off." She shimmied onto a stool, shoving the flyer advertising the pub's Christmas party availability out of the way. "My boss told *me* to deal with it, and I think I made it fucking worse. I always enjoyed social media, but now that it's my job—" Her thumb frantically swept over her phone, searching. "Now customers on the other side of the argument are posting #hailtothekale all over the place. It's chaos. I hate all vegetarians, even Simon. They're always hangry—"

Alex's silence snapped Lucy out of her rant.

"Ah, what am I like? *Sorry*, Lex. You don't need to hear this shit. How'd it go?"

She shrugged and didn't dare speak—opening her mouth would also open up the floodgates, and crying in public was so two years ago.

Lucy wrapped an arm around her friend as the bartender returned with their beverages. "Aw, Lex. Let's get that drink down ya."

The rushed bartender placed their meals—burger for Lucy, fish finger bap for Alex, and fries for both—on the bar.

"Want custard with those fish fingers?" Lucy smirked. Her black turtleneck and high-waisted indigo jeans made her look like a hip cat burglar.

Alex smiled, grateful for the attempt at some *Doctor Who*-flavoured levity. She had better enjoy this meal—it was lunch *and* dinner. "Thanks for meeting me here."

"It's nice to come somewhere new for a change. Why this place?"

"I was watching *Pride* again last night." She loosened the tie-neck of her blouse. "Gay's The Word, the real bookshop in the film? Just down the street."

"Ah, okay, so I *have* been here. I thought it looked familiar." Lucy scattered salt on her fries. "You and your daft movie location hunts."

"No, Mark and *his* daft movie location hunts. He's the one who got me into it."

"You're both certifiable. Running around London finding all the *Pride* places, did me in. Never. Again." Lucy set the saltshaker back on the bar.

"We haven't done one in a while. The last one was months ago—*Scandal.*"

"The Cate Blanchett film?"

"You're thinking of *Notes on a Scandal.* No, *Scandal* is from the eighties. Ian McKellen, John Hurt…it's about the Profumo affair?" Alex shook the bejesus out of the vinegar bottle, dousing her fries. "It's a good film, stars Mark's fave actors. I can see why he liked it as a thirteen-year-old—naked women and lots of sex. He came across it on late-night TV." She tasted a fry and continued the vinegary soak-a-thon.

"I bet he came across it!"

"Lucy!" Alex blushed and abandoned the vinegar bottle.

"You walked into that one, *and* I made you laugh." She smiled. "So, come on then…what happened?"

"I'm in trouble."

"What?" Lucy strangled the squeezy ketchup bottle, shooting a huge blob of sauce on her fries.

"I didn't get it, the Garrick thing."

"But…they were going to develop something with you."

"Yeah, *were.* Their budget's been allocated. They're going with big names—Sir Kenneth Branagh or me, who would you pick?" Shallow breaths escaped from her mouth. "They suggested I submit now for consideration within the next three years, which I *will* do, but…I'm desperate. I need something now, especially with the Donmar commission being…rejected."

"Rejected? But you said—"

"Yeah, I know." She bowed her head. "It's not in the rewrite stage. They decided not to move ahead with my play two weeks ago. With Naomi's wedding, it wasn't the time to… I was too upset to tell anyone."

"Oh, Lex. What did Mark say?"

Alex flinched. "I haven't told him."

"Why not?"

"You know what he's like. If he knew, he'd probably take on another job to make up for *my* financial problems. He's already away far too much." She looked down, warm tears blurring her vision. "I didn't think I'd have to tell him, at least not for a while. The fee from the Garrick would've made up for missing royalties from the Donmar, but assuming the Garrick thing was in the bag was stupid. I've only had one play performed—I'm hardly Andrew Lloyd Webber."

"Thank God." Lucy grabbed a napkin, knocking over the saltshaker. "Shit." She chucked a pinch of salt over her left shoulder. "I don't know how you do it. I couldn't deal if I didn't know when my next payday would arrive. Luckily Mark's earning—"

"You *can't* say anything, Lucy." Alex wiped her nose. "I can't mooch off him. Have you ever asked a boyfriend to pay your rent? I'd feel pathetic. He already pays more than I do. No, I got myself into this mess, and it's up to me to climb out."

"Any chance you could get your old job back at the National?"

She shook her head. "I already asked. If I knew seven months ago what I know now, I would never have quit." Alex stabbed a bunch of fries with her fork. "I should swing by Mare Street on the way home—maybe the ol' Tasty Munch café is hiring."

Lucy snickered through a mouthful of ketchup and fries. "It's not gonna come to *that*."

"I wouldn't be so sure. '*You can make a killing in the theatre, but you can't make a living*'...remind you of someone?" Alex pointed at herself and stuffed the forkful of fries into her mouth.

"I haven't heard that one before."

"Robert Anderson," Alex mumbled through her mouthful. "He's an American dramatist." She swallowed. "That line isn't a quote, it's a mirror held up to my life. I can't even rely on my agent for leads. I asked about sending *Thirteen* to New York and she said it was a waste of time. It's ridiculous—she signed me *because* of *Thirteen*! I'm sick of her passive-aggressive bullshit. I'm seriously thinking of dumping her." A heavy sigh left her lips. "I guess I could submit to theatres myself."

"Why don't you call Isabella? Ask for a favour? That's what mentors are for."

"Last I heard her commission in South America wasn't going well. She goes off the radar when things aren't working."

"Maybe the National will snap up *Upton Park* now that your attachment is over? Who wouldn't want a play about a female teacher inspiring disadvantaged East End kids?" Lucy winked, thrilled Alex's work in progress was set in her old neighbourhood. "Something is bound to come up. Your writing's too good."

"Hopefully, but waiting won't pay my bills or overdraft." She furrowed her brow. "The Hackney Empire usually hires extra ushers for pantomime season. Maybe I can get something short term there? I know it's not writing, but it'll help pay the bills."

"Close to your flat, no shit commute, theatre related—do it." Lucy played with her ruby and gold ring, a beloved piece that used to sparkle on her gran's left hand. "You know what else *we* should do? A graphic novel. I know there's no money in it—yet—but your words, my art…can you imagine?"

"The arguments? Yeah, I can."

"I promise." Lucy crossed her heart with a fry. "I won't boss you around too much."

"Cross your heart and hope to *fry*?" Alex chuckled.

"We *should* swear on carbs—it's a promise we'd both keep."

"But I thought you were too busy with freelance?"

"Not if I stop. I'll miss the money, but I wanna draw my own stuff. I've learned so much, penciling for other people."

"It would be fun. After Christmas?"

"Defo." Lucy blew a raspberry. "I'd like to see Sir Kenneth

bloody Branagh write a graphic novel."

A burly construction guy hammering back the last of his pint beside Alex discarded his crumpled copy of the *National Mail* on the bar and exited through the noisy wall of people. She chewed her fries slowly, lost in the tabloid's sensational headline.

"The morning after the wedding, that article you texted me…" She hid behind her hand. "I looked tragic."

"We've all been there," said Lucy.

"But you haven't had your splotchy face plastered online for the world to mock."

"The best part was the title." Lucy snapped up her phone. "Let me find it—"

"No. Don't."

Lucy tapped her screen twice. "Here it is."

"What? You *bookmarked* it?"

"It still cracks me up. '*Highland Fling: It's Back on For BBC Hunk and His American Love.*' Nice fact-checking fail, *Mail.*"

"If they haven't papped you in a month, the relationship is dead." Alex chomped her last fry. "The editors must've busted a gut, choosing these photos." She pointed at the screen. "I mean, *look.*"

There it was, the ridiculous leaf waving from her fascinator as she tugged on the back of her coat. This shot looked like she was picking underwear out of her ass.

Lucy snickered. "I shouldn't laugh, but…it *is* funny. '*A Wedding Wedgie to Be Be-Leafed.*'"

Alex crossed her arms. "That's it, you're fired—"

"*Punny* headline of the year." Lucy elbowed Alex.

"—for being a crap friend."

Alex scrolled through the photos: caught mid-blink with hair stuck to her flushed face; the straps of her dress shifting under her coat, threatening to expose much more than a shoulder; her mouth agape in a laugh—were those her *tonsils*? There wasn't a single photo that showed her in a flattering light.

"I wasn't slurring when we left. I was tired and a bit giggly, but I wasn't fall-down drunk."

"True. Keegs still had his clothes on."

"It's been ages since I've done *that*." Alex stretched one of the photos with her fingertips, enlarging it on the screen. Its caption: '*Keegan's a Mark-ed Man: Girlfriend is Stage Five Clinger.*' But it was *Mark's* arm holding *her* tight. How badly she had wanted to get home at that moment, to be in their flat, alone together where she could show him how much he meant to her. Mark looked gorgeous—as always—sharing a laugh as they walked towards their Uber SUV. Loosened tie, shirt partially unbuttoned, eyes bright at two in the morning…he looked content, in love, hers—but the paper was determined to serve up a different story, one that its millions of readers devoured. The fugly pictures and snarky captions were still attracting hurtful comments eleven days later.

"Don't read any further." Lucy covered the phone with her hand. "It's a bloodbath."

"I read them last week. At least Mark survived unscathed." The comment trolls were like schoolyard bullies, kicking her self-confidence to a pulp, albeit anonymously. "Maybe I should start telling random people walking down the street that *they* look hideous, fat, and stupid—it's no different than leaving crappy comments like this. I'm not a robot. I have feelings, too."

"People can be such fuckwits, and the paps just feed their trolling."

"It's so different from when we first got together." Alex handed back Lucy's phone, a slight smile taking over her lips. "Riding his Vespa, walking along the South Bank, clubbing with you guys—we could have private moments wherever we went." She stabbed ice cubes with her straw. "But now, a lazy afternoon lounging on deck chairs in St. James's Park would be splashed across the tabloids. Mark can't sneeze without a camera capturing it, they're so sneaky."

"He doesn't seem too bothered by it, though, right?"

"He finds it funny that people are interested in him. Paps follow him to the shops and he'll be chatting away about football or whatever. I've told him not to encourage them, but he says he's just being polite—'*You can take the boy out of Blackrock, but you can't take Blackrock out of the boy.*'"

Lucy shook her head. "If some shutterbug was following me around, making chitchat, I'd take his camera and shove it right up his arse."

"I find it intrusive…creepy." Alex shivered, setting her glass aside. "I get panicky just thinking about it. The photographers are only interested in Mark, but I end up being collateral damage. Out on my own, they don't care who I am."

"Mark's *fans* definitely know who you are."

"The Keeganites know *everything*. They probably knew Mark was going to be at the wedding before we got our invite." Alex shook her head at Lucy's French fry massacre. Had she left *any* ketchup in the bottle?

"You know who *should've* been papped post-reception?"

"Oh, God, yeah—Simon! That split in his trousers, zipper to ass—he was totally balls out." Alex howled. "And Freddie kept snapping photos!"

Lucy creased up. "Si's designer suit…" She struggled for breath.

"If you're going commando, skip the slut-drop dance moves!" Alex held her tummy, much needed happy tears dampening her eyes. "I like Simon a lot, but he's SUCH a bad dancer."

Lucy's smile faded. "Actually, though…I'm worried about Freds. I wasn't bothered when he ditched his secondhand clothes, but dropping out of cons and packing away his collectables?"

Alex sighed. "Freddie needs to stop letting Si call the shots. Did you notice what he ate at the reception? Nothing fun, just broccoli." She munched a fish finger pensively. "He's becoming Si's clone…"

Fries eaten, Lucy dunked her finger into the leftover flood of ketchup and salt on her plate. "It's like he's playing a real-life game of Simon Says. Those crisps at the wedding? I bet he got ten demerit points for that."

"I'd never change for a guy." Alex shook her head and slid her plate away.

# NINE

The FaceTime ringtone trilled from Alex's sofa as the apartment door closed behind her. With the determination of a Premier League goalkeeper, she flung her body across the sofa, arms outstretched, snatching the iPad hidden underneath a *Time Out* magazine. Her leap sent her keys flying across the cushions and the opened parcel in her arms—a care package from her brother Robbie in Florida—to the floor. Six packages of Twizzlers slid in all different directions on the hardwood. She pushed the iPad screen's green *connect* icon, a smile racing through her freckles. "Perfect timing. I was just out with Lucy." She straightened up, lifting the tablet to chin level as she wrestled one arm out of her coat.

Mark's screen jerked abruptly, distorting everything in view like a funhouse mirror. A tall floor lamp appeared, then a blurry glimpse of his bare feet walking across burgundy carpet, and then a flash of charcoal-coloured curtains.

"Hey str—" Mark's greeting crackled as the iPad's picture continued to warp and lose sync with the audio. The camera sailed over a decorative blanket then the screen froze on a shot of his neck.

"Whoops." Alex frowned. "It's breaking up."

She leaned forward, pulling her other arm free, and something sharp jabbed her bottom. She shifted and spied the bum pincher—her keychain, the one that matched Mark's.

"Hello? Mark?"

The image released, revealing Mark propped up on a puffy white duvet. "Ah, there you are. I've waited five days to see that gorgeous face...sorry, Lex, the Wi-Fi here's a nightmare. Did you get my texts?"

"You texted? No. Did you get mine?"

"*No.* Bloody mountains." A smile brightened up his pasty complexion. "It's *so good* to see you. I love you, Mouse. *Here, there...everywhere*, just like that old Beatles song."

"Aw!" She smiled. "I love you, too, babe."

"So, how's Lucy?"

"Crushing on her flatmate, upset about kale."

"Kale?" Mark rubbed his eyes with his fists.

"Don't ask."

"Sorry I didn't call this morning. I *did* text..." Mark exhaled loudly and shifted backwards into a cloud of white pillows, plumped against the bed's headboard. Deep creases travelled across his favourite Manchester United sweatshirt, the same top Alex stole on a regular basis. Random tufts of his hair stood up when he laid his head against a pillow. "I was working with the fight director at four-thirty this morning, and then filming started at six. Talk about *COLD...*"

Alex balanced the tablet on her thigh. "You look exhausted."

"Yeah. Only another week or so, and then I'm all yours for an entire weekend. I could lie in bed for days, but..." He raised an eyebrow. "I know you won't let me."

"Oh, I'll let you. Whether you'll get any sleep, well..."

Mark chuckled. "I've missed you."

"Me too." She reached under her skirt and began pulling down her tights, a coquettish smile growing. "I know what might help—"

"Ah, I can't, Mouse. Not tonight. If I weren't so knackered, I'd be up for more than just a chat." He winced as his hand crept underneath the stretched neckline of his sweatshirt.

Her shoulders deflated. Not tonight, not tomorrow—lately, sex over FaceTime or Skype was as rare as a play commission. No doubt Mark didn't tell Freddie *that*.

"Our call time got moved forward tomorrow morning. Snow is forecast, and we're riding horses again."

"Mark, be careful—"

"I'll be *fine*. I always am." His heavy lids barely blinked. "So, tell me how the Garrick thing went."

"It went." Eyes watering, Alex looked down. "I didn't get it. I'm not even on their radar." She picked lint off the knee of her tights. "Sorry. I didn't want to cry, but with all this, I wish you were here…" She rubbed her nose and glanced back up at the screen, but her boyfriend was frozen, one eye closed. "Mark?"

"Al—" His voice crackled.

"Mark?"

"Mo—se. I didn't catch tha—"

"We're stuck. It's cutting out. Damn." She scowled at his distorted image. "Can you hear me?"

Mark's video blipped to black. Alex's fingers scrambled to reconnect, but a new request to connect filled her screen.

"Hello? Hello? Mark?"

"Sorry Mouse. All good now?"

She rubbed her eyes. "Yeah, but I didn…"

His picture flickered again.

"We've got a bad connection." Alex sniffed. "Fuck!"

"What did you say?" Mark ran a hand through his hair. "You froze."

"We've got a bad connection."

He shook his head, annoyance creasing his forehead. “No, the Garrick. What did *they* say?”

Alex sagged into the sofa. “Try again.”

“Aw, I’m sorry. Looks like bad timing, that’s all.” He yawned through his words. “I’m proud of you, though. You’re handling it so well.”

Alex averted her eyes and picked at an imaginary thread on the sofa. “Yeah…”

“They’ve actually done you a favour. You’ll be free when the National calls in *Upton Park,* and you can give the Donmar project your full attention. When the Garrick sees those new plays, they’ll be begging for their own Alex Sinclair commission. You’ve got a real knack for writing strong female characters. They should be biting your hand off.”

She shrugged.

Mark bit his lip. “I’ve got something big that will have you singing the “Happy Happy Joy Joy” song—”

“I thought you said you were too tired—”

“No, not *that*.”

Alex scratched her head. “You’re bringing home chocolate?”

“It’s better than that.”

“Nothing’s better than that.” Alex broke eye contact.

“Well, this is. What if I told you the *Promise Unspoken* shoot is changing again?”

Alex gritted her teeth. “Urgh, Mark—”

“Wait, hear me out.” He leaned forward. “The *location* is changing. It’s been switched from Canada to Ireland.”

She caught her breath. “What?”

“Yup. Add the production’s senior accountant to our Christmas card list, babe. He’s our new best friend. Apparently, he convinced the producer that a move to Ireland would save tons of cash—”

Alex launched herself upwards with a jubilant squeal. She pictured running into Mark's arms, his stubble riding that cheeky grin, his lips crushing hers, ecstatic to be together again. She bounced on the sofa, sending the tablet floor-bound. Mark got a good view of the ceiling.

"You okay?" He laughed. "They have to recast a few roles because of the change, and we'll be stuck in front of a green screen a lot, but it's worth it. I was dying to tell you earlier, but I couldn't get a signal—"

"We *so* needed this!" Alex whooped, scooping up the iPad. Her shoulders felt lighter; the weight—the worry—of being without Mark for months while he played an 1840s Irish immigrant tackling the wilds of Newfoundland…gone.

"You can visit the set often, and I have several days off at Christmas, so we'll be together. Obviously we can't go to the States, but maybe Manchester? See your dad?"

"What about your mum?"

"Gracie's taking her to Malta. They always go away over the holidays."

"Oh, she'll love that!" Alex beamed. "Dad will be thrilled! I'm so happy, my cheeks hurt."

"Ha, yeah, I know. Can't wait to have your step-mum's bacon sarnies again. I can't stop smil—" His image froze while his voice warbled into a garbled mess. "—be together—"

"Mark? What?"

"—regularly"

"Sorry?"

The picture distorted into low-resolution squares, and then Mark reappeared again. "You're sorry?"

"No, the… I missed what you said."

"The change means I can check in on Mum regularly, make sure all is well at the house."

“Good idea.”

He yawned again and shook his head, trying to clear the cobwebs. “Ah, I’m fading…”

Alex inhaled deeply. “I don’t want to let you go, but…” His screen locked again. “Looks like I have no choice.”

“Mouse?” Mark’s picture came back to life. “Best to wrap up before this thing crashes for good.”

“I love you, Mark. Call me tomorrow?”

“We’ll be in the mountains, so don’t worry if you don’t hear from me first thing. When we’re back here, I’ll let you know I didn’t lose anything important to frostbite.” He winked. “I—”

The screen went dead.

***MARK***
***Thirteen years earlier***
***Dublin, August 1, 2004***

"You awake, ya monkey?" A few hours before sunrise, Finnigan Keegan popped his head around his twelve-year-old son's bedroom door.

Mark was half awake, hoping to catch his father before he left on a three-day trip delivering local beer to Germany. "Yeah, I wish you didn't have to go…"

"I wish I didn't have to either, son, but if you want to see Keano and United play in London, it's off to work I go! All these extra shifts will pay for that holiday, right? Think of it this way: by the time I'm back, London will be less than a fortnight away."

"I can't believe we get to see United play at Chelsea's ground—and fly on a plane!"

Finn perched on the edge of his son's bed. "Well, you and your sister have waited long enough for a *proper* holiday, not just another day trip to Killiney. Besides, I think Gracie's excited enough for *all* of us. She didn't stop for breath at dinner, yammering on about Buckingham Palace, all her Prince William stuff…thank Christ us boys'll have the footy, eh?" Finn smiled warmly. "Look, I don't like being away either, Mark, but money doesn't grow on trees. I promised we'd go, and us Keegans *always* keep our promises, right, ya rascal?"

Mark nodded with a yawn. "Yes, Dad."

"Now, listen, while I'm gone, you're to be good, and look after your mum, okay?"

"I will, but Dad…this lupus thing Mum's got now…" Worry clouded Mark's eyes. "Is she…going to die?"

Finn placed a comforting hand on his son's foot. "I know it's scary, but she's not going to die, son."

"But she had to quit work…"

"It's just the…*stiffness*…it gets to her hands and wrists so she can't sew anymore. She'll be okay, lad, but that's why she needs to take it easy, so you and your sister—best behaviour, yeah? You're the man of the house while I'm away, right?"

"Right. I'll look after Gracie, too. I *promise*, Dad. You can trust me—I won't let you down."

Finn smiled at his son, but even through the darkness, his eyes betrayed a flicker of sadness.

"I *know* you won't, lad." Finn stood, ruffled his son's hair, and kissed him on the forehead then walked to the door. "I'll see you Saturday in time for your footy match. Good-bye, son. Love you."

"Love you, too, Dad."

*The next day*

*Brring, brring!*

Mark's thumbs clicked away on his PlayStation's controller, ignoring the non-stop ring of the telephone downstairs.

*Brring, brring!*

"Gra—ccccie?" He hollered from the edge of his bed, his eyes glued to FIFA 2004 on the tiny television in his room. "Can you get that? I'm…busy!"

A Chelsea midfielder tackled his Manchester United striker. "Shit!" he shouted at the screen. He only had an hour before dinner to play—every second had to count.

*Brring, brring!*

"Gracie!" *Where is she? Helping Mum make dinner? Why aren't they answering the phone?*

With an exaggerated huff, he paused the game and tossed the PS2 controller on his pillow. He lunged off the bed and opened his door as his mother's voice rose up the stairs.

"Hello? Yes, this is Niamh. How may I help…"

His mum's tone was kind yet professional, like she was talking to someone selling something.

Mark spun back around, quickly closed the door, and leapt onto his bed. *Time to finish off Chelsea!* Scooping up the controller, he dove back into his videogame, sending Roy Keane and Ryan Giggs up the pitch. Clicking furiously, his thumbs sent the ball sailing past the goalkeeper and into the net.

"YES!" he yelled triumphantly as the animated fans on the screen cheered, celebrating his best ever score: 5-2 United. He couldn't wait to tell his dad when he called later.

He rifled through the videogames scattered behind him on his bed. What to play next? The on-screen football supporters continued shouting and carrying on.

His door flew open and he threw a perturbed look over his shoulder. "Gracie, don't you ever knock…" His words and annoyance drifted off.

Gracie *was* stood there, looking pale and worried, her headphones looped around her neck, but it was their mum who stole Mark's attention. Her shoulders were bowed as if straightening up would be slow and painful. A shaky hand covered her mouth, partially hiding her damp, red cheeks.

Niamh clasped her fifteen-year-old daughter's hand and slowly walked into Mark's room. "Kids, I need to tell you something…"

Mark pushed his videogames away, making room for his family on the single bed.

Niamh wrapped her arms around her frightened kids.

*Why is Mum crying? Was that her doctor calling? Is she getting sicker?*

"I just had a phone call…from Germany."

"Dad?" Mark frowned. "Is he going to miss my match, Mum?"

"Mark, Gracie…" Niamh inhaled a shuddering breath. "Your dad…he's had a massive heart attack."

"What?" Mark squinted. "Is he going to be all right? Are…Are you going to see him? Can we go, too?"

"Mark, love…" Tears spilled from her eyes. "He died."

Mark's body froze in ice-cold shock. His stomach felt like it did just before leaping off the highest diving board at the public pool: scared…sick…alone…

"But…couldn't they do *something*?" Grace began to tremble within her mother's warm embrace. "A girl…at school, her dad had a heart attack. He had an operation…"

Niamh shook her head. "The doctor said he died instantly, darlin', unloading his truck. There was nothing anyone could have done…"

Grace's eyes scrunched up, tortured with tears.

Mark struggled to catch his breath, his chest tight and stuttering. Sobs burst from his lips. "H-He's never…coming back?"

"No, love. He's with the angels now." Tears streamed down Niamh's face as she pulled her broken children closer.

# TEN

*London, Friday, November 24, 2017*

Alex lunged at an electrical cord dangling from the headboard between her side of the bed and the wall, stuffing the plug into the wall socket. Three strings of intertwined fairy lights came alive, arching over the head of the bed in a soft, romantic glow. A trio of white candles in glass vases on the dresser was next. A quick strike of a match, and Alex set each wick alight—best to take care of that bit of business now since her hands would be otherwise occupied once Mark arrived. She happily blew out the match. The scene was set, and everything was ready, spare one Irish actor.

She exited the bedroom and stepped into the open-plan living room, which gave way to the small kitchen tucked into the corner. Chocolate mousse chilled behind the door of the under-the-counter fridge, the appliance's surface papered in love notes and private photos of Mark and Alex that the paparazzi would probably kill for. Soda bread made from scratch rested on the counter beside a bottle of red wine, and a hearty Irish stew—Mark's favourite—bubbled in the oven, immersing the flat in the comforting aroma of thyme and onions. Alex had followed Niamh's recipe exactly, dicing carrots and potatoes until her hands were sore. That was the easy part—she had also fought her gag reflex and shed a few tears while chopping up raw lamb into precise cubes. Everything had to be perfect. She had been so determined to get the freshest ingredients, she'd charged the whole lot to her already over-extended credit card. The things we do for love.

Mark was due home any minute, no doubt tired from the previous night's wrap party in Vienna. He had texted earlier before boarding his final flight…something about a white-knuckle journey on a prop plane from Tyrol to Vienna and an airsickness bag.

If only he didn't have to start his next movie in Ireland on Monday…but an early Friday night supper followed by unlimited kisses and a weekend in bed was just what they both needed.

She dove her hands into a pair of plump oven mitts and opened the oven, carefully placing the covered casserole dish on the stovetop. One last taste test, just the veggies and broth, not the—*ugh*—lamb.

A key clicked into the flat's lock, right on time.

The taste test could wait.

She whipped off the mitts, tossing them onto the counter. With a cheek-busting grin, she ran to the door.

"Thanks, mate." Mark dropped his keys on the chair and smiled at the taxi driver who rolled his two large suitcases into the flat. "Mouse! I've got a surprise for you."

"I've got one for you!" She lunged at him, airborne.

Catching her, Mark clenched his jaw. "Oof! Careful." A burst of laughter left his lips as he reunited her feet with the floor. "You're a sight for sore eyes. Don't be shy—I brushed my teeth on the plane."

He kissed her eagerly and squeezed her butt. "Mouse, I've been dying to tell you: I'm whisking you away for the weekend…to the Birmingham comic expo!"

"Er, the *what*?" She looked flummoxed.

"The con in Brum. I'm a last-minute special guest. We've got just enough time to toss some things in a bag and go. The train leaves Euston in an hour." He squirmed out of Alex's embrace and gingerly lifted his backpack from the extended handle of one of the cases.

"But, Mark…we've got dinner…I-I made your favourite …"

"Oh, I thought the flat smelled like onions. I'm sorry, Mouse. I had no clue you were going to all this trouble." He hobbled to his left and through the doorway of the bedroom—still wearing his mud-crusted boots—pulling magazines and headphones out of his backpack. "Stew will keep, though, yeah?"

"I just vacuumed…" Alex muttered, following his footsteps. She crossed her arms. "Why didn't you tell me in your text?"

Mark dropped the magazines, headphones, and the little yellow Matchbox car he always had in his bag on the freshly made bed. He opened a dresser drawer, scavenging for socks and boxer briefs. The flames of the white candles bowed with each shift of the furniture. "The arrangements were all last minute. Plus, I wanted to surprise you." His hunched shoulders turned around, his hands grasping her crossed arms, tugging her closer. "A con, a nice weekend away together…it's all good, right?"

Alex frowned.

Mark winced, running his fingers over the *Doctor Who* '*We're all stories in the end…*' quote on the inside of her forearm. "Or so I thought?"

"Aw, babe. My surprise was better. Two days, just us, wine, home-cooked meals…somehow a weekend of hand sanitizer, scary fan-drawn portraits, and greasy con pizza doesn't measure up."

"I thought you'd be excited." Mark let go and returned to the drawer. "Once a fangirl, always a fangirl. You *love* cons."

"I do." She accepted the socks he handed over. "But I also love spending alone time with you, and we're never alone…and I sweated over that meal for hours. I touched raw lamb…"

"Lex, I'm sorry, but Wink thinks it's a great opportunity to promote my guest spot in the *Doctor Who* Christmas special. Now, I know you're excited about *that*!"

"I am—*really* excited—but I've been so looking forward to it being just us." A ghost of a smile raised her lips.

Mark stuffed three pairs of boxer briefs in his backpack and pointed to the socks in her hands. "Can you put those in here?" He strode stiffly to the closet and opened a slim garment bag hanging from the back of the door. "I've got a gorgeous hotel suite—there's a bloody great soaker tub with your name on it." He selected a navy blue button-down shirt and turned slowly with a wink. "Dirty girl."

"It's no fun if I'm on my own." Alex did as Mark asked, stowing his striped socks in the bag. "And you're away again Monday afternoon…"

"Ireland isn't Newfoundland. It's easy to visit."

"A visit isn't the same as a whole weekend at home." Alex ducked over the candles and blew them out with quick bursts of breath. A dark swirl of smoke curled slowly towards the ceiling. "I'm really pissed about this, Mark…"

"Babe, I think you're making too big a deal out of this. You'll have fun once you're there—"

"It IS a big deal! This isn't like when you eat all the Jaffa Cakes. This is the first weekend we've had together in *months*, and you've chucked it—to work. So much for balance…"

He slipped the navy shirt into the garment bag along with two others. "Mouse, I couldn't just say no to this, and I can't disappoint the fans, paying good money…"

"Couldn't or wouldn't? Yeah, better to disappoint *me* than a bunch of people you don't even know."

He closed his eyes, his lips a tight slash. "*Alex*, are you coming or not?"

Alex stared at him, shaking her head. She bent down and pulled her backpack out from under their bed.

# ELEVEN

"I'm counting on you to save me from your fangirl kin." Mark adjusted his belt and smoothed the front of his navy shirt. A final tuck into his skinny jeans, and his smiling eyes returned to Alex.

"You'll be fine. They adore you." Alex grinned, resigned. This comic con fell way short of her planned romantic weekend at home, but at least they were together…in between meet-and-greet sessions, autographs, photo ops, and panel discussions. They would make it work.

A loud chant of "*Mark! Mark! Mark!*" rose above the partition, his impatient fans urging him to make an entrance.

"Hear that? Bonkers." Laugh lines gathered by his eyes. "Lex—"

"Ready to sign your life away?" A smiley BBC press rep barged in, slapping Mark on the shoulder.

Mark winced with a barely audible gasp. It passed his lips so quickly, the BBC guy didn't clue in, but Alex did. Her heart kicked up its pace. *What was that?*

"I haven't seen so many fans queuing for autographs since Cumberbatch." The rep laughed. "Got your game face on?"

Mark's posture was tense, but his smile suggested otherwise. He shot Alex a confident look. "Let's do this!"

A bubbly con employee rushed over, his toothy smile and earnest eyes reminiscent of a children's TV host. "Showtime, Mr. Keegan. Follow me, please."

He pulled back the curtain and Mark ducked through, his beaming smile welcomed by a roar of voices from the surging crowd. He sat beside a con employee in a yellow t-shirt and with a simple hello and handshake, he magically turned her pale complexion bright pink.

Alex followed, lingering in the opened curtain, not sure where to go. The publicist stood beside her.

"Mark saved my neck, stepping in like this." The BBC suit nodded. "I didn't think we could get anyone to replace you-know-who on such short notice. When I called Mark Thursday, I really didn't expect he'd say yes. If I were dangling from cable cars all week, I would be chilling on my weekend off."

Alex sighed. "Exactly."

He returned his attention to the line, now double in size. "Want a coffee, tea?"

"No, thanks. I'm going to wander."

"Smart. These signing sessions are bum-numbingly boring." He vanished through the curtain.

Alex's furrowed gaze darted through the swarm. How would Mark deal with all of this? She had seen him handle a few fans on the street or a crowd of thirty or so program-clutching girls at a stage door, but nothing compared to this disorganized con chaos threatening to engulf his tiny table.

She tightened her grip on the strap of her bag. *Is it hot in here?* Her fuzzy black sweater stuck to her chest. She glanced at Mark—he wasn't sweating—and then back at the crowd, her heartbeat echoing in her ears.

Cancel that…

Never mind Mark—how would *she* deal with all this? The noisy, demanding mob, a beast boasting hundreds of prying eyes and just as many expectations rattled her like she was a cornered animal. Time seemed to slow to an unbearable crawl and yet, her chest pounded quickly as if in a race it was desperate to win. Each gasp from her lips grew short and increasingly shallow, mimicking a hectic response that was becoming all too familiar again.

*Fuck! Not here! Not in front of all these people…how…how do I get OUT of here?* She swallowed heavily as the room swayed around her.

*Crap, everyone's looking at me.*

Texting 'marmalade' was no use here, not now.

Mark turned around and smiled sweetly, beckoning her forward.

*Mark…thinks everything is okay. I can't let him think it isn't…I can't do that to him.* A false grin stretched her lips.

He didn't see through Alex's act and turned back to his Keeganites.

*Everything will be okay, right? If Mark believes it, I should, too…*

*You…can do this…*

She focused on her boyfriend, not the mob…perhaps it was her best chance at riding out this attack?

*You can do this.* She released her stranglehold on her bag's strap, her knuckles so white they practically glowed.

Mark gracefully accepted fan art, not once stifling a laugh at how hideous a few of the portraits were. He was effortlessly charming, engaging…interested in every person without being superficial. Shy little kids dressed like Mark's TV character hid behind their parents, too bashful to say hello. Mark leaned over the edge of the table with a welcoming "Hi, mate!" while coaxing them out from behind a thigh with high fives and compliments about their costumes. He held hands with girls all aquiver and lost for words. He was *so* good, *so* patient. His calm demeanour was contagious, even to Alex—her crazed heartbeat, gulps for air, impromptu sweats, now receding…

*You can do this…you CAN do this…*

*You're…going to be okay—phew!*

Each fan arriving at the table left with much more than an autograph—they left feeling heard, understood, and appreciated. Mark's ease with the fans, his *kindness* wasn't something that could be taught. To him, it was as natural as breathing. To Alex, it was just another of his traits that she loved and made her heart swell with pride.

But witnessing fandom from the *other* side of the autograph table felt surreal, like she had hopped into a TARDIS and time travelled to a strange, parallel universe. Girls crying over *her* guy, the actor who wasn't famous when they met, the one who, like a typical boyfriend, dropped clothes around their flat, ate Nutella with a spoon straight from the jar, and left whiskers all over the bathroom sink.

Alex slipped through the curtain and walked along the 'backstage' hallway. She squeezed through a break in the perimeter's bank of tall white panels where the roving rainbow of cosplayers, comic book aficionados, and pop culture purists on the floor of Birmingham's National Exhibition Centre swallowed her up anonymously. Alex completely relaxed. These folks were *her* people. Take away the theatre world's plaudits, the now-celebrity boyfriend, and intrusive paparazzi buzzing around her relationship, and she was still a geek at heart.

She bought some greasy chips in a paper cone and strolled aisle after aisle, window shopping collectibles, superhero sketches, and sartorial offerings for cosplayers. A puckered face drew her in.

It was a spooky, over-the-head latex mask of the Silence, one of *Doctor Who's* scariest villains. In the Whovian lexicon, the Silence had the ability to make people who looked away from them instantly forget their existence. Alex always thought they resembled the freaky younger brothers of the tortured figure in Edvard Munch's famous painting, *The Scream*: a bulbous head, narrow chin, protruding cheekbones, and deep-socket eyes. The only difference between the two beings was the Silence's pinched mouth, and for the most part, they never uttered a sound, let alone an existential scream.

Alex hadn't cosplayed for at least a year; her Wonder Woman outfit was balled up in the back of the closet she shared with Mark. *Hmm.* The mask was tempting, a chance to wade back in without a big commitment. She surveyed the crowd milling past: Spider-Man, or make that Spider-*Men*—ever so popular, Finnick from *The Hunger Games*, Catwoman...she'd always wanted to put together a Catwoman costume but had never got around to it. The cosplaying itch flared, but would her oversized sweater and dark jeans look too casual to pull it off? The Silence always wore black suits...

She stuffed several chips into her mouth, the saltiness making her salivate. A finger tapped her shoulder.

"Um, hi?"

Her bulging cheeks turned towards the voice.

"You're Mark Keegan's girlfriend, Alex, right?" A freckled-brunette about Alex's height and barely sixteen years old, dressed in a Hogwarts uniform, stared at her through round eyeglasses that pinched her button nose.

Alex raised a hand to her lips and swallowed the mouthful of chips. "Yes?"

"We thought so!" The girl giggled with her friend, a teen with wide-set eyes and scraggly dark blonde hair, the ends dip-dyed sea foam green. They eyeballed her from head to toe.

"You are SO lucky. You and Mark, I mean...talk about OTP."

Aw, fangirl slang—*one true pairing*, a perfect couple. Alex always thought her and Mark were OTP, but then, *she* would.

"Can we have a selfie?"

This was new. "Ah…sure?"

The pair swooped around her, grinning for the smartphone.

"Thanks, Alex. You're so cool!" They scampered off, eyes glued to the phone's screen, reviewing the image just snapped.

Alex knew they didn't really *like* her, not for the right reasons, anyway. Her only relevance to their world was the fact that she had bagged their favourite actor, a clear case of celebrity by proxy. She was a curiosity, nothing more.

She turned back to the latex Silence mask, promptly stuffing her credit card into the seller's hand. Hidden underneath this getup, she could wander around incognito. The Hermione wannabe seemed harmless, but the encounter left Alex exposed and longing for anonymity.

She tossed her half-empty chip cone in a bin and pulled on the mask. *Ugh*. The thing stunk. A sneeze flirted with her nose but never came, the plastic-y aroma of new shower curtain meets stinky feet flooding her nostrils. She set off into the crowd, invisible.

At half past twelve, Alex turned the corner to autograph alley. The line snaking its way to Mark's table looked shorter now but was still a few dozen deep and buzzing with excitement. *Aw, bless.* Still signing his heart out, hunched over glossy publicity photos. He looked stiff, cramped. Mark would definitely need Nurse Sinclair to work her magic with a massage that evening.

Grinning inside the mask, she sidled up to the queue. The Keeganites were still out in full force. Pink-cheeked girls pushed past her, clutching signed mementos and squeeing on a Mark-fueled high. The line inched forward, so Alex did, too.

"The queue ends here." A stocky guy with bulging pecs, threatening to do a Hulk through his t-shirt, closed off the line behind her. "If you're holding afternoon tickets, line up at half two."

Alex bounced on her toes. *Yes!* When she reached the table, she would whip off the stuffy mask and surprise Mark. He would be hers again, the two of them against this new, strange world, for better or for worse.

A girl, stood in front of Alex, wearing a red wig and cosplaying Black Widow, pointed in Mark's direction. "Gawd! He's a total life-ruiner." She elbowed her blue-haired friend. "Talk about hot."

Alex chuckled and stepped closer to listen in.

"I can't even. One glance and…oh, my ovaries, *just stahp*," said Smurfy Blue Hair.

Alex gnawed her lip, trying not to laugh. These girls were hilarious, and yeah, she had to agree with them, Mark brought on all the feels—*full stahp.*

"After I meet him, I swear, I'll DIE." Black Widow took a breath and smirked. "And speaking of walking dead, did you see his girlfriend earlier? God, she's the *worst*."

Alex's eyes bulged. *What?* The mask was seriously hindering her hearing.

Smurfy checked her makeup in her phone's camera. "I thought they broke up, or maybe that was just wishful thinking."

Black Widow nodded. "Why doesn't he date his *Lairds* costar? At least *she's* pretty."

The mask wasn't hindering Alex's hearing *at all*. Nope—these messages were coming through loud and painfully clear. These girls couldn't be more different from the fans earlier. *These* girls wished her ill will; they begrudged her…Mark. She swallowed heavily, their ugly words echoing through her head, shredding her self-confidence and souring her stomach.

Smurfy scrolled through her phone. "She must be a good lay. Fuck knows what Mark sees in that butt face of hers." She held up her phone so her friend could see.

With a clammy hand, Alex grabbed the forehead of the mask and gave it a tug, peeling it from her sweaty skin. The shift adjusted the mask's tiny eyeholes and she spotted the *Mail* header. *Of course.* Her heart broke out into a sprint.

"I bet no one saw her play," said Black Widow.

"I did. It was *shit*. Full of clichés, stereotypical characters." Blue Hair sneered. "She needs to do me a favour: not write another one."

The girls laughed.

Alex's jaw dropped. These words stung more than any anonymous online attack. Maybe it was hearing the venomous slurs in person? Or watching their faces contort with disgust only inches away?

*They hate me...because Mark loves me.*

Their nasty remarks, paired with the suffocating sweatiness of the mask, felt like two hands tightening around her throat. She gasped for air, tears brimming in her eyes—not that this crowd would care. She ducked out of line and fled towards the exit.

"Mouse, did you order me that bacon cheeseburger? I'm starving." Mark slicked back his wet hair and sat on the edge of the hotel bed with a white towel knotted at his waist. A second towel was flung open over his right shoulder, creeping down his chest, and the fresh scent of strawberry body wash hung in his wake. "All I had today was an energy drink and some crisps."

"They said twenty minutes." Alex stood in front of the TV, fussing with the uncooperative remote.

"My hand is so cramped, I could barely shave. Luckily, tomorrow is just photos..." Mark frowned and slipped off the bed. "Hey, stop playing with that." His hands pulled her in. "How's my girl?

Did you have fun?"

Alex spun around, her nose coming within an inch of his shifted towel and an angry purple and yellow bruise that enveloped Mark's entire shoulder and upper arm. Eyes staring, she held her breath. Beads of water trickled down his bare chest.

"Oh, God, Mark! What's *that*?" Worst-case scenarios trampled through her mind: *a plunge down a mountain, a choreographed fist-fight gone wrong, a spooked horse…?*

"It's fine." He smiled. "You should see the other guy."

Alex didn't laugh—her heart was too busy trying to explode through her chest.

"It looks a lot worse than it feels—"

"What happened?"

"I fell on the ice—"

"I *knew* those stunts—"

"—during a snowball fight." He rolled his eyes. "Embarrassing."

Alex gritted her teeth. "How hard did you fall?" Her hand hovered, unsure if she should touch him.

"It's fine, honestly. Would I be here if it wasn't?" He tucked her underneath his chin, his grimace out of her sight. "Did you have fun today? I love your Silence mask!"

"Yeah." She carefully rested her head against his chest, avoiding his eyes and any contact with his poor shoulder. "It's a shame it was too late to invite Lucy. A guy was here, taking pitches. She could've shown her drawings—"

"She can do that any time. This weekend is for us." He kissed the top of her head. "I knew you were off having fun when I didn't see you all day. See? I was *right*, wasn't I? This weekend's been good for both of us, and we still have tomorrow to enjoy."

"Can't wait." Alex shivered.

"You okay?"

"I'm fine. You're—"

"Damp, yeah, sorry babe." He let her go and removed the towel from his shoulder, patting it gently over his upper half. "Weren't the fans great? They're so kind and thoughtful…" His voice trailed off as he walked into the bathroom.

Alex slowly sat down on the bed. Behind the bathroom door, the hairdryer roared to life. "And honest," she whispered to herself.

# TWELVE

*Manchester, four weeks later*

Squeezing through the crush of Albert Square, a passing rain shower did little to dampen Alex's Yuletide cheer. Three days before December 25, the heart of the annual Manchester Christmas Markets was aflutter, its wooden chalet-lined streets playing host to perusing crowds and a rainbow of bobbing umbrellas. The sweet smell of roasted chestnuts competed on the dank breeze with smoky grilled bratwurst, tickling Alex's nose as she searched for her last gift—something special for her grandmother, Joan.

Alex checked her phone: *only twenty minutes!* Soon Mark would be in her arms again, fresh from four weeks of rehearsals and principle photography on his Irish movie. Her National tote bulged with chocolate truffles and wine—sweet treats to share later.

Stopping at a chalet specializing in handcrafted glass jewellery, she closed her umbrella, shaking away any raindrops hitching a ride. There had to be *something* there Joan would adore. Bangles, nope. Earrings, no—she had said, "*they fly around too much while riding my motorbike*."

The *Sherlock* theme erupted from the pocket of her parka, battling the stall's holiday music.

"Hey, Lucy. What's up?"

"Fucking Simon, that's what. Next time I offer to help cook Christmas lunch, give me a smack to the head."

Alex rolled her eyes. "What's he done now?"

"He just texted a recipe *and* a shopping list. Bloody vegans."

"Don't tell me...you're making a nut roast. How *Gavin & Stacey*."

"I wish. No. Curried lentil, parsnip, and apple soup."

"Ew, puke."

"Yup, that's what it looks like in the photo."

Alex shifted backwards, allowing the stall owner to parlez with a frantic Parisian tourist. "Try not to think of us on Christmas morning, lounging by the fire enjoying Helen's bacon baps."

"Yeah, rub it in. I'd kill for bacon Christmas morning. So, where are you, anyway? Sounds like the UN."

"The markets." Alex smiled at the charm bracelets tinkling in the breeze.

"Still shopping? Did you rob a bank?"

"Very funny. I'm using panto money, and I pawned a few things; I wasn't wearing the diamond earrings Mom gave me for grad, so—"

"You what? That's it, I'm returning the gift you gave me and giving you the money."

"You will *not*—"

"Fuck. My boss is back...chat later?"

"Sure, but don't panic if it goes to voicemail."

"I *hope* it goes to voicemail if you and Mark are shagging."

"I would never answer mid-shag. I'm not Freddie!"

Lucy squealed.

"Love ya, babe." Alex disconnected the call and bounced in

her ankle boots.

The *Sherlock* theme rang out again: Mark's mum.

"Niamh, Merry Christmas!"

"Merry Christmas, love. We're all checked in, ready for Malta. I tried Mark but got his voicemail—again."

"Want him to call you?"

"No, love, it's fine. Just let him know we're all set."

"Will do."

"And remind him that he has my present for you. He tossed it into that black hole he calls a backpack, God knows if he'll ever find it again."

"Yeah, what goes inside doesn't always come out. Did my gift arrive in time?"

"I have it in my carry-on. I wish you didn't, Alex. Writers don't make a lot of money."

"That's why I only spoil the people I love."

"Ah, bless you, darling." A smile tinged Niamh's voice. "Mark's really looking forward to Christmas."

Alex's fingers trailed along a velvet box of sparkly rings. "Yeah, me too."

"Oh, they're saying we can pre-board now. I'll call when we land."

"Please. Safe flight, Niamh."

"Lots of love, dear."

Alex stuffed her phone in a pocket. *Oh...wait!* A necklace with miniature comedy and tragedy masks...perfect. Once an actress, always an actress—Joan would love it.

She handed over twenty pounds and rocked back on her heels, watching a baby stroller break through the thick fence of legs like a battering ram.

"Thanks! Happy Christmas, love." The Santa hat-wearing vendor stretched over the table with Joan's necklace tucked inside a paper bag.

"Happy Christmas!" Alex glanced up at the glittery Manchester Santa, the size of six elephants, perched above the entrance of the town hall. He was kinda freaky, his boggly peepers staring blankly over the Square, his gaze all-knowing, never blinking. Alex felt dizzy for a moment and stood still, waiting for it to pass.

*Right.* Time to get a move on—if only the crowds would budge. These shoppers, hypnotized by the staggering array of goodies and snacks for sale, crept along like ants stuck in treacle. Alex didn't know Manchester that well, but she knew the general direction she needed to go. She pulled her National tote into her waist, dodging exuberant office workers let loose at noon, sporting snowman head-boppers and garlands of gaudy-coloured tinsel. Every hand rushing past seemed to be brandishing an arsenal of overstuffed shopping bags.

As Alex headed left onto Mosley Street, the grey clouds overhead burst into an urgent encore, causing umbrellas to bloom from the hands of hurried pedestrians. She pressed the button of her umbrella and ran across the street, clogged with trams approaching in both directions. Their *Thomas the Tank Engine* toots whistled in the damp air as she swung around the corner and splashed through the swollen puddles on the Piccadilly Gardens pavement. Not far now…

To any one else, Mark would have been difficult to recognize, hidden underneath a flapping umbrella, a peacoat, and a black Manchester United cap pulled down over his eyes, but Alex could pick out that slightly crooked stance in skinny jeans anywhere. Nodding his head to some unknown track streaming into his ears from his headphones, he stood outside Pret a Manger with his backpack and suitcase. Alex's lips parted into a smile and her heart turned up its pace another notch, giddy for what was to come.

"There's my girl." Mark yanked off his headphones and surged forward, his hand reaching for her face. He tilted his head and kissed her tenderly as she melted into his hug, her free arm squeezing him like a vice grip while their umbrellas collided into an awkward battle of nylon and metal. "I guess I'm forgiven for missing the earlier flight, then?"

"I'm *so* happy to see you."

Mark clamoured for her hand. "C'mon, Elsa. Inside."

"Who?"

"Your fingers are *Frozen*." Laugh lines creased the corners of his eyes as he kissed her hand. "Let's get you warmed up."

Sandwiches purchased, they claimed a table for two tucked into the back corner of Pret, Mark choosing the seat facing away from the entrance. The welcoming scent of ground coffee beans and freshly brewed java infused the room, while round metal trays clanked on the silver countertop overlooking the glass case housing sugar-dusted crumble bars and mini Christmas mince pies. A barista who recognized Mark brought over two gooey chocolate chunk cookies on the house. She praised Mark's TV role, gushed over Alex's handbag, and then politely left them to it.

Alex blew on the steaming froth of her hot chocolate. "How did the chemistry reads go?" She took a tentative first sip and grimaced—so bitter.

"Good, yeah."

Mark cracked the plastic cap on a bottled water and handed it to her. She gladly took a gulp and then ripped open her bag of cheese and onion crisps.

He peeled away the seal from his Christmas Lunch sandwich, his finger scooping out a taste of its minced pork, herb, and apricot stuffing. "Some of the chemistry reads have been so awkward, you know, like really bad blind dates." He sucked on his finger. "But this morning, it clicked. Luckily, everyone agreed, so now we have our female lead and my male sidekick."

“Just in time, too.”

“Yup. Their first scenes are next Thursday.” He leaned over and brushed her bangs from her eyes. “Any word from the National about *Upton Park*?”

“They passed this morning, but I’ve made a list of other theatres to pitch.”

“Someone will snatch it up. Be sure to mention the Donmar project when you do pitch. It shows you’re in demand.”

“Yeah…” Alex leaned back and swallowed hard. She couldn’t tell him about the lost commission, not yet…not with his first lead role in a movie making him so happy. Her bad news might sour his joy. “I was thinking of taking on some corporate writing, too…”

“Do you have time? I thought you hated that.”

“I do, but it’s money. I kinda got used to the extra cash from the panto.”

Mark peered underneath the table at Alex’s National tote, straining at its seams. “I can see that! Steady on, shopaholic. Did you leave anything behind for anyone else?” He laughed. “As long as you won’t feel too stretched then, yeah, why not? And corporate work is still *writing*.”

*Phew.* She grinned and pulled the chewy ham from her cheese toastie.

Mark’s fingers curled around Alex’s. “Five days. It’s the most we’ve been together in eight months. They’re gonna have to come drag me away on the twenty-eighth.”

Alex squeezed his hand and leaned forward, craving the intimacy she so badly needed. In a few hours, her body would be trading the cosy comfort of Mark’s sweatshirt for his warm lips and gentle touch. Her nerve endings tingled at the thought. “At least we won’t have to wait weeks to be together again. New Year’s—in Dublin! Can’t wait.”

“I promise we’ll make our anniversary memorable.” Mark

smiled at his girlfriend.

They were just an ordinary couple, stealing kisses over their sandwiches, sharing knowing glances. No one else existed; the customers choosing baguettes and soup from the nearby shelves dissolved in an unimportant blur.

Alex reluctantly released his hand and nibbled her toastie without peeling her eyes from him. “I’m so proud of you. Your first leading role, working in Dublin…it’s a dream come true.”

“Yeah, it’s another life-changer, that’s for sure.” He pulled a piece of turkey from his sandwich and popped it in his mouth. “Mouse…” He chewed slowly, buying time. “I’m sorry about New York. If things were different—”

“It’s okay.” Alex cut him off, not keen on getting into it again. She looked at her sandwich and tore off the crust. “You’re here. We’re *together*. That’s all that matters.” A soft smile parted her lips. “A few weeks ago, I didn’t think we would be.”

Mark shook his head. “But I screwed up, and it’s been bothering me ever since.” He reached inside the pocket of his coat hanging on the back of his chair and pulled out a white legal-size envelope. The front was blank—no name, no address, nothing. “I was planning on giving it to you Christmas Eve, but…open it.”

Alex slid her finger underneath the back flap, tearing the envelope open. Eyebrows furrowed, she pulled out a folded sheet of paper.

Mark leaned closer, desperate for a reaction.

She opened the document cautiously.

*London Heathrow (LHR) to New York JFK - December 22, 2018*
*Alexandra Sinclair, Mark Keegan*
*and*
*New York JFK to London Heathrow (LHR) - January 3, 2019*
*Alexandra Sinclair, Mark Keegan*

Flight confirmations…complete with assigned seating—first class, both ways. "New York? A year from now?"

"This isn't your main present." Mark smiled. "That's still coming. Remember in April, I promised we would spend Christmas in New York City? I meant it, but you'll just have to wait a little bit longer." He pointed at the small print. "See? Non-refundable. We are going!"

"But a lot can happen between now and then…"

"That's why I've warned Wink. I'm learning, yeah?" He gave Alex the cheeky smile that always made her melt. "I don't care *what* jobs are offered for next December. That time is blocked off for us. You can be my New York tour guide, keep me from getting lost."

"Great." Alex leaned back in her seat. A year seemed so distant, a mirage she couldn't quite decipher. Mark, by comparison, couldn't contain his glee. His fast-paced banter and ants-in-his-pants demeanour suggested they would be lacing up skates and exchanging kisses on the Rockefeller Center ice rink tonight, not twelve months from now. She wanted to share his enthusiasm, but the trip didn't seem real. It was too far away. But, Mark was pleased with himself, so she faked it. "I can almost taste Serendipity's frozen hot chocolate," she said with a tight grin. She looked at the confirmation again. "I've never flown first class before. I'll feel like Taylor Swift."

Mark chuckled. "Oh, crap. You're not gonna go all Swifty on me, are you?"

Alex folded the confirmation. "She only writes about exes, silly."

He leaned farther over the table, his face bright. "I've booked us a gorgeous hotel, too…"

*Sure, but isn't all this just an apology? For tearing up our holiday, not once, but twice this year?* It was a far-away consolation prize, and like so many things with Mark, it involved an anxiety-filled wait to see if it would materialize.

We can see the Christmas Spectacular at Radio City Music Hall, check out Macy's holiday windows…" He sounded like a tourism website advertising NYC. "Happy, babe?"

Alex nodded.

"Me too. It's you and me, Mouse, always."

"*Mark*?!"

Alex's eyes jagged upwards as Mark turned to his right, a familiar voice in his ears. A tall hulk of a girl around Alex's age hung over Mark's shoulder. Her hands juggled a phone, a deck of promotional *Lairds and Liars* cards, and a Sharpie held aloft in expectation.

"Daisy…hi," Mark mumbled.

"Oh, my *God*! What a coincidence, bumping into you here." Daisy smiled.

To Alex, this fangirl's almost complete lack of self-awareness was annoying and rude and certainly not new. Daisy seemed to operate without a filter, overstepping the line between fan and stalker. Too many times, this self-declared '#1 fan from Belgium' showed up in the right place at the right time…

*Fuck! My tweet two days ago, about visiting the markets, the huge Santa—and my boyfriend. FUCK! I left Daisy breadcrumbs, and she must have followed me here.*

Alex eyed the plastic bag swinging from Daisy's elbow. "Find what you were looking for?"

"I did, thanks." The fan lurched closer, bumping the table with her thigh.

Mark shifted the gingerbread snowman Alex had bought him away from the edge of the table.

Daisy's nosey glance poured over the flight confirmation, the sandwiches, as well as the wallpaper on Mark's phone—a photo with Alex at *Thirteen*'s press night. She waved her cards. "Can I have an autograph?" Her tone was more assuming than asking, assuming Mark would have no problem pulling out of his private conversation to shower her with attention. In a way, she wasn't wrong: Mark never seemed able to say no to fan requests.

This girl had taken up so much of their time over the past eighteen months, hogging the stage door, camping out for TV interviews, showing up on the street, and asking for autographs…*every…single…time*. How many autographs did one fan need? Daisy always wanted *something*, even if Mark was tired, in a rush, or having a private moment—like right now—and her long-winded letters were creepy. Mark had shown Alex a few where Daisy had rambled on obsessively about their 'friendship', and yet in person, Daisy barely spoke. She only asked for signatures or photos, never asking questions about Mark's work or making small talk. Alex almost felt a little sorry for her. Perhaps, she had nothing else in her life…

But today was one demand too many. Alex raised her eyebrows and shook her head. "I'm sorry, but we're in the middle of lunch…"

Daisy turned her back to Alex and pouted. "Please, Mark?"

Alex didn't have to see Daisy's face to know she was staring at him all big-eyed pleading like Puss in Boots from *Shrek*.

Mark surveyed the room, pushing his cap down over his eyes. He nodded at Alex with a look that said, *Sorry Mouse*, and stood up. "Sure, but be fast, Daze. Can't annoy the other customers."

The fan dwarfed Mark by six inches, half of that hair. Five cards were stuffed into his hand, each one with a different publicity image. Just like that, Daisy's request for 'an autograph' multiplied to five. When he handed the cards back, all personalized and signed, Daisy stretched out her arm, phone in hand, and squished her uninvited greasy face against Mark's cheek for a selfie. She snapped a photo burst, then another.

Alex rolled her eyes underneath her bangs and chomped her sandwich, the best way to silence her tongue.

"You good?" Mark offered a slash of a smile, not wishing to encourage Daisy any further.

"Oops, I blinked."

Alex chugged Mark's water. *Yeah, right.*

Daisy clicked another burst as five more teens with phones at the ready flew out of nowhere like pesky wasps at a picnic.

Alex leaned back in her chair. *More?*

"Mark! Oh, God." Mancunian accents flew fast and furious. "Pose with me?"

The shortest girl in the pack shoved forward. "I love *Lairds*. Your accent rocks."

Alex blew out her cheeks. "Sorry, but could we finish eating first?"

The girl launched a death stare at Alex. Face to face with her crush's significant other, her manners melted quicker than a 99 Flake ice cream on a sunny Brighton beach. "Mark doesn't mind." She started to video record Mark with her phone. "He loves spending time with us."

Mark ran a hand over his chin and met Alex's eyes. "Sorry," he mouthed.

Another girl nudged his elbow. "Mark, say hi to my friend Ronnie in Leeds." She held out her phone, the dial tone bleating from its screen. Alex's jaw dropped. This girl was dialing Ronnie in Leeds, fully expecting Mark to FaceTime *right now*.

Daisy hovered with her five autographs and countless selfies, clueless that her moment in Mark's spotlight was over. She scrolled through Instagram but kept squinty side-eye on the girls flirting with her 'friend'. Alex noticed Daisy stopped the Voice Memo app on her phone—she had recorded their conversation!

Alex shoved her toastie against her empty crisp bag. Where did all the *polite* fans go? Were Lucy, Freddie, and her the last of a dying breed, valuing respect, empathy, and self-awareness? Mark didn't owe these fans *anything* apart from common courtesy and a polite hello, but they all seemed to think being interrupted, prodded, and grabbed was part of his obligation as an actor on their TV screens. How could he not *love* it? And who the hell was *she* for standing in *their* way?

After several minutes of high-pitched squeals, additional autographs for friends of friends, and snarky glances at Alex, the pack slunk away. Following Daisy's lead, they bought cola and sweet 'n' salty popcorn then sat a few tables over, riveted in their seats, watching Alex and Mark as if their lunch date was the latest Netflix smash hit. These girls had no shame.

"Fangirls, eh?" Mark winked.

"I've got another name for them…" Alex swallowed hard.

She bowed her head. Mark picked at his sandwich. No further conversation passed their lips.

# Thirteen

*Manchester suburbs, four days later, Boxing Day*

The double bed had surrendered its duvet and most of its plump pillows to the floor, and a discarded white top sheet lay rumpled at the foot of the bed. Damp with perspiration, Mark laid his head down on Alex's bare chest, his breathing still ragged. "That…was the best Christmas gift…*ever*." His fingertips traced small circles over the slight slope of her breast.

Alex hugged him and wrapped one leg around his hips, pressing him closer. "Better than the signed George Best football when you were eleven?"

Mark looked up, eyebrows deep in thought. "Hmmm…okay, maybe not *that* good."

"Ungrateful!" Alex pushed Mark off and onto his back. She climbed on top of him, straddling his abs, her mouth crushing his with a hard kiss. "Give it back, then." She leaned back, leaving the dare between them.

"Oh, I *will*." His hands slipped up her thighs. "Once I catch my breath…" He stretched upwards from the bed, kissing her just as hard.

Alex wrapped her arms around his neck. "We were a bit loud. God, I hope Dad didn't hear, and we'll have to hide the condoms in the trash again. I don't want Dad seeing them."

Mark played with her hair where it pooled over her shoulders. "I think your Dad knows we have sex…"

"I know, but *still.* I don't want to draw him a picture. Let's be quieter next time, okay?"

"Don't tell *me*, tell the ancient springs in this bed. I think it's older than Joan." He leaned in closer, his gaze intense and wanting. "I'll show you how quiet I can be." His hands pulled her back down on top of him and then travelled up into her hair.

Bruno Mars burst into song from the floor.

Alex jumped, and Mark broke away mid-kiss. He sighed loudly, his hands taking flight.

"Leave it." Alex returned to his lips and pinned his hands under hers, pressing them into the mattress.

"I can't." He eased himself out from underneath his girlfriend and followed "Locked Out of Heaven" to his jeans, lying in a heap on the floor. He squatted quickly and stood back up, rifling through the pockets and giving Alex an unobstructed view of his bare ass.

He was a bit leaner than the last time she saw him. A wolfish smile overtook her face. God, he was hot. *Please be a wrong number.* She was desperate to resume what he had started.

Mark looked back at her. "It's Freds…*Hey,* mate! What's up?"

Goose bumps tickled Alex's arms and chest. Without Mark's warmth against her skin, the room felt chilly. She pulled the duvet off the floor and wrapped it around her, flopping back down on her stomach, stretching out like a starfish on the bed.

An ear-to-ear smile rose in the midst of Mark's stubble. "Bollocks are you! Up here? Should I alert the authorities…" He sat down on the bed, listening intently. "No worries, mate. I'll let Alex and Michael know. Hold tight, see you soon!"

Alex stretched, scooping up a Quality Street orange cream from the bedside table, her crinkled brows wondering why Freddie was *holding tight*. "Everything okay?"

"Not sure. Something happened yesterday with Simon, and Freddie's at the train station with Lucy right now."

"I'm sorry for just showing up like this." Freddie's eyes darted from Alex to her dad, Michael. "I didn't know where else to go."

Michael patted Freddie's shoulder. "Our door is always open."

"It was awful. Si's parents flew over from Montréal to surprise him for Christmas. I answered the door in a bath towel, said I was his flatmate. I made up a story about meeting Si volunteering—there was no way I could tell them we met on Grindr." Freddie slipped out of his slim wool coat as he ambled beside Mark, who was walking hand in hand with Alex.

"Sorry, mate. That must've been bloody awkward." Mark gave Freddie a tight-lipped smile as his eyes followed framed images of local football legends David Beckham, Ryan Giggs, and Gary Neville passing by. This corridor at Old Trafford, home to Manchester United, was carpeted, accessorized with potted plants, and buzzing with smartly dressed hospitality representatives and well-to-do football fans—no terrace chants, sloppy drinkers, or vulgar language here. Michael, Alex's step-mum Helen, and her grandmother Joan walked closely behind, all agog at the foreign surroundings inside their favourite football ground. They had sat outside, shoulder-to-shoulder with fellow die-hard Reds in the Stretford End on occasion, but *this*…this posh experience was a world apart.

"Awkward, times a thousand." Freddie hugged his coat against his chest. "Every time I opened my mouth, I worried I'd drop Simon in it." He looked over his shoulder. "Lucy saved me."

"That was the first *and* last time I pretend to be your girlfriend, Freds." Lucy unzipped her puffer and threw Alex a fed-up look. "Worst Christmas ever. When I wasn't fawning over my 'boyfriend', I was hiding photos—shots of them smooching, shirtless holiday snaps—"

"Yeah, all there on display for parental disapproval." Freddie smiled at her.

"And to top it all off, just like Simon, they talked all the way through the *Doctor Who* Christmas special." Lucy scowled.

"I literally *screamed* when you appeared on screen." Freddie leaned into Mark.

"Yeah, that didn't help," said Lucy.

"You should talk," said Freddie. "You practically wet yourself."

"Yeah, well—*our* Keegs with *The Doctor*!"

Mark glanced down at Alex and a proud smile lit up her face. She swung his hand, giving it a squeeze.

The group stopped just short of an open door. The roar of seventy-five thousand football fans mixed with "Love Will Tear Us Apart" by Joy Division—an Old Trafford favourite—echoed into the hallway atop a frosty midday breeze.

"Mr. Keegan, hello." A suited and booted United hospitality employee appeared in the doorway and extended his hand. "Welcome to your private box."

"Thank you." Mark shook his hand warmly and turned to Alex's father. "Happy Christmas, Michael." He stepped back, allowing Michael to enter the east stand executive box first.

Michael gasped and nudged his eyeglasses up his nose. The sight of United's vibrant green pitch outside the window left him dizzy with delight. "Jesus, Mark. If you were thinking of asking for my daughter's hand in marriage, now's the time. If she says no, I'll marry ya…"

"Dad!" Alex squeaked, her face sizzling, no doubt as red as the United shirts Mark, Joan, and Michael wore. *Don't look at Mark. Don't look at him!* She winced and scrunched her eyes as her throat tightened, threatening to strangle her. If only Harry Potter would magically appear with an invisibility cloak. Freddie burst out with a laugh while Joan and Helen exchanged glances, horrified. Lucy froze on the spot and swallowed heavily, cringing for her best friend.

"Um…well…" Mark stammered and scratched his head, an uncomfortable grin raising his cheeks. He quickly looked sideways at Alex and then at her dad.

"Michael Sinclair, what are you like? Leave the boy alone." Helen folded her coat defiantly over her forearm.

He squeezed his daughter's shoulder. "I'm just teasing him, honey." He smiled at Mark, sheepishly. "Seriously, Mark, you shouldn't have spent so much. I feel guilty, like I'm taking advantage."

"It's me taking advantage, more like." Mark pulled Alex close. "You've been like a dad to me these past two years…it's the least I could do."

"Well, it's appreciated by all of us, son." He slapped Mark on the back then grasped Helen's hand and they walked out with Joan to the private outdoor balcony to wait for the players' warm-up on the grass below. Joan proudly removed her winter coat, revealing her United shirt from the legendary 1998-99 season. Freddie wandered over and threw his arm around her shoulder, covering up *BECKHAM* spelled out in white letters.

Alex hid in the nook of Mark's neck, refusing to meet his eyes. "Sorry about that." Her voice cracked.

"I'm just happy he's happy." He smiled. "Hey, look at me." He nudged her chin upwards with his finger and looked her into the eyes. "I love you. Don't ever doubt that."

"I love you, too." Alex didn't know what more to say, so she kissed him.

"Hey…" Lucy shuffled over.

"I'm gonna pop to the loo before it starts." Mark gave Alex a peck on the top of her head, dropped his coat on a chair then slipped away, his United shirt bearing the name of his favourite midfielder as a kid—*KEANE*.

Lucy waited, making sure he was gone. "What is he *waiting* for?"

Alex shrugged, unzipping her coat.

Lucy's eyebrows raised the alarm, even if her voice didn't. "What *did* he give you for Christmas, then? I knew it wasn't the ring when you didn't text."

"A designer dress. It's pretty, but so bodycon—panty line is guaranteed—and…" She opened her jacket. "…this necklace from Tiffany."

Lucy leaned in. The silver scooter charm dangled from a delicate chain. "Super cute, but…it's not THE ring."

"Lucy, shhhh," Alex mumbled under her breath. "It threw me for a second when he brought out the little blue gift bag…I thought he had swapped his mum's ring for Tiffany. I thought *it's all happening*. Even Joan thought so. She elbowed me and said '*Oooh, am I gonna need a new hat?*'"

"Fuck. What did you say?"

"I ignored Joan, opened it, and said, '*It's gorgeous, thank you!*'—what else was I supposed to say after *that*? It was awkward. Mark fidgeted with his tie and wouldn't look at me." Alex's eyes stung. "Shit. I don't want to cry again." She ducked her head just as Mark bounded through the doorway. His hand trailed over her back as he strode past, heading to the outside balcony. Alex grasped Lucy's arm and guided her closer to the suite's entrance, where Irish ears couldn't listen in.

"You cried in front of him?" Lucy whispered, handing Alex a tissue.

"No, later in my room. They went to the pub after lunch. Mark begged me to go, but I wasn't in the mood so I lied about calling Robbie. Mark doesn't know I started those anxiety pills. He would've asked why I wasn't drinking."

Lucy turned her back to the balcony. "And Joan might have asked if you were pregnant."

Alex blotted her nose quickly with the tissue, her eyes unwavering from the big white 16 on Mark's back. *Don't turn around. Don't catch us...*

"I don't mean to sound ungrateful." She played with the charm. "I absolutely *adore* this. It symbolizes our first date, Mark's Vespa rules—'*hop on, hold tight, and remember to enjoy the ride*'. I love it, I *really* do—"

"But it's not what you expected." Lucy frowned.

"Am I fooling myself? I've been so stupid. Mark's already spoken for—he's married to his job, not me."

"Oh, babe."

"I'm holding on, making sacrifices...for what? Every time commitment—a *proper* commitment—is mentioned, he chokes." Alex's eyes bounced to Lucy. "You've just seen it."

"Maybe he's waiting for your anniversary."

"I'm getting tired of waiting. Nothing's going to change."

"It's only a few days away, Lex."

"I'm tired of missing out on normal couple stuff, you know, everyday things? Waking up together, quick kisses in the kitchen, making each other laugh after a tough day. I even miss going to yoga class with him, and I *hate* yoga." Alex winced, watching the balcony again. "And after weeks apart, we're back together—briefly. Our reunions are always so bittersweet, so fleeting, like there's a stopwatch on us, counting the minutes we've got left before he has to leave again. It doesn't play nicely with my anxiety. I worry if I bend any more, I'll break."

"It's like you only get to borrow him for a little while and then have to give him back whenever showbiz calls."

"He says yes to everyone but me, Lucy. I'm starting to feel like I'm wasting my time, living like this, with him half in, half out. I'm not happy."

The white 16 turned around. Mark rushed through the sliding door, a toothy grin growing brighter with each step closer. Alex's stomach rolled. This conversation had to end—stat.

Lucy shrugged. "Maybe you should tell Mar—"

"Tell Mark *what*?" He playfully cocked his head. "Mouse, take your parka off—stay a while." He whisked her coat from her bowed shoulders and hung it on the back of a chair. Alex tugged on the hem of her blouse where it stuck out from underneath her sweater.

Lucy jumped in—rescuing her friends this holiday season had become her new M.O. "I was saying to Lex that she should tell you how much she loves her new dress. All she can talk about is that scooter charm. It's lovely." Lucy winked. "Most blokes are clueless, but you know her so well."

Alex nodded, the desire to give Lucy a huge kiss, top of mind.

"Well, I thought I did," said Mark with a sly smile. "Recently, I've been having doubts."

*Doubts?* Alex swallowed.

Mark curled his arm around her waist. "Living together, I've realized there's a ton of stuff I *don't* know about her. Every once in a while, something sneaks out."

"Oh, I could add to this list…" Lucy played along.

"There's a list?" Alex raised her eyebrows.

Lucy winked. "You are a freak, seriously."

"*I'm* a freak?" The knots in Alex's shoulders began to loosen.

Mark leaned into Lucy. "You know her Paddington Bear? She doesn't just hug him, she sniffs him—deeply. He smells like morning breath."

Alex frowned in protest. "He *doesn't*. He smells like home."

"If home is a dumpster."

"Well, sometimes I think you grew up in a barn, Keegan. You wear your boots around the flat, never wash out your mug, and…you eat and shower at the same time."

Lucy's eyes bulged. "How?"

He shrugged. "Only on weekends."

Alex jutted out a hip. "He goes for a long shower with a plate of toast and raspberry jam. Gets crumbs all over my loofa. Weirdo. And he has freaky nightmares sometimes. He jolts up in bed, mumbling about football. Oh, and he's scared of flowers! If he buys me snapdragons, they have to be covered in cellophane. He can't bear to touch them."

"Lex hates Thai food. How can anyone hate the happiness that is a pad thai takeaway? And she has an unhealthy infatuation with Tower Bridge." Mark scratched his stubble.

"*That* I do know," said Lucy.

"What's not to like?" Alex shrugged. "It opens its arms to welcome big boats…"

"And how have you not watched the entire run of *Friends*?" The actor waved his hands defiantly in the air. "Could that show *be* any more awesome?"

Lucy burst out laughing.

"The last scene in the finale gets him…every…time." Alex brushed her bangs from her forehead. "You know, the one where they leave the keys behind? Cries like a baby."

He tickled Alex's waist. "Yeah, well, you're a sleep farter."

"Mark!" Alex squealed with a half-laugh, shimmying out of his grasp.

"Well! You've exposed all my secrets." Mark laughed. "Fair is fair."

"All of them? Yeah, *right*. I bet there are some skeletons in your closet I've heard nothing about, mister!"

Mark adopted a look of angelic innocence as a roar went up behind him from the Old Trafford faithful. "Come on, it's about to kick off."

# FOURTEEN

*Dublin, New Year's Eve*

Walking into Mark's Dublin hotel suite, Alex gave her boyfriend a flirty smile over her shoulder. "Wow, this room's gorgeous! Happy anniversary, babe."

He grinned and walked past, wheeling her small carry-on along the carpet. "Not splitting hairs, Lex, but our anniversary is actually *tomorrow*…" He turned around and started to unbutton his coat.

"I know, but it doesn't mean we can't start celebrating early!" She removed her parka and hung it up in the closet.

Mark's eyes drifted. "If I'm honest, I've *never* liked New Year's Eve. It's so overrated." He took off his scarf and coat, tossing them onto a clothes-covered chair. "You don't fancy staying in, do ya? We could order room service, watch a film, toast the new year in, just the two of us?"

Alex quickly set her purse down on the edge of the desk. "Babe, you feeling okay?" She narrowed her eyes. He seemed distracted. "It's not like you to bail on a party. I mean, I'd *love* to stay in, but we're in Dublin and…aren't your castmates expecting you?"

"Yeah, but…" He fiddled with his wristwatch.

"It would be kinda rude to bail on them now…don't you think?" She clasped his hand. "Why don't we just go for a bit, have a dance…leave right after midnight…?"

He looked up. "I'm just not feeling in party mode today…"

"Well, *I* know what might help!" Alex clutched fistfuls of Mark's shirt, tugging him into her chest. She returned to his lips, picking up where they had left off when he'd scooped her up at the airport forty minutes earlier.

Mark tripped over her wheelie carry-on, sending his lips skidding off her mouth and down her chin. "Shit. Cary Grant, I ain't. Almost went arse over tit there." He winked lazily and rolled her luggage to the far side of the room, away from distracted feet.

Alex giggled and turned back to her purse on the desk.

Intermingling on its surface with opened packages of Jaffa Cakes and the latest novel he was reading, Mark had a collection of framed photos, a portable shrine in his room dedicated to their relationship: beloved shots of Alex with his red Vespa during their first date, Mark laughing at Alex wearing a Venetian mask on their one-year anniversary trip to Venice a year before, and the pair cuddled together for warmth in a soggy Glastonbury Festival tent.

Alex's eyes did a second loop, revisiting each photo as Mark opened the minibar and removed two miniature bottles of gin. He cracked one open, then the other, downing both without taking a breath.

"Whoa, *steady* tiger—it's not even four o'clock yet! It's early…even for a Dubliner!" Alex chuckled. She glanced down at one special memory holding pride of place in a heavy wood frame. She picked it up.

Wrapped in each other's arms in front of the Royal Court Theatre, Mark beamed at Alex as THIRTEEN BY ALEXANDRA

SINCLAIR sizzled above their heads in red neon. She stared at the image. Mark had chosen to showcase her greatest accomplishment instead of one of his own. "You carted all this stuff over here?"

He slipped an arm around her waist and grabbed the photo out of her hand, returning it to the desk. "Yeah, I always want you with me…"

"That can be arranged." The words barely out of her mouth, Alex met Mark's lips urgently, the gin still potent as she kissed him hard and fast. Her hands dove into his hair, pulling him closer, his kiss deeper. She had to taste him, own him.

Mark didn't back down. Gripping her ass so hard she cried out, he pressed against her with feral intent, blurring the lines of where he ended and she began. His tongue was frantic, devouring her. It had only been two minutes since their last kiss, but to Alex, this one felt different. It was fierce and wild, like Mark's lips were trying to soothe an insatiable need only her mouth could possibly fulfill.

Their second anniversary was the next day, but the desire to show their commitment to each other *right then* was too powerful to resist.

Mark broke free, breathless. "I want you—so badly."

Heart racing, she flung off her sweater and tugged his long-sleeved Henley. "Off, now."

Mark obliged and yanked it over his head, chucking it out of the way. His impatient hands skimmed down her back and unhooked her bra. Normally, Alex would taunt him a little longer, make him wait, but she had left her patience back in London. She let her bra slip to the floor and pulled him close again, craving bare skin-on-skin contact.

He kissed and sucked her neck, his mouth and tongue only pausing to release ravenous moans from his lips as his thumb teased her hardening nipple.

She felt the button undo on her jeans and Mark's fingers slipping into her cotton panties. Gasps left her lips in quick succession. "Keep…going." She gripped the back of his neck, her sighs fueling his hunger.

"Christ, Lex." He groaned between breaths. "You feel *so* good."

She stared at his lips and lunged, desperate to taste him again. Their kisses grew more eager, more frantic as if their time together was running out and their mouths demanded to profess everything they needed to say before the clock struck midnight.

Alex left his lips to catch her breath. One hand slipped downwards, stroking the prominent bulge inside his jeans. "Mark…"

He moaned and removed his hand from her underwear, yanking her jeans to the floor. With a naughty smile, he pressed his lips against her ear. "Hey, sexy playwright lady, this actor needs some direction."

"So eager to please." Alex pushed him onto the bed and climbed on the duvet, unfastening his jeans. Scooting out of them completely, Mark yanked off his socks and grabbed Alex by the waist, flipping her onto her back.

She smirked. "I thought you needed *direction*."

"Plot twist…" His tongue fiercely returned to her mouth, dominating, demanding, as his crotch pressed hard against her.

Alex gasped. "*Hello* stranger!" She cocked an eyebrow and hooked her fingers into his boxer briefs, pulling them down.

"Is it obvious?" Alex clasped Mark's hand and blushed as she dodged between smokers cluttering the sidewalk.

"Obvious that we had mind-blowing sex or that you're not wearing any knickers?"

"Both?"

"Yep, your cheeky smile gives it all away." Mark chuckled as he held open the door to the Stag's Head, a Victorian pub in the centre of Dublin.

She stopped in the doorway.

"I'm kidding. Only *I* know your secrets, and I'm not telling." Mark waved her through the entrance. "Take off your parka, Lex. You look gorgeous."

Alex unzipped her coat and tugged down the creeping hem of her short red dress, her other Christmas gift from Mark. The outfit was a showstopper and unlike anything she had ever worn. The sleeveless dress's scooped neck, low back, and body-hugging seams guaranteed plenty of male attention, whether Alex wanted it or not. Her eyes flitted through the rowdy crowd of anonymous faces, taking in the pub's picturesque stained glass windows, carved wood, and wrought-iron chandeliers. Rosy-cheeked males, toting pints and lecherous smirks, stared. She dipped her chin as she pulled the coat closed. "Mark?"

He held her hand through the dense forest of drinkers. "Don't be nervous. You'll be fine."

A huge wall of a guy in a button-down shirt, his thick tree trunk neck straining to break free of the tie-less collar, shoved in front of the couple, halting their progress. "Mark, you eejit, you're late—I had to start without you!" His loud bark of an American accent—California, possibly—grabbed the attention of nearby revellers. He punched the air with two large pint glasses, the creamy foam of Guinness breaching their rims.

"Christ, they let you in, then?!" Mark fiddled with the collar of his pink dress shirt. "Alex, meet my agent, Coen Winkler. Coen, meet Alex Sinclair, my girlfriend."

"Take one of these, buddy." He stuffed a sloppy pint into Mark's palm. "Don't listen to him. Please, call me Wink." His gaze went to the Vespa charm hanging from Alex's neck. A hand the size of an extra-large baseball glove then shot towards her to shake.

"Nice to meet you…Wink."

His vice-like grip crushed her hand. She caught her breath, grimacing through the discomfort until his sticky paw released her from its bone-rattling shake. Her elbow actually ached. She glanced at Mark, but his attention jerked elsewhere, hijacked by a chatty young couple and their phone's camera.

"I've been working with Mark since what…April? It's about time we met, Sincy."

*Sincy?* Alex hated abbreviating her surname.

A camera flash and a good-bye nod released Mark back to her side. "Sorry, babe." He handed back the pint glass. "Wink, how many times have I told you, Guinness isn't my thing."

"Poor excuse for an Irishman, you are."

A chuckle left Mark's lips as he tugged Alex's parka from her shoulders.

"Hey, did he tell you why he signed with me? What we have in common?" Wink didn't wait for Alex to answer. "I'm Irish, too!"

"You and half of America, mate." Mark rolled his eyes, folding Alex's coat over his arm.

Alex fidgeted with one of the slim straps of her dress while giving Wink a double take. "Your name doesn't sound Irish."

"No, it's German, but my great-great-great-grandmother on my mother's side was from Dingle, so I'm part Irish…I'll leave you to figure out which part!" His booming laugh assaulted Alex's eardrums. Once he finished laughing at his own joke, he leapt into a jerky knee-raising stomp, slopping waves of murky Guinness onto the mosaic-tiled floor and his designer jeans. *Was that supposed to be the Riverdance? Oh, God.* It didn't help that Mark encouraged him by laughing. Did he feel that he had to? Easily six foot four, Wink seemed like the kind of larger-than-life, type-A personality who could make people do whatever they wanted.

Wink's *Riverdance* dried up quickly then Mark slid an arm around Alex's waist and directed her towards the bar. "Come on, love. Let's get a bevvy, stash your coat. Then you can meet everyone. I promise, they're not all mad like this one!"

"Crazy like a *fox*, brother." Wink pivoted to Alex. "Seriously, though, Sincy, I always have his best interests at heart." He glugged half of the Guinness in his left hand and followed, swaying behind them. Alex wondered how many he'd had already.

"Vodka and orange, and a Pale Ale, please." Mark nodded at the bartender and adjusted his black tie. He leaned on the wooden bar and smiled at Alex, but her attention drifted, settling on the majestic stag's head overlooking the pub. Its glassy eyes gave her the creeps. Two guys on the other side of Mark recognized him and started up a conversation.

Wink's massive elbow jabbed Alex's shoulder.

"Have you ever seen Mark so happy? He's in this movie because of me, you know."

Alex looked to Mark for confirmation, but he was busy sharing a joke. She turned back to Wink. *What the—?* His face was now just a few inches away from hers, leaning in conspiratorially. *Bleurgh.* Sweat mixed with booze and musky cologne oozed from his pores.

"Mark talks about you all the time."

Alex blushed. *Aw.*

"At first I thought you were his UK PR rep, his personal manager or something. It was '*let me check with Alex*' this, or '*I have to phone Alex*' that!" Wink laughed, releasing Guinness breath. "Then he said you were his *girlfriend*! I was pretty relieved, let me tell ya! Well, it's finally nice to put a pretty face to the name. Here's lookin' at you, kid!" He raised his glass and supped the creamy head of the black beverage.

Mark handed Alex her glass. "One vodka and orange for my girl." He raised his pint to clink against his girlfriend's drink.

"Cheers." She smiled and took a dainty sip.

Mark took a large mouthful. "Let's find the gang."

As they climbed the stairs to the upstairs lounge, the final gasp of Britney Spears' "Oops, I Did It Again" gave way to the strumming guitar of Ricky Martin's "She Bangs". Alex smirked. *Old school.* These songs used to be played to death on the radio when she was a kid. The other guests didn't seem to care about the trip down memory lane; they were too busy pounding back pints, shouting over each other or staring at her passing ass. Mark, Alex, and Wink had to squeeze through a tight maze of locals in the narrow room until they found the boisterous cast and crew of *A Promise Unspoken* at the back. Stashing Alex's parka in the corner booth, Mark held her tight and joined the party.

A woman, a year or two older than Alex, wearing a makeup counter's worth of shimmery cosmetics, slipped through the crush towards them, her curvy five-foot-eight figure swathed in a clingy crimson cocktail dress. Its high neck and sleeveless silhouette gave way in the back to a deep V that stopped a half-inch above her bum. Her charisma screamed *look at me*, and most of the men in the room obeyed: approving stares followed every shift of the precarious V, their eyes leaving her bare skin only to check out the dark-haired guy holding her hand. Alex overheard the words 'Leinster' and 'rugby' excitedly expressed from a nearby table as the young couple approached. Many of the women did a double take behind their cocktail umbrellas. Where to look, her plunging dress or his muscular physique? Their starstruck reactions didn't register; the woman's crooked yet confident smile and large brown eyes sought out one person.

"Hello gorgeous! You must be Lex. Mark's told me all about you." She extended a soft hand and a welcoming grin. "I'm Fallon Delaney, his co-star." She nodded at the rugby hunk glued to her side. "This is Duff."

Alex perked up, relieved to hand over the title of 'most naked woman in the pub'. She met Fallon's greeting halfway. "Nice to meet you."

Duff placed a hand on Fallon's butt. Alex wasn't keen on guys with over-the-top muscles, but even she stared at his pecs straining underneath his skin-tight white shirt, its buttons ready to pop.

Duff kissed his date's temple. "Drink, Fal?"

Wink raised his pints of Guinness. "Like he has to ask."

Fallon clocked Wink's full hands. "You're one to talk. Nice Irish handcuffs, ya got there!"

Mark and Wink laughed. Duff lumbered off to the bar, leaving a waft of spicy cologne behind. He stopped twice to fist bump and take selfies with several rugby fans. Mark clearly wasn't the only celebrity in attendance.

Fallon fluttered her thick eyelashes in Wink's direction. "Be nice, or I'll trigger that escape clause in my contract. Remember, I'm doing *you* a favour."

She leaned into Alex's ear, Duff's spicy fragrance accompanying her. "I saved his bacon before the Christmas break, taking this role. I even cancelled my holibobs with Duff. Mind you, that bloody read, I swear that's the only '*chemistry test*' I've ever passed." A throaty laugh, defying her young age and worthy of a pack a day, flew from her pale lips.

Her easy charm and playful dig at Wink put Alex at ease. She jumped in, sharing the actress's chemistry joke. "Ugh, I barely passed my sciences except biology. Thank goodness for the arts, huh?"

"I *know*, right?" Fallon's Irish accent was slightly different from Mark's, but Alex didn't know enough about Ireland to place it. "I'd be asking people, *Do you want fries with that?* if it wasn't for acting! Ooh, I *love* your dress, by the way."

"Thanks! Your guy seems nice."

"Yeah." Fallon looked towards Duff, surrounded by admirers near the bar. "We've been dating three weeks. He's fun—and *insatiable*." She laughed and smoothed her pin-straight dark blonde hair away from her eyes. A small tattoo stretched over her inner wrist, a pair of crossed field hockey sticks. "What are you drinking? Vodka and orange?"

Alex nodded.

"That's no way to ring in the New Year."

"And our second anniversary." Alex smiled widely, glancing up at Mark, who hugged her close. "It's tomorrow."

"Really? Well, an anniversary that falls over New Year's calls for celebratory drinks. Mark, I'm *disappointed* in you." She yanked Alex away, dragging her through the tight throng.

"Wait—" Concern clouded Mark's eyes.

Alex glanced over her shoulder, grinning.

"Ahh, leave them to it." Wink smirked. "Besides, it's almost ten o'clock, and you're not even buzzed, man. You've got some serious catching up to do."

Mark craned his neck, trying to spot his girlfriend. "But she's not really a big *party* girl—"

"Stop being so protective." Wink elbowed him in the back. "She's an adult. Let her go. She's made a new friend, and yours are waiting. It's all good, bro." He steered Mark to a crew of raucous males shouting at each other over a table clogged with pints and an ignored platter of deep-fried finger foods.

By quarter past eleven, the Stag's Head was rocking with plenty of good old-fashioned Irish hospitality, unlimited booze, and a standing-room only crowd. Glittery party hats had been handed out along with noisemakers and confetti. Clusters of drinkers hollered and prematurely blew their celebratory horns from the curved red leather booths that lined the narrow space.

"Lexy, darling, get over here!" Fallon unleashed her body-shaking laugh and waved a crimson cocktail that matched her dress.

Alex clung to the edge of the tiny parlour bar. Her heavy eyelids blinked lazily, a cocktail umbrella and wedge of pineapple beside her white knuckles. "No…come here!"

An impatient suit with a stained tie and lipstick on his cheek stuffed himself into the sliver of space between Alex and the wall, weakening her grip. Her blood-starved fingers let go. She fell backwards, crashing into the plaid-covered chest of a tall beardy redhead supping his pint. With nowhere to go but down, she crumpled awkwardly on her hip and his scuffed leather boots. "*He's a lumberjack and…*ow! *Not okay…*" Her tipsy sing-a-long dissolved into uncontrollable giggling.

Wink ducked through the swarm, careful not to spill his latest Guinness. He snatched Alex's arm, tugging her up onto rubbery legs. "Careful there, little lady." He grinned sheepishly at Alex's lumberjack, who shrugged away the nuisance. "Sorry, buddy."

Alex shoved Wink's hand away and dropped her clutch. "Don't tell me what to do. I'm not *Mark*." She weaved on the spot, her right ankle buckling sideways in her heel, causing her to lurch into a lopsided slump.

"Ooh, the mouse that roared." Wink bent down to pick up Alex's clutch and handed it to Fallon. "One of the film assistants is fetching Mark. What the hell happened?"

"We were having drinks, chatting with some blokes from set…" She pointed to two thirty-something guys with Duff near the room's front window. Twinkly fairy lights glowed against its fogged-up glass. "It was great craic."

"How much has she had?"

"Two—three at most!"

Wink blew out his cheeks. “Lightweight.”

Fallon held Alex’s shoulder, keeping her from crashing to the floor again. “She had strawberry mojitos. She wasn’t going to have another, but—”

“*She* told me…” Alex’s head wobbled as she pointed at Fallon.

“What’s she on about?” Wink downed the dregs of his pint and wiped his mouth with the back of his hand.

“I told her about the sex scene—with Mark. She seemed pretty put out by it. He’s done kissing scenes before, but nothing full on like what we shot yesterday.” Fallon chewed her bottom lip. “Once she heard about the nudity, she wanted another drink. Downed it in one.”

Alex rested her head on Fallon’s breast and began to hiccup. “Why…*hic*…didn’t he tell me…*hic*…tell me…?” She sounded like a stuttering CD.

“*See*? That’s the problem with girlfriends not in the biz,” Wink whispered. “They get jealous…dating outside the industry never works out.”

“I thought she’d understand. Isn’t she a playwright?” Fallon backed up. “Lexy, hon—you okay? Here, let’s get this back on ya.” She slipped the wrist strap of Alex’s clutch over her hand.

“Lex!” Mark pushed through the throng, a female production assistant by his side. “What happened?”

Fallon handed Alex over to Mark with concern in her eyes.

“Babe…you wanna play, right?” Alex melted into his arms and hoisted the hem of her dress.

Mark batted her hand, dropping the flirty fabric back down to her mid-thigh. He looked at Fallon. “What’s she been drinking?”

Fallon toyed with the silver coin bracelet on her wrist. “Mojitos.”

“Where did you come from?” Alex touched Mark’s cheek. “Your face, it’s wet…”

“I was in the loo.”

“That loo sees you more than I do...*hic.*”

Mark held Alex tightly and turned to Fallon, Wink, and the production assistant. “Alcohol affects her really quickly.”

“*Fruity* drinksssssss.” Alex giggled and pressed her face into the collar of his shirt.

“Yeah, well, I’m cutting you off...we’re leaving.” Mark looked towards the stairwell.

“But, it’s our anal—verrrsss”—she latched onto his tie as her legs began to slide apart. Mark pulled her up quickly, saving Alex from flashing the bar—“*sorry.*”

Mark cringed, glancing at Wink and Fallon. “She means anniversary.” He hugged her close. “It’s tomorrow, Lex. C’mon. Back to the hotel, let’s get you to bed.”

She fumbled for his belt. “Ooh, *fireworks...*”

The production assistant looked away. Fallon bit her lip. Wink laughed. This time, Mark didn’t join him.

“Lex.” He grabbed her hand and whispered in her ear, “No fireworks, just *sleep.*”

Her right arm curled around his shoulders. “I know what might help.” She kissed his neck while the hand hovering near his belt fought for freedom.

“Lex, no...*listen...*”

A few revellers stared and gestured at the free, impromptu performance by Mark Keegan and company.

“Mark, camera phones, buddy,” Wink mumbled out of the corner of his mouth. “We don’t want this on YouTube...” He quickly ran interference like an NFL pro, blocking the strangers’ view and striking up a loud conversation to distract them. Fallon and Duff shifted back through the crowd, granting the couple privacy.

“Lex, come on.” Mark captured her roaming hand and stared into her eyes. “You wanna enjoy tomorrow, yeah?”

"Yeah." Her scrunched-up eyes popped open with each hiccup. "Okay…*hic*…but promise me?"

Mark squeezed her hand and nodded, anything to get Alex to focus and give up the fight. "Sure, I promise."

She stabbed a wobbly index finger into his chest. "You stay."

"Come. We're goin—"

The production assistant leaned into Mark's ear. "I can take her. It's no problem."

"I don't like leaving her."

"No, it's my turn. I'm leaving *you*—to your party." Alex giggled and ran her hand down Mark's shirt. She poked her fingers through a gap between buttons, her levity slipping into a protest tinged with tears. "I don't want to ruin the party. Promise me I haven't ruined it, Mark?"

"No, Lex." Mark tucked her head protectively under his chin, hugging her close and away from curious onlookers. "You haven't ruined the party."

Wink slapped him on the back. "Listen to your girl, she talks sense. Now, there's someone from LA I want you to meet…"

Mark nodded. "Lex, I'll stay for another hour, two tops." He kissed the top of her head and turned to the P.A., mouthing, "Are you sure?"

The P.A. gave him a reassuring smile. "I won't make it to midnight anyway. I'll make sure she gets to your room."

# FIFTEEN

Mark's shuffle under the sheets bounced Alex awake.

She squinted at his pale back and shifted her head slowly, homing in on the soft blue glow at the bottom of the flatscreen TV—the time, *nine fifteen.* Brightness spilled out from the bathroom around the corner. Dublin was too busy imitating a dishwasher outside, so her eyes were spared the discomfort of stabby shards of sunlight creeping through the edges of the curtains. Her hip ached. A peek under the duvet and her half-off dress revealed a purple and yellow bruise the size of an apple. She scratched her pounding head. "Mark, you awake?"

"Yeah…" His Irish accent barely broke a whisper.

"Kill me now. I'm *so* regretting last night. My head feels like a bashed-in piñata."

"Me too. I should've been here looking after you…" He rolled over and clutched the edge of his pillow.

Alex gulped. Who had kidnapped her smiley boyfriend and replaced him with this mess who reeked worse than a brewery? This guy's hair stuck to his forehead, and his complexion was ghostly, spare smudges of silver glitter on his cheek and chin, no doubt from a party hat long discarded. His brown eyes, bloodshot and puffy, skimmed over her, their usual lively glow extinguished. "Are you cross with me, Mouse?" He sounded like a chastised little boy.

"Hmm, guilty much?" she teased. "No, *I* made you stay. It's my fault I'm in this mess, not yours." She scooched farther up on her pillow, but the room swung around to meet her. "Urgh…don't feel bad. I feel bad enough for both of us." A rub of her eye, and black liner and glitter darkened her hand. "If I look as bad as I feel—"

"You always look gorgeous." Mark's voice cracked, like he was about to dissolve into tears. "Happy second anniversary, Mouse."

"Happy anniversary, babe." Alex swallowed several times, trying to wash away excessive saliva. "What's wrong?"

"My head…is banging. I could murder a glass of water, but I feel like I could be sick. Fucking shots. I can't remember whose idea that was." Mark sniffed and closed his eyes. "If I could do it all over again, I would've come back with you. God, I'm such an idiot."

"But you're *my* idiot, and I love you."

"I love you, too, Mouse, more than anything…you know that, right?"

She squeezed his hand. "My throat's wrecked. I haven't thrown up like that since Olivia stole my play. It was disgusting. When I got up around five to four, you still weren't back."

"How many times were you sick?"

"Twice, maybe…"

"I should've been here, holding your hair back." He squeezed her hand.

Alex's stomach squeaked and bubbled. "I'm tired of feeling like this."

"Me too. Our anniversary isn't going too well, is it? God,

what a difference a year makes. Ah, Venice…" His voice halted. "Never again."

"Never again. I'm done with stupid fruity cocktails… wait, what? Never what…Venice?"

"Promise me we'll never be apart at midnight on New Year's ever again, no matter what."

"That's my line, workaholic." Alex snorted. "And after last night, I think I'm done with going commando…"

"I'm being serious, Lex. No more New Years apart."

A muffled ping came from underneath the bedding. "You don't have to nag. I've learnt my lesson."

Mark groaned. "Me too."

Alex's hand fished under her pillow, pulling out her phone. "Oh." Her eyes lit up. Two unread texts: one misspelled ramble from Freddie that ended with *Stay sparkly* and a delivery notification from the hotel's front desk.

"What is it?"

"A surprise, the good kind." She stared with half-mast eyelids. "So…is there something you want to tell me? Clear your conscience?"

"No…" He picked at a loose thread on his pillowcase. "I don't think so."

"You thought I'd freak out, right?" She dropped her phone under the covers. "Don't worry, my head's too sore to even go there."

"Go where?"

"Mark, please…I know about the nude sex scene. Fallon told me—she thought I knew."

"Oh…" His breath hitched as he looked away. "Yeah."

"Yeah, it would've been nice to hear it from my boyfriend."

"I'm sorry. It should've come from me—"

"You're right. It should have." She sighed. "But I understand why you kept quiet. You didn't need an earache." Alex swallowed, but she couldn't budge the lump in her throat. "I'm angry with myself, and embarrassed. I hope I didn't make you look bad in front of your friends. Fallon's lovely, and I said some things…I wouldn't blame her if she never spoke to me again, and it's my fault for getting blotto with those berry drinks. I should know better. I *do* know better. I can't drink as much as everyone else, and sex scenes are part of your job, end of."

"You're being way too hard on yourself."

"I love you for saying that, but…" She shrugged. "I'll apologize to Fallon when I see her—and Duff…and Wink, and the P.A. I have a long list."

"You don't have to apologize. I should be the one—"

Alex placed her fingers on his lips. "Shh."

Mark kissed her fingers.

"Yeah, you might want to skip my lips until I brush my teeth. I don't blame you." She curled into him and scrunched up her nose. "Ew, you reek. Booze and…something else?"

"I may have had a sneaky cigarette or two last night."

"Ugh."

"I used to smoke, ages ago. That's the problem with Dublin—it's easy to fall into old habits here." He smoothed her hair away from her eyes. "I wish we were done here. I wish we were back in London Fields."

"Me too." She kissed his neck and frowned. "You're sticky."

"Wink spilled a cocktail down me. Bastard." Mark pulled away, flipping his legs out of the duvet. "Fuck, that was a bad idea. The room…" He paused, bracing himself on the bed. "I'm gonna shower. Maybe it will clear my head."

"Need an extra hand in there?" Alex snickered, watching his underwear-covered butt move away from her.

"No, stay there. I'll order breakfast when I'm done." He removed his watch. "If you can stomach it?"

"I'll try. Just some toast, maybe?" Alex pulled up into a sitting position then grabbed the duvet to steady the dizzy sway. "While you're in there, I'll change, pop downstairs, get my parcel."

"Is that a good idea?" He scratched his chin.

"I'll be lucky to make it to the lobby and back without killing myself." She tugged the Vespa charm to the front of its chain. "Nah, I'll be fine. It's something for your birthday. I know how much you love surprises."

Wearing yoga pants, unlaced Converse, Mark's sweatshirt, and a green pallor that would make Kermit the Frog envious, Alex leaned on the hotel's unmanned front desk and typed #MarkKeegan into Instagram. *Lairds* memes rolled under her finger, wishing a Happy Hogmanay and announcing New Year's resolutions to find out what Mark was hiding underneath that kilt. Photos of Mark from Tom and Naomi's wedding continued to pop up along with random fan selfies. A dimly lit, sneaky snap from the previous night of her kissing Mark cropped up in the middle of the Instagram feed—

Her phone lit up: a text from Lucy, sent to her phone and Mark's.

*Hey Marlex. Happy anniversary! Hope you're having a shagging good time. We missed you two last night. Bespoke's Prohibition theme was fun, but Freddie's after-party was dreadful. Don't tell Freds I said that. My head is throbbing, so I'm taking my hot water bottle back to bed! Love you lots. x*

Alex smiled and shifted slowly around, careful not to jar her bruised brain.

A lone figure, chin buried in her scarf, walked across the lobby. An elegant, tight bun reminiscent of a ballerina kept her hair neatly in place—so pretty, but absolute torture with a hangover.

Alex blinked twice, unsure. "Fallon?"

"Oh…hi, Alex. Sorry, miles away." Fallon's skin was luminous, the inch-thick makeup worn at the pub scrubbed away without a trace. Her sparse eyelashes looked like they had never seen a mascara wand in their life. The stunning vixen from the Stag's Head had left Dublin, replaced by a fresh-faced girl next door wearing a parka, yoga pants, and a fat wooly scarf. "How are you?"

Alex groaned. "I've been better. Sorry about last night, I was out of control…"

"Nah." Fallon shrugged, and her scarf swallowed up her chin. "What's New Year's Eve without a laugh, lots of booze…"

"Too right." Alex rolled her eyes.

Fallon smiled. "You're not leaving, are you?"

"Nope. Dublin's stuck with me for a few days. It's Mark's birthday next week and I got him something special, had it sent over yesterday. I'm picking it up…" She turned back to the empty front desk. "…if the staff ever return."

"Did Mark… How is he?"

"He's a bit rough around the edges, but he'll survive. Did you guys stay late, too?"

"The pub did a lock-in. Wink kept getting drinks in. There are going to be some casualties this morning. I'm surprised you're not having a lie-in…"

"It's our anniversary."

"Oh, right. Got plans?"

"Dinner, maybe, if Mark's up to it, or maybe we'll chill, watch a movie or something. His mum wants to see us next weekend when she's back from Europe. We'll celebrate our anniversary and his birthday at the same time."

Fallon's face lit up. "Aw, isn't she lovely? I adore her."

"His mum?" Alex nodded. "Oh, she visited the set?"

"Oh, no. She'd never impose."

Alex squinted, her brain…so foggy. Damn hangover. "Sorry?"

"Oh…I thought Mark would've told you…" Fallon's eyes strayed to the hotel's sliding doors. "I've known Niamh since I was a kid. She was Mum's best friend." Her glance returned with a smile. "They worked together."

"Really?" Alex's voice rose slightly. "I had no clue…"

"Typical Mark, *so* forgetful." Fallon chuckled. "I met him at Mum's work, and then again at a family picnic, freezing by the seaside. We were twelve, *I think*. I bet Niamh still has the photos up on her wall?"

Alex vaguely remembered some beach photos. "Yeah, I think so."

"Our families used to hang out a lot, and Mark ended up in my theatre class—"

"Miss Sinclair?"

Alex pulled her eyes away from Fallon. The breathless concierge darted behind the counter, a parcel in his grip. "Our apologies for this morning's wait."

Alex's stomach rolled again, reminding her of the night's excess. "It's okay. Thanks." She hugged the box covered with stamps and a customs declaration.

"And there's another parcel addressed to Mr. Keegan."

"Okay. I'll take it, too."

The concierge handed over a rectangular courier box. Alex put her own parcel on top and turned to Fallon. "Sorry, you were saying?"

Fallon looked at the glass doors again, clearing her throat. "Look, I feel bad, Alex. Mark really should have said something. I was his first snog, first girlfriend, first…" She bit her lip.

Alex shook her head. Her new friend was delusional. "No, I don't think so. Sinéad was Mark's first girlfriend. He told me. They went out for three months."

"*Three* months?" Fallon's eyebrows peaked. "Alex, this is awkward. I thought you knew…*I'm* Sinéad. Fallon's my middle name. I use it professionally."

"You're…Sinéad?" Alex choked on Fallon's words. "Oh…"

*Why would Mark lie?*

Fallon pulled her parka tighter as she stared at the hotel's exit. A car pulled up. Someone waved. Seconds dragged past. A breath stuck in Alex's throat. She opened her mouth, but no words or air came out.

"My friend's here. Sorry, I wish we could chat longer." Fallon tossed her bag over a shoulder and smiled kindly. "Have a happy anniversary, okay?"

Without looking back, she dashed through the doors to the car, her bun barely touched by Dublin's drizzle.

A strong waft of fragrance, a spicy scent, prickled Alex's nose…

The scent she had detected in bed…

*On Mark.*

*No.*

*No, NO!* A savage coldness ripped through Alex's chest, plunging without mercy into her stomach. She began to tremble. The lobby melted into a wobbly blur of streaky lights and staring guests.

"Excuse me, miss? Are you all right?" A tourist with a Canadian flag pinned to her coat's lapel smiled kindly.

"I-I…don't know." Alex shuffled past the woman, up the hallway leading to the elevators, and leaned precariously against the wall. Juggling the two parcels, her fingers jabbed at the phone screen quaking in her palm. The last photo she'd seen before receiving Lucy's text—the fuzzy image of her and Mark pressed against the wall in the pub—lit up her screen. Her eyes poured over the image.

The back of Mark's pink shirt was at a diagonal angle to the camera. His arms looped around her waist, and his face was hidden, lost in a kiss. A glimpse of her red dress peeked out from behind his body, but beyond that, only her arms, squeezing him tightly, were in view. Her fingers dug into his back, their embrace verging on desperate. The silver bracelet on her wrist caught the light.

Alex blinked. Something wasn't right. Some parts of the night were still a fog, but Alex did remember that she hadn't made out with Mark at the Stag's Head, not once, not at all…and she didn't own a silver bracelet…

The photo of Mark pressed up against the wall in lip lock—was with Fallon.

# SIXTEEN

"The truth is rarely pure and never simple." – Oscar Wilde

*Oh, God! Oh, God! Please…be wrong. Please be WRONG…*Hot tears pooled in Alex's eyes. She gulped for breath as her mind spiraled.

She flicked her phone's screen, searching for Fallon's Instagram account—if she had one. Fallon…*no, wait… Sinéad* Delaney. Yep, there it was…public for all to see, plastered with party photos date stamped from the night before. Pictures with Duff and Wink, plus, the cast and crew they chatted with at the bar—and then *that* photo. The embrace she had already seen. A Keeganite must have reposted it under Mark's hashtag.

But it had company…a kissing photo, close up with revellers smiling and kissing in the background…and another shot of two people holding hands in the back seat of an SUV. Only the hands and wrists were visible, but Alex could make out Fallon's unmistakable field hockey tattoo…and the pink cuff of Mark's dress shirt, as well as his watch—the one Alex had given him just seven days earlier for Christmas.

*Fuck! NO!*

Fallon didn't use Mark's hashtag but made up her own: #reunited.

*Oh, God! I wasn't wrong. I wasn't fucking WRONG!* Alex gagged, but her tortured stomach refused to comply.

The elevator door opened, empty—*thank God.* She stepped inside.

Now it all made sense. Why Mark hadn't been back when she'd crawled off the bathroom floor at five to four. Why he hadn't kissed her on the lips that morning. Why he had jumped into the shower so quickly.

That spicy scent on his skin, mingling with stale cigarette smoke…it was Fallon's.

She couldn't feel her fingers. The two parcels slipped from her hands, thudding onto her Chucks. Alex barely reacted. She couldn't. All the air had been sucked out of the elevator. Her ears filled with the tuneless theme of an old adversary: the frantic pounding of her broken heart.

*This can't be happening…*

The elevator door slid open. A young couple smiled and bounced their cooing baby in their arms. Alex scrambled for the fallen parcels. "Happy New Year," they chirped, but Alex fled before they expected a reply.

Stumbling down the hall, her quivering legs somehow did their job, carrying her to their door. She stopped. *Am I in the middle of a sick dream? Mark and Fallon…*

A thought struck: *first love.* After her parents' tumultuous divorce, her dad had reunited with Helen, his first love from back home in Manchester. *Fuck!*

She held her breath, leaning against the door, unable to ignore her heart's urgent rhythm beneath Mark's sweatshirt. The shower was quiet. Mark was inside, waiting. He was a *liar* like her ex, Devin.

*Just like Devin.*

She stabbed her keycard in the slot and shouldered the door open. There was Mark, hips wrapped in a towel, his freshly washed hair slicked back with a few tufts misbehaving over his forehead.

"Hey Mouse." He smiled broadly, pointing at the desk and two room service trays crowded with English muffins, Nutella, Frosties cereal, a small vase blooming with snapdragons… "Surprise!"

Alex unleashed her arm like an Olympic shot put thrower, hurling his birthday parcel towards him.

Mark ducked, the box skimming the top of his head. "What the FUCK—"

The parcel swept the cluster of picture frames off the desk and they landed with a sickly crash. Their happy life, protected underneath glass and wood, lay exposed and splintered on the grey carpet.

"Why the hell didn't you tell me?" Her chest felt like it was collapsing, crushing her heart.

"Christ! Tell you what?" Mark's voice went up two octaves.

"About *Fallon*."

He sank onto the bed. "What?"

"You told me she was just some actress…" Tears poured from her swollen eyelids as she slammed his courier box to the floor. "But she's not, is she?"

"Mouse—"

"IS SHE?" Alex jabbed her finger at his face. "You *lied* to me. She's your ex, the first girl you fucked." Her ribs closed in, squeezing her lungs.

Mark looked like he had been kicked in the groin. "Lex, I can explain—"

"Actually, Sinéad…Fallon—whatever the *fuck* she's calling herself these days—has already done that."

"What?"

"I bumped into her downstairs. We talked. I mentioned your mum. She said she's known your family for *years*. Said you two…" Her hand flew to her mouth. "…you and her…you two have shared things I could never…" She gasped for breath through her sobs. "She thought I knew. She thought I *knew*!"

Mark rose to his feet, weaving unsteadily. "Mouse, calm down."

"Calm down? I find out my boyfriend lied about being naked on screen with his ex and you're asking me to calm down? *Fuck you*!"

"We were together a long time ago. It was *over* a long time ago."

"And here I thought your sex scenes with some *random* Irish girl were a huge deal, but she's not random, is she? I can't *believe* you hid the truth from me. I liked her, thought we might even be friends. She was right there, in my face, and you didn't tell me."

"I didn't tell you because she's not important. She doesn't mean anything to me."

"If she doesn't mean anything, you should have told me."

"I didn't tell you because I knew *this* would happen. You'd freak out on me. Mouse, we're both actors." He tightened the knot of his towel. "Reading lines from a script."

*No, NO!* He wouldn't get away with this. Glass shards crunched under her Chucks. "Was *this* in the script?" She foisted her phone with the close-up Instagram kiss in his face.

"What is this?" He blinked, trying to focus.

"It's you, kissing Fallon." Nausea swirled in her stomach. Just saying those words out loud…

"Kissing?" Mark slowly shook his head. "Yeah, that's when midnight struck. You know what it's like, everyone kisses everyone else. I kissed Fallon—I kissed Wink, for God's sake—"

Her finger swiped across the phone. "And this one?" The grainy embrace against the pub's wall glowed from the screen, impossible to ignore. Alex flicked her finger. "*And* this one?" The cosy handholding image in the SUV stared back at him.

Mark clutched his throbbing head as if he feared it would explode. "What are you showing me?"

"It's Fallon—*Sinéad's* Instagram. You're Devin all over again. You're a cheat, just like him! I *trusted* you!"

He grabbed the phone and squinted at the screen. His eyes widened as he stared at the images and swallowed hard, his silence retracting his denial.

Her heart shattered, as broken as the picture frame glass scattered on the carpet. "Mark, you fucking ASSHOLE!"

He squeezed his eyes shut. "Alex, please listen." Sweat beaded on his upper back and chest. He shook the phone in his hand. "This isn't what it looks like."

"Oh, God! Oh, *God*!" Her hand covered her mouth. "Why is this happening…? '*Happy anniversary, Lex*.' How fucking *dare* you!"

"Lex, I was completely off my tits drunk—I can't remember anything after one in the morning!" He stepped around the broken glass, his arms reaching for her. "Mouse, c'mere—"

"Don't touch me." She backed up. "I can't even bear to look at you. I'm such an *idiot*. I should've known. You were never going to ask me—"

"What?"

"The *ring*, Mark!"

"What ring?"

"I found an engagement ring in your bag. This summer? In Dublin? I found it and put it back."

He shook his head. "An engagement ring…? I don't know what you're talking about."

"Oh, so I imagined it, did I?!"

"Lex, you're not making any sense. You have to believe me. I want to be with you, not Fallon—she means nothing to me. I love *you*. I'm telling the truth."

"You wouldn't know the fucking truth if it—"

"Would you just stop, please? For a second? I'll tell you everything. Let's sit down."

Alex paced, refusing to comply with Mark's command.

"Look, not long after you left, someone, probably Wink—"

"Yeah, well, he's a fucking asshole, too."

"Lex, let me finish. *Please?* Someone bought all these trays of shots: tequilas, absinthe, sambuca…I got carried away. I might have taken a hit or two of weed." He glanced down. "I was trying to unwind but went too far—"

"*That's* your big excuse?"

"Look, I'm not proud of myself, okay? *Fuck*!" He covered his forehead with both hands and stared at the floor. "I've been really stressed out and tired lately…maybe it's being back here in Dublin…" Mark's chin dropped as his arms crossed his bare chest. "I just wanted to…oh, I don't even *know*—get out of my own head for a little bit? But after one in the morning, it's a complete blank."

"Really? What time did you crawl back to me, then? I was up just before four and you weren't here."

"Lex, you *told* me to stay—"

"*Tell me*! When did you get in?"

He scrunched his eyes tight and dragged his hand over his mouth. "Around nine."

Alex swallowed, silent tears racing down her red cheeks. "And you weren't out boozing till nine, were you Mark?"

He opened his eyes as his hand dropped from his face.

"So, when you woke up…" She choked, barely getting the words out. "*…in her bed…*were you dressed? Was *she*?"

His chin trembled. “No,” he whispered.

Alex wiped her eyes and shoved past him into the bathroom.

“Lex, I swear last night was…was just a drunken mistake. I was so out of it. There’s nothing going on between us—what are you doing?”

She stormed back out with her toiletries bag, glass splintering with each heavy step. She snatched her jeans and yesterday’s sweater then crouched down in front of her wheelie case. “I’m leaving.”

“No, you can’t. Alex, wait.” Mark lurched towards her, kneeling down. “Let’s talk this through, properly.”

Flipping open the lid to her case, another wave of tears streamed down her cheeks. She chucked her belongings inside and slammed the case closed, her designer dress discarded on the chair in the corner. She couldn’t bear to look at it or the man who gave it to her. How wrong she had been about both. “I’m done talking. I’m going home.”

“No, stop.” Tears glistened in his eyes. “Mouse, *please*.” His hand hovered over her back, desperate to make contact.

Alex’s fingers trembled, scrambling for the zipper pull.

“Don’t go. Please listen to me.”

She ignored him, yanking the zipper around her case. It snagged on the leg of her jeans.

“Let me fix—” Mark’s hands lunged at the stuck denim.

“Don’t!” Alex leaned away and stared straight ahead.

Mark’s hands retreated from the zipper’s path. With a final shove, she dislodged the troublesome jeans underneath the lip of the case and tugged the zipper closed.

“Mouse, I made a HUGE mistake.” He grasped her shoulders, fighting for her attention and their future together. “I love *you*, more than anything. *Please*. How can I fix this? Name it and I’ll do it, I promise.”

She rolled her shoulders, desperate to shake him away. “Get

off me."

Tears swelled in his eyes as he let go.

"I don't want any more of your fake fucking promises. I've had enough." Alex stood up, grabbing her handbag from the desk. She rummaged through it for her passport, her fingers scrambling over her wallet and medication.

Mark rose to his feet. "Lex, there's nothing going on between us, last night was just…a terrible, drunken mistake. It meant nothing. I don't even remember what *happened*!" He reached for Alex's arm, but she flinched. "You've got to believe me! I'm so sorry. Please, Lex, believe me!" His apology fought through his tears.

"That's the problem, Mark: I don't—not anymore." She grabbed the suitcase's handle and her parka then stepped over the rectangular courier box addressed to him on the floor.

Cramped in economy waiting for all the passengers to board, Alex mindlessly shook her leg and sagged against the plane's window. Her eyes dropped to her phone's screen, its volume muted. The voicemail tally jumped from four to ten to a dozen. The higher the number climbed, the more her determination grew to ignore Mark's beautiful accent; her heart couldn't bear it.

Then, he started texting.

*Mouse, where are you? Please call me, I'll come get you. I'm so sorry. Love you. xo*

Alex pounded her phone into her thigh and stared out the window. Icy rain stabbed the glass while two soaked ground crew flung suitcases onto the conveyor belt. Was anyone in Dublin having a good start to the year?

Her phone buzzed again, a new text.

*Alex, love. Happy anniversary from all of us here in Malta!*

*I'm looking forward to this weekend. I'll make that chocolate biscuit cake that you love. Enjoy today and the surprises my son has up his sleeve! See you soon. Lots of love, Niamh. x*

The words began to blur. Her hand scrambled into her pocket, finding a fresh tissue. It felt like sandpaper on her raw nose. Before today, she would have dashed off a warm reply to Mark's mother complete with smiling emojis, ending with kisses. Now, she just felt another wave of loss.

Another buzz…

*Lex. I've never hated anyone as much as I hate myself right now. I'm so, SO sorry! I know how much I've let you down, but you're the most important person in my life. I don't want to lose you. I love YOU.*

She blinked, and another text from Mark arrived.

*Marmalade.*

She dropped her head against the window and scrunched her eyes, but the tears snuck through her eyelashes. *Just stop, Mark. Just…stop.*

Enough. She couldn't read any more. New texts arrived, scrolling earlier messages upwards, off her screen. They piled up, ignored, just like the cracks in their relationship. Her phone continued to buzz intermittently, like a fly dying on a window sill. She dragged the cabin's cooled air into her lungs and stabbed the device's settings, swiping into airplane mode.

Farewell, texts. Farewell, Dublin.

Farewell, Mark.

# SEVENTEEN

*London, four hours later*

The chugging taxi exited Henshaw Street, leaving Alex hunched protectively over her laptop bag, quivering in the whipping rain. She retreated into her parka's hood and banged on the red-painted door of the south London terraced house, regretting it immediately. Maybe going there had been a mistake…what if Lucy was still in bed—or worse, her flatmate Charlie answered? Footsteps stomped down the stairs behind the door. *Shoot.* Too late to make a run for it now.

The lock clicked. The door opened three inches.

Two sleepy brown eyes squinted through the crack. "Lex?" Lucy croaked, her voice raspy and exhausted.

For the past few hours, Alex had held it together—barely, but with a single word from Lucy, her trembling chin gave way. The dam burst, hot tears pouring down her face, mixing with the icy January sleet. Her best friend became a watery, welcome blur.

"Honey!" Lucy flung open the door, her oversized Hufflepuff sweatshirt not quite long enough to cover her lacey knickers. "It's pissing down. Get in here." She tugged her friend into the dark flat.

Alex wiped her streaming nose with the edge of her hand. Her rain-splattered carry-on dragged along behind her, its squeaky wheels clogged with mushy leaves. "I'm so sorry. I didn't mean to ruin your lie-in—"

"What are you doing here?" Lucy peered behind Alex into the road and nudged the door closed. Her hands flew to her hair. No amount of flattening worked: her rebellious dark curls bounced back into bedhead mode, refusing to play nice. She gave up. "Where's Mark?"

Alex gulped for air and shook, her body wracked with uncontrollable tremors. Tears slid down her splotchy cheeks, muting her usually vibrant freckles, and her eyes itched. Was it from the constant crying or the dusty flat? Lucy wasn't fussy about vacuuming every week like Alex had been when she lived there.

"Lucy?" A tired male voice whispered in the darkness atop the narrow stairwell.

"Oh, God." *Charlie.* Alex's swollen eyelids blinked at the shadowy figure upstairs. "I should go—"

"No, don't be daft." Lucy's gaze flitted up the stairs as her hand stretched the hem of her sweatshirt.

Pale feet jogged down the stairs, revealing equally pasty white legs, a flapping dark blue bathrobe, and—*was that pubic hair? No underwear alert!* Alex blushed, her watery eyes flying to the grey carpet. In her peripheral vision, she caught the guy's hands fumbling with the belt of Lucy's plush TARDIS robe. He reached the bottom of the stairs.

"Wait…what…?" Alex hiccupped through her tears. "What are *you* doing here?"

Harry's eyes widened. "Oh, jeez, Lex. You're trembling. What's happened?"

"Holy crap!" Alex straightened up. "*Harry's* your hot water bottle?"

With a wry smile, Lucy bit her lip. "Busted."

"But…you? Charlie?"

Harry gave Alex a double take. "What's going on?"

"I bet Charlie's asking the same thing." Alex blinked her puffy lids.

"Stop dodging our questions." Lucy pulled her bestie into the lounge and flicked the light switch.

Alex flinched under the bright light. "*Our* questions?" She looked back at Harry.

"Where the hell is Mark?" Lucy tugged the hem of her sweat-shirt again. It sprung back up, her undies playing peek-a-boo.

Alex drooped, her shoulders rising to meet her ears. Fresh tears raced down her face to her chin. Drop by drop, they leapt from her jaw onto her rain-splattered laptop bag. She dug in her pocket for tissues, but her hands resurfaced with her phone.

Harry glanced at Alex and then Lucy. "Want me to leave, yeah…?"

Lucy nodded.

"I'll go put the kettle on." He tightened the robe and disappeared behind the wall separating the pokey lounge from the kitchenette.

"Let me take that." Lucy winced as she helped Alex remove her laptop bag and her dripping coat, the fake fur trim on its hood all matted and stuck to her friend's messy hair. She stuffed the parka on top of the room's old radiator and leaned the bag against the TV table. "Aw, babe. What's happened?" Returning to Alex, she hugged her tightly and pulled her down beside her on the loveseat.

The faucet ran hard and stopped abruptly. Mugs and spoons clinked on the kitchenette's counter. Harry was making just enough noise so he couldn't be accused of listening in.

"You weren't supposed to be back for another week."

Another wave of tears tumbled through Alex's eyelashes. "I…walked…out." She trembled and gasped between words, dragging the cuff of Mark's sweatshirt under her nose.

"I can see *that*." Lucy stretched towards the tiny coffee table and grabbed a handful of tissues, placing them in Alex's lap.

"It was the worst…"

"No ring?" asked Lucy

Alex shook her head.

"Aw, Lex. We talked about this. You can't—"

"He slept with his ex." Alex ran her fingers over her necklace. The skin underneath felt cold and clammy, and yet vulnerable, like a layer had been pulled back, exposing her nerves. Even the slightest scratch would tear her open.

The whistle from the kettle jumped into a high-pitched squeal.

"*What*?"

"Fallon…"

"Who?" Lucy squinted.

"Fallon Delaney." Alex abandoned her phone in her lap and clasped a tissue. "From the film, his love interest…"

"Wait, the new actress? They just hired her."

"Turns out, she's not new…not to Mark." She blew her nose hard, her ears popping. They hurt. Her nose hurt. Bright red blood speckled the tissue. She balled it up, hiding it from Lucy. Any pain that distracted from the crushing ache in her heart was welcome.

"You're fucking joking." Lucy seethed.

"I thought she was *nice*. I thought I made a new friend." Alex's lips quivered. "Happy anniversary to me."

"But when—?"

"After I left the party last night. I don't know if it was a one-off or…"

"*Fuck*." Lucy wrapped her arm around Alex's shoulder.

Harry returned and solemnly set down two steaming mugs on

the table. Lucy mouthed, “Thank you.”

He picked at the robe’s belt and shifted from foot to foot, unable to stay still. He cleared his throat. “Lex, if there’s anything you need…”

She shook her head, releasing him from any obligation. Lucy looked up at him with a tight smile.

“Is it okay if I maybe have a shower?” he asked.

“’Course, just don’t use up all my body wash again.”

Harry nodded, reached over and softy touched Alex’s shoulder, and left the room.

Alex’s tearful eyes widened. “*Again*?”

Lucy shook her head. “Never mind that. How did you find out?”

Alex told Lucy about her sloppy party exit, the morning’s conversation with Fallon, the intimate Instagram photos, and confronting Mark. She used the entire box of tissues in the process.

“The *wanker*! I could fucking kill him. He gives a whole new skanky meaning to taking a trip down memory lane.” Lucy gritted her teeth and picked up her phone. “I need to see this minger. Can I look at her Instagram?”

“Oh, she’s a lot of things, but a minger isn’t one of them…” Alex leaned onto her knees, burying her face in her hands.

“Fallon…Delaney, right?” Lucy searched the name on her app.

“It’s under Sinéad Delaney. She posted three photos with Mark.”

Lucy’s thumbs flew over the phone’s screen at lightning speed. “No, she’s made her account private.” She held her phone up for Alex. “See? Someone’s got a guilty conscience…”

Alex frowned. “They might be in the Mark Keegan hashtag. One of the kissing shots was there earlier.”

Lucy searched #MarkKeegan, her eyebrows raised. “Bitch…”

The midnight kiss photo, clearly showing Mark and Fallon attached at the lips, was now the top post in #MarkKeegan with 3,279 likes, the tight embrace by the wall at a close second with 2,980 likes. Both photos were screen captures of the actress's Instagram, posted into the hashtag by a Keeganite. The back seat SUV photo wasn't there. Alex guessed most fans wouldn't realize that the guy with the watch holding Fallon's hand was Mark.

She raised a hand to soothe her throbbing temples. "I keep replaying everything. Was it me? Maybe none of this would have happened if…He wanted to leave *with* me, Lucy. I *made* him stay, and I definitely shouldn't have been drinking."

"Bullshit, Lex. It was New Year's Eve—it's all about drinking."

"Not when you've been on anxiety meds. I screwed up."

"I thought you stopped taking them. Dizziness or something?"

"I *did* stop. Three days ago. I thought they would be out of my system…"

"Shit."

Alex nodded. "I got wrecked on half a vodka and orange, and two mojitos. One minute I felt fine, the next I could barely stand."

"Mojitos?" Lucy half-smiled. "That's one step up from a mocktail. It's like getting drunk on tap water."

Alex tugged the cuffs of Mark's sweatshirt over her hands.

"Well, they *are*. Did Mark know about the meds?"

Alex shook her head, avoiding eye contact.

"So, he thinks you deliberately got rat-arsed in front of his castmates?"

"I guess so. I don't know…"

"Jeez, Lex, you two have to stop with all these secrets. You're as bad as each other—"

"I didn't sleep with my *ex*!"

Lucy held Alex's hand. "Did he *admit* it? What did he say, exactly?"

Alex scowled. “He didn’t go into the smutty details. He admitted they woke up in bed together, and they were both *naked.* Doesn’t take a frickin’ *genius*, does it?”

Lucy widened her eyes. “So, how did you leave it? Did you text on the way here?”

“No…it took all my willpower not to burst into tears again. He left a ton of messages and texts. I put it in airplane mode.”

“Want me to see if he sent any more?”

“You can’t. Battery died.”

Lucy leapt up to the small dining table and dug underneath a pile of comic drawings, rescuing a phone charger. “You might want to look later…” She plugged in Alex’s dead phone.

Alex chipped the glitter polish off her nails and rocked back and forth on the edge of the loveseat. “What do I do now? I wanted to spend the rest of my life with him. All I thought about was our future, waiting for it to happen…but it’s been shattered. Was it all a big lie? I *trusted* him. I thought he was different. He wouldn’t cheat on me. He wouldn’t hurt me…Lucy, tell me what I should do?”

“I don’t know, honey. I mean, on Boxing Day you said—”

“I *know* what I said.”

“But now…are things clearer?”

“You think I should end it?”

“I’m not saying *that…*”

“I love him, Lucy, and the thought of losing him, really losing him—” A sob broke out from her lips.

“I could fucking strangle him.” Lucy sat down beside her friend, swallowing her anger for Alex’s sake. She pulled her friend into a gentle hug. “Remember what you said about Devin?”

“I know. *I know*! Cheating is a deal breaker—end of relationship. But it’s Mark, Lucy. It’s *Mark.*”

The creaky stairs alerted Lucy. She looked up from the dining table, covered in comic sketches, pencils, and markers, hinting that no meals had been eaten there recently. "How you feeling, sleepy head?"

"Numb. I can't warm up." Alex shuffled into the lounge, pulling Mark's sweatshirt's sleeves over her pale hands.

Lucy shot to her feet. "Hot sugary tea coming right up—"

"No. I feel pukey." Alex sniffed. Non-stop crying had left her eyelids swollen as if she had gone ten rounds in the boxing ring. "Thanks, though. What time is it?"

"Just gone quarter to six." Lucy sat back down. "At least you got a few hours kip in."

"I didn't really sleep…" Alex hovered over the table, taking in the scattered drawings. "These new?"

"I wasn't going to show you yet, but you're here, so…" She held up a few sketches. Most panels were in pencil, but a few had been inked.

"Lucy." Alex squinted her plump eyelids. "Fuck."

"I know, they're shit. I'll bin the lot and start over—"

"They're stunning." A smile brightened Alex's grey complexion.

"You're just saying that."

"I'm not. Why are you so critical?"

"I'm preparing myself for the inevitable."

Alex scrunched up her face.

"I don't mind people hating *me*, but my drawings…I don't know how you do it. How do you put your heart and soul out there like that?"

"I just figure that if *I* feel something, someone out there must feel it, too. It's the hope that you're not alone. When someone says they love my play or a character, it's the best feeling in the world. It makes it all worth it, even the risk of rejection."

"I think that kind of rejection would kill me..."

"Yeah, depending on the day and the project. Sometimes I'll shrug it off, sometimes I'll spiral into a weepy *I can't do this anymore* puddle." Alex smiled, revisiting the drawing in her hand. "Lucy, you've outdone yourself. She's fucking *awesome*!"

Lucy pointed at the black female superhero confronting a hulk of a politician. "But it's so...me."

"That's the best kind of art. It's authentic."

"It's edgy. I don't do safe. It might make it a tougher sell."

"She *is* so you, but that's a good thing. She's raw, real. You can tell what she's feeling at a glance—her personality leaps off the page. I love that her superpower is her mind, Yoda-style persuasion, thought control. I wouldn't change a thing—"

Alex's muted phone, tethered to the wall by Lucy's charger, lit up with a text. She froze, staring at the glowing screen on the arm of the loveseat.

"I turned it on...just in case." Lucy raised her eyebrows.

Alex set Lucy's drawings on the table and peered at the screen. "It's...Dad. I-I can't. He'll want me to put Mark on the phone, wish him a happy anniversary..." She swallowed hard, unmuted the volume, and yanked the phone from the charger. The screen lit up: sixteen texts from Mark.

"You don't have to answer that—you don't have to do *anything*. Just stay here and chill."

"Won't Charlie be home soon?"

"He's not back until the third, and even then, he can kip on the loveseat if you want to stay—" Lucy's phone buzzed. She shoved it aside.

Alex sat down on the chair beside Lucy. "Harry didn't have to leave."

"Nah, he did. He's expected at his parents' annual New Year's Day supper."

"And who made *you* Harry's social secretary?"

"Yeah, well, it's just sex. I'm sure it won't last. Let's face it: he's destined to be with an Olivia, not a Lucy."

"Oh, shut *up*. You're talented, funny, and gorgeous. I'd kill for your boobs, *and* you're the most caring person I've ever met." A soft smile fought Alex's cheeks, still tight from crying. "I'd choose a Lucy over an Olivia any day."

"Aw, babe, thanks. Sorry I didn't tell you. Me and Harry…is uncharted territory, and you're so protective of him. It's felt a bit…weird, you know? Almost too close to home?"

"Like dating my brother?" Alex smirked.

"Argh! I *knew* that comment would come back to bite me."

"Wow, you're dating *my* Harry. I love seeing friends fall for each other…no awkwardness—"

"Yeah, until we break up…"

Alex's face fell.

"Oh, fuck. My big mouth."

Alex swallowed and set her phone on the table. "So…when did you go off Charlie?"

"After I shagged him."

"*What*?!"

"Yeah. It was only once, in October. Turns out he's a typical City boy, all mouth and no trousers. He went at me like a jackhammer, rolled off after two minutes, and fell asleep. Talk about *rubbish.* I have thongs that are more stimulating."

"Well, good. You two together made me think of some pervy *Peanuts* comic, 'Charlie and Lucy'—" The *Sherlock* theme erupted from Alex's phone.

"Mark?"

"No, Dad again." She smiled at Lucy. "So, all Charlie left you with was a broken headboard and a hickey to wear to Tom and Naomi's wedding?"

Lucy furrowed her brows, glancing at her friend's phone. "Lex, maybe you should call your Dad back."

Alex crossed her arms. "Well?"

"You mean my *straightener burn*?" Lucy smirked. "Nope, Harry's work."

"What…?" Alex's finger poked her phone's calendar, counting weeks. "That means you two have been at it…" Her eyes bulged. "…for *eight* weeks?"

Lucy winced. "Try ten."

"And you've been mad at *me* for hiding things. I thought you just hooked up over Christmas or something!"

"Don't rub it in. I already feel like a shit friend. Harry wanted to tell you straight away, but I thought it best to stay mum for a bit. Plus, I must admit, sneaking around was fucking hot."

"If you've been dating for ten weeks, it's not just sex, Lucy. Why aren't you at his parents' dinner? Surely he asked you?"

Lucy shuffled her drawings. "It's a family thing."

"Sausages in the garden, a post-meal stroll around the Berkshire estate, Scrabble in the library—Harry's family are rich, sure, but they're really nice."

"*Sausages in the garden*? Is that a euphemism?"

Alex laughed. "Maybe that can be your code for sex from now on."

Lucy's phone lit up. "Bloody hell, that's number *seven*."

"Mark again?" Alex caught a flicker of a frown on Lucy's face. "You shouldn't be in the middle. I'll text him—"

"No." Lucy smacked her hand on top of Alex's. "You want time, I'll buy you time." Lucy's phone buzzed again. "For fuck's sake, Mark." She snatched it from the drawings. "Oh, it's *Naomi*. What…? Oh…Mark's been texting her, too. Want me to text her back?"

"Why is he bothering Naomi? I can understand Freddie—"

"I spoke to Freds while you were napping. Mark called him first thing."

"So, everyone knows?"

"Lex, Freddie and I debated telling you…"

"What have you guys done?"

"We haven't *done* anything. Mark's flying back. He's landing in two hours."

"I *don't* want to see him."

"I figured as much. I told Freddie to tell Mark to do one."

"I'm serious, Lucy."

Lucy's shoulders deflated. "We argued about something else, too." She tapped her phone and turned the screen around, exhaling forcefully. "I found this."

*NationalMail.com* boasted a New Year's Eve exclusive: an article with photo after grainy photo of Mark and Fallon pressed against a wall at the Stag's Head. Each image was credited to a name Alex didn't recognize, a fan most likely cashing in on her heartbreak.

Alex's phone lit up with yet another text.

*Honey, we saw the photos. Worried about you. Call me. Dad x*

"Well, that's it then. If Dad knows, everyone does."

Alex closed her eyes and laid her head on the table.

# EIGHTEEN

*Later that evening*

Freddie set a plate crowded with runny fried eggs, veggie sausages, and beans in front of Mark.

"Urgh, mate." Mark gagged. "The smell." He covered his nose and mouth then slumped his shoulders away from the cramped breakfast bar in Freddie's north London flat.

"Care for something else?" Simon raised an eyebrow. "A conscience, some truth serum, an STI test?"

"Si…" Freddie scowled.

Mark squinted, avoiding Simon's leer. "What are you doing cooking a fry-up at nine at night anyway?"

"Turning your stomach, are we?" Simon's knife and fork slashed his eggs and a blob of Worcestershire sauce into a swirly abstract design of yellow, white, and brown. "Imagine how Alex feels."

"I haven't thought of anything else."

"You still determined to head to Lucy's?" Freddie gulped tea and patted Moriarty, slinking along the counter past a cluster of prosecco bottles and two trays of half-eaten vol-au-vents. The black feline poked his nose in one and recoiled.

"Why are you encouraging him?" Simon slapped organic honey on his multigrain toast as he stared at Freddie. "What's he going to say to her?"

"I *am* in the room, Si." Mark nudged his untouched plate.

"Unfortunately."

Freddie whipped off his *Licence to Grill* James Bond apron. "Si, please—not helping!"

Mark's eyes began to water and itch. *Great. Thanks, Moriarty.* "Whenever you're ready, Freds. Thanks."

"We can go now."

"Yeah, cheers, Freds." Simon nodded. "You swan off. I don't need any help cleaning up *your* party."

"*This* mess can wait. Mark's can't." Freddie grimaced at his best friend. "God, remember that New Year's when I barfed up a brewery, snogged the face off some rando at midnight?"

"Ah-choo*!* Ah-*choooo!*" Mark half-smiled, holding back another sneeze. "Yeah, sickly suave, mate."

Freddie caught Simon's disapproving eye. "I was much younger then."

"How's *your* hangover?" Mark asked, cradling his throbbing head, his allergy to the cat not helping.

"Barely there." Freddie sipped his tea. "We went for Thai, and I skipped the bubbly at Bespoke. Stuck with white wine and switched to club soda when we got back here."

"Who *are* you, and what have you done with my best friend?"

Freddie laughed and went to scrape Mark's plate into the trashcan. "Have you remembered anything more—"

"Christ, how good would *your* memory be after absinthe, tequila, and God knows what else?"

"So *why* should Alex take you back?" Simon's honey-covered

knife clanked against his plate. “Talk about falling down the rabbit hole of celebrity self-indulgence. Hardly reliable boyfriend material.”

“Simon!” Freddie said over his shoulder.

“No, he’s right. I deserve that.” Mark’s bloodshot eyes stared at a photo of Alex, Freddie, and Lucy on the wall. “But I have to make her see, this was all a horrible, drunken mistake. I never meant for anything like this to happen…”

“You’re wasting your breath.”

“Si, I know, okay. I know. You don’t care, but hopefully Lex still does. I hope I haven’t completely lost her trust, though I wouldn’t blame her if I have.” He leaned on the counter, propping up his head with his hand. “Christ, I’ve really fucked up. I’ve kept her in the dark about so many things.”

“Like what?” asked Freddie.

“Austria for starters…”

“Oh, Keegs, you didn’t—”

Mark clenched his jaw. “No, Freds, I *didn’t.* I fell on some rocks—from a horse.”

Freddie sputtered on his tea, all colour draining from his face. “What? You could’ve died.”

“I dislocated my shoulder. Hit the ground at the wrong angle, and it just…popped. Lex was always worried about the stunts.”

“For good reason.”

“Freddie, if she knew the truth, she would have panicked the entire shoot. It was better that she didn’t know—for both of us—but in Brum, she saw the bruising. I tweaked the truth a bit, but it wasn’t a total lie. I said I fell during a snowball fight.”

“A snowball fight?”

“Sometimes it’s best to gloss over the details, you know?” Mark sniffed his runny nose. “The occasional white lie? It’s easier on both of us…”

"I guess…" said Freddie.

"But this time, I should've been completely straight with her. If I had told Lex the truth about that chemistry read, who Fallon was, the sex scenes in the script—"

"You have *sex scenes* with her?" Freddie lowered his tea. "Proper nudity with grinding and orgasm faces—the whole meal deal?"

"Yep. Bare butts, breasts, you name it, you see it—well, *almost* see it."

"Shit, Keegs. No wonder Lex got blotto when she found that out. *You* should have told her."

He slowly sat up. "Don't you think I know that? She wouldn't have been too happy about it, but at least it wouldn't have come as a shock last night. New Year's would have been completely different."

"Mate, be honest." Freddie leaned on the counter. "Did you know Fallon was coming to that read?"

"No. Fuck!" Mark winced, unable to get comfortable. "I don't stay in touch with her. I haven't seen her in four or five years. Last time I saw her was at her mum's funeral. I didn't know she was coming to read until she showed up. I have wanted to tell Lex everything, but she hasn't been herself lately. That morning in Manchester, Lex seemed…distracted. I asked her what was wrong—a few times—but got the same answer every time: she hates us being apart. Maybe there's more to it?"

"Like that's not enough…" Simon chomped his toast.

"*You* haven't noticed anything, have you?" Mark rubbed his eyes. "Panic attacks?"

Freddie shrugged. "Don't think so."

"Carrying this movie has been so fucking stressful. When Lex left the party, I just…let loose. I thought I could handle it…stop before I went too far, yeah? I didn't plan on blacking out or waking up starkers in Fallon's bed." His Adam's apple bobbed heavily. "I lifted the duvet, saw her naked…I just…*knew* we must have…" He closed his eyes tight and inhaled slowly. "I panicked—got out of there as quick as I could. It was only when I slipped into bed beside Alex, I realized I could still smell Fallon's perfume on my skin."

"Oh, *Mark*," said Freddie.

Simon stopped chewing.

Mark glared at Simon. "Fallon was as horrified as I was, by the way. She was in tears, worried about Duff."

"Duff?" asked Simon.

"Some rugby player she's been seeing a few weeks."

"Nice, *more* casualties." Simon snorted. "Where was he when you had your tongue down Fallon's throat, then?"

"He left after Lex. Curfew—" Mark fought back a sneeze. "He had a match today."

"So, you just missed spending New Year's in a full-body cast." Simon shook his head. "Luck of the Irish."

"Right. Come on, Mark. Get ready to grovel." Freddie slammed his mug on the counter.

# NINETEEN

Alex tugged a scratchy afghan—Lucy's first and last attempt at knitting—up to her chin. Riddled with dropped stitches, it looked like Joseph's Technicolour Nightmare. The weathered cotton of her plaid pajamas, paired with Mark's sweatshirt, offered warmth, and yet the combo left her unsettled, reminding her of what she was at risk of losing—her boyfriend, their cosy home, his loving family. She stared at the TV but saw nothing, the events of the previous twenty-four hours playing on a loop in her head.

"Let her 'ave it, judges!" Lucy howled, watching the precarious layers of dark chocolate goo and spongy gateaux fall to the floor. "That cow is finally going to get hers."

Her laugher shook the loveseat as her hand dove into a banged-up box of Cadbury Heroes, chocolates left over from Christmas. Discarded Dairy Milk and Twirl wrappers flew out of the cardboard and settled on her bathrobe-covered boobs. "Lex." Lucy nudged her friend's knee with a sock-covered foot. "Want a baby Wispa?"

Alex swallowed, but the acid taste in her mouth lingered. "I feel like I could be sick again."

"I'll get you a bin bag in case you can't make it upstairs." Lucy dumped the chocolate box on the loveseat and padded into the kitchenette.

*BANG BANG BANG BANG!*

Alex jumped.

"What the fuck?" Lucy shouted from the kitchenette.

"LUCY?! IT'S MARK." His voice, hoarse and urgent, emanated from the front door.

Alex's breath stalled as her heart took flight, its escalating beats filling her ears.

Lucy ran into the room, foisting a hastily snatched plastic bowl in Alex's face. "Stay there."

Alex gripped the bowl, lowering it to her lap. *Holes?* Her puffy eyes focused on the object in her hands. "A strainer?"

Lucy peered through the sheer curtains. Henshaw Street, dimly lit by the streetlights across the road, seemed darker than usual thanks to a bone-chilling downpour. Freddie was to Lucy's right, his usually out of control bangs hidden under a woolly hat, his shoulders hunched in his black wool coat. He planted his hands in its pockets and swayed from foot to foot like a fidgety penguin. Mark wasn't visible, but from his loud announcement, it was obvious that he stood in front of Freddie in the small alcove by the door.

Freddie's head turned, his water-splotched eyeglasses catching the light streaming from Lucy's lounge. "I see you, Hardy. C'mon, open up. It's bucketing down."

Lucy leapt backwards, her curls flying over her shoulders. "Lex, hide in the kitchen. I'll get rid." She tightened her robe and strode through the doorway that separated the lounge from the small landing at the bottom of the stairs. She flicked a switch, the outside light illuminating the front window. Staring at the door, Lucy's chest rose and fell as if she was running an uphill marathon.

Alex left the strainer on the loveseat and grabbed the DVR

remote, hitting pause on all the sweet talk of cakes and fondant icing. The constant tip-tapping of icy rain on the window filled the silence.

*BANG BANG BANG!*

"Lucy, open the door, please?" The tone of Mark's voice hinted that he wasn't really asking a question.

Lucy squinted through the door's peephole. Mark's tense brows and dark eyes stared back underneath the brim of his United cap. "Jeez, Mark! Are you trying to wake up all of Southwark?"

She pried the door open a few inches, just a sliver of her face revealed. A blast of frigid air brushed past her into the lounge. Alex hugged herself, willing the sweatshirt and pajamas to fight off the chill, but goosebumps riddled her skin.

"Lucy, thanks." Mark's shoulders relaxed with a sigh.

"Thanks? Are you *kidding* me? I'm this close"—she held her thumb and forefinger an inch apart—"to having your balls on a plate. You've got a nerve showing up here." She clasped her robe tightly at the neck. "Besides, you're wasting your time. I don't know where she is, and I'm *hungover*, so if you don't mind—"

"Nice try." Mark blew on his cupped hands as he weaved back and forth. "I can tell when you're lying. Your voice gets all high and you forget to swear."

Lucy scrunched up her face. "You want swearing? I'll give you swearing: she's not *fucking here*!"

Alex left the loveseat and followed Mark's voice, staying out of Lucy's sight behind the wall. Despite her heavy heart and the chill creeping around the corner, part of Alex yearned to move closer to hear his comforting Irish lilt again. Her present, her future—everything—depended on his words and whether she chose to believe them.

Mark pulled out his phone and hit redial. The *Sherlock* theme burst from Lucy's loveseat. Alex's eyes flew to her phone.

"Please…" Mark's lips trembled. "Let me speak to her."

"Piss off, Mark—"

"Christ, you can't keep me from seeing her. Let Lex decide, eh?" Mark dropped his phone into a pocket, wrapped his arms around his waist, and craned his neck, trying to see past Lucy. "Mouse, I know you're upset, but please, babe…come to the door." His voice faltered. "I need to see that you're all right…please."

Alex picked at the peeling wallpaper and slumped against the doorjamb. Ignoring his texts and voicemails was hard enough but this? *What to do?* Her bruised heart screamed, *Go to him*, but how could she live with herself if she gave in so easily? She pulled away, but Mark's sweatshirt kept her tethered to the wall. A loose thread had snagged on a sneaky nail and wouldn't let go.

"Mark, she's *not* interested." Lucy shoved the door closed.

"Wait! Lucy! FUCK!" Mark threw his arms into the air and turned to Freddie, lowering his voice. "Any chance you still have a spare key?"

"Lucy, at least let me in. I'm dying for a wee—"

Mark gave his friend a double take. "Mate, *really*?"

Freddie shrugged. "Too much tea."

Alex fought with the sweatshirt, but the more she struggled, the more the stitching unraveled.

"Better hurry, Freds," Lucy hollered. "The kebab shop closes at eleven. You've got five minutes."

"Lucy, come on, *please*." Mark pounded his fist on the door.

Outside, a sudden brightness lit up the right side of the front window. Alex froze.

"Nice one, Keegs. You've woken up the widow next door. Go. HOME. Before she calls 999." Lucy stared through the peephole. "Do you *want* a New Year's mug shot? The press will *love* that."

Mark slumped. "Lucy, I'm not giving up. As long as Lex is here, I'm staying." He clamped his mouth shut, tugged his cap over his eyes, and plunged downwards, revealing a blurry blob of Freddie standing in his shadow.

"Mate, what the hell?" Freddie's voice rose. "You can't stay here. You've already got the hangover from hell. You...You'll catch the lurgy."

Lucy stomped past Alex to the window, yanking the curtains aside. "Mark, stop being a knob!" She turned to Alex. "I think that daft boyfriend of yours is having a sit-in on the doorstep."

Freddie shivered, drenched from the unrelenting rain. "Great! You've totally lost the plot, and I'm bursting for a piss..." He turned towards the road, keeping his back against the driving wind and rain. "I'm off! Give me a bell if you're coming back to ours."

Lucy banged on the window. "Don't even *think* of leaving him here, Freds."

"It's okay, you go," said Mark, nestled into the alcove. "You don't need to stay."

A bolt of lightning lit up the skies. With a violent clap of thunder, the dark sky doubled its efforts to drown the streets of London.

"Ah, *fuck it*! Shift your arse..." Freddie sunk into the alcove where Mark had hunkered down, disappearing from Lucy's view.

With a sharp tug, Alex finally freed herself from the wall. *Fuck!* A huge tear now separated the bottom hem from the shirt. She retreated to the stairs, torn between running to or running from Mark.

Before, that had never been a decision to make. Being reunited with Mark had *always* been the answer, but the previous night, the morning after—they had changed *everything*. Fallon's damning Instagram photos, Mark's lying about knowing her, his almost tangible guilt—he had betrayed her trust, completely.

Alex no longer knew what to believe or what to do. Had she been duped all along? Was Mark just pretending to be serious about her? All those times he couldn't say no to Wink, the broken dates and cancelled holidays—was it his cowardly way of putting space between them? Had he been pining after his first love all this time?

Or maybe he was telling the truth—maybe he *was* in the wrong place at the wrong time with the wrong people, fueled by a stupid, misguided bender then exploited for sex by an unscrupulous ex? He had come to her, after all. Would he have done so if she didn't matter at all? Mark had always been the answer, always, but…their universe had shifted.

Sat near the top of the stairs, Alex stared down at the front door. Mark was only a dozen yards away, but in reality, there had never been a greater distance between them.

Lucy returned to the front door. "Better cuddle up, then, boys," she hollered through the wood, switching off the front light. "You're in for a bloody long wait—and Freddie, don't even *think* of weeing in my wheelie bin."

Bundled up in Charlie's duvet, Alex splayed one hand on the bedroom window as she clasped her Vespa charm in the other. She angled to look straight down, squishing her forehead against the glass. The iciness jolted her skin, but the chilly ache couldn't compare to the heaviness in her chest. The rain had stopped a half-hour ago and a thick fog now cloaked the street. An eerie glow from the streetlights set off the reflective orange, yellow, and blue striped markings on the side of the police vehicle that had just arrived. Two Metropolitan police officers made their way towards the house.

Alex shivered, desperate for a glimpse of Mark or Freddie, but they were still tucked away.

The female constable adjusted her cap. "Good evening." Her voice echoed in the damp street. "We're from Borough High Street station. There's been a complaint about two men loitering and exhibiting antisocial behaviour—causing a disturbance and public urination. Could you tell us your names and addresses, please?"

Down in the alcove, Mark and Freddie's responses were a mumble.

The female constable did a double take. *Did she recognize Mark?* "So, what brings you to Southwark?"

Mark stepped forward, the top of his cap appearing. "I…surprise my girlfriend…" Alex jammed her ear against the glass. The alcove made his voice hard to make out. "…didn't want to miss her…I'm sorry…too loudly…the neighbours."

Freddie came into view, fidgeting with his glasses. Alex had never seen him so nervous—he was bricking it, as Mark would say.

The male constable nodded his head. "Mr. Keegan, this behaviour—loitering, watching a person—can be classified as a Section 2A offence for *stalking*. Now, we'll give you a warning, provided you leave the property immediately and don't return within the next twenty-four hours."

"Yes officer, no problem," Freddie jumped in, his shoulders leaving his ears. "It won't happen again. *Right*, Mark?"

He stepped forward. "Right. Thanks for letting us go on a warning. I'm sorry for any misunderstanding."

The female constable smiled. "Have a safe trip home."

The officers walked to their car while Freddie mouthed, "Come on!" and speed-walked in the opposite direction.

Alex lifted her face from the glass. The show was over.

Mark stepped into the alcove again, out of sight, and then reappeared with his backpack and a courier box—the rectangular box she had claimed for him from the concierge. He took a few steps towards the road then turned around, looking up at the window.

*Damn!* She jerked backwards.

He kissed his palm and raised it at the empty window before turning and walking away.

# TWENTY

The stalls of Borough Market yearned for company—hungry tourists, fresh from the Shard, were long gone. Alex checked Lucy's whereabouts: yep, still lined up at the Pieminister stall, making faces at her and drooling over the Moo & Blue pie that would soon be hers. Alex pulled her phone from the pocket of her parka. No texts. No voicemails. Nothing. After last night's drama, Mark had gone silent.

She dove into #MarkKeegan on Instagram. Someone had posted two photos from the BBQ she and Mark had attended last August in Greenwich—an industry-only get-together. No press had been invited as far as she could remember. *So much for privacy.*

Alex scrolled to the second photo. *Ah, that top.* Her lips loosened into a slight smile. The pink halter top, worn bra-less, was breezy and pretty—perfect for a warm summer evening. Paired with her purple diagonal-striped cotton skirt, she looked polished and presentable without trying too hard. Mark, fresh from filming *Lairds* season three, gave off a relaxed holiday vibe in a Bruno Mars concert tee, cargo shorts that barely hugged his hips, and a month's worth of whiskers. He had arrived from Scotland an hour before, in town just for the weekend, and hadn't yet reunited with a razor or event-appropriate trousers. His arm was slung around Alex's shoulder as they chatted to another guest. They looked happy, picture perfect, albeit in Mark's case, dressed more for the beach than an industry garden party in a posh London borough.

How had everything fallen apart only a few months later? There were certainly no hints, no cracks to be found in these photos. Alex's finger swiped tentatively up the screen to see if any comments had been left…

*Mark looks hawt, his date tho—NIPPLES! Too casual! Go home and change, bitch.*

*Doesn't this girl realize who she's with? Put in some effort.*

Alex kicked the pavement with her Converse, ignoring the rest of the post. Now she was sad *and* insulted. *God, I should have known...*

Lucy danced towards her, proudly holding a box.

Alex tugged her hat down over her stringy, unwashed hair and the sore pimple in the middle of her forehead, so large, it was probably visible from space. Stress zits, yay! "You're going to regret pulling a sickie when someone spots you. We should've stayed in."

Lucy shoved her change purse into her cross-body bag, her Christmas gift from Alex. "My boss never ventures south of the Thames, so it's all good." She blew on her mini steak and Stilton pie, a spiral of steam rising above the pastry. "Are you sure you don't want a grilled cheese? Brownies, cookies…you *never* say no to the cookies here!"

Alex shook her head.

"I feel bad, though, eating in front of you…"

"Don't. I'm not hungry." Alex stared at the Bread Ahead stall with its decadent orange and chocolate donuts.

"I'm sorry my plan to cheer you up with pricey plonk fell through. The Shards' rule about no trainers is stupid as fuck."

"Don't worry about it. I don't think they even looked at my shoes. I look yuck. This"—Alex pointed at her face—"is all they needed to see: huge zit, puffy eyelids. I'm a total mutt. *No dogs allowed*."

"You *do* have the dark eye circle thing going on, babe. Very Pug-like, but cute in a *Frankenweenie* kind of way."

"You're comparing me to a Franken-dog? Are you planning to shock me back to life, too?"

"I'll do whatever it takes! And don't diss Frankenweenie. He's small, faithful, adorable—just like you." Lucy nudged her friend, trying to raise a smile. "We'll try the Shard another time. Harry says the view is really something, better than the London Eye."

"New year, new Lucy. Listen to you…*Harry says*."

"Erghh, what am I like? You don't need me swooning."

"Lucy, just because Mark and I have imploded doesn't mean you can't be excited about Harry. Talk about him. I love seeing you happy."

Lucy bit into the chunky steak pie, closed her eyes, and chewed in silence until a large smile overtook her cheeks. "Oh, my God, that is *soooo* good. Look, give me a smack if I ramble on about him too much, okay? I don't want to be one of those women who gets lost in her relationship."

"Like me, you mean…"

"No! Well…kinda? *Don't hit me*! I'll drop my pie."

"No, you're right. I did lose myself a bit…everything revolved around him."

"Yeah, Marlex…but with the life he leads, how could it not? It's easier with Harry. Even if he's busy, he's here. Plus, he does exactly what I tell him to." Lucy laughed and bit into her pie.

Alex admired the nearby stacks of boozy cheese wheels drawing in customers at the Drunk Cheese stall beside them. "There's no denying it. *Yooooou liiiiike Harry*. Admit it!"

Lucy beamed. “I do. *There*, I said it! Any second now, I’m gonna burst into flames. I wish Gran were alive. She’d love him. She always hated my ex.”

“Yeah, Harry’s a good one.” Alex held up her hand like she was swearing a pledge. “My name is Alex Sinclair and I approve this relationship.” The phone buzzed in her other hand.

“That from Mark? He better pay for my door knocker.”

Alex nodded.

*Lex, please text me. We need to talk. I love you. x*

“Hmm, just the one text this time? He better not be on my doorstep again when we get back.” Lucy swallowed another bite of her pie. “If he is there, what’s the plan?”

“I think we should talk, but I’m afraid I’ll cry.” Alex and Lucy began to stroll towards the Middle Market entrance. “I want to have my shit together.”

“How long did you sit by the window last night?”

“An hour.”

“Did you see them leave?”

“Yeah…”

“An hour my arse.” Lucy pursed her lips. “I know you were sat there for at least three, Lex. The slamming car door woke me up, just gone two.”

“I wanted to make sure they were okay.”

“Personally, I don’t think Keegs deserves your concern. I would’ve been quite happy to let him freeze his balls off or get arrested by the cops, but I’m not you. It must be doing your head in, not running after him, but really, it’s the only way to see things clearly. You need to figure out what’s best for *you*—not him.”

“I don’t know what to do. I don’t think I can trust him, and I can’t forgive him…at least, not yet—”

“If at all,” said Lucy.

“The minute I do, I lose my self-respect, and taking him back makes me a hypocrite. But, if I *dump* him, I…honestly don't know if I'll ever get over him. It's lose-lose."

"Total clusterfuck. I still can't believe this is Keegs we're talking about. You think you know someone… He's fooled all of us. Never trust the super-smiley ones—they're always hiding something." Lucy's voice boomed. "I could have his guts for garters for what he's done to you, the fucking lying cheating *arsehole*—"

Two stroller-pushing mums shot disapproving glares at Lucy.

"Oh, you know what might make you feel better? *Revenge fantasies*! Worked a treat when my ex dumped me. Look, I made you a list!" Lucy shoved her pie into Alex's hands and dug her phone out of a pocket. She swiped a few times. "Okay—you could edit his Wiki page, say he had a secret porn star past? Or you could sell his precious signed football on eBay for a quid? Then we could puncture the tires on his stupid Vespa—"

"Damn, girl! God help Harry if he ever wrongs you!" A twinge in Alex's chest took away her breath. "I *wish* I could be angry, but right now, I just feel…I feel empty, sick."

"Oh, the anger's coming. It's only been twenty-four hours." Lucy rescued her pie.

"Yeah, I know the drill; not my first time at the cheating rodeo, remember?"

Lucy wrapped an arm around her friend.

Alex looked sheepish. "Did my crying keep you up last night?"

Lucy smiled. "Nah, I was awake anyway. Too much adrenaline—and chocolate." Her lips morphed into a devilish grin. "I wonder what the widow next door was thinking, though? Bonking noises one night, tears and drama the next. She spied through her curtains at Harry when he left yesterday. He said he gave her a cheeky wave."

"She probably thinks she's living beside a real-life *Fifty*

*Shades of Grey*." Alex glanced at the Spice Mountain stall. "Anyway, on that bombshell, I'll get back to my flat tomorrow. You and Harry deserve some privacy—"

"Lex, there's no need—"

"Lucy, I *know*…I know what you did yesterday."

"What?" Lucy juggled her phone and half-eaten pie. "You *saw* it?"

"I'm sorry. I wasn't snooping…"

"That's embarrassing! I told Harry to put it away—"

"Put? *What*? Wait…oh, God, NO, don't tell me!" Alex covered her ears, her eyes scrunched.

"Good, 'cause I'd rather I didn't have to." Lucy laughed. "Hey, it's been a while. I've got needs, what can I say?"

"And I'm happy you're satisfying them!" Alex chuckled as they exited the market. "We're obviously talking about different things. I saw Harry's *text* last night, the '*Wish you were here*' one? Your phone lit up beside me when you were in the kitchen. You said Harry didn't invite you to that family dinner, but he *did*, didn't he? And you skipped it—for me."

"Yeah, that's me, completely selfless."

"You are."

"Oh, please! If you want to know the real reason…" Lucy popped the last morsel between her lips. "I…" She mumbled through a mouthful, holding her finger aloft. "…didn't fancy meeting the parents with a brain-crushing hang."

"I *know* you've already met them. I read the whole text, Lucy. His dad? Disappointed that he didn't see you *again*? And Harry got all mushy. He said he was lucky to be dating a woman who wouldn't dump her heartbroken BFF for some '*overpriced crustaceans.*' Whatever that meant."

"They were having lobster. It's actually yummy. Who knew? Don't hate me."

"Lucy Hardy, going all posh. I'd only hate you if you served nothing but seafood at your wedding."

"Woah, steady on. Cart, horse!"

"So, you *have* met his parents. When did *that* happen?"

"Christmas Eve."

"What's that—nine, ten weeks in? Wow. Mark made me wait almost two years."

"I was shitting myself. Harry has never dated a black girl, and I figured they might have a problem, but his dad—I mean, Budgie—couldn't have been kinder."

"Budgie loves everyone," said Alex.

"His mum was a bit Baltic at first, but we got talking, and she couldn't apologize enough for the initial chill. She blamed Olivia. I'm the first girl Harry has brought home since, so she's a bit overprotective, you know? After a few cocktails, she wouldn't leave me alone! She invited me to tennis, she wants to see my drawings…Lex, she won't stop texting me now. I might need a restraining order."

"She knows a good soul when she meets one, can't fault her for that." Alex swallowed heavily as they walked along Southwark Street. "You know, I'll never be able to thank you enough for the past two days. I don't know what I would have done if you weren't home."

"And you'll never have to find out. We're family. I'm going nowhere."

"Right back at ya."

Lucy smiled. "Hey, want to circle back, get some donuts? My treat."

"Still not hungry, but thanks."

"Aw, I hate what he's done to you." Rihanna's "Umbrella" burst from Lucy's pocket. "Fuck."

"Is that your boss?"

"Shit. I can't take this here…traffic noise." Lucy looked back towards Borough Market. "I'll let it go to voicemail and call back from the market. It's quieter there. You okay for a minute?"

"Yep."

Lucy rushed back up the street.

Alex walked a little farther and gasped, stopping in the middle of the sidewalk. Mark's face, unsmiling and stern, stared at her from a poster-size bus shelter advertisement. *Lairds and Liars* was returning to TV for its third season next month. Branded underneath Mark's stubbly chin, four white letters—*LIAR*.

Her pocket buzzed. Speak of the devil… *Mouse, please check your email. Love you. x*

She waited a few seconds. *Lucy's still gone, right?* She jabbed her email icon.

*From: Mark Keegan*
*To: Alexandra Sinclair*
*Sent: 2 January, 15:37*
*Subject: My side of the story*

*Mouse,*

*You can rest easy now. I won't be showing up at Lucy's again. I'm flying back to Dublin tonight.*

*I didn't think I could make things worse, but I did, didn't I?*

*Truth be told, I don't regret pounding on the door or shouting at Lucy. I don't regret bunking on her step, refusing to leave, or the cop visit. I was desperate. I'd do it all again in a heartbeat, trying to prove to you how much I love you, but your silence has made me realize that you're just not ready to talk. I guess I proved the casting agents wrong last night, eh? Turns out, I can play a realistic psycho. I never intended to freak you out. For that, I'm truly sorry. I know I keep saying it, but I am. I just keep hoping you will accept one of those sorrys, and we can fix what I've broken.*

*I keep going over everything in my head, trying to figure out how I got into this mess. I swear on my life, Alex, I don't remember what happened or how I woke up in bed with her. Dublin has always been a tricky place for me. It's my hometown, but it's also a place I've left behind on purpose. Maybe like you with Tallahassee—there are too many bad memories mixed in with the good ones, you know?*

*Here's the honest truth then, about me and Fallon. I want you to know everything.*

*Fallon and I—*

"Fuck it."

Alex jumped. Had Lucy seen the email?

"I didn't need this today." Lucy inhaled deeply, her eyes wide.

"Huh?"

"I swear I could hear the veins popping in his neck from his voicemail."

"Oh…your *boss*?" Alex breathed easier. "He knows you're playing hooky?"

"Don't think so, but I was supposed to launch the New Year's 'eating well' initiative on social media today! It completely slipped my mind." Lucy grabbed her hair at the temples. "I have to post it before six tonight or I'll be in deep shit. Can we head back?"

"Yeah, sure." Alex started walking towards London Bridge Tube station.

"Thank God my call went straight to his voicemail," said Lucy. "If I'm lucky he'll believe I'm tucked up in bed with a fever and *The Chase* on TV."

Alex crawled into bed, nesting with Charlie's overstuffed duvet and her laptop. It was only half past five, but Lucy was busy downstairs on her computer, tweeting the nutritional merits of "rainbow super bowl salads" and coconut porridge, so Alex took advantage of the alone time. She put in her earbuds, hit play on her iPod, and opened Mark's email again.

*...have known each other since we were twelve. I met her at the dry cleaners where our mums worked. To me, she was just a stupid, snobby girl, taking tap and drama classes.*

*Dad had passed away two months earlier, and I was having a tough time. Mum and my teachers agreed that afterschool drama classes might boost my confidence, so I began to see Fallon regularly. They cast us opposite each other in our first play. She was the obvious star—everyone said it, but she was full of herself, cocky, ambitious. She announced early on, "I'm going to marry Leo DiCaprio," which I took to mean, "I'm well out of your league, Keegan, don't get your hopes up." But by the time we were fifteen, we started to fancy each other. I lost my virginity to her soon after at a house party. For the most part, it was a normal teenage relationship with long drives in my beat-up Mini, snogging behind pubs, and having sex—*

She glared at the screen and punched a pillow. *Great! An insider's guide to Mark and that bitch fucking their way through high school? NOT HELPING!* She slapped the screen of her laptop closed and dissolved into the pillows, determined not to cry.

***MARK***
***Seventeen years earlier***
***Dublin, May 2001***

"Gracie, do you like this house?"

"Yeah, I do."

"I don't. I liked it better when we lived above the pub. Mum and Dad were home all the time at the pub." Mark scraped the baked beans off his toast. "It's my fault we moved, isn't it?"

"It's not your fault." Grace pointed at the nine-year-old's plate. "Eat your dinner before it gets cold."

"But Dad doesn't want to spend time with me. That's why he's gone all the time."

"Fappy, he's gone all the time so he can make *money*. Driving a truck means long hours."

"Can't he do something else?"

His twelve-year-old sister scooped up a forkful of beans. "I heard him tell Mum that he can't *do* anything else."

"I wish he was home more. I wish Mum was home more, too. She's never here when we get in from school."

"Fappy!" Grace swallowed her mouthful. "How many times have I told you? She has to go *out* to work now, to help make ends meet. We're not as rich as we used to be."

"We was rich?"

"No, I didn't mean *rich* rich. We just had more money when we lived above the pub, that's all."

"Why can't she do that mending stuff at home and be here with us?"

"Because she has to be at the dry cleaners and sew *there*. Look, you can always go there after school. Do your homework in the back room beside her. It's okay, you know."

"It is?"

"Yeah. The owners don't mind. Mrs. Delaney is really nice. She has a daughter around your age. On Monday when I was there, she was waiting for a lift home."

"Ugh, no. It's okay." Mark scooted baked beans around his plate. Given the choice, he would rather come home to an empty house than meet a smelly girl.

# TWENTY-ONE

*London, Tuesday, January 9, 2018*

Alex's mind wandered as she tiptoed over a sheet of ice that made the pedestrianized walkway of Tower Hill one face-plant away from a lawsuit. The bright sun did little to take the edge off the freezing temperatures or melt the glistening hazards that lingered after the sleet storm the night before.

"Shit!" Freddie pushed his glasses up his nose. Six busloads of boisterous eight-year-old schoolchildren clogged the Tower of London's entrance. "Don't people believe in birth control anymore? We'll be stood here forever. Freezing my dick off was *not* on today's agenda."

"We can do something else." Alex pulled off a glove and opened Google on her phone, wishing she were back in bed. Lucy had insisted she join her friends this Tuesday morning instead of being "a mopey arse" alone at home. It was a big ask—January 9 was circled in red on her *Lairds* calendar.

"No, you've always wanted to come here, and we've got tickets." Lucy glared at Freddie. "And besides, we're English—queuing is what we do best."

"Do they have anything to drink here that's hot, low sugar, low fat?" Naomi shivered, her over-the-knee black leather stiletto boots tapping out a tune on the cement.

Lucy rolled her eyes.

"What?" The actress peered over Lucy's head towards the riverside café. "The wardrobe mistress will *kill* me if I pop the seams on my costume tonight."

"One hot bloody chocolate isn't going to make you sprout hips like mine, Naomi," said Lucy.

Alex's fingers scrolled her phone. She flashed a quick smile, determined not to be that irritating, heartsick girl that bummed out her friends. "We could tour Westminster Abbey instead—"

"And risk bumping into my boss on Victoria Street? Fuck that." Lucy steered Freddie and Naomi to the line. Alex followed.

"At least your boss knows you exist." Freddie pressed his lips tight. "The promotion went to someone else."

Alex's face fell. "What, again?"

"Freds, that's awful," Naomi scowled.

"Yep. Third time unlucky." He flung his scarf over his shoulder, just missing the nose of the woman lined up behind him. "My boss can officially go fuck himself."

"So that's why you were so quick to skive off today." Lucy hugged him.

"Screw 'em. I'll end up making a mint with my YouTube channel, and one day, the BBC will come crawling back to me, crying, *We used to know him.* Fuckers." He released Lucy and exhaled, a cloud of breath rising skyward. "But all is not lost…bunking off work, the Crown Jewels, hanging with my girls—things are looking up." Freddie laughed with a shiver. "As long as my dangly bits don't fall off."

Naomi turned to Alex. "Have you talked to Mark today?"

Lucy gritted her teeth. "Naomi—"

"It's okay." Alex shook her head. "I don't know what I would say right now other than *fuck you*."

"How 'bout *off with his head?*" Lucy's attempt at Tower of London humour missed its mark.

Alex jumped back in. "I hope he feels even a fraction of the pain I feel and can't show up to his precious job. But I bet he'll get up, arrive on set, and pretend—that's what he's good at. Asshole."

Naomi patted her arm, her eyes darting to Freddie. "I know *you've* talked to him. It's written all over your face."

"It's my best friend's birthday—of course, I've talked to him."

Alex sighed.

"You didn't mention that we were taking Lex out today, did you?" asked Lucy.

"No…" Freddie looked through her towards the Thames.

"You did, didn't you! *Freddie*!" Lucy dug her thumb and forefinger into his upper his arm and twisted.

"Ow, ow, OW. Okay—OKAY." He shook her off. "All right, I did…sorry, Lex."

She mouthed, "It's fine."

"I knew it." Lucy stuck her finger in Freddie's face. "You're picking sides."

"I'm not. Shit, I've totally lost feeling in my arm now."

"You're here to report back to him. Admit it, *spy*."

"I'm *not*. Jeez, Lucy. I wanted a fun day out, not a trial by fury…" The four friends edged forward in line.

"Freds, if I discover that you've told Keegs anything, I will tell Simon all about you skipping spin classes."

"You can't prove that!"

"Oh yes I can. I screen-capped your lunchtime Insta stories, wandering around Topman eating Cheesy Wotsits." Lucy laughed, a visible puff of her warm breath floated away.

Alex stifled a giggle.

"Nice one, Luce," said Naomi.

Lucy shot her a dirty look.

"Fine." Freddie crossed his arms.

"Your arse is mine, Mr. Ryan. So, maybe *now* you'll tell us what really happened in Dublin?"

Freddie maintained a poker face.

"You said you're not picking sides, so what's stopping ya?"

"Keegs' *memory*, that's what."

"Of course, you would take Mark's side," said Lucy. "Mark could spin Moriarty over his head, fling him into the Thames and you'd still say he's innocent."

"Lay off. It's not like that. Would *you* remember anything after a skinful and an E?" Freddie's eyes bulged and he slapped a fingerless gloved-hand over his mouth. "Ah…shit."

Alex's face blanched. "E? He took *ecstasy*?"

"Er, yeah." Freddie turned away, biting a fingernail.

"He didn't tell *me* that. He said he smoked a joint…" Alex's stare darted from Freddie to Lucy and back to Freddie.

"Don't look at me." Freddie's shoulders crept up to his ears. "That's all I've got. End of."

"If Keegs was *that* trolleyed on booze and drugs…" Naomi blew out her cheeks. "…anything could have happened."

Lucy looked at Naomi. "Why? Did Mark cheat on you, too?"

"No, but you know what he's like when he's drunk. He's giggly, flirty…forgetful."

Freddie sighed. "Aren't we all?"

"Some of us more than others. It doesn't make us bad people." Naomi wrapped her arm around Alex's shoulder. "I'm not telling you anything you don't know, right?"

Alex nodded.

"I bet he was boozed up and BAM—a momentary indiscretion, a mistake." Naomi squeezed Alex's arm and let go.

"Oi, get your tickets ready." Lucy pointed at the entrance, now five people away. A chilly gust blew in from the river.

Naomi tugged her faux fur leopard print coat tighter. "I slept with an ex behind my boyfriend's back once, at drama school. I still feel bad about it."

A blue-haired senior began punching their tickets at the gate.

Naomi rambled on. "That said, I *have* shared my boyfriends with others, though—at sex parties."

The ticket puncher's cheeks reddened, but she pretended not to hear.

Freddie's eyes lit up. "Ding dong! Do tell."

Naomi nudged him. "I could tell you things that would make your toes curl…"

"Why am I not surprised?" Lucy whispered to Alex as they left the speechless Tower of London employee behind.

Freddie rubbed his hands together. "Oh, goody. Why sample one sexual entrée when you can devour the entire buffet?"

"Freds, would you? *Have* you?" Alex handed him a Tower of London pamphlet.

"Actually, no." His shoulders deflated. "I just like to file those images into my wank bank, all those fingers roaming, plunging—"

"Not just fingers," blurted Alex.

Naomi leaned into Freddie. "And I'm partial to an occasional ménage à trois."

"With Tom?" he asked. "I can see him up to his knob in three-way shenanigans."

"With Tom." Naomi smiled. "A few times now."

Lucy sneered. "Ugh. *Caprice*?"

"Oh, good God, no—never."

Alex tugged her hat down over her ears. "I thought when you got married, you guys stopped…"

"Shagging around?" Naomi laughed. "We did, but we're married, not dead! We both like a *featured player* now and then. That's the thing, Lex: what you see publicly isn't necessarily the whole story."

Alex inhaled sharply, her hand squeezing the pamphlet. "Did you have threesomes with Mark?"

"No, sweetie. He's Mr. Monogamous. That's why I reckon New Year's was a shitty fluke. He's been falling all over himself, trying to prove that ever since. If I were you, I'd give him a second chance."

"See?" Freddie nodded, his nose beginning to run. "Naomi agrees."

"Oh, sure, give the guy a medal—he only cheated once!" Lucy shook her head. "What's the difference between cheating once and a million times? It's still *cheating*."

Naomi put her hand on her chest. "I know the pain Mark's feeling, breaking the trust of the person you love." The corners of her eyes crinkled as she looked back at the entrance.

"She's right, he is." Freddie sniffed, glancing over Lucy's head. "Oh, lock up your chastity belts, ladies."

"Hello, skivers." Tom strode over to his friends with a cigarette bobbing between his lips.

"Bite your tongue." Lucy handed Freddie a tissue for his nose. "I booked today off."

"Hi, mate, all right?" Freddie patted the newlywed on the back.

"Hello, Miss America." Tom smiled at Alex but got a smirk in return. "Okay, what have I done?" Tom's gaze swung around the group, settling on Naomi.

"What *haven't* you done, Tommy boy." Naomi kissed him on the lips. "Good audition?"

"Bollocks. I thought it was a modeling gig for a health magazine, but it was info pamphlets, you know the STI ones at the chemist?" He snapped his knuckles. "Crikey. Do I look like Gonorrhea Guy?"

Lucy snorted. Alex stepped on her friend's foot.

"Not at all, babe," said Naomi.

"They can shove their STI propaganda. Guess who's off to Dublin and the *Promise* shoot?"

Alex and Lucy looked at each other.

"But they turned you down…" said Naomi.

"Some dude dropped out. I got the call on my way here. They need someone who can do a French-Canadian accent. I leave *ce soir*." He waved his cigarette with a Gallic flourish.

"Congrats," Alex and Lucy chimed in at the same time.

"Looks like hanging out with Simon paid off." Freddie gave a thumbs-up.

Naomi laid a smacker on his mouth. "Did Mark put in a good word?"

"Maybe." Tom stuck out his bottom lip. "Don't know. I'm just chuffed to have a proper acting gig for a few days." He dropped a lanky arm around his bride and looked over his shoulder. "Man, this place brings back memories…my first proper snog was in the Wakefield Tower on a school trip."

Freddie looked up from his pamphlet, the cold making his eyes water. "Says here the Wakefield Tower is home to *instruments of torture*." He snickered. "Rather fitting, eh, Tom? You BDSM beast, you."

"Hey, if the fetish gear fits…" He laughed and kissed Naomi on the forehead. "We joining one of those Yeoman Warder tours, then?"

"We can now." Naomi pulled her hubby towards the sign listing the tour departures. Alex, Lucy, and Freddie followed, their noses stuck in their pamphlets.

Tom extinguished his cigarette with the heel of his boot. "I need a piss first. Be right back." He set off in search of the washrooms.

"I need one, too." Lucy chased after him.

Freddie sniffed his runny nose. "Lex…you know, Keegs got in real shit for flying out after you on New Year's Day. He was due on set the next day, but he blew it off, hoping to patch things up with you."

Alex smirked, her gaze settling on Traitor's Gate. "This is Mark we're talking about. He doesn't skip work."

"On January 2nd, he waited at your flat. When he didn't hear from you, he caught the last flight back."

Her expression softened.

"The director gave him a right old bollocking." Freddie shoved his hands deep into his pockets. "They had to scrap filming. Keegs was in every scene."

Naomi nodded. "I've seen directors tear into actors when they're late but not showing up *at all…*" She winced at Freddie. "Did they fine him?"

Alex blinked rapidly as her eyes volleyed back and forth between her friends.

"Yup."

"That won't do his reputation any good," said Naomi. "If directors or producers hear he's unreliable, fat chance he'll get hired again. Word gets around."

Freddie rounded his shoulders, seeking warmth. "Well, let's just say he's not the most popular person on set right now. The cast and crew waited hours—in the cold. He said his agent was terrific, trying to smooth everything over with the production staff."

"I wanted to make him pay for what he did, but not like this." Alex's phone vibrated in her coat pocket. Joan hadn't been feeling well lately, so she peeked.

*Mouse, your present...thank you. I don't deserve it. I don't deserve you, but you're all I want. I miss you. I love you. x*

She hid the evidence in her pocket.

"I've never seen Keegs in such a state. He's beside himself over what he's done to you," said Freddie. "I'm not saying he's not been an arse, Lex, but he was trashed—he didn't even know his *name* that night, let alone who he was in bed with. Won't you even *try* to make up with him?"

Naomi laid a reassuring arm around Alex's shoulder. "I don't think one terrible error in judgment is worth ending your relationship. He risked a lot, coming here. If last week doesn't prove how badly he wants to fix things, babe, I don't know what does."

Dump him…keep him. Never mind the Tower—Alex was imprisoned in her own thoughts.

# TWENTY-TWO

Placing her tea on the coffee table, Alex sat down, tucking her feet under her bum while steadying the rocking laptop on the sofa. She was used to being alone in the small apartment, but since leaving Lucy's flat, it had never felt emptier.

Yesterday's diversion to the Tower of London was a welcome reprieve, but…she couldn't put it off any longer.

An anxious hand dove into the box of Lucky Charms lying on its side. Not so lucky—only the blue marshmallow moons rattled around at the bottom. She stared at her laptop's screensaver, the slideshow of her and Mark in Venice flickering past.

Her stomach snarled. Opened packages of Twizzlers and Percy Pig sweets beckoned from the table, but she resolved to avoid another round of comfort eating.

Her eyes crept to the table and the rectangular courier box addressed to Mark. The same box *she* had collected for him from the concierge in Dublin. The same box *he* brought with him to Lucy's doorstep. He must have left it behind in the flat after waiting for her that day. An anniversary gift, maybe? Opening it now would be…weird…

She couldn't put it off any longer.

She woke up her laptop and with a tap of her finger, minimized a scene in *Upton Park* that just wasn't working. Her cursor hovered over the mail icon. She clicked, scrolling to the half-read email, now over a week old.

*From: Mark Keegan*

*To: Alexandra Sinclair*

*Sent: 2 January, 15:37*

*Subject: My side of the story*

*Mouse,*

*You can rest easy now. I won't be showing up at Lucy's again. I'm flying back to Dublin tonight.*

*I didn't think I could make things worse, but I did, didn't I?*

*Truth be told, I don't regret pounding on the door or shouting at Lucy. I don't regret bunking on her step, refusing to leave, or the cop visit. I was desperate. I'd do it all again in a heartbeat, trying to prove to you how much I love you, but your silence has made me realize that you're just not ready to talk. I guess I proved the casting agents wrong last night, eh? Turns out, I can play a realistic psycho. I never intended to freak you out. For that, I'm truly sorry. I know I keep saying it, but I am. I just keep hoping you will accept one of those sorrys, and we can fix what I've broken.*

*I keep going over everything in my head, trying to figure out how I got into this mess. I swear on my life, Alex, I don't remember what happened or how I woke up in bed with her. Dublin has always been a tricky place for me. It's my hometown, but it's also a place that I've left behind on purpose. Maybe like you with Tallahassee—there are too many bad memories mixed in with the good ones, you know?*

*Here's the honest truth then, about me and Fallon. I want you to know everything.*

*Fallon and I have known each other since we were twelve. I met her at the dry cleaners where our mums worked. To me, she was just a stupid, snobby girl, taking tap and drama classes.*

*Dad had passed away two months earlier, and I was having a tough time. Mum and my teachers agreed that afterschool drama classes might boost my confidence, so I began to see Fallon regularly. They cast us opposite each other in our first play. She was the obvious star—everyone said it, but she was full of herself, cocky, ambitious. She announced early on, "I'm going to marry Leo DiCaprio," which I took to mean, "I'm well out of your league, Keegan, don't get your hopes up." But by the time we were fifteen, we started to fancy each other. I lost my virginity to her soon after at a house party. For the most part, it was a normal teenage relationship with long drives in my beat-up Mini, snogging behind pubs, and having sex whenever we could.*

*Fallon liked to party and could look a lot older than she actually was. She would get into bars and clubs underage with no problem. She was pretty—but God, did she know it—and older guys constantly hit on her. I found out much later that she had cheated on me at least once. Would I have broken up with her, had I known? Probably not. I had it bad for her and didn't want to be left behind, so I did everything I could to keep up with her. I'm not proud of it, but I tried ecstasy with her at Excuses, our cheesy local nightclub. I had smoked weed before, but pills were new to me. I was sixteen at the time. It just became a thing we did whenever we went out. It helped us forget all the crappy stuff in our lives, for a few hours anyway.*

*But it didn't take me long to figure out that using wasn't a good idea. I felt drained all the time, and my football coach benched me; I wasn't playing up to my usual standards. I even had trouble memorizing my lines for theatre group. The short-term buzz just wasn't worth it, so I stopped. I only took it once or twice after that on special occasions like birthdays.*

*Anyway, things went from bad to worse. There was a pregnan-*

*cy scare, and she would lash out over the time I spent at my part-time job or football. She said I wasn't fun anymore. I got accused of not loving her enough because, by skipping drugs, I was judging her. On my eighteenth birthday, we split. The breakup was mutual and inevitable: she was always keeping an eye out for someone better, I was headed to London to study drama in a few months, and she was staying in Dublin to attend Trinity. She moved on within a week or two, started dating a pro rugby player (some things never change, I guess).*

*When she showed up out of the blue for the chemistry read and got the part, I didn't know how to tell you that Fallon was Sinéad or that I had lied about how long we had dated. I guess I had fibbed about the three-month thing because it made our relationship sound like a teenage fling, nothing serious. I wanted you to think you were my first big love, and in many ways—all the ways that count—you are. Fallon and I were a lifetime ago. She's my past, like Devin is your past. She's a footnote, a wrong turn, nothing more, but I was scared if you knew who she really was and how long we were together, you would feel threatened and anxious. A nude scene with an ex is kinda hard for a girlfriend to shrug off, and our separations are upsetting you so much; I didn't want to add to your anxiety if I could help it.*

*I was wrong. I should've told you. It was me who couldn't deal with digging up the past, not you. The strength you've shown when dealing with your own problems is inspiring, Mouse. I wish I had that faith in myself. I wish I had told you, but instead I bottled it and ended up slipping back into my old destructive habits on this fucking Dublin job.*

*I got plastered, then took an E (at least that's what I thought I took...who knows what shite they put in pills these days) at the Stag's Head because I think I wanted to forget I'm 'Mark Keegan' for a few hours. This new life, Mouse—everyone recognizing me, wanting their slice of me—I don't think I'm handling it well. I feel this constant pressure, like I'm faking it and people will realize I'm a fraud...I'm frightened of letting people down.*

*I wanted to vanish for a few hours. I thought I could handle it, but I couldn't. I drank way too much booze before and after the pill, and my stupid (and fucking selfish) lapse in judgment brought me here, paying the ultimate price—the loss of your trust. I just hope my behaviour won't result in losing your love, too. I need you, Mouse. I want to be with you, more than anything. All I want is for you to let me prove that. I want to rebuild your trust. I'm desperate to know what you're thinking. Just say the word and I'll fly home to talk.*

*Love, Mark. x*

*P.S. Please don't be cross with Freddie. He's not taking sides. He only wants us back together. I gave him money to fix Lucy's doorknocker. I'm sorry about that, too.*

She read it again...and again. Mark and Fallon split on Mark's birthday—eight years ago, yesterday. There was something she had to check.

She pulled up Google and typed a web address she knew too well. The usual headlines popped up on her screen: celebrity baby bumps, beach body-ready starlets in bathing suits, and famous couples toting to-go coffees. When the final piece of the *Mail*'s landing page loaded, her fingers pushed along her laptop's trackpad, her eyes searching.

And there it was: *Mark Keegan's Birthday Booze Up*. She clicked.

*He may be one of the most in-demand actors of the past year, but Lairds and Liars hunk Mark Keegan managed to squeeze in a few celebratory drinks for his twenty-sixth birthday. Castmates, crew, and friends joined the rising star last night for festivities at the Long Hall, a traditional Dublin pub dating back to 1881. The*

*Dublin native is home filming his first leading role in* A Promise Unspoken, *a historical action/drama.*

A large photo of Mark, Wink, and a few co-stars—Alex couldn't remember their names—leaving the pub sat between the paragraphs. She recognized two members of the production crew, including the woman who had helped her back to the hotel on New Year's Eve. She read further.

*Mark wore a knee-length black coat over a blue button-down shirt...* blah blah blah…

The next photo was Mark alone in a cab.

*With filming scheduled to resume in the morning, Mark and his squad called it an early night, and a fleet of cabs whisked away the revellers by ten p.m. One person was notably absent: the woman locked in Mark's New Year's Eve embrace. Fallon Delaney, 25, his co-star in* A Promise Unspoken, *was nowhere to be seen. When asked about her whereabouts, a source said the two actors dated as teenagers but couldn't comment on their current relationship status.*

Alex grabbed her phone, her thumbs flying over its screen, texting Mark.

*You there?*

She held her breath. If he was filming, it could be hours before he responded—if he responded at all. He might be pissed off that she hadn't answered his email. Mark knew it wasn't her style to ignore them.

Ten seconds later, her phone buzzed—Lucy.

*Help! Harry's mum is suffocating me! She won't take no for an answer. She's texted me three times this morning about their annual Alps skiing vacation. Harry's busy, but she wants me to go even if he can't.*

Alex responded. *Go! What do you have to lose?*

The three dots bounced as Lucy composed a response.

*My lunch, my cool rep, MY LIFE? Fuck. Of all the guys to*

*date, I picked one with pseudo-Olympians for parents. Why can't they be couch potatoes? Why do they like me SO MUCH? Help! I'm not used to this parent-thing!*

Alex smiled. Another text landed on her screen.

*I'm here, Mouse x*

Her eyes widened. Breathing in slowly, her thumbs took their time to answer.

*Did you have a good birthday?* She waited…reading it over—twice. With an exhale, she hit send.

Mark replied within seconds.

*No. Worst one yet... for obvious reasons. How are you doing?*

She bit the inside of her cheek as she typed her response. *Sad, nostalgic, lonely.* She paused and tapped the delete key, erasing 'sad' and 'nostalgic'. Lonely could stay.

*... for obvious reasons. FaceTime this week? We need to talk.*

*Yes! But I'll come to you. Does Friday afternoon work?*

*Yes. x*

# TWENTY-THREE

Alex's stomach churned as her eyes circled back to her *Sherlock* clock. Fifteen minutes and Mark would be here, home together for the first time since he dragged her to the Birmingham comic expo—forty-seven days ago. She reached towards her bedside table to grab the final touch to her outfit—

The lock clicked. *He's early.*

A quiver rose from her chest and wouldn't stop vibrating. *Please, no sweating.* Maybe the sleeveless dress would have been better?

"Lex?"

Too late to change.

"Coming."

She marched from their bedroom, her heart racing three times as fast as her feet.

*Mark*...hair disheveled, two weeks of stubble darkening his pale face, closing the door behind him. He set his backpack on the floor, a carry-on baggage tag curled around one of its straps. Straightening up, he shrugged off his wool coat, propelling a familiar scent into the air. Not too strong, not too faint...perfect, the scent of home.

Alex couldn't slow her breathing. He looked *hot.*

Mark removed his Ray-Bans. His eyes, weary and serious, met Alex's.

The giddiness that had flushed her cheeks while getting ready dissolved within seconds. She stopped short, running her hand over her neck—no necklace. She hadn't had a chance to put it on.

The keychain in his hand clinked against his sunglasses.

Alex swallowed, but the lump in her throat wouldn't budge. "Hi." Her voice barely rose above a whisper.

"Hi." Mark mirrored Alex's posture, stiff and still, but his eyes darted to her lips.

She felt that flick of his eyes deep in her stomach. What she wouldn't give to kiss him and turn back the clock twelve days to New Year's Eve…to stay in and skip *that* party. Tucking her hair behind an ear, she smiled and turned away. *Stay on script!* "Want a beer or something?"

"No, I'm good…thanks." Mark placed his keys and sunglasses on the black chair by the door and yanked off his boots.

"I'm gonna grab some water." She walked to the kitchen, wondering if he was following her ass in her grey dress. A glance over her shoulder—*yep*, but once caught, his gaze swept across the few furnishings they owned and landed on the shelving unit to his right. Chairs, area rugs, and end tables might be in short supply in their flat, but they didn't want for happy memories collected in picture frames. Clusters of photographs congregated on the shelves, each one celebrating a cherished moment: birthdays with friends, her comic con coups, and their whirlwind Venice vacation—Mark's surprise anniversary gift last year of a three-day stay over New Year's in the City of Bridges.

He was staring at one photo in particular, the two of them huddled up for warmth under a blanket in a wobbly gondola on the

Grand Canal. Her heart beat in her throat as she turned back to the sink and filled two glasses. That shot captured the heady bliss of their first anniversary. On that swaying boat, they had made a vow: every year, the first of January would be unforgettable. They had more than fulfilled that promise this year.

She turned around and walked back to the sofa, two water glasses in her hands. Mark sat down, legs wide apart, and shoulders hunched. He put his phone on the table beside the still unopened courier box. Midafternoon sunlight slipped through the west-facing balcony windows, settling on Mark's argyle socks and a vase holding a burst of red snapdragons. The flat felt spotless and orderly, warm and welcoming.

"My flowers came, then."

"They're gorgeous. Thank you." She placed a glass in front of Mark and perched on the edge of the sofa to his right, knees together, back straight. Her left foot jittered, betraying her practiced cool.

"You look lovely. Did you have a meeting today?"

Butterflies fluttered in her stomach. "Thanks. Uh, no, not today." She forced a half-smile.

They sat in silence for a minute.

"Lex, there's so much—"

"Mark, I need you—" Their words collided, spoken at the same time.

"Sorry." Mark ran a tentative hand through his hair. Dampness shadowed the material underneath his right armpit. "You go first."

She sipped her water and shakily relinquished it to the coffee table. "This all feels surreal…" She cleared her throat.

Mark stared at the water settling in her glass.

"I've felt for a while that I'm way down your priority list. You're never home. Our stable, loving relationship has turned into a painful long-distance one. I worry every time you leave you'll come back a little less in love with me. I'm always waiting for the worst to happen, scared that missing me will fade into forgetting me, replacing me…with someone else—"

"Lex, there's never been anyone els—"

"Mark."

He nodded and leaned forward, clasping his hands between his knees.

"Maybe there's never been anyone else *before*…but there is now. You don't get brownie points because you didn't sleep with another woman until a few days ago."

"Lex, it was a *mistake*, a *stupid* mistake."

"A mistake is tossing a red sock into a washer filled with white clothes. This isn't a *mistake*, Mark. This is a wrecking ball. It's shattered what we had. You've broken *us*."

"I know. I'm not trying to minimize what I've done or make excuses…sorry, poor choice of words." He crossed his legs and uncrossed them again, unable to find a comfortable position. "Guilt has been gnawing at me. I keep forgetting my lines. I've barely slept—"

Alex huffed and crossed her arms.

"How I've been feeling doesn't even compare to what I've put *you* through, Mouse. I know my word isn't worth much right now, but it will never happen again—I don't want to be with her. That is the God's honest truth."

"But you did that night." Alex pinched her lips tight. "Know what hurts the most? Your blatant dishonesty. You shared your life and bed with her *for years*, but didn't tell me. It was like I was relegated to a need-to-know basis, but Fallon knew who *I* was. She blurted it out: '*Mark's told me all about you.*' You should have told me *all about her*, Mark. For fuck's sake, I'm your girlfriend! Your lying is unforgivable."

"I don't expect you to forgive me."

"Good, because I can't—"

Bruno Mars burst into song from Mark's phone, facedown on the table.

"Aren't you…?" Alex glanced at it.

"No." He raised his voice to be heard above the music. "Lex, I know all the sorrys in the world won't erase what I've done, but everything in my email was the truth, every word, and if I could, I would pick apart every minute of that evening to figure out why I…let myself…why I let *you* down so badly."

Bruno's warbling abruptly stopped.

"I wish you could, too. I'd like to know what you two got up to. I'd like to know why you would even *want* to go there—"

"Lex…"

"Well, come on! It must have been a pretty epic reason to have sex with her on *our* anniversary." Alex gave him a pointed stare.

Mark glanced away and pawed a hand through his hair.

"Was she on top? Did you do it in a hot shower? No, you couldn't have—you reeked of her. Shame we can't relive the magic of Fallon coaxing you to finish—"

"Lex, *don't…*" He scrunched his eyes. "I swear on Freddie's life, I can't remember a thing, not a single bloody second, and even if I could, it meant sod all."

"I'm sure Fallon filled you in when you woke up."

"She was crying, frantic…worried about Duff finding out."

"Crocodile tears. Hope he dumps her." Alex paused. "Did you use a condom?"

"I think so."

"I thought you couldn't *remember.*"

"The wrapper was on the duvet…" Mark forced the words out. "When I stumbled out of the bed…there was a used condom in the bedside bin." His eyes fell with his shoulders. "Mouse, I'm so so sorry."

Her nose prickled. *Dammit. YOU are in control, Alex. YOU.*

She looked away and reached for her glass, but thought better of it, burying her hands in her lap.

Mark stuck his fingers inside the strap of his watch and spun it around and around his wrist.

Neither spoke for half a minute. The squeals of a baby, the girl belonging to the lesbian couple next door, reverberated from the hallway.

Alex brushed imaginary fuzz from her dress. “At least Mark Junior won’t be making his debut nine months from now.”

Frowning, Mark continued to spin his watch.

“Our relationship has meant everything to me.”

“It means everything to me, too, Mouse. Meeting you changed my life.”

“I think *Lairds* did more to change your life than I ever did.”

“That’s not true.” Mark angled towards her. “I was at a low point when I met you. Six months of rejections, and not a *single* role, not even a radio play. Every audition came to nothing. The doubts started…was I good enough? Was I wasting my time? I was thinking about giving up.”

“I doubt that!” She huffed. “You seemed so confident.”

“Yeah, ’cause I was trying to impress you! It’s not every day I meet a cute American girl who writes plays.” His face softened with a smile. “After twenty minutes talking to you, I realized—she *gets* me. Unlike most people, she doesn’t think I’m stupid for hanging out in drafty theatres, getting paid next to nothing. She gets my need to disappear into a character, because *she* craves that escape, too. Lex, the joy you have for writing your plays—for taking that leap of faith that *maybe* one day they’ll be seen by an audience—that inspired *me* to keep trying. I felt like I had found a kindred spirit.”

“I felt that, too.”

“See?” His eyes crinkled. “Other than my mum, I’ve never had *anyone* in my life who believed in me as much as you—and to top it off, you laugh at my stupid jokes and love my Vespa! And your talent—Christ, Lex…your first play staged at the Royal bloody Court? I wasn't surprised—I knew all along you could do it. You, gorgeous girl, are a force to be reckoned with." He pointed towards the shelves. "You'll need to shift those photos for Olivier Awards soon."

"I love those photos."

"I do too." He moved closer to her. "Those memories are special because you were by my side, Lex. God, we have *so many*. Remember when the *Doctor Who* Christmas special script arrived?"

"Yeah. I cried." Her eyes moistened, recalling the memory, wishing she could revisit that simpler, happier time. "I'm so proud of you, Mark. You deserve all the accolades, the success…" A heavy breath landed on her lap. "We almost survived it unscathed, until now…"

He clutched her hand. "We can get *through* this."

"I've thought about nothing else, Mark…"

"Neither have I."

"You can't remember, but I can't forget…"

His forehead creased briefly as her words stung.

"I love you, Mark, but once trust is broken…" She winced, her heart pounding faster…faster… "We can't go back to the way things were."

"I know. I *know* that." He swallowed heavily, squeezing her hand. "I love you more than anything. I don't care how long it takes or how hard it will be, I *will* prove you can trust me again. Just tell me what I need to do." His eyes lit up. "Just name it."

"I think we should break up."

His face fell. He blinked a few times, stunned—as if the words Alex had spoken were a foreign language. "*What*?"

Alex pulled her hand away. "I can't see a way through this.

I'm sorry."

"Mouse." He leaned closer, his eyes wide and pleading. "No! We *can* make this work. I know it will take time to rebuild your trust—"

"There's more to it than that." She slanted away from him. "We're never together…and when we are, we have zero privacy. I haven't been happy for a while."

"I know you haven't been, but we can fix this—"

She shook her head. "You and I deal with things differently, you and I *want* different things. I would like to get engaged; you want to wait. I wanted us to have time together; you couldn't say no to a *single thing* Wink suggested. I can't *do* this anymore, Mark. I'm done with being patient. I'm done with *always* being the one forced to compromise."

Mark clasped her knee, his thumb rubbing back and forth. "It won't always be like this—"

"I want a partner who spends more time *with* me than away from me, but that's not our life, is it? And if you were serious about making time for *us*, you'd have done it by now…"

"Babe, I am serious. That's why I'm gonna carve out more time for us. You can visit set more often. We can FaceTime every morning, before bed—"

"Waving through a tablet screen or having sex in your dressing room every few weeks doesn't cut it. I want to wake up beside you in *our* bed. I want to decorate this flat together. I want to cook for us—simple things. What we have, it's not enough."

He dragged both hands through his hair. "Lex, it's not enough for me either."

"You say that and yet every time we've talked about it, I can see you're *torn*. I know you don't *mean* to let me down, but if it's a choice between disappointing me or Wink, I lose, *every* time. It's like Wink has this hold over you." She threw her arms up. "Fuck, he's even got you doing action movies, Mark! We used to make jokes about those films. When we first met, you said your dream was to follow in the footsteps of your favourite actors, doing roles that *meant* something, but since Wink arrived, you've abandoned that. Since when do you want to become Vin fucking Diesel?"

"I *don't*. I'll still do theatre." He pointed at the table. "Look, why don't you open the box—"

"Wink dictates *everything*: the jobs you take, how often you're home. It's a tug of war, and I'm tired of always being on the losing end—"

"Not anymore. I talked to him."

Bruno sang out again from Mark's phone.

"Ignore it." He refused to pull his eyes away from Alex.

"We can't, Mark, that's the point…"

Bruno kept singing.

"It doesn't *matter* what Wink thinks." Mark shook his head, turning his phone over. "Shit." He sagged with a sigh. "I hav—"

"Yep."

"Wink." Mark snapped his eyes shut. "Can I ring you—"

Alex exhaled.

"Er, really…? *They* want me to read…? Wow, okay…if you think…no, not a problem… Yep. Thanks."

Alex shook her head. "Go on. You were just saying 'it doesn't matter what Wink thinks'?"

He pinched his lips and dropped his phone on the table. No words were necessary. His hesitation spoke for him.

She placed her fingers to her temples. "You haven't been around to notice, but…I've spent hours at my keyboard these last few months but nothing comes. It's like an instrument I've forgotten how to play. My writing's a shadow of what it was last year. Producers and directors are passing on my work…it's just not good enough—"

"The Garrick is just one theatre, Lex. There's plent—"

"The Donmar rejected my commission—"

"*What*? When—?"

"Back in October. See? I've become a theatre has-been at twenty-four. No one is returning my calls. Being ignored is even more brutal than being rejected. It's soul crushing."

"I know that better than anyone. Look, I can help—"

"And do what? *Make* them take my calls?" Alex clenched her jaw. "Everything is a mess. My credit card is maxed out. I had to sell stuff to pay rent—"

"Why didn't you tell me? *I* can support us."

"*I* want to be financially self-sufficient, but I can't, not without my writing voice. I've lost it. Can't you see how that feels, Mark? It's like…it left with you one day and hasn't come back. What if I never get it back?"

"Lex, it *will* come back."

"Yeah? When? Because I'm tired of waiting, turning myself inside out over writing, bills, the future…*you*—it's not helping. I just…*can't*…not anymore." She fought to catch her breath.

His posture stiffened. "Why didn't you tell me you were having panic attacks again?"

She bowed her head.

"Lex." He scooted closer, wrapping his arm around her shoulder. "I would've come home, rearranged…" The rest of the sentence stuck in the back of his throat.

"And what?" Alex slowly shook her head. "Get fined like you did on January 2$^{nd}$? Or worse? Mark, I don't want you resenting me. I don't want you regretting *being* with me."

"I don't regret being with you. I *love* you. You're the most important thing in my—"

Alex's hand pushed pause on Mark's chest as tears gathered in her eyes. "We both know that's not true, not anymore."

"It won't be this crazy forever...just hold on a little longer." Mark pulled her closer. "Please...don't give up on us."

"I'm not giving up on us. *You* gave up on us...the moment you slipped into Fallon's bed." Her voice cracked, each word tearing them further apart.

"No. *Lex*—"

"Mark, it's over." The tears she choked back clogged her throat. "Please go."

His hand slipped from her shoulder, his jaw slack. He stared at the wall for a moment before scooping his phone from the table. He stood up, eyes glued to the floor. "We'll...We'll have things to sort out, living arrangements...all that." Dazed, he blinked and turned to his left, walking around the back of the sofa so he didn't have to face Alex or squeeze between her and the table. "They'll have to wait until filming wraps next month. I've gotta...head to the airport..." His chin trembled.

Alex rose to her feet, but her knees wobbled like jelly. Tears trickled down her cheeks.

Keeping his back to her, Mark wiped his nose with the edge of his wrist and tugged on his boots, ignoring their laces. He slipped on his coat, dumping his keys and phone in the pockets.

The half-dozen steps to the door took all of Alex's energy, her chest tightening with each sob and gulp for air. The room began to sway ever so slightly. She reflexively reached for the Vespa charm, but it wasn't there.

Mark leaned towards the chair and his sunglasses but changed course, turning around quickly towards Alex. He threw his arms around her shoulders, crushing her body with his and leaving a tender kiss on her forehead. Clinging to her, halting breaths shuddered through his chest as he finally gave in to the tears he had fought to suppress.

Alex pressed her face into his neck and dug her fingers into his waist, pulling him tighter, trying to commit his scent, his heartbeat, the warmth of his body to memory. If only New Year's hadn't been spent in Dublin. If only Mark didn't choose Wink each time…if only…*if only*…he hadn't cheated on her. Letting go was the right thing to do, but her disintegrating heart begged her to reconsider. There was nothing she could do. Their time had simply…run out. Another wave of tears spilled from her eyes.

He inhaled purposefully and trembled upon its release. With a final squeeze, he let go. "I love you, Mouse, always."

She swiped her wet cheeks with a hand and licked her lips, tasting a melancholy mix of salty tears, hers and Mark's. She wrapped her arms around her quaking chest, barely holding herself together.

Mark put on his sunglasses, grabbed his backpack, and pulled open the door. He walked away without turning back.

# Twenty-Four

"Sorry I took so long." Lucy shoved through the door, her eyes hidden underneath the wet, faux fur trapper hat that was swallowing her face. "Fucking Elephant and Castle." Exhausted, she placed an umbrella and two full shopping bags on Alex's apartment floor with a thud.

Cheeks streaked with tears, Alex plunged her swollen nose into a handful of disintegrating tissue. "How am I going to get through this?" She clutched a rectangular blue, green, and pink tin decorated with hearts and birds against her chest.

Lucy's arms flew open. "One shitty day at a time, babe. Come here…"

Alex's knees buckled, her body collapsing into Lucy's embrace. "I feel like I've fallen under the wheels of a bus—*on purpose*." Her body shook with sobs as Lucy held her. "Freddie texted me, '*What have you done?*'"

"Oh, ignore Freddie. And *fuck* Mark." Lucy pulled back, making close eye contact. "What you need right now is the *Bezzie Mate Treatment…*" She opened her shopping bags. "See? Ice cream, wine, vodka, oven chips, Lucky Charms, Pizza Express dough balls, triple chocolate cookies, cheese strings…oh, and I can confirm… *Kick Ass*, *Kill Bill*, and *Waiting to Exhale* are still on Netflix. Or if you need comfort and the soothing tones of Whishy, there's always *Bright Star* or *The Hour*, even *Spectre* if you fancy some Q in a wooly hat. We're all sorted for the weekend."

Alex chased breaths between sobs and dove a hand into a bag. "Chicken Christmas trees with…BBQ dip?"

"The chicken trees were marked down—clearance. Actually, most of this stuff was on offer."

"Thanks, Lucy. I need a food hug."

"Hey, wanna mainline carbs? I'm your girl." Lucy dumped her backpack on the floor and frogmarched Alex into her bedroom. "C'mon, let's put on our jim-jams. I want to hear everything."

Alex placed her untouched bowl of chocolate and cheese strings on the table beside a small white box and the rectangular hearts and birds tin. A ratty tissue fell out of her sleeve. "Oh, God, look at me—I'm such a mess. If I'm not bawling, I'm in the bathroom. Pathetic."

"It's only been two and a half hours since you split, Lex. There's no fast-forward button for heartbreak."

"He'll be landing in Dublin soon."

Lucy wrenched the belt of her bathrobe.

Alex rubbed her cheek, further smearing the mascara and eyeliner that had smudged underneath her eye. She looked around their flat. All their photos…shared books…memories. Landing in Dublin or not, Mark was *everywhere* here. "I wonder what he's thinking…"

"Probably how stupid he was to fuck up the best thing he's ever had."

"His face…" A breath caught in Alex's throat. "He was crying when he left—"

"It's not helping, worrying about him, and please, stop with the pathetic crap. You're the opposite of pathetic. You took control and chose the tough option. Fuck, I can't imagine how hard it is—dumping someone you still love. I've never been there. The easy way would have been to accept his cheating, all those absences, and take him back—better the devil you know and all that bollocks."

"Trust me to ignore the easy way…"

"When have you *ever* taken the easy way out? Drives me bonkers, but this time, lady, you played a blinder. You had enough and you pulled the plug—nothing pathetic about that. If anything, you're…*indomitable*."

"Indomitable? Where did you pick that up? Playing Scrabble with Harry's parents?"

"No, Simon's word-of-the-day calendar at Christmas."

"Are you sure it wasn't *abominable* like the snowman in the *Rudolph* Christmas special?"

"The what?"

"The Abominable…*the Bumble*?"

Lucy flashed a blank stare.

"Never mind. It's an American thing. So, if I'm indomitable, why do I feel like I've flung myself from the Shard? I'm in freefall, about to splat across the pavement." Alex popped open the tin. "Look." The blue, green, and pink rectangle was filled to its rim with cookie birds and hearts, hand-iced in all colours of the rainbow. "Mark ordered them from that Biscuiteers café."

"They're so detailed and pretty but…why?"

"He had them couriered to the hotel for our anniversary…" She held a pink and white bird. "I've always wanted to visit that shop."

"What did you get him?"

Alex shrugged, sadly. "It doesn't really matter now, does it?"

Lucy picked up a heart with a crack down the middle. “Hmm, that’s fitting.”

“It’s my fault. I dropped the box in Dublin.” Stray tears trickled down Alex’s cheeks. “There was something else in the parcel, too.” She lifted the lid on the small white box. “Diamond constellation earrings. Aren’t they pretty?”

“He gave you *star* earrings?” Lucy snorted. “Fame is going to someone’s head. What happened to Mrs. Keegan’s humble son?”

Alex crumpled. “Oh, God, his *mum*. She would’ve known something was up when I didn’t answer her text on New Year’s Day…”

“It’s not *your* job to tell his mum.”

“I owe her a good-bye, Lucy. I can’t ghost her.”

“If she’s as empathetic as you say she is, she’ll understand. I’ll bet she freaked when she found out what he did.”

“Oh, fuck. I have to cancel our holiday.”

“The Florida one?”

“Yeah. Next month.” Alex pressed her flushed face into her hands.

“Leave it to me. I’ll take care of it.”

“I’m going to lose this place, too…”

“You’ll stay with us.”

“There’s no room.”

“Well, if not mine…Harry’s.”

“Sofa surfing? No.” Alex rubbed away the tears with her hand. “I might move to Dad’s…get my bearings, start over.”

“Moving? Not permanently?”

“It will hurt too much seeing Mark around with Freddie…”

“You won’t have to worry about that. He’s never *here*, remember?”

Alex snapped the lid closed on the cookie tin. “You said it yourself: friendships often fall apart when there’s a split.”

"No, I didn't."

"Yeah, New Year's Day? I said there would be no weirdness with you dating Harry because we all knew him and you said—"

"Oh yeah…'*until we break up.*' Fuck."

Alex sniffed. "I won't make Freddie choose. His loyalty lies with Mark."

"No, Freddie's loyalty lies with *me*. I've known him a good two years longer than Mark."

"If I go away, you guys won't have to juggle your friends. I won't bump into him, and maybe it'll be easier to pull myself together again. I'll paint on a smile, fake it till I make it…whole on the outside but in pieces on the inside." Alex pointed at a small blue and orange box lying amongst a smorgasbord of snacks on the table. "Like that Terry's Chocolate Orange…"

"Want it?" Lucy tossed it over. "Lex, don't rush into anything."

Alex tore open the box and slammed the foil-wrapped chocolate into the table's edge. The table wobbled, swirling her untouched wine around its glass. "Mark never did fix that damn leg…"

"You gonna drink that?" asked Lucy.

"Go for it." Alex got up, dragging her bathrobe behind her. "I haven't touched a drop since New Year's. I need a clear head. There's so much to mull over."

"I don't like this booze-free clear-headedness, not if it's telling you to leave." She sipped Alex's wine. "Where are you going?"

"Dad's. I just said—"

"No, right now."

Alex opened the cupboard under the sink and pulled out a beat-up shoebox. She walked back to Lucy. "Can you help me shift this stuff? On the sofa, floor, wherever."

They moved the food, glasses, cookie tin, and snapdragons onto the hardwood floor.

Alex lifted the small table onto its side and dug through the box, each movement of her hands clinking and clanging the contents inside.

"Dad's house will be quiet during the day. Joan will be teaching, Helen's busy at the hospital…"

Her hand reappeared with a screwdriver.

"Shame that thing's not sonic." Lucy laughed.

Alex slowly tightened the loose bolt at the base of the table leg. "I might stay for a few months, concentrate on writing. I could work on our graphic novel up there."

Lucy looked hurt. "Come on, Lex. Don't go up north. I'll miss you."

"You'll be fine. Think of it as more time with Harry." Alex tugged on the leg. Now stable, it wasn't going anywhere. She returned the screwdriver to the box and the table to its feet.

"Look at that," said Lucy. "Indomitable AND handy. Forget Harry, I should be dating you."

Alex starred at the smashed chocolate orange, ignoring Lucy's silliness. "When we were in Manchester on Boxing Day…did you notice Mark's behaviour? I keep thinking about it. He went to the bathroom like, four times during that football match. He nursed one pint the whole visit, so I doubt he was peeing in the toilets. Maybe the ecstasy on New Year's Eve wasn't a one-off. Maybe he's doing other stuff, too?"

"You think he was doing drugs? In the loo?"

Alex shrugged and set their snacks back on the table.

"I didn't have Mark down as a pill popper." Lucy reunited their glasses and the flowers with the table. "At least based on what I've seen."

"I couldn't get him to take aspirin when he hurt his shoulder, so what's up with the recreational drugs?"

"Hurt his wha'?"

"His *shoulder*. Austria in November? He said he slipped during a snowball fight. It looked nasty, like the Hulk had stomped on him…all purple and yellow, really bad."

"So much for him channeling Action Man, getting his arse kicked by Buddy the bloody Elf. Unless…do you think he was high, hurt himself that way?"

"He's lost weight, too. He was thinner before Christmas, before Fallon. I thought he looked skinnier in Birmingham, but it was really noticeable in Manchester."

"Really? Wow, maybe it is a drug problem, then. I never thought Mark would be one to have a quarter-life crisis. God, Lex, no matter how you slice it, you *had* to kick him to the curb."

"It's just been one thing after another."

Lucy sneered. "Stupid guy. I think he came here figuring a few snapdragons, apologies, a box of cookies, and you'd be ready to forgive and forget. He doesn't deserve you."

Both women sat in silence for a minute.

"Lex, what you told me on Boxing Day…it's been stuck in my head. Don't get cross at me for asking but, if the cheating hadn't happened, Fallon hadn't come back on the scene…if it was just you and Mark and his bonkers schedule…would you still be together?"

Alex exhaled. "I don't know. I love him, but a big part of me hates what our life had become, you know? That's the problem: Mark's a package deal now. The lack of privacy, the constant absences—it's a huge part of him, just like panic attacks are part of me. *And never the twain shall meet.*"

"But what if he *had* proposed in Dublin?"

"But he didn't. I'm done mulling over what-ifs. Things don't always work out in the end. Life isn't a fairy tale, Lucy—we both know that." She scooped up her shoebox of tools and walked back to the kitchen.

# TWENTY-FIVE

*Two weeks later*

Freddie hopped out of the rental car and slammed the driver's side door.

Mark winced. "Christ! Freds!" He snatched at his messy hair as he slowly slid off the front seat. Gently closing his door, careful not to jar his thumping head any further, he nudged his Ray-Bans up his nose. His red, watery eyes would remain his secret. He looked up at the four-storey building in front of him, trying to focus on the top floor window—the flat he used to call home with Alex.

"When we've got your stuff, I'm calling Tom." Freddie strode around the car to face his hungover friend. He curled his lip, taking in the chaos that was Mark's appearance. "Giving him a right ol' bollocking for all *this*."

Clutching his bubbling stomach, Mark stared back. "I've already told you, this isn't Tom's fault. I'm having a hard time dealin—" His shoulders lunged forward. *Cough, cough, cough!* His fit sent puffs of warm, boozy breath into the chilly January air.

Freddie wrinkled his nose and waved a hand in front of his

face. "Jeez, Keegs! You reek! Please tell me you didn't drink Dublin dry?"

*Cough, cough!* "I drank beer"—*cough*—"nothing else," he wheezed.

"Yeah, a whole brewery's worth—"

Mark sniffed. "Tom was looking after me..."

"Tom's the worst babysitter—*ever*. I mean, if '*looking after you*' means putting you on a plane completely shit-faced, well I—"

Mark squinted behind his sunglasses. "For fuck's sake! GIVE IT A REST!" He flinched at the loudness of his own voice. "I don't need this, not today."

"Keegs..." Wilting under Mark's outburst, Freddie gave up. "Let's get this done."

Ushering a weaving Mark inside and towards the first flight of stairs, Freddie mumbled under his breath, "You're in absolutely no state to move *fuck all*..." He planted his hands on Mark's back, pressing him forward.

Above their heads, the stairs creaked. Rushing feet galloped downwards from an upper floor.

"*Mark*...?!"

He jolted, tripping up the next step. His sunglasses slipped down his nose.

Alex met him on the small landing, her eyes wide, mouth agape. With a stuttering sweep, she looked him over from head to toe and back again. His wool coat was buttoned wrong and one of his boots' laces was untied.

His sweaty face softened as he swayed closer. "Lex..." He plucked his sunglasses off his face and tried to smooth down his disheveled hair.

Lucy pushed past her best friend, creating a barrier. "Keegs, back OFF!" Her eyes flew to Freddie. "What the fuck? We agreed!"

Freddie shrugged. "The car was ready early so..."

Lucy clenched her jaw, her eyes shooting to Mark.

The corners of his mouth rose, ignoring Lucy and Freddie. Only Alex mattered. His eyebrows creased as he looked over Lucy's shoulder. "It's good to see—"

"Freds," Lucy interrupted, a vein pulsing in her temple. "We'll talk about THIS later!"

Mark inched closer, sandwiching Lucy. Alex's eyes fell to the floor, but her lips parted like she was about to say something…

Lucy turned and snatched Alex's upper arm. "COME ON!"

"OW!" The playwright winced, digging in her heels. "That hurts!"

Lucy tugged, propelling Alex into Mark's side. He stumbled backwards, blinking at the sweatshirt peeking through Alex's open coat. *She's wearing my shirt! Maybe she's regretting this…* "Lucy, please…give Lex and me a minute—"

"Time's up, Mark." Lucy scowled over her shoulder, marching Alex down the stairs. "Just get your fucking shit out of here!"

Alex didn't look back.

Mark didn't look away until Alex was through the front door, out of sight.

# TWENTY-SIX

Alex's leg shimmied under the table, making their plates shake. The Cat and Mutton's upstairs space was packed with loud groups of friends, young families, and wide-eyed tourists devouring the 300-year-old pub's Sunday lunchtime specialty: heaping plates of roast sirloin, Yorkshire pudding, potatoes, and a medley of honeyed carrots and parsnips.

"It's too soon."

"No, it's time. You've been glued to that sofa for two bloody weeks." Lucy dunked a piece of beef into the thick gravy. "Your wheelie bin goes out more than you do."

"No. I mean—I didn't expect Mark to *move out* today. Everything's real, now it's happening…"

"The faster he moves out, the sooner you can move on, do your Manchester thing, and come back to London…and can you *please* stop shaking the table?"

"He looked awful…"

Lucy impaled a potato with her fork. "Karma's a bitch."

"*I* look awful." Alex glanced down at her sweatshirt and jeans which hung from her curves. "Splotchy, pale—I'm such a catch."

She rubbed her eye without fear. Her mascara and eyeliner hadn't left her makeup bag since the afternoon she called time on their relationship.

"What the hell are you doing in *his* sweatshirt?" Lucy's glare dropped to her plate as she sliced her Yorkshire pudding into pieces. "You've been sleeping in it, haven't you?"

Alex slid her Vespa necklace underneath the shirt's collar while Lucy wasn't looking. "It's comforting."

"Yeah—for all the wrong reasons. Besides, it smells and it's got a huge hole in it." Lucy stabbed a baby carrot. "I could *kill* Freddie. Why couldn't he just fucking LISTEN for once and follow simple instructions?"

Her loudness attracted furrowed brows from the next table.

"I told him to wait until we'd left but ohh, no! He *had* to bring Mark over an hour early. He did it on fucking purpose. You weren't supposed to see him, and he definitely wasn't supposed to see you, especially in *that* sweatshirt."

"Mark looked green. Do you think he's sick?"

Lucy exhaled with a huff.

"I could ask Freddie…"

"You *could*, but you *shouldn't*. He's not your concern anymore."

"I can't flip a switch and stop caring. It's only been two weeks—"

"Fine," Lucy interrupted. "Yes, he's been out getting wrecked again in Dublin. Happy now?"

"Was Fallon—"

"No, according to Tom. Does it make a difference? It shouldn't."

"It doesn't."

"Liar." Lucy shoved aside her parsnips with her knife. "You are pining *big time*. You're binge-watching *Friends*, haven't started packing. There's unopened mail, dust bunnies, unwashed clothes."

Alex half-heartedly took a bite of her Yorkshire pudding. "I ran out of underwear. I'm wearing my bikini bottoms—"

"See? Neat Freak Lex would be horrified. And I love junk food, but your eating habits—"

"What?" Alex scooted untouched carrots around her plate. "Naomi brought casseroles—"

"That you don't eat. She finds them morphing into science experiments in your fridge. And I know you read this morning's *Mail* story. I saw it on your laptop."

"Naomi said Tom was in some of the photos. I just wanted to see—"

"Don't use Tom as your latest excuse. You're the one who broke it off, not the other way 'round. It's over. There's no going back. Just stop, okay? Stop! Eat your lunch and quit shaking the table."

Alex's leg picked up speed. "Come on, Lucy, give me a break. All you've done lately is harp at me for being sad. *I* may have ended it, but it still hurts." She avoided eye contact. "At least Freddie's been understanding."

"Yeah, 'cause Freds wants you two back together."

"Maybe Freddie's right. I keep having doubts…" Alex lowered her voice. "…asking myself, *Did I do the right thing?* Living with Mark's clothes, his bathroom stuff, the Vespa…it's a daily reminder of what I've lost."

"Well, then you won't mind when I chuck that United shirt in the bin when we get back."

"You might as well toss me in with it."

"Don't tempt me." Lucy gestured with her fork as she talked. "In an hour or so, all those reminders will be out of your flat for good, and I'm changing my Netflix password, so you'll stop with the *Friends* marathon. It's not helping."

Alex poked at a small roast potato. “But the absence of his stuff is a reminder, too.”

“For fuck’s sake, Lex, you’re doing my head in. The cheater *had* to move today, okay? Once the film finishes mid-Feb, Freddie said he’s straight into rehearsals for some play.”

“What play? Where’s he doing it?”

“I don’t care. You shouldn’t either. You were doing so well two weeks ago. Now you’re…*regressing*, yeah, that’s the word.” Lucy picked up the menu, giving the desserts a once-over. “Oh, I forgot to tell you—I called to cancel your Spring Break Florida trip, but Mark had already done it. At least he’s taken responsibility for something.”

“Fuck, I miss him.”

Lucy’s phone buzzed on the table. “It’s Freds. *If* he’s telling the truth, they’ve just left the flat.”

Alex jolted to her feet sending her chair squealing across the floor. “I’m going back. Now.”

Tearing off her coat, Alex’s eyes landed on the black chair inside the flat. “His keys…”

Lucy closed the door. “What about them?”

“They’re not here. He always leaves them right here. Maybe he’s not done—maybe he’s coming back.” Without stopping for breath, she raced into the bedroom, her keychain—the one that matched Mark’s—clasped within her grip.

“Lex…” Lucy called out even though Alex was around the corner, out of sight. “Don’t. His Vespa’s gone…”

Heart pounding, Alex whipped open the closet at breakneck speed. Half of it—Mark’s half—was bare. She ran to his drawers, heaving them open two at a time, their hollow *clunk* a punch to

Alex's stomach. She spun around, eyes wild and roving, the room dissolving into a streaky blur. His record collection, his signed football, his dog-eared novels—all gone, off to live someplace else…someplace without her.

"Babe, don't do this."

Chucks thumping across the hardwood, Alex ignored Lucy and strode through the living room to the bathroom, her eyes scrambling over the vanity, through the medicine cabinet, over the edge of the tub: Mark's hair products, razor, and toothbrush that had lived alongside her lotions, potions, and bottles…all taken. With a shaky hand, she shoved her bangs off her forehead, creased in despair.

The fridge…the fridge would tell her. Smothered with photos and loving Post-Its—that's where she needed to look. She careened from the bathroom, all hope pinned to that under-the-counter appliance.

The surface of the fridge was like a baseball bat to the knees. Alex reached for the kitchen counter, steading herself. Mark hadn't taken *anything*. She stared at the memories left behind, deemed dispensable by the man she had hoped to spend the rest of her life with.

He hadn't *left* anything, either. "No note, no…nothing? Doesn't two years mean anything to him?" Alex squeezed the keychain in her hand, the engraving on the silver rectangle branding its significance into her palm and scarring her heart.

Lucy placed a hand on her friend's shoulder. "Actors are like nomads, moving from job to job, Lex. He's used to leaving people behind."

Tears slipped down Alex's cheeks and landed on her sweatshirt—Mark's sweatshirt—her new reality seeping into her heart as quickly as the tears soaked into the cotton top. Not only had Mark taken all his belongings, he had also snatched away her hope, her breath, her heart.

Looking across the counter, Lucy spied a propped-up bubble envelope with 'Alex' scrawled across it.

"Lex, what's that?" She grabbed the medium-sized package for her friend.

The handwriting with its looping A and sweeping X was as familiar as Alex's own. She fought back tears, taking a hopeful breath.

Ripping open the parcel, her shaky hand met the waxy dust jacket of a hardcover book. The ache in her chest squeezed tighter. It was the signed autobiography of Manchester United's most celebrated manager, Sir Alex Ferguson…her birthday gift to Mark—the one she had hurled at his head in Dublin. A page fell open, revealing a piece of hotel notepaper.

*Alex, you've always known what to get me, but this left me speechless. It's Michael's copy, isn't it? I spent so many hours with my nose stuck in its pages, your dad always joked that I should have it. He gave it to you, to give to me, but I can't keep it, not now. Please make sure Michael gets it back and tell him I'm sorry for the pain I've caused your family.*

*You must wish we never met. I deserve your disappointment, your disgust in me. It mirrors mine. Love always, Mark x*

She stared at the paper, hovering over the last line: no goodbye. Mark *knew*. He knew how much they both hated saying that word.

She looked back inside the envelope and gasped what felt like her last breath. Her hand slipped inside the bubble wrap sleeve, her fingers meeting cold, jagged metal—surrendered, never to be held in Mark's hand again.

A sob let go in her throat, releasing wave after wave of tears.

The final thread connecting her to Mark had been severed. Mark Keegan, loving boyfriend, was now Mark Keegan, the next big thing. All news of him would be gleaned from Google or maybe a slip of Freddie's lips. No more kisses. No more rapturous reunions or easy smiles. The next time she'd see his face would probably be through a TV or cinema screen—*you can look, but you can never touch.* He would land bigger roles, collect even more enthusiastic fans—and probably have a new A-list girlfriend. He was no longer hers.

It wasn't supposed to end this way. It wasn't supposed to end at all.

She swallowed, digging out Mark's keys. The landlord would be happy…at least someone would.

One key. Two keys. They were Mark's unspoken, unwritten good-bye. Her whole body ached.

She reached in again, but her hand came back empty.

Mark was always careless, losing things; his silver keychain that matched the one in her hand wasn't there.

"I guess it's official then…" Alex gulped for air, sinking into Lucy. She released her grip on the beloved object. "I'm one of those people, left behind, forgotten."

Through a veil of tears, her eyes settled on her palm: the *June 5, 2015* indentation from the keychain was fading fast from her skin.

# TWENTY-SEVEN

*Three and a half weeks later*

"Lex, I've always thought of you as my little sister—albeit a perfectionist, pain-in-the-arse of a little sister—so I can't help being protective…" Harry stretched back into the onyx leather booth. "Please, let me take care of your rent."

"You sound like a broken record." Alex smiled. "I appreciate your offer, but I'm not changing my mind."

Her eyes strayed to the Bespoke waiter arriving with two plates. He slid Alex's lunch—posh mac 'n' Gruyère cheese—on the table with oven mitts. "Careful—don't get burned."

"Thanks." Alex waited for the guy to walk away. "You're not paying for this."

Harry unfurled a smile along with his black cloth napkin. "I knew you would say that."

"Paddington and I may end up living in a box, eating untoasted Pop-Tarts under Marble Arch, but at least it will be on my terms. Just think of the writing material it will generate—and maybe even the headlines: *Homeless Playwright Brings Down the House with*

*Olivier Win!*" Digging her fork through the breadcrumbs, parsley, and cheesy pasta, wisps of steam evaporated from her plate.

"An Olivier Award won't keep you warm at night."

"No, but it would make a handy weapon to fend away any junkies coming after my Pop-Tart stash…"

Harry scooped up a mouthful of his grilled potato, salmon, and lentil salad, careful not to spill any on his suit. "Look, think of it as a loan—"

"Harry, I move next week." She blew on a forkful of pasta and took a delicate taste. She closed her eyes, savouring the hot cheesy happiness on her tongue. "Mmm. Want some?"

Harry sipped his sparkling water. "No, thanks. I'm watching my figure."

Alex snickered. "So is Lucy."

"That's why the mustard cream sauce is on the side." He tapped his fork against a small bowl riding shotgun with his plate.

"The furniture's been sold. Even the bed's gone. Simon's been a huge help. He even dropped everything to fix my leaky sink. He's a good guy, despite what Lucy says."

"I think he just wanted to show off his old plumbing skills, and he's Team Alex. He has always had a jealous hate-on for Mark."

Alex exhaled heavily.

"You know it's true." He flicked through his salad with his fork. "Actually, I'm coming around to Si's opinion. I mean, I don't *hate* Mark, but I hate what he's done to you, and his behaviour lately is not like the bloke I know *at all*."

Alex scooped up some pasta. "Harry, you don't have to choose sides. You and Mark are such good friends, I—"

"*Were* good friends. Hurt my loved ones or betray a trust like that? Sorry, I want nothing to do with you." He smiled softly. "There's no competition. I am, and always will be, Team Alex."

"Harry, do me a favour?"

"Anything, little sis!"

She cocked her head, wincing. "Stop saying Team Alex. It's cheesier than this pasta."

He laughed. "Done!" He watched Alex eat, choosing his words carefully. "Have you contacted him?"

"No." She squinted. "Have you?"

"No. Would you tell me if you had?"

"Did Lucy put you up to this?"

"No."

She pinched her lips tight and swallowed, abandoning her fork. "I never knew I could I miss someone so much."

Harry reached for her hand across the table. "Oh, Lex—"

"I can't leave the flat…those *Lairds* posters are *everywhere*, and a red Vespa will pass and I…" She stared at her plate. "London feels *tainted*…all the places we've been…"

"It'll take time."

"I can't watch TV in case I see him—or *hear* him."

Harry nodded. "I thought that was his voice on those Irish tourism adverts."

"And stupid little things. I can't eat Nutella, or Jaffa Cakes, and sleeping alone in our bed…knowing he'll never come home…" Her eyes began to well up. "I couldn't sleep it in anymore. I had to get rid of it. So, despite what everyone thinks, I'm trying *everything* I can to forget him…because clearly he's forgotten me."

Harry squeezed her hand.

She sniffed back tears. "I *know*…*I'm* the one who said it was over, but he was the one who broke us up. I thought maybe he'd email me since he took his stuff but…" She shook her head. "I haven't emailed him. I haven't searched his name on social media. I haven't even Googled him. Why would I? To hurt *more*? Like that's even possible." She took in a shuddering breath. "I stopped wearing his necklace…"

"I'm sorry, Lex, I didn't mean to make you cry—"

"Can we talk about something else, please?" She pulled her hand away and used her napkin to dab at a stray tear.

Harry let out a sympathetic sigh. "Sure. How's your writing?"

"Good."

He smiled kindly, not buying her response. "Lex…"

She looked up from her plate.

"That bounce you get when you're passionate about something? Still missing."

"That's why I'm going to Dad's—a fresh start. *A change is as good as a rest*, right?"

"Right—" Harry did a double take over Alex's shoulder and dropped his fork. "Bloody hell?"

Alex followed his gleeful stare.

Harry couldn't climb out of the booth fast enough. "Mate! I didn't expect you until tomorrow."

"Come here, ya pillock." The tall stranger manhandled Harry, yanking him into a bear hug punctuated with back slaps. They laughed like a pair of naughty schoolboys.

Their smiles were contagious. Alex fought it, but she broke out into a grin, too.

Pulling away, the new arrival locked eyes with her. "Hel-lo."

"Tarquin Balfour, meet Alex Sinclair, my unofficial little sister from America. Alex, meet Tarquin. This bastard is the bane of my existence."

Alex was sure his face matched a name she had seen commenting on Harry's Facebook.

"Harry's telling porkies." Tarquin's accent was an odd mix of upper-class polish and lad-on-the-piss. He scratched his scruffy reddish-brown hair and smiled.

*Holy cheekbones and dimples*…you could fall in and never climb out. Realizing she was staring, Alex's eyes darted to her plate.

“I’m his brother from another mother, his partner in unspeakably salacious crimes…” Tarquin gave Harry a playful smooch on the mouth and laughed, his face giving in to an even wider grin, dimples in full effect.

Harry wiped his mouth with his napkin. “I’ve been stuck with this berk from day one. We were born on the same day in the same hospital ward!”

Tarquin winked conspiratorially at his friend. “Come now, Harry…that’s not *all* we’ve shared.” He swooped down, all charming and gregarious, kissing Alex on both cheeks. He smelled fresh like soap…regular drugstore soap.

“Lovely to meet you, Alex. I’ve heard all about *you*, so I’m sure Hazza’s filled you in about me…”

*Hazza?* Alex squinted.

“Nope, spared her. Sit. Have a drink.” Harry waved over the bartender. “You hungry?”

Tarquin shook his head and planted his jeans-clad butt beside Harry. He dropped a packet of cigarettes on the table and dove back into his blazer’s pocket, pulling out a ratty cocktail napkin. A silver ring on his thumb caught the light. “Look what I found from my leaving do.”

“Is that…from three years ago?” Harry pointed at a phone number written in smudged ink.

Tarquin raised an eyebrow. “You know it, my friend.”

“Why on Earth would you save that?”

“Oh, come on! It’s not every day you shag a WAG.”

Alex scrunched her eyebrows. “WAG?”

“Wives and girlfriends…of footballers.” Harry leaned across the table. “In this case, emphasis on *wife*.”

“Oh.” Her mouth pinched.

Harry nodded at the bartender, an immaculate brunette with a bouncy ponytail. "Pint, Tarq?"

"Sparkling water, please. I'm picking up my Porsche after this."

"No booze?" Harry smirked. "You've been in America too long."

Tarquin waved the napkin. "I kept this because it's the football wives who control the purse strings." He looked at Alex. "Her husband is England's captain. You never know, maybe they'll be in the market for a penthouse or something. I made a list of potential properties."

"Tarq only played football to meet girls. Like father like son."

"You're just jealous because Olivia had you on a short leash. Alex, let me tell you, before Olivia got her hooks into him, dear Harry and I dropped more panties than Agent Provocateur. We bedded most of the field hockey team before we graduated from Eton."

"Talk about overachievers." Alex smirked. "Your parents must have been so proud."

"Oh!" Tarquin chuckled. "Remember that time, Hazza, when I DJed that uni bash?"

Harry hid under his hand. "Don't remind me, DJ Klimaxxx."

Alex gasped. "DJ *what*?"

"Klimaxxx—with three Xs." Tarquin snickered. "My old DJ name in uni."

She groaned.

"Hey, I *earned* that name!" He scratched his chest where his v-neck t-shirt met a hint of sparse chest hair. "It was brilliant. Then Olivia came on the scene and ruined everything."

"Says the bloke who was supposed to be my best man."

"Happiest day of my life was when you broke it off, mate. Granted, I missed out on delivering my *brilliant* speech. I had some great lines that would have left Olivia's knickers in a twist."

"You win some, you lose some." Harry shoved his friend.

"Anyway, I come bearing gifts. Property for your Manhattan club." He turned to Alex. "Despite what this bellend is spinning, I've been working on property deals in New York for Budgie the past two and a half years. Life isn't all drinking and fornicating as delicious as that sounds."

He raised his eyebrows, digging for a reaction from Alex. She didn't bite.

"So, what's next?" Harry rested his arm on the back of the booth. "Dad's Docklands project or the Square Mile skyscraper…"

"Both."

"I figured as much."

"Well, if you hadn't gone rogue with this place, these plum assignments would've been yours."

"I'm just happy Dad has someone he can trust. You're the next best thing."

Tarquin burst out laughing. "It's great to be back." He cocked his head, his eyes returning to Alex.

"Did you get that Tower Bridge flat?" Harry nodded to the bartender as she set Tarquin's water in front of him.

"It's stunning." Tarquin's eyes followed her ass back to the bar. "You can practically reach out and touch it."

Alex felt the weight of Tarquin's gaze fall on her again. "Where do you live, Alex?"

She didn't look up from her plate. "Manchester."

Harry stepped in. "Lex is off to Manchester next week, staying at her dad's for a month—and if she stays any longer, Lucy and I will storm his house and drag her home."

"Lucy?"

"My new girlfriend. She's an artist. You have to meet her."

Alex smiled. Harry didn't hesitate to refer to Lucy as his girlfriend or an artist. She couldn't wait to tell her.

Tarquin's phone buzzed. "Hold that thought. I should take

this." He excused himself and walked towards the exit.

Alex waited until he was out of sight and leaned over her plate. "How are you friends with someone like that?"

"The vulgar, laddish crap? He's just having fun." Harry chuckled. "He's showing off because you're here."

"Like I'd be attracted to any of *that*."

"If you weren't here, it would be much worse."

"What did you tell him about me?"

"Nothing personal, don't worry! He knows how close we are. He knows you're the antithesis of Olivia. He hated her, she hated him—"

"Wow. I actually agree with Olivia on something."

"It didn't help that he dated her best friend and it ended badly. Remember Rosamund?"

"No wonder. If he disposes of women like used condoms—"

"Actually, she cheated on *him*." Harry spied his friend walking back to the table. "He's a good guy and a lot of fun. Actually, I bet you'd have a laugh with him—"

"Hazza, you've outdone yourself. This place is smashing." Tarquin sat back down and pulled out a cigarette and matchbook.

Harry shook his head. "You can't smoke in here."

He lit up anyway. "Oh, it's okay, mate—I know the owner."

Harry rolled his eyes. "A few puffs then, Balfy, but no more."

Alex wrinkled her nose.

Tarquin leaned back, smiling at her. "Know what you need, Sincy?"

Only one person ever called her Sincy. She narrowed her eyes.

"Unadulterated, no-holds-barred fun—"

She glared back, refusing to look away first. "Tarquin, I have zero interest in ever sleeping with you—"

"Blimey!" Tarquin raised his hands in defence. "I don't mean sex. I *mean* fun…you know, cinema, nice dinner out? Harry said you need cheering up." His cigarette smoke collected over his head like an ironic halo. "And I *always* deliver on fun."

Harry nodded. "I *did* say that. You do, and he does." He grimaced. "Sorry, Lex, I meant to talk to you about this today—"

"See?" Tarquin blew smoke over his shoulder. "Hazza knows best."

Alex stared at Harry. "Does he now? I never thought"—her fingers made air quotes—"*Hazza* would pimp me out—"

"Lex, I'm not setting you two up, I just want you to have some fun, forget you-know-who for a few hours."

Alex winced.

"Look, *I'd* take you out, but I'm drowning in meetings. As it is, I don't see Lucy enough."

Tarquin's face became a picture of concern. "Mate, what have I told you? Never *ever* settle for a wank." He stopped the act. "Seriously, Hazza—always make time to see your woman."

"Believe me, I'm trying." Harry looked at Alex. "How about it, Lex? Tarq needs to go to restaurants, galleries, work some new business contacts—"

"And not as Billy No Mates." Tarquin flicked an ash onto a spare side plate.

"I don't have time to accompany him, and you…you have nothing *but* time, in a way—"

"Thanks a lot!"

"You know what I mean. You write all day then, what? Write all night, too? That's not healthy." Harry's eyes pleaded. "It could make perfect sense. He needs you, you need him."

"That's a bit rich," said Alex.

"I am, actually, but don't let that put you off." Tarquin's smile taunted her. "You might be interested in this…I know the producer of Sir Ian McKellen's play."

Harry sat up. "Really?"

Alex pretended not to listen, digging through her pasta with intent.

"Yeah, she took a shine to me." Tarquin stubbed out his cigarette on the side plate. "I have two freebies for Friday, third row. I know it means breathing the same air as me for three hours, but I'll get the champers and ice creams in at the interval. How 'bout it, Sincy?"

Alex clenched her jaw and stabbed the air between them with her fork. "Keep calling me Sincy, and you're leaving here without a testicle."

"Good thing I carry a spare then, eh?" He winked.

Harry jumped in, redirecting the conversation. "Lex, you did say earlier you wanted to see that production—"

"So I'm a charity case now."

Tarquin smirked. "Au contraire, ma chère, *I'm* the charity case here."

Eyebrows raised, Harry gazed across the table, like he was trying to do a mind-twisting Derren Brown on her. "Come on, Lex. Do it…for me?"

Harry rarely asked favours; how could she say no? And she did want to see that play…third row, too…

"Fine, but I'm paying for my ice cream."

"You'll come?" Tarquin jerked back.

"I'm doing it for Harry, not you."

His lips snaked into a confident smile, turning on those dimples. "Meet me at the theatre for half six?"

Alex nodded.

"Smashing." He stood up. "Must be off. My chariot awaits."

Harry laughed. "Get out of here."

"See you Friday, Sincy." He snatched his cigarettes and walked away.

She exhaled heavily.

"I know what *that* means." Harry dropped his napkin on the table. "Look, you really are doing me a massive favour. Tarq's been away for too long. He used to be the life of every party, but now it's like everyone has moved on, you know?"

"I know he's your best friend, but he just seems all flash and no substance."

"I'm not blind. I know he can be full on and inappropriate at times, but there is a good heart buried under all that testosterone. He just hasn't had many opportunities to show it, especially around women."

"*Please*! It sounds like he slept with all of Kensington!"

"No, I mean, in terms of real relationships. He's only had one. Final year at Eton."

"Rosamund?"

"Nope. Some girl from a nearby village, none of us ever met her. They lasted maybe five months, and when they split, he snapped back to his old ways—flings without strings."

"I was half expecting you to say he fell for a buxom gym teacher."

"Oh, she was hot. I wouldn't put it past him."

Alex pursed her lips. "Honestly, if you weren't such a good friend, I wouldn't go anywhere near him."

"Lex, you need to get out, have a laugh. You never know, you might thank me."

# TWENTY-EIGHT

"Aw, now *that* feels better." Tarquin stroked his leg.

Alex groaned and rolled her eyes. *Typical.*

"What? My legs went to sleep!" He stood up straight.

Jeez, he really *was* tall—taller than Mark, definitely taller than Harry's five foot ten.

He pointed at his grey trousers. "My kecks? They're too tight. Blame my footballer's thighs. Last time I buy off the bloody rack." His eyes roamed down their row. "Are you enjoying the play?"

"Yes." A hint of a smile brightened her face. "I *love* Sir Ian McKellen."

"Good. So, no dramatic exit, then?"

"Not yet. You said there'd be ice cream."

He waved a hand. "Follow."

They shimmied through an obstacle course of knees and feet in the third row. Once in the aisle, Alex caught up to Tarquin. "The ice cream dude is…back there."

"Thought we'd grab some drinks first."

She smirked. "Why? So, I can get sozzled, forget being here with *you*?"

"No, because it's on me and my platinum card needs a workout."

"I haven't touched a drink since New Year's."

"Ah, right—the famous New Year's. So how *is* Liam Neeson?" Tarquin led the way, weaving through an endless stream of patrons carrying glasses of wine.

"Who?"

"Your ex—the Irish action star."

"His name is Mark, and for the record, Liam Neeson is from *Northern* Ireland, and he's much more than an *action star*."

"Do you miss him?"

Alex ignored his question as they joined the crush at the bar.

"You need to stop pining. He sounds like a self-absorbed prick." Tarquin jammed his hands in his trouser pockets.

"Takes one to know one…" she murmured.

"Sweetheart, if no one has your back, pick up that slack." Tarquin laughed. "Hey! That sounded a bit Dr. Seuss, didn't it?"

Alex's expression pinched. *Ow*. Her blouse…its label was attacking her neck. "Ahh, so that's your reading level, is it? Second grade." She shrugged, but the label poked even more.

"Ooh, *salty*! If looking after number one makes me self-absorbed, so be it. At least I've never put my job ahead of someone I supposedly loved—"

She glared sternly. "Who made you a relationship expert?"

Tarquin ignored her question. "This Mark bloke *definitely* put his career before you."

Alex narrowed her eyes and shoved her purse under her arm.

"Oh, I've heard it all, Sincy. Cancelling a third holiday on the trot, desperate to fanny around in costume? That's *selfish*."

"He didn't." Alex twisted, trying to reach the label under her collar without elbowing the people breathing down her neck.

"Weren't you supposed to be in Florida this month? If you

were still together?"

"Yeah…so? What's it to you?"

He shook his head, eyebrows raised.

"We cancelled Florida because we broke up."

"You sure about that?"

"Yeah. Lucy was cancelling it for me, but Mark had already taken care of it."

"Yep, but *when* did he take care of it?"

Alex stiffened: the itchy label, the suffocating crowd, Tarquin being an annoying dick…her heartbeat began to race. "*What*? Does it matter?"

"It does, yes."

"Tarquin, if you want to slag off Mark, just do it, okay?" She clenched her jaw. *Stupid label!* "I'm in no mood to play games—"

"He cancelled on January 4th."

Alex's brow furrowed. "What? How would *you* know?" She snatched her hair off her neck and fanned her face with the program. Too many people in too tight a space, and her throat—so parched; forget ice cream, she could drink the Thames dry.

"When did you dump him?"

A few theatregoers squeezing past recognized her with grins and hellos. Alex let go of her hair and reciprocated with a flashed smile. "Oh, hi…hello…hi…"

"When, Alex?"

"January 12th. There! *Happy now*?" she sneered. Causing a scene in front of influential theatre folk was the last thing she wanted. "I thought you were getting drinks…"

Tarquin gave an I-told-you-so smirk.

"What?" Alex slowed her furious fanning.

"Do the maths, dear."

"No…" Alex blinked, her mind filled with *twelve minus four*. She cleared her throat, but it began to tighten. She swallowed again, her program upping its furious pace. A man at the far end of the bar caught her eye and nodded with a smile. *Is that...the artistic director of the National?* She waved back, and then felt silly for doing so.

"He cancelled a week *before* you broke up. Why is that?"

Flustered, Alex looked at Tarquin. *So hot in here.* Cramps rolled like waves through her lower abdomen. *Is the restroom nearby?* She clutched her stomach with her free hand. "We weren't talking…" The label clawed her neck. "I don't know…" She gasped as the program grazed her cheek.

"I do: Mark knew he had a play coming up, the one he's rehearsing now. He must've accepted the role before January 4$^{th}$. I bet he knew *before* Christmas. God knows what else he wasn't telling you…"

She asked herself that question constantly.

Tarquin leaned into her, allowing a portly man, his hands held hostage by three wine glasses, to exit the drinks' scrum. "If you *were* still together, you wouldn't be in Florida right now. Mark would be on stage, stroking his ego while you wondered for the millionth time if he would *ever* put your relationship first. If that's not prickish and self-absorbed, I'm Drake."

Alex inhaled deep breaths but came up short each time, an out-of-body sensation tingling her temples and twisting the sound of Tarquin's words into a garbled, underwater warble. *You wouldn't be in Florida…Mark would be on stage…*

Black spots peppered her vision as the floor dissolved beneath her heels. "I don't feel—"

A boa constrictor was crushing Alex's bicep. Her eyes jolted open. "Where am—oh!"

A paramedic, pumping a blood pressure cuff, smiled. "Hiya Alex, you're at the theatre. You fainted, do you remember?"

Tarquin hovered sheepishly. "You fell just as I was about to get the drinks in. If that wasn't a protest vote for ice cream, I don't know what is."

The paramedic tore the Velcro strap from Alex's arm. "You're going to be fine, love. Keep taking deep breaths: in through the nose, out through your mouth. Lucky your boyfriend caught you, so you didn't bang your head."

"Boyfriend..."

A woman wearing a name tag stepped forward. "There's no rush, Miss Sinclair. Stay until you feel better, okay?" She turned to the paramedics, thanking them while they packed their cases.

Still groggy, Alex looked around. Somehow, she had been transported to a chaise lounge in...a backstage space? The area was stuffed with racks of costumes and spare props. She shifted up onto her elbows, but the room swayed, nudging her head back down on a silk pillow.

"Oh, God. I'm so *embarrassed.* Of all the places to pass out..."

Tarquin winced. "The house manager did say he loved your play—"

Nametag Lady jumped in. "*Thirteen*? Oh, yes it was wonderful." She smiled and escorted the paramedics towards the exit.

"Shit!" Alex hid behind her hands. "Did the National Theatre guy see me fall, too?"

"National?" Tarquin looked puzzled. "A few people rushed over, but...I didn't catch any names."

She pulled herself up. The evening had just gone into the record books as the most humiliating ever. At least the panic attack two years earlier in front of Isabella Archer hadn't ended with her collapsing at her idol's feet.

Alex waved him away. “You should go, catch the second act.”

“And cut off my circulation again? I don’t think so.” He smiled and handed over a bottle of water. “Relax. Once you feel better, I’ll drive you home. It’s the least I can do.” His dimples flirted. “I’ve never had a girl fall for me like *that*.”

“I didn’t *swoon*, I fainted. Trust me, you’re not my type.”

“Ouch.” Tarquin grinned. “Someone’s feeling better.”

“I’ve had anxiety and panic attacks my whole life.” *Maybe that will get rid of him.*

Tarquin shifted from one foot to the other. “Ohhh, blimey! I’m…sorry…if I caused this one, shooting my mouth off. It’s the old Eton debater in me. I can be a bit heavy-handed—”

“Tarquin, what *was* that all about?” Her face pinched. “How would *you* know when Mark cancelled our holiday?”

He frowned, avoiding eye contact. “Fuck, my *big* mouth. I shouldn’t have said anything.” He turned to Alex. “Look, I’ll spill, but you’ve gotta promise to tell Harry that tonight was a success. We had a good time, I cheered you up—job well done? Please?”

Alex sat up straight. “Fine, I promise.” She crossed her fingers underneath her thigh.

“I was just trying to make you *see*, in my not very tactful way, you absolutely did right getting shot of the actor. I know what it’s like, when you keep having second thoughts after a split, wondering if you could’ve done something different, but you did the right thing, everyone says so…”

Her eyebrows creased. “*Everyone*?”

“I met Harry and Lucy last night for dinner. They filled me in on everything…well, not *everything*, of course—nothing girly or private! But Lucy did say that when she called the travel agent, they confirmed the trip had been cancelled much earlier. That was all true…sorry.”

Alex’s face fell. “Well, at least I know. But Lucy should have told me…" she murmured.

"She was going to—eventually. She said you were barely functioning the day she found out, so she just let it lie…"

They sat in silence awkwardly.

"So, these panic attacks…what's the deal? I want to be more…careful—to avoid them next time."

*Next time?* Alex shook her head. "Stress triggers them, but they also happen when everything seems fine—when I'm buying groceries, at the cinema, anywhere. They sneak up on me."

"Does it happen *a lot*?"

"It varies. I've had more since last April, though."

"What happened last April?"

"What didn't?" Alex squeezed the water bottle. "I quit my job, moved in with Mark, and his new agent, Wink—"

"His name is *Wink*?!"

"His surname is Winkler…he prefers to go by Wink."

Tarquin shook his head. "*Wink*! What a wanker."

"Yeah, *wanker* sums him up perfectly. Wink convinced Mark to take a last-minute shoot in Thailand. That film cancelled our holiday—the *first* time. Mark was gone for a month."

"And is fainting…the *norm*?"

"No. This was only the second time."

"You scared the shit out of me! I almost didn't catch you. You got a bigger audience reaction than the play's murder scene."

Alex winced. "*Great*! I'll be forever known as the playwright who gets the vapors."

"Maybe it just adds to your mystique."

"Mystique doesn't pay the bills."

"There is that, but you're not alone, you know. Most people have *something*. Maybe they're just better at hiding it." He beamed. "Hey, I grew up with a fear of heights! I pissed myself on a Ferris wheel at Alton Towers once when I was eight. Figures, right? I end up building skyscrapers for a living. *Shhh*! Don't tell Budgie!"

Alex smiled briefly, despite her annoyance.

"Listen, you promise, yeah? We'll tell Harry tonight was a success? If he hears that I made you pass out—"

"It's fine—"

"I *hate* disappointing him."

"You really care what he thinks, don't you?"

"He's my boy."

"I know what you mean." She exhaled heavily. "Yes, Tarquin, we had a *fun time*."

He smiled. "You know, actors never make good partners. They're all about trying new people, new faces on for size. Then, *boom*, straight out the door—onto the next one."

"You sound like Lucy."

"That's the first compliment you've given me. She's spunky—love that."

"I'm a bit pissed she didn't tell me that you were having dinner last night. *Conspiring…*"

"Spoilers, sweetie!" He grinned. "See what I did there?"

Alex snorted.

"What? Only you and Lucy can share *Doctor Who* humour?"

"You're seriously a Whovian?"

"The best people are, gorgeous." He leaned against the chaise. "Maybe Lucy didn't say anything because she wants you to make up your own mind about me."

Alex glared.

He held his hands up, palms facing her. "Seriously, don't worry, Lucy didn't betray any confidences. All I know is that she wants you to be happy again—and actor boy definitely wasn't the man for you."

She rolled her eyes. "Tarquin, if you're trying to get into my pants, you are *so* wasting your time."

"I'm not trying to get into your pants..." He grinned, shifting his weight from one leg to the other. "I just want out of mine! Well, these cheap trousers at least. I can't sit down. When you're ready to leave, just say the word. I'm dying for a smoke."

Alex scooted to the seat's edge, desperate to send Tarquin, his cigarettes, and his contempt for Mark off into the night along with their disaster of an outing. The world '*shame*' didn't begin to cover it. How dare a panic attack take her down *there*—of all places—at the theatre...her safe place.

She knew how anxiety burrowed into her mind, how it left behind spores of doubt to feed and grow another attack. She would do just about anything, even the absurd, to dodge situations or places associated with anxiety meltdowns. Once an attack happened, that place was tainted, on her no-go list, a hall of shame that was long and riddled with lowlights. The memories made her grimace: the Florida store where she had fainted, the laundromat near college, Heathrow terminal three arrivals, Bridgewater House—even London's Boris bikes. She and Mark took a spin once, and the insane traffic roundabout near the IMAX on Waterloo Road left her a hyperventilating puddle on the curb. Now, new to the list, her beloved theatre.

Alex pouted. There was no way she would allow panic to tarnish the theatre or banish it to the growing tally of places to be avoided. *Hell no*! Something else—someone else—would shoulder the blame. Her eyes crept up the towering figure standing in front of her, watching crew members shift a piece of unused scenery past the doorway.

Avoiding the theatre was out of the question. Avoiding Tarquin? Her answer.

She snatched her purse. "I'm ready. Let's go."

Trudging up three flights of stairs, Alex shoved her key in the lock and pushed inside her dark flat, setting her purse on the chair where it shared real estate with mail yet to be posted: Tom's birthday card, packages addressed to two London theatres, and a box destined for the States.

The flat's eerie quiet weighed her down; only a vague cry from the infant next door punctured the silence. She looked around the space, purged of belongings, spare three boxes of books, two lonely suitcases, a backpack, her laptop bag, and the dishes she had yet to pack. Her happy, heady life with Mark was being erased and stored away like it had never happened. In five days, another couple would call this place home, collecting memories, reaching milestones, and building a future…together.

Her nose prickled. *No.* She wouldn't cry. She had never felt more alone…or determined. She started texting Lucy.

*Hey. Need a favour. Here are my social media passwords. Please change all of them, and keep the new ones to yourself.*

# TWENTY-NINE

*Manchester suburbs, ten days later*

Alex sat on the edge of the comfy blue couch, reading over two handouts: one about anxiety, the other, panic attacks. The radiator in the cosy office hummed calmly, almost drowning out the unrelenting March rain and the splashing car tires on the road outside. A perky box of tissues and a full glass of water rested on the low table, just in case.

Waiting patiently with a warm smile, Catriona, a psychologist specializing in anxiety disorders, jotted notes down on a pad.

Alex looked up, biting her cheek. Her eyes darted past the window and over the serene flower photographs hung on the walls. A quote she had spotted spray-painted on a derelict building on the way there popped into her head: '*Nothing can bring you peace but yourself.*' She fiddled with the cuff of her sweater. *Ralph Waldo Emerson better be right.*

"Now that we've discussed your situation, your preference to avoid medication, and your treatment goals, I think the best approach is cognitive behavioural therapy. Are you familiar with

CBT, Alex?"

She met the therapist's eyes and nodded. "I've read a bit online…doesn't it involve coping strategies?"

"You're right, it does," Catriona agreed in her Scottish burr. "The premise of CBT is that it helps you identify negative thoughts that can trigger anxiety or panic attacks. Once they're identified, we work to replace them with positive or more realistic thoughts, so you'll be able to deal with anxiety-causing situations."

Alex's heart began to pound. *What have I put myself in for?* "It sounds hard."

"Well, it takes practice. Negative thought patterns can be a tough habit to break, but CBT is very effective at treating these underlying habits." Catriona leaned on her notepad. "We'll work together during our weekly sessions, and I'll give you homework to do on your own."

"How many sessions do you think I'll need?"

"Everyone's different. Some people come in for ten sessions, others, twenty or more. There's no quick fix, Alex, and you'll have to keep practicing what you've learned, even after you're finished therapy. CBT might not cure your anxiety or completely eliminate attacks, but it can give you the tools needed to deal with negative thinking patterns in a healthy way. If you look at CBT as a lifestyle change, the benefits can be long-lasting."

Alex broke eye contact, drifting back to the papers in her hands. "So…" She swallowed heavily. "…part of me will always be an unsolvable riddle?"

"I wouldn't say that you're unsolvable…or a riddle." Catriona grinned. "But as long as you're committed to our sessions and practice what you've learned, you should feel better."

Alex nodded, exhaling a tense breath. "Well, I can't feel any worse."

"It takes courage to ask for help," said Catriona. "Just the fact that you're sitting across from me says that you want to make a change for the better. We'll take this one step at a time…together. Ready to start?"

"I think so." Alex's hand drifted to her neck. No Vespa charm, no Mark. *No.* She knew who she had to believe in—herself. "No…*I am*." She smiled and sat up straight, ready to move forward.

# THIRTY

*Two weeks later*

"Holy shit, she LIVES!" Lucy huffed.

Alex cringed and pulled her phone away from her ear. She tightened her scarf against the grey March morning and speed-walked down her dad's street. She'd known *this* was coming.

"So you call to say you've arrived, said you might be offline for a bit, and then…you ghost me—for three weeks? Thanks a bunch!"

"Come on, Lucy. You know I wasn't ghosting you. I was trying to settle in here without… I *needed* to focus and not think about—"

"I haven't even seen *he-who-shall-not-be-named*. Don't punish me and Harry. We're on your side, remember?"

"I'm not punishing anyone. I'm busy with my therapy sessions and writing. My phone kept buzzing, and I stuck it in a drawer so I could concentrate. I got used to being without it."

"I just wish you had told me! My mind was all over the bloody shop. Were you pissed at me? Were you ill? I was *freaking*, so I put

Harry on standby…" Her words drifted away from the speaker. "Didn't I, Haribo?"

"I just do what I'm told. Hi, Lex!"

Alex's laughed at Harry's—a.k.a. *Haribo's*—barely audible response in the background. She pictured him sat in his robe, thumbing through the paper, sugary tea at the ready, but wait…it was *Monday* morning. Why was Harry home with Lucy at twenty past nine?

"Why's he on standby?"

"To drive me to your dad's. I made him take the day off, that's how much I was bricking it, Lex."

"Crap. Sorry. I'm just working through things. Didn't Dad tell you—"

"Yeah, when I finally reached him, but I didn't know if he was telling the truth. I can't *read* parents."

"Well, you can trust him—he's a terrible liar, even on the phone." Alex waited for a car to pass before crossing the street. "So, what's new with you guys? How's work? How's the drawing coming along?"

"Nice try, Lex—you're not ducking and diving around *my* questions. How's life in the sleepy suburbs? Have you had a chance to visit Manchester city centre?"

"Just once, two weeks ago. Like I said, it's been therapy and writing—nothing thrilling."

"Want your new passwords, then?"

"Not yet. It's too tempting. I deleted the apps off my phone and everything. I'm determined to stick with this break. I'm only dipping in for work emails."

"God, I'd shrivel up and die—and be jobless—without social media. How's the withdrawal? Sweats, shakes, dizziness?"

The sky began to darken, so Alex upped her pace. "All of the above. I even had the beginnings of a panic attack after the first few days. Despite that, going cold turkey has been good for me."

"Ah, Lex. I'm so shit! I didn't mean to make light of your attacks."

"You didn't," she answered breathlessly. "Hey, if *we* can't joke about it—"

"Wait, you're not having—"

"No, I'm not having one *now*. I'm rushing to meet Joan."

"Thank fuck. I thought I—*never mind*."

"Joan's worse than a drill sergeant. Here's my typical day: Zumba together first thing, then her two-hour computer class, either pottery studio in the afternoon or a therapy sesh, and then a couple of hours writing."

"Why are you in her computer class?"

"I'm not *in* her class. I just go along and write while she teaches."

"Least your evenings are free."

"Nope. I help Helen make dinner, we all eat together, and then I do therapy homework and that corporate writing gig before bed. I'm splitting the cost of therapy with Dad and paying for my food and necessities, so I need the cash."

"Joan scheduled all this?"

"To the minute. She won't let me sleep in, eat sugar, or surf the web—and she nicked my phone from the drawer in my bedside table and hid it. I had no clue until this morning. I was looking for an old CD to make a workout playlist and there it was, wedged behind her Guns N' Roses collection."

"Joan for the win!" Lucy snickered. "Best hiding spot ever. God, I *love* her."

"I'm just relieved that when she took my phone from my drawer, there was nothing else battery-operated lurking in there!"

Lucy laughed even harder.

"Luckily, she's open to bribery. I can skip Zumba if I go for a jog. I also had to agree to help her tutor a difficult computer student."

"Yeah, you gotta watch those dodgy pensioners."

"This one you do! He booty-calls Joan. Has a prescription for blue pills and everything."

"Ewwww!" Lucy wailed. "I don't know what bothers me more, *that* image or you becoming a Zumba-ing jogger. I want my couch potato bezzie mate back!"

"It's part of my therapy. My psychologist says exercise releases *endorphins*, helps with anxiety symptoms."

"Lex, you're not becoming one of them, are you?"

"One of *what*?"

"Those boring workout people like Simon—tracking your steps, eating kale, and blending your meals into disgusting green drinks. Mind you, Harry's mum would love you..."

"No, she wouldn't. I'm not *you*." Alex smiled as she dodged two teens on skateboards. "Anyway, just because I'm doing it, doesn't mean I *like* it. I can barely jog two blocks without collapsing, but I like how it lets my mind wander. I've come up with a bunch of play ideas while doing it."

"I'd rather Zumba."

"Yeah, but I've been craving alone time. Joan, Helen, and Dad have been amazing, and they mean well, but they're *suffocating* me. Helen just wants to mother me—"

"Aw, bless her!"

"It's sweet, but she won't let me do *anything*, even washing my own clothes. Everything comes out with a stinky flowery fragrance—I can't stop sneezing. And I swear Dad asks me ten times a day how I'm feeling but never mentions Mark. None of them do, but I *want* to talk about the split. Thank God for my psychologist. She isn't always Team Alex—which is good—but she's never judgmental."

"Unlike me?"

"Yeah, but I still love ya, Lucy." Alex laughed and waited at a red traffic light.

"So how *is* therapy going?'

"Good. I've ugly cried too many times to count, but I think it's helping. It's *got* to help. Fainting at the theatre was an all-time low. I can't be that girl again."

"You won't be, Lex."

"It's going to take time, training my brain to react differently, but I'm committed to it. I need to *own* my anxiety, manage it, and not feel embarrassed by it. That's the only way I'll feel better, and I WILL feel better."

"I'm really proud of you, Lex. We both are."

Alex switched the phone to her other ear. "I've realized that a lot of my anxiety comes from worrying over the future, and I need to live in the here and now, focus on what I'm dealing with in *this* moment instead of what might never happen down the road. Take it one step, one minute, one hour at a time."

"Um, hello? Didn't a certain someone say that to you…I don't know, at a certain wedding?"

"Maybe? Okay…you *did*, but sometimes—" Alex's eyes followed a red Vespa zooming past.

"You need to hear it from someone else, I get it."

*Vespa rules.* The memory made Alex pause.

"Lex…where'd ya go?"

"Sorry…*traffic*…" The light changed to green and she ran across the street. "You missed your calling. Maybe you should've been a comic-drawing psychologist."

"I'm a woman of many talents." Lucy's voice trailed away from the speaker. "Button it, Manville!"

"When are you coming home—" Harry's voice rose from the background. "We miss you!"

Alex smiled at a hint of sunshine breaking through the clouds. "I miss you, too, Harry, and Freddie and Si…*everyone.* Please tell them."

"I'm not talking to Freddie." Lucy took over the phone again. "The cheater is staying at his place…well, until his allergy to Moriarty's hair makes him cough up a lung. When *are* you coming back?"

"A few weeks, once I feel confident enough to manage my anxiety on my own."

"Can't wait. It's not the same, hanging with Naomi."

"Lucy! Come on. She's *fun.*"

"She thinks Superman and Wonder Woman are married…"

"Aww, but at least she's trying!"

"Yeah, I find *her* trying. She came with me to the con this weekend, the one at Earl's Court?"

"It was *this* weekend? Oh my God, how'd it go? Did you take your drawings?"

"Lex, I don't mean to rub it in, but it was freakin' awesome! I showed my drawings to an editor and he *really* liked them! He said my sketch work was 'original and raw', and he loved the story outline, her superpower of persuasion, all that. I think we might be onto something."

"LUCY! That's incredible. I knew they'd love your stuff. God, I wish I had been there."

"He gave me pointers for improvement and invited me to send more samples, so get your writing cap on. We've got work to do."

"The cap's already on. I've been fussing over copy for it the past two weeks. I'll email it to you from the community centre."

"She's got copy!" Lucy relayed the news to Harry.

Alex shook her head. "Just put your phone on speaker…"

"What?" Lucy's muffled voice distorted through the phone. "Sorry. Harry reminded me that you might want to tread carefully when you're back."

"Why?"

"Remember those *Mail* photos? Tom on set with Mark? Well, apparently some old one-night stand saw the story and tracked him down. Lex, he's been hit with a *paternity suit*."

Alex stopped in her tracks. "Who? Mark—"

"No. Tom!"

Alex clutched her chest. *Phew.*

"I know your plan was to rent a room from Tom and Naomi when you get back but—"

"Jeez! Naomi must be freaking out!"

"She hasn't slept with Tom since he was served."

"It was recent, then?" asked Alex.

"Being served, yeah, not the kid. The boy's *two years old*! Tom's doing a genetics test."

"Tom got around. That kid could be one of many!"

"Lex?" Harry's loud and clear voice made her jump. "Greedy Lucy wanted you all to herself, but I've put you on speakerphone. Thanks for my birthday present."

"Glad it got there. I hope it arrived on time." Alex walked across the community centre's parking lot.

"Yours always do. As lovely as it was receiving post from up north, would you please get your arse back down here? We all miss you. Hell, *London* misses you! When you're ready, please come home."

"Well, give London a hug from me and tell her I'll be home soon." Alex smiled and pulled open the door.

# THIRTY-ONE

*Three and a half weeks later*

"Are you sure you only need one more session?" Michael leaned forward in his chair, the comfy basement dining room of Annie's restaurant still bustling with its Saturday lunchtime crowd at five minutes to two.

"Yeah." Alex nodded. "Catriona and I agreed—I'm ready. I mean, this is the longest spell I've gone without an attack in a year: five weeks."

"No, six." Joan smiled. "I logged it in my phone. There was no way I was letting this milestone pass." She waved her debit card at the server, who returned with the handheld payment machine. "My shout."

"Thanks, Joan." Alex swirled her spoon in a pool of chocolate ice cream. "I'm definitely coming back here for that cheese and onion pie."

"I'm surprised you wanted to come into town." Joan inserted her card into the debit machine. "You've been eyeing up that Italian place near the pottery studio for weeks."

"We can go there any time. I've missed Manchester city centre."

"Ooh, does this mean you might stay?" Helen scooped up the last spoonful of the jam roly-poly she was sharing with her husband. A hopeful smile raised her chubby cheeks.

Alex glanced from Helen to her dad, her eyes resting on Joan beside her. "I love being here, but…"

"It's not *home*." Joan winked, punching in her PIN.

"Lucy and Freddie will be happy to hear that," said Michael.

"I'll have to tell Freddie myself—Lucy's still not speaking to him."

"She'll come around. God love her, that girl has a big heart. She won't be cross with Freddie for long." Joan raised her eyebrows. "Mark, though…"

Helen looked at Michael, who became suddenly interested in the framed Grand Theatre poster that hung beside their table.

Alex breathed deeply. "Joan, it's okay. Just say it."

"I promised I wouldn't." The server handed Joan her receipt, which she slid into her wallet a little too carefully, buying time before she had to say another word.

Michael's eyes bore into his mum.

"Promised who? Dad?" Alex's stare travelled from Joan to Michael. "I know you guys made a pact. So obvious."

Michael blew out his cheeks. "We didn't make a pact—"

"Dad, I've seen the looks you've shared. I've been here almost two months, and you haven't mentioned Mark once. That takes a scripted effort."

Joan wrapped her arm around her granddaughter. "When we saw you blocking social media, love, we realized you were doing everything you could to move on and feel better. We just followed your lead. Us having a bloody great whinge about how terrible he behaved—well, it wasn't going to help you, was it?"

"Believe me, whatever you were thinking would have paled in comparison to what *I've* already thought or said to Lucy. I don't need to be protected in bubble wrap. What I *do* need is for you to be honest. I won't shatter if you tell me the truth."

"It's just with the panic attacks…" Helen looked at Michael. "We would do anything to make them go away…"

"We didn't want to undo the good Catriona was doing, that's all." Michael patted Helen's arm.

"Mark was a lovely lad," Joan blurted out, staring at the fairy lights strung across the ceiling. "But he's made me so angry. I just want to deck him."

"Join the club," said Alex. "I think Lucy has first dibs."

"I'm not naïve." Joan tilted her head. "Every actress has seen affairs begin behind the scenes. Back in '56, my best friend fell for the lead in our musical. They both had sweethearts at home, but maybe sneaking around was exciting? I don't know. I don't understand why people do it. And Mark, he had you, a pretty, talented girl, and a family here who loved him like our very own…I feel like he cheated on us, too."

Helen nodded.

Joan leaned in. "I've been so close to telling you exactly how I felt, but I bit my tongue because, well, like those *Cosmo* articles say, if you two got back together, I'd regret everything I said—"

"We are never ever getting back together."

"Ha! *Taylor Swift*!" Joan elbowed Alex. Helen and Michael just looked confused.

"No, I'm done with actors. Two was two too many."

"You'll find someone who deserves you, pet." Helen set a reassuring hand over Alex's.

"Maybe one day. Right now, the only company I'm keeping is my laptop."

Michael stood up, holding his wife's coat. "Alex, did you hear back?"

"I did! Late yesterday. One of the theatres is interested in *Suffragettes*. Three years on, and it might finally see the light of day. And for the heck of it, I applied to the TV development scheme with Channel Four..." Alex's phone buzzed on the table. Tugging on her coat, she squinted at a new text. "...so I've got a few things in the pipeline. I can't wait to get back."

Joan shoved an arm through her parka's sleeve. "Everything okay, love?"

"Yeah, it's Lucy. She emailed new scans of her drawings. Wants my feedback ASAP."

"She's such a bossy boots!" Joan laughed and zipped up her coat. "Why don't you come with us to the National Football Museum? There's a new Fergie exhibition!"

"Nah, I need to get Freddie a card. His birthday's next Saturday. Then, I'll head straight back and edit my play a dozen more times."

Joan smiled. "If you change your mind, you know where to find us."

"And watch you drool over that big United team painting again? It's not an *interactive* exhibit, Joan. I think they're serious with the *Do Not Touch* sign."

Michael nodded. "Yeah, I really don't want to get chucked out again, Mum."

"Bloody Nora." Joan threw her hands up. "You reach up and touch Beckham's pecs the *one time* and you're branded for life!"

The Sinclairs zigzagged through the tables and climbed the stairs, trading the restaurant's homey warmth for a cloudy Manchester April afternoon. Alex shivered as the damp chill pierced her coat.

"There are some lovely card shops in the Arndale Centre." Helen ushered her family down narrow Old Bank Street. "Rain's held off. Why don't we take the scenic route down to King Street and then up Spring Gardens? Isn't that Italian restaurant there? The one owned by that United player? What's it called?"

"Rosso." Joan nodded enthusiastically and turned right onto Cross Street. "That randy old git in my class wants to take me there. I'd love to go, but not with him. It'll turn into grab-a-granny night. He's handsy."

"The Arndale, it's a bit out of the way. I was going to pop into the card shop in the arcade…" Alex pointed over her shoulder in the opposite direction. "…right there."

"We'll walk with you," said Helen.

"Yeah, for all of one minute!" Alex joked.

"Embarrassed to be seen with us, love?" Joan nudged Alex with her elbow. "Wouldn't be the first time."

"We just want to spend more time with you, Alex, that's all." Michael smiled.

"Dad, I'm rarely out of your sight." Alex hugged him. "I'm just gonna grab a card and get back. Yesterday's session was a double, so I'm behind in my writing."

"What type of card are you looking for?" Helen clutched her stepdaughter's waist and steered her along Cross Street.

"For Freddie?" Joan laughed. "Has to be a cheeky one."

"Has Simon told his parents yet?" Michael pulled his coat closed against the breeze.

"Freddie would be a lovely son-in-law," said Joan.

Alex's head pinged back and forth, dizzy with their non-stop interrogation. She swerved left to the arcade's entrance. "Okay, twenty questions ends now." She laughed. "Bugger off. Go enjoy the football museum. I'll see you at home."

"Okay, well…" Michael nodded. "Call if you change your mind."

"I won't. Go." Alex backed up towards the arcade's entrance.

Joan's eyes roamed to the darkening sky. "Don't dillydally. Looks like rain."

"If you hurry love, you can catch the 2:25 train home." Helen didn't budge.

Alex's eyebrows met in the middle. "Okay, weirdos. *I'm* going…even if you're not." She skipped under the stone arch and into the Royal Exchange Arcade.

Finding Freddie's card proved more difficult than Alex thought. Ten minutes and three cards later, she stood underneath the arcade's Cross Street entrance, watching the pummeling rain flood the road. What to do? Buy a cheap umbrella? Grab a taxi? All the cabs splashing through the dirty puddles were occupied. Alex looked at her phone: only two fifteen p.m. *Hmm.* The entrance to the Royal Exchange Theatre was next door, just a quick dash away. If she had to wait out the rain…

Pulling up the collar of her coat, she ducked her head and dodged the fat raindrops. She ran up the theatre's stone steps and through its glass doors. Craning her neck, Alex's eyes climbed the soaring columns that reached upwards to the ceiling of the Great Hall, a historic meeting space once used as the epicenter of Manchester's booming 1920s cotton trade.

"Gorgeous," Alex sighed aloud, happy to revisit the beauty of the hall's massive glass domes dominating the ceiling. Even with the unrelenting downpour outside, natural light spilled through the glass, illuminating the floor.

Cafés and a gift shop hugged the perimeter of the cavernous space. The steel and glass theatre, suspended from the building's four columns, commanded attention in the centre like a seven-sided spaceship. Alex weaved around theatre fans, their anticipation contagious as they rushed to their seats for the matinee's start.

*Why not?* Since she was here… head down, texting furiously, she strode over to the box office line. She hit send.

*Dad, change in plans. Seeing a play! Be back for tea.*

The play would be…research. *Yeah.* Not only would she chill out for two hours or so, but she would also get a grasp of the stage size, how intimate the space was for the audience, all need-to-know details if she was to submit work there.

She dug for her wallet but got interrupted by a buzz in her hand.

*Alex, your writing won't get done sat in a theatre.*

*Oh, Dad.* She shouldn't have mentioned at lunch about falling behind in her writing. His motto was always *work now, play later.* She didn't reply and stuffed the phone in her pocket as the woman ahead of her turned away from the ticket window.

Alex looked up.

*Fuck?!*

She did a double take, her heart stuttering beneath her coat. For the first time in six weeks, her lungs felt heavy, uncooperative. The pale Irish skin. The dark eyebrows. The jet-black hair, misbehaving and tumbling over his forehead. The parted lips that had softly touched hers so many times. The poster's artwork was abstract, but the identity of the male was unmistakable: Mark. *Her* Mark was in Manchester on the poster for *this* play—*Constellations*—a play she had read and always wanted to see. The beautiful story was a romantic wallop to the gut about fate and what-ifs and clumsy communication; a tale about falling in love, cheating, and breaking up; the cruelty of forgetting and the desire to remember. Her jaw fell open as an unbearable ache pressed down on her chest, her family's words replaying in her mind: *We'll walk with you…Don't dillydally…Your writing won't get done sat in a theatre…*

They knew.

The poster was all she could see, the two people who had broken her heart, lost in each other's eyes: Mark's intense gaze, drinking in his co-star, his hands cradling her face. Fallon's body offering the unspeakable: longing, want…love. Mark and Fallon. A couple. On stage. *Here.*

"Hello, can I help?" The chirpy voice of the woman behind the box office window snapped Alex back into the room. "You all right?"

No, Alex wanted to holler. She breathed deeply, her mind racing, desperate to hold on and not allow this shock to unravel the past six weeks' hard work. She wouldn't allow it.

"The performance starts in less than five minutes…"

Alex smiled tightly. "One…please."

"There's one seat stage level, back row?"

"I'll take it."

Mark's hand touching Fallon's lower back, pulling her closer…that sweet smile that crinkled the corners of his eyes…the urgency in his kiss…the nuances he had shared with Alex triggered memories: warm, loving, painful memories that would never be relived and would be forever altered.

Alex's hands flitted from her collar to her abdomen to her face, unable to lie idle. Each time Mark touched Fallon, Alex's stomach dropped, an endless rollercoaster ride—her worst nightmare—except here, she couldn't scream. She had to take it. Watch it. Even looking away, their voices intermingled like their lips. Was this what it would have been like in Dublin? To watch them together after midnight struck and "Auld Lang Syne" had been sung? Did Mark like the way Fallon's skin felt? How she tasted? How much of this was acting? How much was real? Alex couldn't tell.

The theatre had always been her safe place, a port in the storm, but right now it was pushing her under, locked in an undertow that threatened to drown her once again. She squirmed in her chair, nausea swirling in her stomach. Her usual response—her old response—would be to cry and run. Her eyes darted down her row. G10, her seat, was one of three that made up the short back row. It was on the end beside the wall, and the only way out was to her left, past two people sitting beside her. She was blocked in, trapped. She checked her phone: forty of the play's seventy minutes left to go. *Damn.*

Catching Alex's lit phone screen, the woman on her immediate left shot her a dose of side-eye. Alex sat back in her seat. WTF? She *knew* better. Leaving during a performance was impolite, disruptive, and potentially…revealing. Mark might see her. Fallon might see her. Humiliating if she fled. Heartbreaking if she stayed. Why the *hell* had she bought that stupid ticket?

She closed her eyes and concentrated on one breath at a time. *Inhale…exhale…inhale…*

Mark and Fallon's voices floated to the back of her mind. A new voice took over…her own.

*These negative thoughts aren't good for me. I know this anxious feeling will pass. It always passes. I will be fine.*

She captured her roaming hands, squeezing them together in her lap.

*Mark and I wanted different things. I believe I did the right thing to be happy, to be healthy. I'm confident I WILL be happy. I know I'm strong and able to have an even better life without Mark.*

She continued her measured breathing and opened her eyes. Mark, in character as Roland, was kneeling down in front of Fallon—playing Marianne—with a tiny black box in his hand. Alex inhaled slowly…exhaled…inhaled…

*It's a PLAY. He's reading his lines. She's reading hers. He will kiss women on stage. It's just his JOB...everything is okay. I'm okay.*

Her throat was easing, along with her pounding heartbeat. Alex sat back in her seat and breathed in.

*I'm determined to enjoy the play and have a good time.*

She concentrated on the play, getting lost in the rhythm of its words. Tears collected in her eyes, not for the boyfriend she had lost, but for his mesmerizing performance. Mark wasn't playing Roland—he *was* Roland.

The actors spoke their last words. The audience leapt to its feet, showering Mark and Fallon with applause.

*I feel better. I'm fine. I really am.*

In the back row, Alex stood up. No fleeing, no hiding, although her lack of height and the tall man in the row ahead of her did keep her attendance a secret.

*Everything is going to be all right.*

Alex applauded as much for herself as the actors on stage.

# THIRTY-TWO

"As soon as Lucy heard about *Constellations*, she called Michael." Helen leaned against the train's window as it chugged away from Manchester Piccadilly towards the suburbs. "When was it again?"

"January 2$^{nd}$," Joan answered, popping the lid off her tea.

"Lucy and I were at Borough Market that day." Alex fiddled with a discarded newspaper left on the table between them. "Her boss—"

Michael shook his head. "No, it was Freddie who left her that message. Lucy was still talking to him then. She called me from the market, but got my voicemail. We chatted when she got home."

"She told me she had a work emergency."

"Lucy's a pretty good actress," said Joan.

Alex narrowed her eyes. "So, Mark found out about doing *Constellations* that day?"

"No, he knew a few days before Christmas," said Joan. "Just his part. The female lead hadn't been cast then."

"He knew *before* Christmas?" Alex frowned. "We were together. He never said anything."

Joan shook her head. "Apparently, he was going to tell you on your anniversary. He reckoned you'd be thrilled: living with him during the play's six-week run, close to us. You could write and be together every day. It would have been perfect…"

"Yeah." Alex slumped back in her seat, her mind drifting to the star earrings Mark had bought as an anniversary gift—*constellations…*

Michael sighed. "When it became clear that Mark was flying back to Dublin without you, Freddie told Lucy about it. I guess he figured that maybe if you knew about the play, you might patch things up with Mark." He shrugged. "But Lucy didn't want to interfere. Nor did we, love, and when you decided to come up here, putting all your effort into managing your anxiety…we thought it best that you didn't know. It would be easier for you to move on if you didn't know he was in Manchester."

"Didn't I say, Michael? We should've told her." Joan put her arm around her granddaughter's shoulder.

Michael crossed his arms. "Now I'm wishing we had, too."

Alex sighed. "It was a total shock, but…once I knew, I had to see him…"

"I'm glad we found you afterwards. I hated the thought of you stuck in that theatre with Mark and that hussy," said Joan. "I had a lovely vanilla slice while we waited for the play to finish, and the café girl gave me it for nothing."

"You hate vanilla," said Alex.

"You can't truly appreciate chocolate without a little vanilla, love." Joan smiled.

"How you could eat, Joan…I was worried sick." Helen looked at Alex. "You had been crying…"

Alex shook her head. "I didn't cry over Mark. I cried because the play really touched me."

"Or maybe a bit of both?" Joan squeezed Alex's shoulder.

She stared at the sports headlines on the newspaper's back

page and flipped it over. A familiar face smiled from the top corner. "Is that Mark?" She grabbed it for a closer look.

"A play review?" Joan leaned in.

"I'm gonna read it."

"Is that a good idea?" asked Michael.

"Dad, I just sat through seventy-minutes of Mark acting out a relationship with Fallon. I think I can handle a review. Despite…everything, it was a great play. I'd like to see what they thought."

Alex flipped to the article: *Lairds and Liars Star Talks Fans, Theatre, and Manchester.* "It's a Q&A."

A slow breath left her lips. She began reading. Michael and Helen kept an eye on her, and Joan read over Alex's arm.

*Q: Two and a half years after graduating from drama school you landed* Lairds and Liars. *Did luck play a part in your success?*

*A: "Luck has everything to do with [my success]," Keegan says, sipping his water. "I've worked hard, but so have all the talented actors I went to drama school with. The struggle to get noticed, bouncing back from rejections, the times I wasn't asked to audition—which still happens, by the way—is always on my mind. If it wasn't for* Lairds, *I'm sure I'd still be bartending, running to auditions between shifts, and waiting for my phone to ring. I think 'why me' daily."*

*Q: Were sacrifices made to get where you are now?*

*A: "Sometimes you have to make choices you never thought you'd make. Even with a little success, things don't pan out the way you think. I've learned that achieving your dreams has a cost; it's bittersweet. Sometimes you end up losing what's…what's very important to you."*

Alex pulled away.

"You okay, love?" Joan looked up from the page.

"Yeah. It's just…"

"You don't have to keep reading..."

How could she stop?

*Q: How does it feel following in the footsteps of Benedict Cumberbatch and Kit Harington as the internet's boyfriend?*

*A: "It's flattering, but fans might be surprised. I'm actually a rubbish boyfriend, but I'm learning. I won't repeat the same mistakes."*

*Q: Your film and TV schedule has been non-stop. Why did you decide to tread the boards?*

*A: "The theatre community embraced me straight out of drama school when no one else would. I owe it so much; it just feels like home. But since* Lairds, *I've been offered mostly outdoorsy movie roles that require lots of physicality. I love the films I've shot so far, and I'm looking forward to the action-thriller I'll be starting in August. We'll be shooting in Mexico, Russia, Portugal—"*

*Q: Is that* Full Throttle 3: Blood Lust, *the Dwayne Johnson blockbuster franchise?*

Alex's jaw fell. "He's in *Full Throttle 3*?"

"*Ooh*!" Joan squeezed Alex's arm. "I love those movies!"

Alex looked at her grandmother and went back to reading.

*A: "It is! I'll be spending spring and summer in the gym, bulking up for it. But like I said, I'm thrilled to get back to my roots on stage, taking on* Constellations. *It's very intimate."*

*Q: Was that what attracted you to the play? The emotional range required?*

*A: "Yes. It's a sexy, heartfelt story about boy meets girl, boy loses girl, and what might have been. I think anyone who has been in love will relate to Roland and Marianne, especially if you've questioned what you did or didn't do in a relationship. That aspect especially resonated with me, and I'm sure it will touch audiences. I jumped at the chance to perform here again. Manchester and its people—they'll always have a big place in my heart."*

A smile tugged at the corners of Alex's mouth.

*Q: You just completed filming* A Promise Unspoken *in Dublin with your* Constellations *co-star, Fallon Delaney. Your play's director praised what you both bring to your roles. He said: "The reason Fallon was cast is because she has a sizzling chemistry with Mark. You can't fake that, especially live on stage." Mark, care to say a few words about her?*

*A: "Fallon and I have known each other since we were kids, so yeah, there is a shorthand that we bring to the stage. She's a very talented actress."*

*Q: There are rumours that you two are dating...*

*A: "I've learned the hard way that a private life should be just that—private. I'm protective of it and those I hold close." Keegan smiles. "Nothing to see here."*

Alex sighed as she pushed the paper away.

"All right, love?" Joan patted her hand.

Alex stared out the window at the slow-moving shops and buildings that signaled their stop was next. "That Q&A left me with more questions than answers."

"Maybe that's a good thing," said Joan. "Sometimes we don't like the answers we're given."

# THIRTY-THREE

*London, ten days later*

"Hi, Lex. You going out later?" Tom leaned on the doorjamb leading into Alex's room.

"Yeah, I'm heading out around five-thirty…time to mend some fences." She looked up from her laptop.

"Please tell me you're not off to see Mark?" He scowled as he walked in, staring at her screen.

"I'm seeing Freddie. I was away for his birthday so…" She glanced back at her work in progress. "Need me to pick up something on my way back?"

"No…" He snapped his knuckles. "Naomi's off work tonight, so I'm planning a romantic evening, get a takeaway in…"

"Oh." Alex sat back and nodded. "Okay."

"I feel like a shit friend. You've only been here two nights and already I'm pushing you out."

"Tom, it's your house."

"You don't have to stay out all night…"

"If we're done early, I'll catch a late movie."

"Aw, cheers, Lex." He stopped cracking his knuckles and hovered.

"Things still aren't…"

Tom shook his head. "Since it's been confirmed, Naomi barely looks at me."

"Give her time. It's a massive shock." Alex's eyes flitted back to her laptop as the screensaver—now set to con photos with Lucy instead of Venice with Mark—took over her screen. "A two-year-old child with someone else? Not how she envisioned her first year of marriage."

"Me neither." Tom smiled sheepishly. "He is something, though. Want to see a photo?" He pulled out his phone. "Meet Rex."

A redheaded toddler dressed in a Chelsea football kit grinned from the screen.

"Wow, Tom." Alex's eyes flew back to her friend. "You made a cute kid!"

"I know, right? My mini-me, albeit a ginger mini-me. It's weird but kinda cool." He laughed. "When you think about it, it's amazing how *one shag* can change everything."

Alex sighed. "Yeah, change it forever."

"We have to take Lex *here* after we're done." Freddie leaned across the boardroom table in the Teenage Cancer Trust offices, showing Simon a website on his phone. "It's a Tube-themed cocktail bar in Soho. She'll die! Apparently, it used to be an underground air raid shelter."

Simon squinted at the screen. "You only like that place because it's Instagram-worthy. You're not shooting a vlog there, too, are you?"

Alex peeked around the doorjamb. “Happy belated birthday, Freds!”

“Aw, come here, Sparkly Girl!” Freddie jumped up from his chair and hugged her. “You’re the best prezzie. I’ve missed you.”

“I’ve missed you, too,” Alex mumbled into Freddie’s chest, his embrace tightening by the second.

“It didn’t feel right, you being up north away from us, but now you’re back, it’s almost May, and everything is right with the world again…well, *almost*…oh, fuck it, you know what I mean. It’s just good to have you back.”

Alex’s heart dipped. How long would it be before *that* stopped happening?

Freddie released his clinch. “Okay, lady, ready to work?”

“Definitely.” She removed her coat.

“Welcome back.” Simon stood up, kissing Alex on the cheek. “I’ll get us some plastic banners. Be back in a minute.”

“I’m so glad you came.” Freddie smiled. “I figured if you saw me with my big boy charitable pants on, you couldn’t possibly be cross with me anymore. I’m a good ’un, see?”

“I see.” Her eyes swept over the table filled with bang-bang sticks, ponchos, and temporary tattoos for Teenage Cancer Trust’s ‘Cheer Kits’. “I wasn’t angry with you, Freddie. I was in self-preservation mode. I needed time away.”

“Yeah, from me.”

“Not just you.”

“But I went *way* overboard. That ‘*What have you done?*’ text? God! And bringing Mark around early for his move? Lucy’s *still* pissed at me. I thought if you saw how sad Mark was, you might buckle and take him back. It almost worked, too. You had that *look*, like you really wanted to hug him—and you were wearing his shirt! My heart ballooned, and then Lucy popped it by pulling you away.”

“I was having huge regrets—”

"Really? I thought so—"

"But not anymore."

Freddie's face fell. "Well…I'm happy you're back. I miss your snarky comments on my Insta."

"Don't hold your breath. I might extend my social media sabbatical."

"Aw, come back, Lex! I'm *bleeding* followers. That annoying silver mime artist in Covent Garden? He's got more followers than me! How messed up is that?"

He plucked an armful of ponchos from the table. "So, here's the deal: each envelope gets one tattoo, one poncho, and so on. Don't seal them up, though. Si's fetching the banners…*if* he ever comes back. He's probably stuck offering plumbing advice to the manager again—she's in the middle of loo renovations, apparently."

Alex sat down, picking up a tattoo. "You know, it still shocks me…teenage *you*, with cancer. I had no idea."

"I know I can be a blabbermouth, but even *I* have secrets. I threatened Lucy and Mark with pain of death if they ever spilled. I wanted to be the one to share my past."

"Absolutely."

"I almost said something when you told me and Lucy about your anxiety, but it wasn't the right time. I wanted to know you a little better. Some people get super freaked by the c-word—especially when it involves a kid. I can't blame them, really. You're supposed to be all hormones at fifteen, trying to cop off for the first time, and there I was, having a ball removed." He stuffed ponchos in his envelopes. "I never wanted to use cancer for sympathy. I wanted you to know *me* first. That way, if you did end up feeling sorry for me, it would be because of my terrible singing or my shitty taste in rom-coms…not because I had testicular cancer."

"I understand why you waited. I didn't tell Mark about my panic attacks for seven months."

"I know. You kept telling us not to tell him, and *I* never did."

She smiled. Her anxiety was a secret Freddie had guarded like it was his own.

"I wish I had told you differently. Toasting my latest all-clear check-up at *Thirteen's* closing party was a bit too *Freddie*, even for me."

Alex giggled. "You gave us a big reason to celebrate that night." She added inflatable bang-bang sticks to Freddie's packages. "Until then, I always thought you were off shopping when you weren't around. I had no clue you were so *philanthropic*."

He shoved his hair from his eyes. "It worked though, didn't it? I like to keep up the illusion of Fun Freddie, twenty-four-seven in glorious technicolour, darling!" His finger flicked through a stack of tattoos. "Are you still volunteering with that lupus charity?"

"Yeah, it's been eight months now. I'm writing for their newsletter, just minor pieces."

"Minor, my arse, Lex. I'd say that's pretty major, still doing it. You don't have to, you know."

"I know, but I don't want to let them down." Alex shrugged. "Niamh meant a lot to me."

"Mark said she misses you."

"Freddie…"

"You can still talk to her—"

"No."

Freddie leaned in. "But if something happens…if her lupus gets worse, you'll feel awful."

Alex opened up a new box of ponchos. "I know…she was like a mom to me, but it's awkward now. Ditch the guy, keep the mom? Don't think so."

"Awks but not impossible," said Freddie.

"Maybe in a few months, I'll reevaluate but…" She shrugged.

"Lex, I don't want to come off all *I had cancer and now I*

*know what's important* because I don't. I'm still figuring things out, but I *do* know that there's no time for regrets or putting things off. That's why I came out a day after my diagnosis—there was no way I was going to die in the closet. Life gives you no guarantees. You never know when that bus will hit you or cancer will show up."

"Do you worry a lot? About it coming back?"

"The worry—the threat—is always there, like your panic attacks. In my own silly way, I look at cancer like a crazy-ass ex who might knock at my door out of the blue. I just hope he's lost my address and I never hear from the bastard again."

Alex bumped his arm. "*Your* crazy-ass ex might kill you. At worst, I might faint when mine shows up. They're hardly the same."

Freddie chuckled. "We all have our terrors, Lex. That's why I love hard and make merry every day…even if some people think I'm OTT. Today isn't a dress rehearsal for tomorrow. Do things *now*. Live in the moment—don't worry about what's ahead."

A sentiment she knew too well floated through her mind: *Hop on, hold tight, and remember to enjoy the ride.* She swallowed, not prepared to give Mark credit. "My therapist said something similar, said living in the moment will ease my anxiety."

"See? Great minds!" He widened his eyes. "That's why I asked Si to marry me after four months of dating. I love him. Why wait?" He paused. "I know you and Mark had talked about it…"

Alex looked up from her envelopes.

"He told me, Lex, and I told *him* to pull his finger out, but you know Mark—work, work, work…" Freddie shrugged. "I don't blame you for leaving him. Your split broke my heart, though."

"Have you seen him much?"

"You want me to go there?"

She inhaled deeply and nodded.

"Well, now that the play's over, he's back living at my place, so…yeah. And we have been out, a few times…" He pushed up his glasses, gauging Alex's reaction before finishing his answer. "I don't want to hurt you—"

"I asked. Whatever you're going to say, I can handle it."

Freddie swallowed. "Mark and Fallon are seeing each other."

Her stomach flipped. The unspeakable, spoken.

"I give them credit though…" Freddie grabbed several bang-bang sticks. "New Year's Eve aside, they didn't hook up until earlier this month, up in Manchester."

"Right…"

"At least nothing more happened until you were broken up and living separately, and to be honest, it's Fallon who's all in…"

Alex looked up from her pile of filled envelopes. "Why? Did Mark say that to you?"

"*No*…just a feeling I have." He shifted in his chair and looked away. "Lex, I'm sorry. I wish he was still with you."

"I wish he didn't still mean so much to me." She bowed her head. "It wasn't meant to be."

"But *we* are, right?" Freddie shifted closer, ducking down to look into her eyes hidden beneath her bangs. "I might be a constant reminder of Mark, but I promise I won't talk about him or tell him what *we* talk about. We're okay…aren't we?"

Alex hugged him. "'Course we are. I might have moments when I just *can't*, but that doesn't mean I don't love you, Freds. I know this hasn't been easy, stuck in the middle."

"Tightrope walking…" He smiled over her shoulder. "…one of my many talents." He pulled back. "Perhaps you can work on Lucy, though? She's still freezing me out. Both Moriarty and I are blocked on Insta. I even started unboxing collectables on my YouTube channel, hoping to grab her attention, but nope."

"You're buying again?"

"I shouldn't have stopped. I love collectables, I love cons. I love Simon, too, but I can't keep sacrificing who I am to keep him sweet. Relationships shouldn't be like that. It's got to be give *and* take. Sometimes I think Simon didn't get that memo—his parents still don't know he's gay, still don't know about our engagement. I want to marry him, but I'm done trying to twist myself into someone I'm not. That's why I came out in the first place—to stop pretending. I *hate* pretending." He chuckled. "God, I'm preaching to the converted, aren't I? I'll shut up."

Alex smiled.

"Hopefully, Simon will realize I'm just as *adorable* without the vegetarianism and Cross-Fit bod."

"Freds, you've never had a Cross-Fit bod."

"Fair enough. I'd choose cheese and onion pasties over having six-pack abs *any* day. So…you'll talk to Lucy?"

"Yep. Promise."

"Her and Harry, eh? I was the last to know."

"They're cute together. I'm happy for them."

"Oh, you're a bigger person than me, honey. After breaking up with my ex, I hated all lovey-dovey couples. I dove into dancing, drinking, shagging randos…worked a charm. If *you* ever want to get off your tits, I can leave Si with his pipe and slippers. You and I can stay out till all hours. We'll give London's most notorious party animals a run for their money!"

"If Tom and Naomi patch things up, I might have to." She leaned in, her voice lowered discreetly. "I'm *dreading* the first time I stumble over a threesome…"

Freddie roared with laughter. "Oh, my God! Did you ever think that sentence would pass your lips when you moved here three years ago?"

"Never in my wildest, Freddie." She laughed and grabbed another pile of envelopes.

# THIRTY-FOUR

*One month later*

Rihanna meant business and so did Alex. The booming chorus of "Only Girl in the World", in sync with her pumping arms and determined feet, surged her forward along the narrow Regent's Canal towpath, past rows of moored canal boats. She weaved around cyclists, Saturday morning walkers, and fellow joggers, seeking a big finish to her run—just what she needed after receiving *that* email earlier in the morning.

Pushing herself, her breathing upped its pace to match her full-on sprint. She squinted into late May's overdue sunshine, across the canal at two steel gasholders towering into the blue sky. Their presence and the railway and street bridges looming ahead signaled that the first half of her daily run was almost over, and the steps leading to Mare Street were, thankfully, around the corner.

Third chorus in, RiRi gave way to the *Sherlock* theme. Alex's phone, strapped to her upper arm, kept the caller's identity out of sight. "Hello?"

"Sincy, it's Tarq!"

"And good-bye." Alex pushed her earbud cord's disconnect button as her eyes scanned the puzzling *'break a leg'* graffiti spray-painted underneath the railway bridge.

Ten seconds later, the theme played again. *Ugh.* She stumbled to a stop just beyond the second bridge overpass, her chest rising and falling with breathless abandon. "What?"

"Sorry about *Sincy*. It has now been deleted from my vocab. You all right?"

"I'm fine."

"Your breathing is heavy…"

"Not for the reason you think."

"Shame, that."

"Tarquin, what do you want? You've ruined my jog."

"A fellow jogger? Blimey, a girl after my own heart."

"I'm not after anything, Tarquin. What do you *want*?"

"Someone to hang with this afternoon. Harry said you were back."

Alex winced and slowly climbed the steps leading to Mare Street.

"Meet me on the South Bank."

"I can't. I'm in Hackney."

"After your jog. After your shower."

"I have writing to do."

"On Saturday? Look up. The sky's glorious. Shame to waste it. I'll buy you ice cream outside the National Theatre. Go on, Sunshine, say *yes*—you know you want to!"

He had a point: this May day was a stunner. And…if they did sit outside the National, maybe she would see the literary manager, or someone from the New Work department…remind them she still existed…but she couldn't stay out all afternoon.

"I'm meeting Lucy later."

"I'll have you back before she shows. Harry says she's always late, anyway. Come on! A wander and a chat, that's all I'm after."

"Okay."

"Brilliant. Meet me at the foot of the Golden Jubilee Bridge—you know, in front of the Royal Festival Hall? Half past twelve?"

Waiting on a concrete bench, Alex ignored the Thames view and flicked through a cheap magazine she had found discarded on the Tube. Just a few pages in and…surprise! Yet another slap to the face—photos of Mark and Fallon leaving Soho House. Fallon was all over him, like he was her personal jungle gym. A twinge of jealousy pinched her heart. Mark was laughing, moving on…

"Junk food for the brain." Tarquin's hand reached over her shoulder, snatching the magazine from her grasp. He joined her on the bench. "A mind is a terrible thing to waste."

"I guess you'd know."

He dismissively glanced at the page Alex had open and slapped it down beside him. "I came early to shop." He opened a red plastic Foyles bag. "See, I read more than Dr. Seuss."

Alex checked out his stash—a memoir about the guy behind PayPal, a Steve Jobs biography. "You surprise me—no football bios, no trashy thrillers, and…the updated *Star Wars* encyclopedia? Really?"

"I'm a massive *Star Wars* geek. My dad hired actors to play Han Solo and a Wookie for my tenth birthday party. Tread carefully, I'm skilled at Jedi mind tricks."

Alex snorted and stood up. Following her cue, Tarquin rose to his feet, too.

"I know who was in that magazine. Breakups are hard enough, but spotting your famous ex everywhere? Jeez." Tarquin steered her back with his free hand. "No magazines on my watch."

"And Jedi mind tricks will make that happen, Geek Boy?" Her glaring eyes, shooting over her shoulder, told him to remove his hand from her back—immediately. "Obi-Wan would be horrified. You should put those skills to better use."

"Oh, I am. You'll see." He swung his bag of books and smiled into the sun and gentle breeze. "There's no better place than London on a day like today."

"Is that why you moved back? Missed it too much?"

"No. Things in New York ran their course. I took advantage of everything it had to offer, but after almost three years, it was time to come home. It's funny—I felt *most* like a Londoner when I was there. All the differences, like their lack of salt-and-vinegar crisps? It's the only flavour I like. Couldn't find them anywhere."

Alex's eyes followed a tour boat down the Thames. "I could say the same about Twizzlers here."

"Those awful sweets? The red chewy ropey things?"

"They're delish, candy snob."

"Have you tasted the chocolate ones? A shop in Times Square sells them."

"That's just wrong." Alex shook her head. "It's strawberry or nothing."

"Who's the candy snob now?"

"I like what I like."

"You're too *picky*."

"Says the dude who only eats one flavour of crisps."

"Touché." He laughed. "You figure out what's important when you're away, don't you think?"

Alex shrugged. "I guess."

"My dad took us travelling during most school breaks. I've skied all over Europe, surfed the Australian coast. I've had a lot of opportunity to visit other cultures and learn from them, but no place compares to London." He glanced across the river at the Shell Mex

House's large clock and back to Alex. "Have you travelled much?"

"Nowhere exotic or beachy—I hated sunbathing, growing up in Florida. I lived in Atlanta during college, and I've visited New York, Chicago, New Orleans, Dublin, Venice, and a few places around England—"

The slamming of polyurethane on cement drew Alex's attention away from Tarquin. A crew of skateboarders were showing off their noseslides and grinds in the graffiti-covered undercroft of the Southbank Centre.

Tarquin's grin grew twice its normal size. "My people!"

Alex scoffed.

"What?" His phone buzzed in his pocket, but he ignored it.

"Everything about you screams polo, rowing for Cambridge, and reading poetry to swooning debs. *Skateboarding*? Yeah, right."

"Sorry to burst your bourgeois bubble, but I hate polo, and I can't row for toffee. Poetry? Not if I can help it. I *did* go to Cambridge, but I ran cross-country, played footy, lived at the skatepark, and DJ'd, but I never got my kicks riding a polo pony. I'm more a coasteering, bouldering, snowkiting guy…"

Alex laughed. "Did you just make those up?"

"No! They're extreme sports."

"I thought you said you had a fear of heights?"

"Actually, it's a fear of falling, but extreme sports have made that almost disappear. You have to be so in the moment, there's no room to be scared. I felt amazing after my first rock climb. I felt like I could do anything."

"Ah, so you're scared of nothing and cocky about everything."

"Yes and…yes." He laughed and started walking again. "But my free time isn't all fun and games. I've done my share of honest grafting, too."

Alex rolled her eyes.

"I have! Volunteering…building hospitals in Nepal and

schools in Senegal. I may come from old money and privilege, but that doesn't *define* me—just like being blonde, blue-eyed, and from Florida doesn't define you, Sunshine."

"Touché." Alex nodded as they approached a cluster of tables selling secondhand books underneath Waterloo Bridge.

"We're not that different, you and me…"

"You barely know me." Alex stopped at a table filled with hardcover books. A busker, strumming a guitar nearby, sang a tune that sounded familiar. She prided herself on recognizing old songs, but this one…

"You use words to build worlds. I use my hands…although nowadays I'm more hands off than on." Tarquin slipped a finger along a row of book spines. "See anything you like?"

Tarquin's question hung in the air, unanswered; Alex's mind was elsewhere. *I hate it when I can't ID an earworm! I know this…what IS it?*

Tarquin touched her arm. "Alex? Anything you want?"

"Oh!" She jolted to attention, scanning the tables. Her eyes stalled on a book with giant green letters on its spine—MARK.

She caught her breath as his name unlocked the mystery tune: "Here, There and Everywhere" by the Beatles. *Mark used to play his dad's old Beatles records all the time, and we'd dance and sing around the flat...*

"Hey, Earth to Alex..."

She looked at Tarquin. "No…thanks."

He held up a copy of Maurice Sendak's *Where the Wild Things Are*. "Day made! Love this book." He broke into a wide grin.

*Damn.* Never mind Jedi mind tricks…those dimples—hypnotizing. His smile was self-assured, used to getting its own way—sexy, but in a completely different way than Mark's. She pulled her eyes away while simultaneously grabbing the nearest book: *The Kama Sutra.* A blush warmed her cheeks.

"Blimey. Steady on, girl!" He laughed and walked to the vendor, leaving Alex in a sweaty haze of embarrassment.

*What am I doing? Comparing a guy I barely know to Mark? And that sex book? Nice one, Lex.*

When Tarquin returned, he pointed to the Sir Laurence Olivier statue outside the National. "He named one of his sons Tarquin. Larry had good taste."

"So, you *are* a theatre fan?"

"Uh, no. I'm just a keeper of banal facts about my name."

"But you took me to that play?"

"Yeah, because Harry said it would cheer you up." He nodded towards Kitchen, the National's café. "Feeling peckish?"

Alex's heart dipped. The National was her place—and Mark's. She didn't want to share it with someone who didn't appreciate it. "No. Let's keep going…"

"As you wish."

They stopped in nearby Gabriel's Wharf, an open-air shopping enclave, for fries and ice cream, passed by the Tate Modern, Shakespeare's Globe, and Southwark Cathedral. With each step, Alex felt a little more at ease, a little less judgmental of Harry's best friend. He was funny and sharp, definitely less braggy. He asked questions—and listened to Alex's answers—about her writing hopes.

"It will be my first piece performed in a theatre since *Thirteen*, so I'm pretty excited about it."

"When did you write it?"

"Eleven months ago. It's just a scene. I wrote it at the Court during an invite-only group session. I forgot all about it until they called three weeks ago. They're performing ten different scenes next month, all from emerging playwrights."

"Can I come?"

"I'll be lucky if *I* can grab a seat. It's a fundraising gala, so every penny goes towards new works and writers' schemes. Anyway, you're not a theatre fan!"

"But I'd like to see your work. I bet the after-party will be epic."

Alex shook her head as they walked under London Bridge. "I won't stick around. I got an email this morning listing all the actors participating…"

Tarquin raised an eyebrow. "Mark?"

"His girlfriend. At least she's not in *my* scene."

"She should be so lucky." He smiled. "Speaking of lucky…*Thirteen* sounds incredible. You should send it to Broadway."

"Maybe."

"I know a woman. Want her details?"

"Do all your hookups owe you favours? Thanks, but no thanks."

"Alex! She's a lesbian in her late fifties. I helped her get an apartment, not an orgasm. Our interaction was professional, like my dealings with the producer of Sir Ian's play." He threw his arm in the air. "Look, despite the over-sexualized banter you witnessed at Bespoke, I'm really *not* a douche. I didn't spend the last three years in the Big Apple keeping Durex in business. I was there *to work.* Budgie's always been more of a dad to me than my own father, and there was no way I was going to blow it.

"*And* for the record, I dated three women—*three*—the entire time I was in New York. One was my flatmate. The other two were model/actresses who did my head in. Actually, they reminded me of my mother."

"Eww."

"Not in that way. My mum was a model, an actress."

"Wait a minute…" Alex's eyes climbed up the Shard, looming behind London Bridge Station. "Balfour…Balfour…*Kiki* Balfour?

Kiki Balfour is your *mum*? Wasn't she in a sci-fi series, mid-nineties?"

"Yep. *Equinox Ten.* Not exactly *Doctor Who* level, but yeah…how do you know that? You're too young—and American."

"Dad's a sci-fi freak. We used to binge-watch British shows on PBS when I was a kid. Your mum's name stuck in my head because Joan's—my grandmother's—cat was called Kiki, after KiKi Dee, the singer?"

"God. Don't go breaking my heart…"

She laughed. *Musical cheese! Tarquin knows KiKi Dee!*

"My mother didn't take *that* song to heart. Her first love was acting, and Dad was way down the list. My brothers and I didn't fare much better."

"How many brothers?" asked Alex.

"Just two. You?"

"Sister and brother. Both older."

"I'm youngest, too. Before I was born, Dad and my uncle sold their share of the family's oil company. They split over eighty million quid. He used his portion to start Sports Now, the bargain sports apparel chain?"

"I bought my running shoes there."

"Well, thanks for supporting my cold, dysfunctional family." He grinned and guided Alex to the entrance of Hay's Galleria, a converted riverside wharf that boasted shops and restaurants.

"My mother was pissed Dad didn't pour that money into a TV production company she wanted to bankroll. They fought a lot. She took off several times, shacking up with various male co-stars. Her leaving, her ego…the constant phoniness of her profession—it left me with a perpetual showbiz hate-on. Mum *always* chose her job over us. I did everything I could to grab her attention: I excelled at sports, deliberately crashed my skateboard a few times." He glanced at Alex. "I remember being seven, maybe eight, and thinking: *if I hurt myself badly enough, Mum will have to love me*. Stupid, eh?"

Alex's gaze travelled along the Galleria's vaulted glass and steel ceiling. "It's not stupid. I know exactly how that feels."

"Do you? Did *your* mother ever change?"

"She showed a shred of interest when *Thirteen* got picked up, but she never flew over to see me. We haven't been face to face since I left Florida three years ago, which is fine by me. Mark always wanted us to get along. We argued about it. He's close to his mum and never understood why I stopped trying with mine. I think there's only so much rejection you can take."

"Exactly. Einstein's definition of insanity sums it up nicely, don't you think?"

"Totally."

"I think my mum loved her TV kids more than she ever loved us. I hated them, precocious stage-school shits."

Spotting Tower Bridge, Alex pulled out her phone for a photo. "Crap, it's almost three. I need to get back for Lucy."

Tarquin smiled. "My Millennium Falcon awaits!"

# THIRTY-FIVE

"Okay, I admit it—I *love* your car! It's so Austin Powers." Alex smiled as they reached the steps leading up to Tom and Naomi's semi-detached Victorian house in Hackney.

"Used to drive a Porsche, but it wasn't a good fit." Tarquin looked over his shoulder at his shiny car parked around the corner. "The '66 Alfa Romeo Spider feels more *me*…more shagadelic."

Alex laughed. "*Yeah, baby*!"

Tarquin's eyes lingered along the street. "Albion Square, eh? Mature trees, the garden…these 1840s properties sell at a premium." He chuckled and turned to Alex. "Sorry, blame the day job."

"Don't get too excited. My stay is temporary."

"Hey!" Lucy hollered from across the street.

Alex squinted into the bright sun. "Hey!"

"Tarquin…in Hackney?" Lucy threw her arms in the air as she skipped over the sidewalk, careful not to land on any cracks. "What the fuck, dude?"

"I'm stepping outside my comfort zone."

"Suits you." Lucy winked.

He smiled at Alex. "Till Tuesday?"

"Yep." She nodded. "Thanks, Tarquin."

He waved and rounded the corner towards his car.

Lucy bumped Alex's hip. "Tarquin's got a not-so-secret-boner for you."

"Lucy!" Her eyes widened.

"The way he looks at you—he's gagging for it."

Alex scoffed and started up the steps. "He looks at *all* women that way."

"No, he doesn't." Lucy followed close behind.

"Someone needs a history lesson."

"Oh, I know all about *that*. That's old news. Even Harry says so. He says Tarq only has eyes for you."

Alex screwed up her face and looked away, pausing on the top step. "So, Freddie says you spoke last night—"

"Stop ignoring what I just said."

"I'm not ignoring it, I'm just not *acknowledging* it."

"That's rude, Lex."

"No, rude is pushing a topic I don't want to discuss."

"Tarq thinks you're gorgeous, smart, and different. I mean, hello? He used the word 'smart' to describe a girl he likes?" Lucy chuckled. "Harry practically fell over."

"He also used *different*—"

"Lex, you don't give a shit about his money. You're not intimidated by it, and you don't take his crap. *That's* different. He finds it sexy."

"Well that's…flattering, but we're friends—that's it."

"Didn't you have fun today?"

Alex pursed her lips. "Yes, Lucy. I had *fun* today."

"And you two are hanging out again next week?"

Alex put her hands on her hips. "Just say it. I know you're dying to."

Lucy leaned in. "It's been *five months*. You can't stay on the shelf forever."

Alex shook her head, looking away.

"Stop putting up walls. The longer you wait, the worse it's going to be."

"So, you want me to *date* Tarquin?"

Lucy smiled with a shrug. "You're already halfway there, babe. Hanging with him. Lex, *really*…time to move on…"

"Well, Mark certainly has. If he can move on so quickly, what does that say about what *we* had? It wasn't special? *I* wasn't special? It hurts. It makes me doubt everything. I'm scared to open myself up again. I took that risk after Devin cheated on me, dating Mark, and look how that worked out…"

"I know, but that's why I'm suggesting you wade in slowly with Tarq. You're already friends. See where it goes, and if you *do* decide to have sex…with mutual respect and protection, knowing it's a bit of fun…what's the harm? Plus, you could do far worse than Tarq. I mean, *phwoar*! *Swipe right.*"

Alex rolled her eyes.

"After your theatre date—"

"Lucy, it *wasn't* a date."

"Outing, night…*whatever*, Tarquin wouldn't shut up about you while you were in Manchester. I like the guy. He's even trying to quit smoking 'cause you hate it—and he's *fit*. I bet he's *goooood…*"

Alex crossed her arms.

"You *have* to stop comparing everyone to Mark."

"I'm not."

"Think of it this way: would you turn Tarquin down if Mark didn't exist? That's your answer, right there."

***MARK***
***Seventeen years earlier***
***Dublin, March 2001***

Mark covered his face with his pillow. *Not again!* These arguments between his parents were happening almost nightly, but this one was louder, angrier. The nine-year-old crept out from the refuge of his pillow and warm quilt, nudging his bedroom door open. He stood silent and still, listening in. As long as his parents didn't move around too much in the living room, they wouldn't spot him.

"I told you time and time again, Finn, a pub is no place to raise a family…now look at us!" His mum sounded stuffed up, like she had been crying again. "I can't live here anymore. It hurts too much."

"Niamh, *shhhh*! You'll wake the kids." His dad lowered his voice. "Look, none of the breweries were interested, you know that. Maybe I'll call a local developer, see if he'll make me an offer, but a fast sale comes at a price. He might not give us what the pub's worth—"

"I don't care if you have to *give* this place away. I want out, Finn—now."

"A quick sale won't help us financially—"

"A quick sale will help us *emotionally*…and right now, we're hanging by a thread. Grace has become so overprotective of Mark. She barely lets him out of her sight. And Mark's so withdrawn. He's having nightmares, wetting the bed almost every night…"

Mark winced. On top of feeling sad and lost, he also felt like a sucky baby. He had started having nighttime accidents immediately after it happened. If the kids at school ever found out…

"…We need a proper family home, Finn. A nice little house on a quiet street."

"You know I would do anything for Mark and Gracie…but this pub, it's been in my family since the *forties*. To leave it all behind, everything my family built up—"

"I know it's hard, love, but your parents, your brother…if they were alive, they wouldn't expect you to keep it, especially now, after what we've been through. It's time to start over, to move on…before it's too late…"

Mark sank back into the shadows, closing his door quietly. *Moving? On top of everything*? He climbed into his bed and hid under his pillow, muffling his tears.

# Thirty-Six

*North London, Tuesday, June 5, 2018*

Freddie's flat lay quiet. Then Bruno Mars began a muffled warble.

Startled from a deep snooze, Mark fumbled under the blanket for his phone. Bruno kept singing. *Shut up, Bruno! Shut up! Ah...found it.*

His hand and the phone surfaced. Mark's puffy eyes squinted at the bright screen, his finger jabbing the red disconnect dot. His phone had been busy: missed calls from Fallon, Wink, and Freddie, plus a text from him all in caps: *GET UP, KEEGS! I'LL CALL EVERY 30 MIN. UNTIL YOU'RE UP. STOP MAKING THIS A HABIT. LATERS.*

The time came into focus—half twelve—and the date…June 5. Mark's mind wandered to a sunny London day, riding his Vespa with the wind in his hair and the girl of his dreams hanging on tight…three years ago, *today*…

Mark dropped the phone on his tanned chest and stared at the crack in the ceiling, its focus blurring. His stomach throbbed as past mistakes haunted his mind. Sweeping hair from his eyes, he winced as he rose up on an elbow. The springs of Freddie's lumpy sofa bed whined in solidarity.

Back arched, tail waving back and forth, Moriarty hissed from his lofty perch atop the breakfast bar crowded with dirty dishes.

"Yeah, judge all you want, mate." A frustrating itch tickled Mark's nose. "Ah-choo, *ah-chooo*!"

His gaze fell to his backpack and suitcase, still sporting airline baggage tags. He had been back in London a week and still hadn't unpacked.

"Fuck it." He sniffed, clutching his stomach. "I can't…not to-day." He returned to his phone, typing a quick text to Wink: *Got laryngitis. Please tell the studio I'll be in for ADR tomorrow.*

He hit send and pulled the blanket over his head, retreating from the day.

*South London*

*Done!* The act in *Upton Park* that Alex had been revisiting for months was finally finished. She sat back in her chair and let out a satisfied sigh, absorbing the breathtaking view beyond her laptop: the Tower of London, the Thames, Tower Bridge. She never tired of it, and thanks to Tarquin's rooftop terrace, it was hers for the sum-mer.

Last week, he had given Alex keys to his riverfront penthouse in Anchor Brewhouse, a historic converted warehouse, so she could write away the summer overlooking her favourite bridge. Tarquin's place was quiet, free of Tom practicing his audition pieces, and close to the theatres she was pitching.

Tarquin's generosity may have removed her from London Fields during the day, but it didn't remove London Fields—or

Mark—from her thoughts, especially today. She had pushed through their shared memories, the unanswered questions, the lingering hurt…determined to finish the latest draft of *Upton Park*. She was *determined* not to allow June 5 to derail her progress, and neither would the presence of Fallon at the Royal Court's fundraising gala in nine days' time. Alex would show them. She would show everyone.

# Thirty-Seven

*Nine days later*

Mid-June was colder than usual, but Alex didn't have time to ponder the weather. In between *Upton Park* edits, rehearsals for her scene in the fundraising gala, and Tarquin's social calendar, she barely had time to sleep, or think about Mark—much.

Smoothing the skirt of her favourite plum dress for the eleventh time, she jittered on Tom's sofa, her toes tap-tap-tapping on the hardwood floor. Their frenetic dance matched the conga line traipsing through her stomach. Tonight, her words would be performed on the Royal Court's stage. Her piece would be over within fifteen minutes, but that didn't matter: two years after *Thirteen*'s surprise triumph, she was back.

And so far, so good. Rehearsals had gone without a hitch, and she hadn't bumped into Fallon once. The last run-through had been that morning, and by the time Alex arrived to watch her scene—the second-to-last piece being performed—most of the actors had already left. Tonight, Fallon would be too busy preparing her scene, so the preshow dinner would be guaranteed Delaney-free. Mark, though, was another concern altogether.

A text from Tarquin lit up her phone: *Hey, Sunshine. 'Will you succeed? Yes, you will indeed! (98 and 3/4 percent guaranteed.)' Dr. Seuss believes in you—so do I. Go smash it. x*

Bless. Tarquin had offered to come…several times. Over the past weeks, he had earned her trust with his thoughtfulness and dependability. Like clockwork at one p.m. on Tuesdays and Thursdays, he would check in, calling to discuss that evening's adventure. Unlike Mark, he didn't spring surprises on her; he always consulted with her first—a trait that soothed her inner control freak. Sometimes nights out were his choice: exercising his expensive tastes with dinner in the clouds at the Sky Garden, or tickets to the hottest plays. Sometimes Alex called the shots, choosing cheap fry-ups at Pimlico's Regency Café, edgy theatre performances in found spaces, or lazy window-shopping strolls through Seven Dials. She even took him to his first comic con, a small Saturday-only *Star Wars* celebration in Brighton.

With each excursion, Alex realized Harry *was* right. Getting out and about was exactly what the doctor ordered—for Tarq and for her. He was forging new business contacts amid cocktails and theatre outings, and Alex's writing muse was back with a vengeance. These dates between friends were a permanent fixture in her bullet journal, unlike her panic attacks, which, thanks to her continued diligence, had taken a back seat for almost three months.

But through it all, Alex couldn't ignore the fresh lilies or packets of M&Ms Tarquin left for her in his flat, or the new novels she wanted to read, bookmarked with handwritten Dr. Seuss quotes on his personalized stationary. His laddish persona? Gone. He was actually funnier without the pervy innuendos. Alex laughed a lot with Tarquin, and yet, she still wasn't sure she could make *that* leap.

She typed and hit send: *Thanks, Geek Boy. Will let you know.*

*Phew*. Five minutes, then she'd head out. The house was quiet.

Naomi had a *Mamma Mia!* performance, and Tom was visiting Rex. She checked her makeup again, vetted the contents of her clutch again, and texted Lucy…again.

*Leaving soon. Wish you guys could come, but the Court doesn't have rubber walls! xoxo*

Lucy replied within seconds.

*Thought you should know about THIS. I don't want you walking in there blind...keep me posted. x*

Lucy's text included a link. *Blind...to what?* She tapped it, and Fallon's—Sinéad's—Facebook page appeared. *Oh, Lucy.* Alex had resisted for months; why look now? But…Lucy wouldn't have raised the alarm for nothing.

The page was locked down, but it displayed five public pictures in addition to her profile and cover photos. All featured Mark. *Of course.* Two pictures were lovely dovey Fallon and Mark circa 2008 and 2009. Alex couldn't deny it—they had been a cute teenage couple once upon a time. The other images were recent: downing shots in a Manchester bar, on set in Ireland, and frolicking on a sun-kissed beach. *…wait, a beach?* Two weeks ago…*in Florida. Her* home turf. Alex curled her lip but couldn't look away.

Mark, clad in soaked swim trunks that left little to the imagination, was clutching Fallon and her drenched bikini as waves crashed around them. Four months of dating and already, Mark had taken Fallon on holiday. *That was fast.* Mark had taken Alex to Venice when they hit twelve months—for their first anniversary. Three times Mark had cancelled their U.S. trip—*his first trip*—to her home state. But here he was, his first time in Florida, romping in the surf with Fallon and her see-through bikini. *Fucking bastard.*

Her cheeks burned. *What else is out there?*

*Fuck it!* She downloaded Instagram on her phone, punched in #MarkKeegan, and…an official blue-ticked account popped up. *You're kidding me?* Thirty-seven photos scrolled under her finger:

promotional shots from *Lairds*, *Constellations* images, beach photos. *When did this happen?* She read his profile. It included a link to an official website. With one click, a moody black and white site filled her screen. Mark was doing studly things: straddling a Harley (not his cute Vespa) and squinting into the sun wearing jeans and a wife beater—*a wife beater?!*—with his burgeoning biceps bulging to attention. *Tacky!* There were links to official Twitter and Snapchat accounts, too. *Mark…on Snapchat? Mission accomplished, Wink!* Mark's action-hero makeover was obviously speeding ahead, full throttle.

She took a deep breath. Calmly, she placed her phone in her clutch. Time to go. Time to show Mark, Fallon, and everyone else that the last six months hadn't broken her. Alex painted on a smile, shoved her bangs from her eyes, and grew three inches in her heels. The show must go on.

The evening's actors bowed for a third time, eating up the rapturous standing ovation of the Royal Court faithful. Alex beamed from mid-stalls at her own actors, Pete and Sara, but her eyes had a mind of their own, drifting to centre stage where Fallon smiled like a newly-crowned Oscar winner. Alex followed the actress's gaze but couldn't spot Mark in the audience. *Strange.*

The house lights brightened to full strength, the actors exited the stage, and patrons lumbered down the aisles, anticipating the free bar and live music at the post-show party.

Alex hung back, lost in her phone. The screen was clogged with texts.

Lucy: *What's happening? I'm dying here.*

Harry: *Drinks are waiting. Come celebrate.*

Tarquin: *I'm on stand-by. I can pick you up.*

Alex answered Lucy. *It went really well.*

*See Mark?*

*Not a whisker.*

*Workaholic. For once, that's a good thing. U coming?*

*Yes. Saying good-bye to my actors first.*

*K. x*

Alex slipped down the aisle and out the exit, walking past the red wall overlooking the bar. She stopped at the top of the stairs, surveying the lively party below. Finding Pete and Sara in this crowd would be a struggle. She followed the flow of people down the steps and the familiar wall of heat and noise waiting at the bottom unleashed happy memories of *Thirteen*'s press night party, of Mark beaming at her across the bar…of his promise that he would never lose her again…*Vespa rules*…

She closed her eyes and took a deep breath, pulling herself back to *this* moment—here, now. Her so-called 'friend'—nostalgia—could piss off. She was here to create *new* memories, and nothing—and no one—would stop her.

Inching farther into the fray and passing an overstuffed photo booth spilling random legs and arms, she bumped into the stage manager. "Hey! We did it!"

"*You* did it, Alex. You must be chuffed. Want a drink?"

"No, I'm good, thanks. I had two glasses of champagne during dinner." She squinted into the crush. "Have you seen Pete and Sara?"

"Not yet." The pretty brunette shook her head. "Maybe they're upstairs? The DJ's up there."

"Cool. Thanks." Alex smiled and craned her neck, scarcely looking over the people around her; even aloft in heels, she was still a short ass amongst this crowd. She huffed and turned around, squeezing her way back towards the front of the room.

"Hey, Alex, all right?"

"Welcome back, girl."

"Congratulations, wonderful scene!"

She shook hands, hugged, and laughed through the crush. It felt amazing to be back, to reunite with familiar faces she hadn't seen in two years, people who remembered—who loved—her work. She made lunch plans and exchanged phone numbers. Their vote of confidence left her with perma-grin, sore cheeks, and a revised action plan for the coming weeks. Who knew that a ten-page script could make such a splash? She was back on Theatreland's radar and fit to burst.

Nodding her head along to the DJ's beat, she wriggled through swaying bodies and shouty conversations and got stuck behind a raucous pack of actors toting handlebar moustaches and oversized sunglasses outside another photo booth. Her phone vibrated in her hand: a call from an unknown number, stealing her attention as she hightailed around the scrum—

She slammed chin-first into a woman's back, draped in silky straight hair. "Ooof!" The playwright stumbled backwards, juggling her ringing phone.

"Ow! What the—" The long dark hair took flight, fanning out as the woman spun around, away from her well-dressed clique. Alex's victim stared, her delicate features disdainful.

*I'm such a klutz!* Alex wished she could hide behind a pair of those giant photo booth sunglasses and blame this hit-and-run on someone else. "I'm sorry. Did I hurt you?"

"No, I'm *fine*," the woman snapped, rubbing her shoulder blade as she turned back to her loud cluster of friends.

Brown eyes, soft and wide, peered around the woman. "Christ! Alex?" His lips quivered, not sure whether to smile, laugh, or curse again.

*That voice...* Alex's heart dropped to the floor, taking with it the false sense of security that had protected her until six seconds ago. She had come *so close* to getting through the night without seeing…him.

"Are you okay?" Mark stepped forward, ignoring the suspicious looks and headshakes of his associates. His left hand reached towards Alex's arm but hesitated and withdrew before making contact. His other hand strangled the neck of his beer bottle.

She half-smiled, preventing an honest answer from leaving her lips. "I'm okay…sorry for crashing into your friend."

Mark looked tanned. His hair was longer, like he hadn't cut it since she last saw him in *Constellations* three months earlier. His voice sounded incredible, his unmistakable scent teasing her closer. The urge to touch him vibrated all the way down to her fingertips.

His chest rose and fell in time with some nervous nodding. "Um, Alex Sinclair, meet Chelsey Wu. Chelsey's my personal assistant."

Mark didn't have to explain Alex's relevance to Chelsey. The mere mention of her full name unleashed a head tilt of recognition.

"Chels, can you—"

"Absolutely." She gave Alex a knowing smile and wrangled their gang of six. "Come, meet Mark's American PR. She's setting up an interview with Graydon Carter's people…"

Mark paused as they moved on, his eyes briefly swept down Alex's body and back up again. He hovered over her lips before reuniting with her eyes. Chills raced along Alex's arms and neck, every second of his gaze, torture.

"Lex, you look…great." His eyes did that crinkly thing at the corners that Alex loved. "Your dress, it's from the wedding, right?"

The *wedding*…their awkward marriage convo…their sensuous morning after…like dominos, the memories toppled, one after another. She nodded, lost in his voice and their past, unable to function.

"How *are* you?" A surge of longing lifted his voice. "How's

Michael…Joan…?"

"Good. Thanks. You? Your…mum?"

"Good, yeah…" He stepped closer.

He smelled *so* good.

"Mum's well. She misses y—" He cut himself off, his eyes darting through the swarm of bodies an elbow away.

Alex held her breath, fearful that exhaling would release the wave of loss and sadness that was threatening to flood her heart all over again.

"So…big night, eh?" Mark smiled again. "So much talent on show."

"Yeah. I was flattered to be included."

"You *deserved* to be included. Your scene blew the others off the stage."

She let her breath go. "You saw it?"

"Yeah! From side stage. Wink and I got here just before Fal's…" He cleared his throat and looked away. "Wink looks after both of us now."

"Right." Reality slapped Alex out of her nostalgic stupor. *How cosy.* Mark and "Fal" shared an agent. They shared holidays. They shared a past…and the present. Alex's face began to flush. *First loves*. Like Helen and her dad. Despite the teenage angst, years spent apart, and relationships with other people, they would always find their way back into each other's arms. Mark's future had never been hers—it was Fallon's.

Tonight's Facebook discovery, his total 180 on social media, his stupid makeover…*this awkward conversation* reminded her once again that this guy was not the unspoiled Irish actor she had met in the lobby of this theatre three years ago. This rising star was not the Mark she had fallen in love with. Things were different now. Her world hadn't just slipped off its axis; it had been flung from it.

*What am I doing? Feeling sentimental? Missing him? No.*

No sadness, no yearning, no regrets would seep into this conversation. She clenched her jaw, a renewed sense of cool, detached anger—of purpose—rising from her chest.

"Congratulations on *Full Throttle 3*."

"Thanks. Yeah, it's exciting…" Mark smiled.

"How's the script?"

"Actually, I haven't seen it. Soon though. I signed on because, well, it's a massive…"

His eyes searched hers; for what, Alex had no clue. If it was words he needed to finish that sentence, she could offer a few: 'piece of shit' immediately came to mind, as did 'sell-out', but she remained silent. This new Mark was just doing what he did best—following Wink's advice, even if *Full Throttle 3* was sure to be void of creativity, heart, truthfulness, or any of the qualities he used to hope for in a script. The urge to shout, *You've become the celebrity we used to LAUGH about!* while smacking some sense into him was overpowering.

"…opportunity." His grin stretched farther. "The movie of next summer, they're saying."

"Well, if *they're* saying it, it must be true…"

Mark dragged his hand through his hair, his smile softening. He leaned close to her ear. "Lex, there's something you should know—"

"There you are!" An arm snaked around her waist from behind.

Alex flinched. Her eyes dropped, catching a flash of silver—a ring—on a determined thumb, stroking her side.

*Tarquin.*

The smile glued to Mark's face dissolved.

A strange mix of relief and unease quivered in Alex's chest. She closed her eyes, hoping that when she opened them again, she would find herself anywhere but there. The Court wasn't the place for a scene.

"Car's waiting, Sunshine..." Tarquin's eyes took in Mark like an afterthought. "Oh, hello. I'm Tarquin." He extended his hand. "You're Mark, right?"

Mark stood up straight and met Tarquin's handshake. "Hi."

He dropped Tarquin's hand quickly, his eyes narrowing as they flew to Alex's waist. They flitted back to her face, questioning. A sharp swoop of his hand swept his hair from his forehead.

A blonde in an ankle-length silver dress slipped around the corner of the photo booth and pounced on him. "Babe, did you see who I was talking—"

Fallon's hand halted its journey along Mark's chest, her attention leaping towards the subject of his stare. "Alex...*hi.* Congrats on your scene." Her eyes jumped to Tarquin.

"Thanks, Fallon. You...were terrific." A rehearsed fake smile trespassed across Alex's cheeks. If it stretched any farther, she worried her foundation might crack. She looked up at Tarquin and squeezed his hand where it held her waist. "I'm ready."

He nodded.

Her eyes bolted to her ex. "Take care, Mark...Fallon."

Alex guided Tarquin away from the couple, weaving her way through the crowd to the stairs.

Once in the lobby, out of Mark's sight, Tarquin stopped, forcing Alex to hit the brakes. "You okay?"

She nodded. "I can't talk here."

"Okay, so, Bespoke? Or...home?"

"Not mine. Yours."

# Thirty-Eight

Tarquin didn't push Alex for answers. Driving across London, he kept his attention on the road, leaving Alex to her texts with Lucy. Once at his building, he carried her high heels and followed her into his private elevator. The floor numbers counted upwards…two, three, four…but nothing seemed to lift the distant look in her eyes.

The door slid open to his four-bedroom penthouse on the tenth floor, and Alex strode in, past Tarquin's framed medals from the London and New York City marathons and photos snapped atop mountains and inside caves. She turned left into the living room and headed straight for the floor-to-ceiling windows overlooking Tower Bridge, all lit up and commanding attention like London's biggest showoff.

"I'll get you a drink." Tarquin set down her shoes and kicked off his own before walking into the kitchen. Removing two glasses from a cupboard, he set them on the counter, free of crumbs and dishes. His place resembled one of those impossibly neat apartments showcased in glossy home décor magazines.

Alex rushed past his life-size Stormtrooper and took up residence in front of his London telephone box, filled with biographies and reference books, listening to a message on her phone. A minute in, she slowed down her pacing, lowering the phone from her ear. *Oh. My. God.*

"Everything all right?" Tarquin handed over a vodka and orange and took a sip from his boulevardier.

"Better than all right…" She set her clutch on a table beside the window and with a smile, downed a large mouthful. "Do you know I made a checklist for tonight?"

"You know I love a good list. Go on, then, what was on it?"

"Number one: get through it, stay calm, don't panic. Number two: make sure to talk to new people, new theatre contacts." She grinned. "Not only did I *not* get overwhelmed, but my phone is stuffed with contacts."

"I couldn't have played it better myself." He laughed and leaned against the window in front of Tower Bridge. "What else was on that list?"

"Only one more: prove that *Thirteen* wasn't a fluke. My scene flew by so quickly tonight, but the audience loved it—Pete and Sara bowed four times. I don't know if my former agent was there, but even if she wasn't, I felt vindicated, and people at the party kept coming up to me. Tarq, they didn't forget me or *Thirteen*."

"Didn't I say you would boss it?"

"I had one wobble…" She gulped her drink. "Seeing Mark…it was like the previous three hours didn't count—the previous *six months* of healing didn't count. That broken girl from the Dublin hotel room was stood in front of him again, Mark and his Coen Winkler-approved career makeover, yanking me back down."

She set her glass beside her clutch. "But then I became so fucking *furious* that I could barely see straight. It all came flooding back: why I left him, how he's changed, why I deserve more. At that very moment, everything became clear. I knew what I needed to do. I felt empowered again. And then *you* arrived—"

Tarquin raised his glass with a grin. "How was my timing, good?"

"Impeccable." Alex tapped into her voicemail. "I crashed into Mark's friend because I was distracted by my phone ringing. I let it go to voicemail and forgot all about it until we got here and I had a listen…check this out." She put her phone on speaker.

*Good afternoon, Ms. Sinclair. It's Peggy Ward calling from the 59E59 Theaters in New York. It's four fifty p.m. Eastern, nine fifty British time. I'm calling regarding* Thirteen. *We love it and want to arrange a meeting with you in New York. Please call us at your earliest convenience at 212-555-5959, or just reply to the email I'll be sending shortly. Okay, look forward to chatting soon. Thank you, bye.*

Tarquin's jaw dropped "You sly fox! You *did* send it?"

A grin stretched her cheeks. "To an off-Broadway theatre, four months ago—the morning after I fainted."

"Blimey. Talk about picking yourself up after a fall. Well, I couldn't be happier for you. Congratulations, Lex!" He raised his glass in her honour.

"Let's *celebrate…*" Alex took the glass from his hand, leaving it on the table beside her drink. "…properly."

He rubbed his hands together. "Now you're talking! Champagne, it is. Moët or Veuve—"

Alex grabbed his belt, yanking him close and forcing his shoulders to bend towards her. She stretched up on tiptoes, her mouth delivering an unexpected answer.

He leaned forward in shock, but the urgency of her lips woke his senses. His hands rose to her face, cupping her cheeks and pulling her closer.

His kiss was warm and persistent but undemanding, waiting for Alex to decide where it would go next. This restraint was not what she expected, not after his banter with Harry. Tarquin was letting Alex take the lead; it was sexy and respectful and made her want him even more.

To her annoyance, it also made her think of Mark. She thought of their kisses, perfect in their impatience and unforgettable in their desperation, the type of kisses that inspire love songs, the type of kisses against which *all* kisses were measured—and measure, she did. Comparing Tarquin—available, caring, smitten Tarquin—to Mark, the man who spent more time away from her than *with* her, who took almost two years to introduce her to his family, who cheated on their anniversary. Who was being cruel and unfair now? What was she doing? Was Tarquin's only crime that he wasn't Mark? It didn't make this kiss wrong or unwanted. Mark had moved on; it was time she did, too.

She threw her arms around Tarquin's neck and slipped her tongue between his lips, exploring his mouth with abandon. He tasted spicy, the rye from his cocktail lingering on his tongue.

Tarquin responded to her invitation, kissing deeper, urgently, with a passion he could no longer fight. His hands slipped from her face to her waist, his fingers hitching her dress up her thighs.

She widened her legs and pushed closer. Following her cue, Tarquin's hands roamed to her hips, lifting her off the ground, the subtle shift up against him causing a gasp to escape her lips. His body…felt so damn *good.*

Tarquin reluctantly tore his mouth away, his breaths coming hard and fast. "Alex…are you sure?"

Pressed against his trousers, Alex could tell Tarquin was *very* sure.

She opened her eyes, taking him in. His smouldering gaze silently beckoned, like he hoped Alex wanted him as much as he wanted her. Patient, unselfish, empathetic Tarquin—never pressuring her, never living up to his wild, womanizing reputation. How her perception of him had changed since the day they met.

Catching her breath, a naughty smile lit up her face as she wrapped her legs around him. Her hand slipped down his neck and underneath the placket of his shirt. His pecs were firm with a trace of fine hair. Lucy had been bang on: *swipe right.* She stroked his chest, desperate to feel him, to break down the final barrier between them. Under her hand, his heart pounded as hard as hers, and in his eyes, she saw lust, but also tenderness…respect. For the first time in months, Alex didn't care about Mark. She didn't care if tonight was a one-off or something more. Feeling safe, desired, turned on…paired with tonight's successes—it was all too heady a cocktail to resist.

"I want you. I *only* want you—"

She claimed his mouth, kissing him recklessly, her tongue encouraging him, taunting him, rewarding him for waiting…*for her.*

He pushed her backwards against the floor-to-ceiling windows overlooking the Thames. Locked against the glass, she grasped the back of his neck, forcing his kiss deeper, showing him that she had no doubts. She needed him as much as he wanted her.

With each passing minute, their kisses became more bold and urgent. Hands explored, lips travelled, and the couple slipped to the floor, joining Tarquin's shirt. The hem of her dress flirted precariously high, coming close to giving the tourists snapping photos on Tower Bridge a souvenir worthy of a visit to a Soho peep show.

Tarquin breathlessly broke away, glancing past Alex at the glittering city below. He straightened the skirt of her dress, covering her thighs again. "Lex, snogging in public is totally hot, but…" He squeezed her hip, his eyes flitting over his shoulder.

"You've read my mind." Alex pulled him back to her mouth, their kiss dissolving into a mutual laugh. He picked her up and carried her to his bedroom.

# THIRTY-NINE

"We must be willing to get rid of the life we've planned, so as to have the life that is waiting for us." – Joseph Campbell

"I *told* you he'd be good," Lucy whispered through Alex's phone. "And sex releases endorphins and happy hormones—it's way better for you than jogging! *So*, how do you feel?"

Alex propped herself up in the once-crisp bed sheets. "Okay, but…odd."

"*Odd*? You just said last night was totally uninhibited."

"It was. But…" She yanked her fingers through her tangled hair. "…it's so real now. I'm naked in his bed, waiting for him to return from the shops to make me breakfast."

"Ooh, you lucky bitch."

"What? Breakfast in bed?"

"Yeah. *Love. It.* Harry makes me brekkie every weekend. Maybe it's a posh boy thing?" A smile raised Lucy's voice. "Either that, or I have him perfectly trained."

Alex giggled. "Tarq insisted on making me Belgian waffles.

I've never had a guy make me breakfast in bed before."

"I like that Tarquin didn't have anything in. Nothing on hand for breakfast proves that he wasn't expecting to sleep with you."

"He didn't have condoms, either."

"Fuck. *Lex, you didn't—*"

"Lucy, chill. I had some in my clutch, left over from New Year's." She pulled the duvet tighter. "But that's why it's awkward. We've crossed that line, and there's no going back. He's been inside me—I have intimate knowledge of his knob! That changes a friendship into something else."

Lucy laughed. "It does! You regretting it?"

"No. I wanted him last night. My God, Lucy…he can *kiss*. But this morning, it feels like…I don't know, like there's something missing."

"Oh, Lex…"

"I know Tarq cares for me—a lot. I don't doubt that for a second, and I *really* like him." She stared at a skateboard deck, painted with graffiti-style scenes of London, mounted on the wall. Tarquin had been speechless when Alex gave it to him last week. "We always have fun. I feel safe, appreciated, but sleeping together…I miss feeling that magical *something*."

"Okay, wait a minute. So, you *didn't* orgasm—?"

"I didn't say that! I mean…being *in love* with the person. Sex without love, for me, is…strange. It's like having hot chocolate but there's no marshmallows. I want marshmallows. I *need* marshmallows. Hot chocolate goes from good to out of this world."

Lucy muffled her laugh. "Sorry…don't want to wake Harry. Sex and love don't *have* to be a package deal, you know? Lex, this is all *new* to you, right? You might fall in love with him. It's not uncommon, you know, to develop feelings *after* you've shagged someone."

Alex shrugged. "I guess I'll have to sleep with him again to figure that one out."

"Well, it's only quarter to seven. Have fun *figuring that one out* before he leaves for work!" Lucy snickered. "I'm glad you're okay, though. I was worried I pushed you into something you weren't ready for."

"I was ready. I wouldn't have condoms in my purse if I wasn't…I'm moving on—*literally.*"

"Literally?"

"New York called last night."

"No shit!?"

"They want to meet me. Lucy, *Thirteen* might actually be happening over there."

"Fucking *amazing*! Lex on Broadway!" Lucy whooped. "Oh…! *Haribo, sorry.*" Her voice strayed from her phone. "Lex is headed for Broadway!"

Harry mumbled a raspy congrats in the background.

"Not Broadway, Lucy. Off-Broadway."

"But hang on…how long will you be gone?" Lucy sounded worried.

"Don't know yet—depends. If they actually go ahead with it, a few weeks, maybe?"

"But…what about all the buzz from last night, the theatre interest—can everything *here* wait?"

"I've been asking myself the same question. I *hope* it can. New York is…*well*, it's New York! I have to try."

"That's true." Lucy's voice still carried a hint of sadness.

"Maybe you and Harry could come over? We could finish the graphic novel, get our synopsis and pitch ready. You're overdue for a holiday—"

"Fuck, yeah! We're going to New York, Harry…" Lucy's voice trailed off.

"Hi, Lex." Harry laughed, stealing Lucy's phone. "Don't mind

Ms. Hardy. She's doing a happy dance around the bedroom. Let me call Dad, see if you can stay in his place in the West Village. As far as I know, he's not heading Stateside this summer."

"Oh, my God, Harry! That would be amazing! I would be in the middle of everything."

"No sweat. So…I couldn't help overhearing…you and Tarq, eh?"

"Yeah…is it weird?"

"No! Tarq hit the jackpot. You, on the other hand…"

"Harry!"

"I jest. I'm happy for you both."

"I mean, we only decided this morning to start dating…it's not like we're professing our love to each other yet…"

"One step at a time, Lex."

"So, New York…can you come?"

"We could definitely fly over for a week. I could take some meetings while I'm there, and Tarq can show us his favourite haunts. I think we might be in for several all-nighters if his war stories are to be believed."

Alex laughed. "Prepare yourself, Harry. What happens in New York, stays in New York."

Tarquin peeked around the doorjamb, a worried expression creasing his brow. "*Harry* knows?"

"Yep. The secret is out, and he's fine with it."

Tarquin's face warmed up into a wide grin, waking up his dimples. He sauntered into the room and sprawled across the duvet, his lips diving for Alex's neck.

"Harry, I've gotta go." She bit her lip. "Breakfast is ready. Tell Lucy I'll call later?"

His voice left the phone. "Lucy, Lex says she'll speak later." He chuckled. "Lucy gave me a thumbs-up and…"

Lucy's voice mumbled something in the background.

"She said 'good luck with your marshmallow experiment.' Yeah, I don't even want to know what *that* means..." Harry laughed.

Alex stifled a giggle as Tarquin kissed her ear. "Bye, Harry." She dropped the phone in the covers.

Tarquin skimmed a finger across her cheek. "Fancy some homemade waffles, real maple syrup, strawberries—" He leaned in for a peck, but Alex tugged him closer, slipping her tongue between his lips. He smiled into their kiss. "Someone's hungry, but not for waffles..."

"Did you get the whipped cream?"

"I did. Also, condoms."

"Call your assistant—Mr. Balfour's going to be late this morning."

# Forty

*Two weeks later*

The private-hire SUV lurched ahead in the drop-off queue outside the Royal Albert Hall. Alex finished emailing Lucy a revised section of graphic novel copy and grinned at Tarquin, sat beside her on the middle seat.

She clasped his hand, her eyes squinting in the late June sunlight as they skimmed down his tailored dark grey suit. "You look extra handsome tonight."

He kissed her temple and pulled back, admiring her slim, long white dress. "Just trying to make a good impression."

"You and me both." Alex exhaled heavily.

"Sunshine, you already have! You've sealed the deal." Tarquin's smile squinted his eyes. "Channel Four is in the bag."

"I hope so. Their TV development scheme is an *in*, but that's all it is." Alex picked at the beading on her new clutch. "There's no guarantee they'll take what I write, and as their guest, I need to make sure they see me as a good fit tonight—"

"You're a *great* fit: smart, talented…gorgeous." He nuzzled into her waves, inhaling the beachy scent of jasmine and amber left behind by her shampoo. "Only a showbiz idiot would think otherwise. Honestly, *these people…*" He huffed and leaned back, his eyes shifting to the window. His dimples slowly evaporated into a pout.

Alex tightened her grip of his hand. "Tarq, I meant it. We'll stay two hours, tops, okay? Then, I'm all yours until my flight tomorrow morning."

A sharp exhale left his lips. "What's this bloody thing called again?" He pulled a ticket from his jacket's inside pocket. "*A Celebration of British Television.* God, if *that* title is any reflection of how boring it's g—"

"We won't stay long." She let go of his hand. "You might surprise yourself—you might have fun."

"Hanging with self-absorbed C-list celebs?" He stuffed the ticket back in his pocket. "I knew I should've packed a flask—"

"I told you…you didn't have to come—"

"I *want* to support you, Lex…"

*Whining? Some support...* She rolled her eyes. "Well, why *are* you so pissy, then? Is it your mum? Was she invited tonight?"

"Now, there's a boner killer." He flung his head backwards on the seat, staring at the SUV's ceiling. "No, she wasn't."

Alex shook her head and looked away. The SUV slowed to a stop.

"Hey…" Tarquin pulled her in, kissing her cheek. "What am I like? I'm being a dick. I'm sorry."

"It's okay." She half-smiled. "I know you hate these things, but sometimes they're part of my job…sometimes I have to socialize with *these people…*"

"I know, it's just…I didn't want to share you tonight. Two weeks apart, Lex…? I'm going to miss you."

"I know. I'm going to miss you, too."

He left a kiss on her shoulder and glanced out the window. "Uh, why aren't we moving?" He leaned towards the driver. "Excuse me, mate, is there a problem?"

"Paparazzi at the backstage entrance," the driver replied, looking in his rearview mirror at Tarquin. "Someone up ahead just got ambushed from the looks of it."

Tarquin lowered his window and leaned outside. "Blimey." He blinked several times. "They're surrounding an accessible van. That's not cool."

Alex climbed across his lap and stuck her head out the window. Her stomach flip-flopped. "It's Niamh!"

"Who?"

"Mark's mum." She frowned.

The photographers, at least twenty or more, baited Mark and crowded closer.

"Mark, mate! Pose with our old mum!"

"Mrs. Keegan, you must be proud of your son? Give us a smile, eh?"

"Mark! Just need the one shot—hug your mum and girlfriend. Happy families, yeah?"

Face like thunder, Mark tried to shield Niamh's wheelchair from the swarm, but he was outnumbered. "Guys, come on, would ya back up! She can't move. Give her space. Please!"

Fallon appeared through the scrum, waving the pushy paps away. A few fans stormed the crush, including the notorious Daisy—no surprise there.

"Niamh must be here for Mark…for *Lairds*. He's introducing the salute to Scottish TV." Alex swallowed. "She's a sweetheart. She doesn't deserve this."

"Tabloid wankers…she looks frightened," said Tarquin. "Should…I help?"

Alex's mouth opened and closed, unable to find the words as

her past tugged at her heart.

Mark posed briefly with his mum and Fallon, giving the paparazzi what they demanded. Amidst a storm of flashes, Fallon beamed warmly as Niamh attempted a nervous grin. Not a hint of a smile graced Mark's face. Satisfied, the photographers cleared a path, allowing Mark to steer his mum into the hall's entrance.

"Lex, you okay?"

Alex retreated from the window and Tarquin's lap. "Yeah, everything's fine."

Tarquin smiled, pressing a gentle kiss into her hair, and closed the window.

"Tarq..." Alex leaned onto her date's chair and squeezed his arm, jolting him awake. "I'm going to pee myself if I don't get to the restroom."

The event's host bleated on and on about tax credits for TV productions.

"Make a run for it. Save yourself." Tarquin mimicked shooting himself in the head.

She chuckled quietly and snuck past, joining a wave of women with the same idea. Unfortunately, the restrooms at the Royal Albert Hall weren't large, and the famous Loggia boxes where Alex was seated shared toilet facilities with the extensive stalls section. The line snaking into the women's restroom was long and barely moving.

Alex popped open her clutch, took out her phone, and got lost in Freddie's non-stop backstage texts. He was there tonight with Simon volunteering as talent wranglers.

*Fuck me sideways. I'm wrangling bat-shit crazy, you know, that red-nosed car show host? He's drunk already!*

*Simon got the diva from Dance-Off. Hopefully she'll teach him some moves. Don't tell him I said that!*

Freddie and Simon, along with several of Freddie's BBC co-workers, were each assigned a TV star, and their task for the night was making sure that their 'talent' got from point A to point B during the program—"*celebrity babysitting*" was how Freddie described it. From his texts, he was the worst talent wrangler ever.

*Shit! I can't find him!*

*Idiot stole some bloke's disability scooter, found him doing doughnuts backstage!*

*They're trying to get it off him now. He wants to drive it away. Train wreck!*

Alex typed a response:

*You get all the excitement! I'm in the loo queue behind a barmaid from* Eastenders.

Three minutes passed. Alex didn't get a response or hear if the boozy presenter with the stolen scooter made a clean getaway. She hoped he did.

Dumping her phone in her clutch, she spied a small packet of chocolate Buttons: her emergency reserve. She tore it open and munched, oblivious to the mascara-coated glances coveting her rapidly disappearing chocolate stash.

Inching closer, the line dancing was non-stop: a step to the left and a slip to the right, allowing access to the sinks and mirrors. The loud roar of the hand dryers to Alex's immediate right overpowered polite conversations and a burst of dirty laughter. She stuffed the chocolate wrapper in her clutch and smiled, turning towards the hilarity.

*Shit! Fallon?!* She was with two friends, talking excitedly in her sing-songy Irish accent. With the drone of the dryers and background noise, Alex couldn't catch a word. At least they hadn't seen her.

A glint drew Alex's eye. *That's not...is it?*

The petite diamond ring from Mark's backpack—Niamh's ring was *there*...on Fallon's hand, sparkling under the pot lights as she waved it back and forth underneath a hand dryer. Alex's heart threatened to thrash through her ribs. She inhaled, but the sudden tightness of her chest didn't allow further breaths to depart her lips.

*Wait*... The ring was on Fallon's *right* hand.

Alex gasped for air and clarity as the dryers continued their thundering drone. *What are they saying? Damn! I can't hear anything!* Only three women stood between Alex and an empty stall. Figures, the line would speed up now.

The dryers' howling abruptly ceased.

"—story behind the ring." Fallon's friend placed her hand over her heart. "Oh, my God, Fal. It makes me want to cry."

*You want to cry?*

"I know, right?" Fallon stared at her hand. "I can't believe it's mine now."

The woman behind Alex nudged closer—so close her breath tickled Alex's neck. *Shit.* Alex stepped ahead, next in line for a free stall. Her eyes darted back over her shoulder.

Fallon beamed at her friends, unaware of Alex a few feet away. "Of course, I have to wear it on *this* hand, otherwi—"

"Uh, excuse me?" An elderly woman's voice invaded Alex's ears.

Alex squinted. *Otherwise? Go on!*

"Hello? Excuse me...if you're not going to use that stall, would you mind letting me go ahead of you? I have a urinary tract infection, and my doctor says that..."

*Fuck fuck fuck!* Alex's eyes widened at the close-talker complaining all over Fallon's story. She slipped sideways, waving UTI lady ahead, Alex's need to pee overtaken by the need to hear Fallon. *What came after 'otherwise'?*

Fallon tossed her hair over her shoulder and for the first time, clocked Alex. She dimmed her wide smile and nodded awkwardly, a flicker of sympathy in her eyes.

*Shit! Spotted!* Each second felt like an eternity. Alex froze on the spot, her legs heavy and uncooperative, like they were made of lead. She couldn't escape anyway; all the stalls were occupied.

Hiding the surprise guest star on her finger, Fallon turned away and followed her friends out the door.

Walking away from the restroom, Alex loitered outside the entrance to the Loggia boxes, hastily typing 'Mark Keegan engaged' into her phone's browser. A story date-stamped that evening popped up: *A Promise Spoken: Irish Star and First Love Set to Wed.*

*No!* Her knees started to buckle.

*Fresh from the set of* A Promise Unspoken*, the Dublin movie that rekindled their teenage romance, Mark Keegan and Fallon Delaney, both 26, are set to become co-stars in a real-life love story. Friends say the Irish lovebirds are secretly engaged. "Fallon and Mark are thrilled to be back together and aren't wasting any time," said a source close to the couple. "Expect an engagement to be announced before Mark leaves for Mexico in August to begin* Full Throttle 3*."*

"He proposed," Alex gasped quietly into her hand, tears welling up beneath her eyelashes as she took in new photos snapped at the hall's backstage entrance.

"Excuse us." Two couples squeezed past, making their way back into the hall.

Alex blinked repeatedly, swallowing her sadness. Now was not the time, nor the place. She couldn't let the Channel Four people see her like this—or Tarquin.

*Mark's no longer your concern. He isn't yours, Lex. YOU broke up with him.*

Alex drew a deep breath to calm herself; she felt more numb than angry. She walked through the doorway to the boxes and paused, her eyes locking on the stage. Mark was strolling up to the microphone and she stared, unable to look away. He began to introduce the Scottish TV segment, but Alex didn't hear a word he said.

*Mark's getting married. Mark's happy...without me.*

# FORTY-ONE

"Morning, Sunshine." Tarquin rubbed his sleepy eyes and smiled, catching Alex in his en suite's soaker tub. "Care for company?"

"Sure."

She shifted forward and Tarquin climbed over the tub's side, easing himself slowly into the warm bathwater. "I thought you were going to have a lie-in." He sat down behind Alex and stretched his legs out around hers.

"I did my packing instead."

He kissed the back of her head. "Want to talk about last night? You seemed…distracted—"

"Did I?" A Stormtrooper rubber duck bobbed past her elbow. "Sorry, I was just…annoyed it took so long to get back to you. I missed most of the show."

"Consider *that* a blessing." Tarquin pumped the bottle of body wash. "Thanks for not prolonging my agony."

"Agony?"

"Yeah." He lathered up his hands and slowly massaged Alex's shoulders. "You barely sat down before we made our excuses and left. And here I thought *I* was the one desperate for a steamy sesh between the sheets. Wow, Lex, last night was…"

She sighed quietly and submerged the rubber duck under the water.

"Sure you're okay?"

"I'm *fine*." She released the bath toy and stroked his thigh, feeling guilty for letting her past cloud their present. *Enough!*

"You know, I could change my plans…fly out next weekend instead of two weeks' time, be there for your birthday…"

"My birthday…well, *yeah*…" She smiled. "…but aren't you too busy—"

"I'll have to cancel some meetings, stack up a few conference calls…but what's more important than your birthday?" He squeezed her shoulders. "Can't have you celebrating turning twenty-five on your own."

"Can't have that!" Alex leaned back into him and giggled. "When Harry and Lucy arrive the week after, you guys can hang out while we finish our book."

"How hot is that? My girlfriend…creating graphic novels."

"You find that *hot*, you big nerd?"

"Can't you tell?" He pressed hard against her lower back as he groaned and kissed her neck. "Lex, while we're in New York…as a birthday present, I want to take you away for a long weekend. A beach—Bermuda, Virgin Islands, Barbados—wherever you want to go, as long as it's hot, romantic—" He gasped into her hair. "*Secluded*."

His offer was a kind one, but Alex hated roasting in the sun, and with work, the timing wasn't ideal. "Tarq…uh, isn't it a little *early* for romantic trips? We've only been dating two weeks—"

"Seventeen days—I've been keeping a tally." He washed away the soap from her shoulders with a cloth. "Lex, when you know, you know."

She blinked rapidly, her arms gliding under the surface, rippling the water. "Tarq…"

"*Quick*: name the Quality Street chocolates that you love and hate."

"What?"

"Just name them."

"I love the orange cream. I hate the toffee penny."

"I *despise* the orange cream!" he said gleefully.

"And?" Alex scrunched her nose.

"The key to a happy, compatible relationship is finding someone who likes all the Quality Street that you *hate*…you hate the toffee penny—my favourite—and I always leave your fave in the tin. See, we've passed the Quality Street test. Compatible as fuck."

Eyebrows raised, she looked over her shoulder.

Tarquin broke into a laugh. "Sorry! Just trying to lighten the mood! Do you really think I'd base our compatibility on what chocolates we like and dislike?"

Alex winced. Shame compatibility wasn't that simple, but after two weeks of dating, she felt uneasy discussing vacations or their future. "I really like you, Tarq, but I don't think I'm ready—"

"Lex, I don't want to hide things, not from you." He left a kiss in her hair. "I mentioned the holiday because I'm falling for you, but you knew that already, didn't you?"

She knew it; hearing it out loud made it real, though. "I thought you had a fear of…falling."

He hugged her from behind. "Look, I *get* it. I know it might take a while before you can reciprocate my feelings, and that's okay." He smiled. "Truth be told, I've had a bit of a head start. I spotted you on Harry's Facebook page a year back. When I found out you were The Girl Who Slayed the Dragon, I wanted to meet you: looks, brains, courage of conviction? Sign me up!"

Alex shifted out of his embrace to face him, unintentionally splashing water over the tub's side. "Dragon?"

"Olivia." He smirked. "When Harry broke off their engagement, he told me about her stealing your play, how you took her down in front of your mentor. Hearing that, I knew you were a bit special. Plus, *duh*—you're gorgeous."

"Tarq—"

He pulled her close so she straddled him. "Lex, don't be freaked out. I'm having a great time and want *whatever this is* to continue. Forget about the holiday, no pressure. We'll go another time, when you're ready, okay?"

"Okay…but don't think that I don't like being with you, Tarquin, because I do—I *really* like you…a lot, and I don't want to see anyone else…" She wrapped her arms around his neck.

"Good, because the last thing I want is to scare you off." He placed a gentle kiss on her lips.

She slipped a hand under the water and down between his thighs. "Does this feel like I'm scared?" Her mouth covered his, kissing him slowly, with intent.

Tarquin's hand swept down her back and squeezed her waist. He inhaled sharply as her hand found a rhythm between his legs. "Does this mean I can have your toffee penny?"

Alex bit her lip. "You can have more than that."

"What kind of a boyfriend lets his girlfriend board a seven-hour trans-Atlantic flight without a homemade breakfast?" Tarquin spooned golden batter into his professional-grade waffle maker as Alex, fresh from the bath and wearing just a bra and panties, sauntered into his kitchen.

She cuddled him from behind and softly kissed his back. "You spoil me." With a squeeze, she left him to it and raised herself up onto the counter across from him. She swung her legs from her perch, her eyes strolling down Tarquin's muscular bare back to his tight butt, clad in navy boxer briefs. "Tarq, I can't wait for you to join me in New York."

He closed the lid and turned around, grinning. Alex giggled. Tarquin was wearing his *May the Forks Be With You* apron she had bought for him—now he never cooked without it.

"See, Sunshine?" He pointed at his temple with the spatula. "My Jedi mind tricks worked like a charm this morning. Now, *you* want the next week to fly by at lightspeed, too." He joined her in a soft kiss. "Waffles will be ready in two minutes."

He stepped backwards, taking her in, and with a sigh, turned back to his culinary work in progress. Alex grabbed a piece of crispy bacon and dipped it in the maple syrup flooding her plate. She chewed, savouring the salty sweetness.

"Lex, when you get to the loft, remember to turn the air conditioning on straight away." Busy with his back to her, Tarquin cracked open a jar of blueberry compote. "It takes a while to cool with the twelve-foot ceilings." His phone on the counter vibrated against Alex's hip.

"I will." She looked down at the screen, her smile contorting into a twisted frown. "What the…hell? Is someone playing a joke?"

"Sorry?" Holding a melon, Tarquin looked over his shoulder.

Alex stared at the image. Her jaw dropped: two breasts straining through a wet bikini top, sent from a 646 area code…from Olivia Chadwick-Smythe.

"Why is Olivia sexting *you*?" She lifted the phone to show him. "Of all people!"

Tarquin dropped the fruit. "Fuck!"

"*Fuck* is right. Is THIS why you're always ignoring texts?"

"Lex…" Tarquin blinked rapidly, his fingers flying to his forehead. "It's not…*listen*, we…dated in New York—"

"*What*?!" She squeezed the phone.

"—but, it's over, has been for ages. She's trying to lure me back, but I'm not interested! I'm with *you* now." He reached for her hand.

Alex flinched, abandoning his phone. "I have a flight to catch." She scrambled off the counter.

"Lex!" Tarquin followed her through the living room to the bedroom. "Harry had just dumped her. She showed up in tears at my Manhattan flat. I couldn't just turn her away…"

"Ah, so *she's* the flatmate with benefits. Got it!" Alex stumbled into her jeans and threw a t-shirt over her head.

"It was nothing, Lex, we weren't hurting anyone."

"What about Harry?"

"He doesn't know. We only slept together a few times—"

"What's a few? Twice…? Every day with a Y in it?" She dug in her purse, her shaky hand resurfacing with a compact. She checked her face in its mirror. "Whatever. I don't fucking *care*. I'm so out of here. What is it with guys hiding the fucking truth! So sick of it." She snapped the compact closed and threw it in her bag.

"I didn't say anything because I didn't want to hurt *Harry*!"

"If you didn't want to hurt Harry, you should never have fucked his ex-fiancée."

"It's not like that…" he stammered. "Alex, she was mine *first*."

"Whatever." She stuffed her feet into a pair of wedge sandals.

"Me and Olivia, we were together as teenagers—*before* she dated Harry…and no, Harry never found out."

She stopped, mid-buckle. "Oh, you're fucking *kidding me*! *She's* the relationship at Eton?!"

"I met her at a cricket match nine years ago. I was seventeen, very sexually experienced and not after anything serious, but Olivia…changed all that."

"So, why didn't you tell Harry?"

"Lex…the girls we met, socialized with—they always preferred him over me. He was this sweet, blond tennis star. I was a skateboarding showoff with a bad faux hawk. Olivia was *mine*. I didn't want to lose her. So, I kept her a secret. It was easy to do—she went to Cheltenham Girls, ninety minutes away."

Alex shook her head and finished fastening her sandals.

"I got the train to see her every weekend, except one in November, thanks to Mum dragging me to a showbiz thing. Olivia went with friends to a school tennis tourney. Harry was there, representing Eton—he won, of course. They met at the banquet afterwards, and Harry was a goner. He texted me on the ride home, wouldn't shut up about her. He didn't know she was the 'girl from the village' I'd talked about. Sure enough, two days before Christmas, she dumped me and began reeling him in, playing hard to get. I told her we should come clean, but she wouldn't have it…" He followed Alex across the room to her open suitcase. "Olivia knew the score. If Harry knew that she was *the girl,* he wouldn't date her—the bro code, right? And I didn't say anything because he was completely love sick, acting like she was the one. By spring, they were the golden couple. Harry never found out that the girl who broke my heart was Olivia, or that the bloke who took Olivia's virginity wasn't him but me. The hating each other thing was an act to cover our tracks."

*Zzzzzzip.* Case closed, Alex stood up, shaking her head in disbelief.

The alarm on the waffle maker started to beep. Tarquin ignored it. "Olivia would have done anything to keep Harry—you know that better than *anyone*! And I love him like a brother, but even brotherly love has limits. The longer he was with her, the more determined *I* was not to tell him I'd slept with his future wife. It *had* to stay secret, or our friendship would have been toast…"

"Oh, bullshit! You're a coward! You could've said something

when he broke off their engagement. Sure, he would have been pissed, but he's *a guy*. He would've gotten over it—water under the bridge. But, no! She turns up in New York, damsel in distress…" She scoffed, yanking the extendable handle of her suitcase. "Right there, you crossed the line. You never fuck your best friend's ex."

Tarquin held his palms up, his posture conciliatory. "In New York, Olivia said she was serious about giving it another go—her and me. I felt flattered. She said we'd tell Harry when the time was right. It was good for a while…until Olivia landed some Wall Street wanker after a few weeks of us shacking up. She moved out, set up her charity. She played me like a bloody fiddle. That's what Olivia does, she *uses* people.…come on, Lex, you've seen her in action. You *know* what she's like!"

Alex stared at the floor.

"Then, these *titty texts* started out of the blue, a week after I moved back here." He huffed. "I'm actually the VICTIM here, Lex. I'm being *zombied*."

Alex didn't react.

"Zombieing…it's when an ex resurrects a relationship from the dead via text…"

"I know what it *is*, Tarquin." She turned away from him, checking her purse for her passport.

"Come on, this is crazy. I never cheated on her *or you*. Please. Don't leave like this…"

Alex tossed her laptop bag on her shoulder and pulled her suitcase along, leaving the bedroom. The smell of scorched waffle emanated from the kitchen.

He paced after her. "Look, I get it. You need some space. I'll call you in a few days—"

"No, you *don't* get it, Tarquin." She jabbed the elevator button and spun around. "Don't text, don't call, don't fly to New York. *We're done*. You *say* you love Harry like a brother? Well, I *really* do, and the difference between you and me is that I would *never* betray him."

He spun the ring on his thumb. "You're not going to tell him?"

"I don't know, but the truth will come out eventually. It always does."

"Seriously, he'll never trust me again. I could lose my job with Budgie—"

"Good-bye, Tarquin." She dragged her case into his elevator, closing the door on their relationship.

# Forty-Two

Standing on Tooley Street outside London Bridge station, Alex sent a text to Lucy before descending into the hellish heat of the Underground.

*Headed to Heathrow early. I finished with Tarq. Don't worry, I'm FINE. Getting on the Tube. Unreachable until Paddington. xo*

Twenty-five minutes later, Alex's phone erupted with text after text. She ran for the express train to Heathrow, hopping on as the doors slid closed. She plopped down on a seat inside the door, hurried breaths escaping her lips as she checked her phone.

Texts from Lucy, Tarquin, Lucy, Tarquin…

Alex had never been in such demand. What a mess.

She called Lucy—she answered on the first ring.

"You *really* okay? Your text sounded surprisingly okay."

"I am. My mascara was never in danger…"

"But…?" Lucy knew her best friend too well.

"I *liked* him, Lucy—a lot. He was funny and kind. He was *here*. Maybe that sounds like a stupid thing to list as a positive, but after Mark…"

"Shit, Lex, I'm sorry."

"We planned things and did them. Tarq said he wanted to fly over early for my birthday—have a weekend away. I bet he would have, too. How's that for a novelty? Booking a trip with your guy and following through with it. I bet in *time* I would have fallen in love with him…"

"So, what the hell happened? Had to be major."

"Is Harry with you?"

"No. I slept at mine last night. Why?"

"Harry's going to be upset."

"Well, yeah. That's the risk, right? When friends date friends."

"No, Lucy. This goes beyond that. Tarquin dated Olivia in New York."

"FUCK OFF?!"

Alex told Lucy everything.

"*Eww*! *Tarquin and Olivia*? I don't think Harry will care about *her*, but he'll be upset about Tarquin. He might overlook the teenage stuff, but hooking up with her again post-engagement? What best friend thinks *that's* okay?"

Alex winced. "Lucy, sorry. I'll be at Heathrow in five minutes and my phone's draining…"

"Don't worry, babe. I'll bring Harry up to speed. Call me when you're in the Big Apple, okay?"

"I will."

"God, what a way to start your trip, eh?"

# FORTY-THREE

*New York City, fourteen hours later*

The hazy, early evening sun stretched through the large windows of Budgie's three-bedroom loft in New York's West Village. Alex picked one of the smaller bedrooms, reserving the large king-sized suite for Lucy and Harry. She turned on the air conditioning, plugged in her dead phone, and started to fill the closet with her clothes.

Her phone came alive like it was possessed, buzzing and then switching to the *Sherlock* theme and then back to buzzing again.

"Shit. Okay, Lucy, I'm *coming*!" She hollered over her shoulder, leaving her wrap dress to swing from a wooden hanger in the sizeable closet. She ran around the bed and pounced on her phone, not stopping to read the texts, phone alerts, and FaceTime requests that battled for space on the screen.

She typed quickly and hit send: *Sorry! Phone died. Here safe.*

Lucy replied within seconds. *We're FaceTiming NOW.*

"Wait!" Alex shouted aloud. *Tarquin's escapades must have turned Harry's world upside down.* She didn't have time to dig out her iPad from her computer bag before the FaceTime request appeared, but it was from…Freddie?

"Lex!" Freddie looked so tiny on her phone's screen. His chest rose and fell like he had sprinted up the steep escalators at Angel Tube station. "Thank GOD. I can't hold it any longer."

Simon squeezed in from Freddie's left. Lucy was sat on an armrest. Harry was…missing.

"Where's Harry? Is he okay?"

Lucy nodded. "He's on his way back from Tarquin's."

Alex bit her nails. "Guys, what happened?"

"Lex!" Freddie leaned forward, hogging the entire screen. "Are you sitting down?" He was on the verge of hyperventilating.

She sat on the edge of the bare mattress. "Freddie, take a breath…you're scaring me—"

"Lex…" Simon yanked Freddie back. "New Year's—*it never happened.*"

Alex's brain had to backpedal. *New Year's…?* "What?"

"Mark didn't have sex with Fallon in Dublin!" Freddie yelled, bouncing up and down on Lucy's loveseat.

# FORTY-FOUR

Alex struggled to catch a breath, this emotional wallop sucking all the air from her lungs as time slowed to a crawl. "Wh-Wh-*What*?" Her eyes bore into her phone.

Lucy's smile ran riot across her face. "Simon overheard Fallon and Wink last night at the TV thing. It's true—Mark didn't cheat on you."

*Mark didn't cheat.* Lucy's words echoed in Alex's mind, overtaking the heart-pounding *thump-thump-thump* tormenting her ears. *Mark didn't cheat.* Three words she never imagined could be spoken, least of all by Lucy. A shaky hand rose to her mouth. "But how?"

Simon nodded. "The dancer I was wrangling last night was in makeup for ages. I was waiting in the hallway just across from a small greenroom, so, I did a Freddie—"

"Hey!" His fiancé scowled.

"And aren't you glad I did?" Simon squeezed Freddie's knee. "I've never been around so many celebs before, so I earwigged. I wanted to hand out a business card or two for the boutique and thought maybe—"

"Si, get on with it!" Freddie jittered like he had downed a dozen espressos.

"Anyway, I hear a girl with an Irish accent, and thought, *Shit, is that Fallon?* She's talking to a guy, loud voice, definitely American. I hear her laughing, glasses clinking—sounds like they're celebrating. The Yank congratulated her on a wonderful job—he used her name then, so I knew it was definitely Fallon. I thought he was talking about her movie or something, but then I heard him say '*Alex*' and '*New Year's*' so I moved closer to the door. Fallon thanked him—for everything—and called him Wink."

Simon caught his breath. "Wink then said something like, '*I told you, didn't I—you'd get it ALL doing things my way? I never expected losing the deadweight writer to be THAT easy...*'"

Alex sat open-mouthed.

Simon continued. "He said you getting wasted did them a huge favour, and I remember this part clear as day: '*Mousetrap snaps, girlfriend out of the picture.*' I couldn't believe my ears."

Wide-eyed, Alex slowly rocked back and forth. "Fuck! I got the feeling Wink resented me but..." Her voice faltered.

"I could strangle the bastard." Lucy's nostrils flared.

Simon scratched his beard. "It went on from there. Wink laughed about plying Mark with booze and offering him an E just gone midnight. Apparently by one-thirty in the morning, Mark was so trashed, he was barely standing—"

"Putty in Wink's hands," interrupted Freddie.

Alex stared at the screen, dazed. "But how...do you know that Mark didn't..."

"Fallon's rugby bloke left after you did, so she was free to 'look after' Mark." Simon shook his head. "I'll never forget what Fallon said: '*It was the best sex I've NEVER had.*' I didn't catch anything after that as my dancer came out of makeup and I had to escort her to the stage area."

Alex slumped in her chair. "It was all a lie…?"

"A complete setup by the sound of it," said Simon.

"Wait—does Mark know?" she asked.

"He does *now*!" said Freddie, his face filling the small screen once more. "I couldn't tell him last night because his mum was staying over, but when he came back from taking her to the airport, I sat him down with a full English and told him. Lex, he wept like a lost little boy. It broke my heart." Freddie sat back.

Simon shook his head. "I feel bad. I totally misjudged the guy."

"Me too," said Lucy.

Tears began to pool in Alex's eyes. She blinked quickly, halting their progress. "Where is he now?" Her voice broke.

"It took him a while to compose himself," said Freddie. "Then, he got PISSED. I'm talking, *Irish-temper-I'll-skin-you-alive* furious. He was pacing, swearing, muttering under his breath. Around nine tonight, he reached Fallon on her cell and told her he was coming over. I said to text when he was on his way back, but I haven't heard a peep since."

Simon tilted his head. "You okay, Lex? You look shaken. Aren't you…happy? Maybe now there's a chance…"

She dabbed at her eyes. "I'm *relieved* he didn't cheat, but it doesn't fix what was broken between Mark and me. He'd changed a lot. Besides, it's too late, anyway."

"Too late? Whatcha on about?" Freddie frowned.

"They're engaged."

Freddie burst out laughing. "No, they're not!"

"I saw the ring, Freds. Fallon was wearing it last night." Her sad eyes darted to her best friend. "Lucy, the one I told you about? His mum's ring?"

Lucy raised her eyebrows. "The backpack ring?"

Freddie scrunched up his nose. "Bullshit. Mark has *never* mentioned getting engaged!"

"See for yourself." Alex sighed. "Check the *Mail* website, their gossip column from last night."

Simon handed Freddie his phone. He tapped and scrolled the screen. "What? Okay, THAT question tops my list when I hear from him! You can't believe anything in these tabloids, Lex, you know that!"

She shrugged. "Freddie, it won't change anything."

"But do you *want* it to change things?" asked Simon.

"*Of course* she does." Freddie rolled his eyes. "She still loves him—"

"Freddie, stop—" Alex protested.

"The truth might change more than you think. The mood Mark was in, I was certain he was going to dump her!" said Freddie.

Alex shook her head. "He's been gone two hours? It's just past eleven p.m. there, right?"

"They've got a lot to discuss," said Simon.

"Or they're making up." Alex looked away.

Lucy smiled kindly. The lock on her front door clicked open. She leapt from the armrest and disappeared from the screen. Alex could hear Harry in the background.

Simon stood up. "You look shattered, mate. Have a seat." He walked off screen.

Harry dropped down beside Freddie and rubbed his eyes with the heel of his hands. Lucy reclaimed her spot on the armrest, and Simon pulled up a chair.

Harry waved at the screen. "Hey, Lex."

"How did it go?" she asked, Freddie's big announcement still sinking in.

Harry tugged his hand through his hair. "So, I saw Tarq. I can forgive the teenage relationship…I mean, he *did* date Olivia before me, so I'm the one who broke the so-called 'bro code'—although I had no clue *I* was breaking it." His eyebrows furrowed. "But sleeping with her *straight after* I ended our engagement? He crossed a massive line. Maybe down the road we might be able to laugh this off, but I doubt it…"

"What about his job?" asked Lucy.

"That's Dad's call, not mine. I don't think Tarq's extracurricular activities interfered with his job performance." He grimaced. "Lex, I'm so sorry…if I hadn't introduced you to him—"

"Harry, don't. I can't be with someone who would betray you. It's for the best. My heart…is still bruised, anyway."

Harry balled his hands into fists. "Fuck! I'm *so* pissed at him."

Freddie's mouth opened into a huge molar-exposing yawn. He slowly stood up, his head and shoulders disappearing from Alex's phone screen. "Si…time to go…let's get back, see if Mark's home."

Lucy stole Freddie's place on the loveseat and nuzzled into Harry, trying to cheer him up with soft kisses.

Freddie's face filled the screen. "Lex, text ya when I hear."

"Hear what?" asked Harry.

Freddie yawned again. "About Mark's convo with Fallon—she made it all up. Mark didn't cheat on Alex!"

Harry's eyes bulged. "What!?"

"I'll fill you in." Lucy's hand stroked Harry's loosened tie.

"I'm texting Lex as soon as I hear." Freddie looked pleased with himself.

"Freds, no rush. It's late for you. I'm gonna turn in…" Despite Alex's outward resolve, thoughts of Mark flooded her mind, pushing away Tarquin and everything else. She stifled a yawn. "I've been up since five a.m. London time—"

"'Nuff said." Lucy nodded. "After today, I think we'll all sleep like logs."

"Definitely." Alex smiled, thinking she would be lucky if she slept a wink.

# Forty-Five

*London suburbs*

Mark barged past Fallon into her small living room.

"Lovely to see you, too." Fallon shook her head and tightened the belt of her robe with a sharp tug.

He dropped onto her loveseat, his fingers yanking the zipper of his leather jacket. "Sit down."

"No kiss hello? Who pissed on your corn flakes?" Fallon crossed her arms and sat down beside him.

"I'm looking at her."

Fallon rolled her eyes. "Babe, chill. I told you already, I won't share any more childhood photos with the *Mail*—"

"This isn't about kiddie photos, Fal. This is about fucking honesty."

"When have I ever *not* been honest with you?"

"Try New Year's Eve." He pulled off his jacket, chucking it on the armrest. "Did we have sex in Dublin?"

She laughed. "You travelled over an hour to ask *that*! You already know the answer—"

"Do I? Last night a friend overheard you and Wink backstage—"

"So?"

"I know what you said. Do you want me to fucking repeat it? Does '*It was the best sex I've never had*' sound familiar?"

Her shoulders deflated. "Babe—"

"Why, Fal? Why would you do this to me? Why lie—"

"Mark—"

"What did Wink promise you, eh? In exchange for ruining my relationship with Alex? 'Cause I know you wouldn't just do something like this on a whim. He promised you *something*—that's what he does." He leaned in, his face reddening with rage. "TELL ME!"

Fallon flinched, keeping her voice low. "Mark, for fuck's sake. Settle. Down. You'll wake my flatmates."

Mark stared, refusing to relax. "Tell me—" He gritted his teeth.

"Okay, okay!" She straightened her robe. "Before you arrived at the read, Wink wanted to know my story. I told him you and I knew each other as teens, how we dated. I figured it might give me an in, and he seemed genuinely fascinated. He asked what acting jobs I had done and if I had representation. The timing was perfect; my agent and I had...parted ways, a while back. He offered to sign me right there—so straight after the read, I did."

"Without due diligence?" Mark shook his head. "That was stupid—"

"He seemed *nice*, okay?" She snatched a hand-rolled cigarette and a lighter from the table. "And *you* were signed with him. You seemed happy enough, joking around with him."

He crossed his arms, exhaling heavily.

"Anyway, that evening, after the reads with you went well, Wink took me out to a posh steak place, to celebrate signing me AND my first proper movie role—he told me that the job was mine, right then, said our chemistry was 'electric' and the director loved me. I was so happy, and he was so *nice*. We talked for hours. I told him how our families knew each other, and he blurted out that he was *worried* about you, about your *career*. He said you and Alex were having problems: she didn't understand the biz, was getting in the way…" Fallon lit the cigarette and inhaled slowly.

"*And…*" Eyes wide, his nod prodded Fallon to continue.

"I told him…I felt *bad* for her." She blew smoke away from Mark. "I *get* it. Kissing, sex scenes, lots of time apart—it's a big ask for any partner to be okay with all *that*. I remember exactly what he said next." Fallon adopted a convincing American accent: '*Mark could break America, Fallon. He's a special talent, but he's gonna throw it all away for some girl with issues.*'"

Mark scowled. "Go on…"

"He said Alex was manipulating you, had some weird hold over you. How she'd deliberately have 'anxiety issues' when you needed to focus, like before a big shoot or audition. How she'd show up on set sometimes, make a scene…"

"What a load of *shite*." Mark's eyes darkened. "*None* of that is true, you know."

"How was I to know that?" She inhaled deeply on her cigarette and tapped it into an ashtray. "So, he asked for my help…"

"And *that* wasn't an unprofessional red flag? You should have walked—"

"That's easy for you to say!" She sputtered, exhaling smoke. "You're the golden boy of Wink's client roster, in demand, working all the time. Some of us don't have it as good as you, okay?"

He waved her smoke away from his face. "Oh, come on—"

"NO!" She tucked her feet underneath her bum, leaning closer. "We *don't*, and you know what makes it worse? Some of us were *supposed* to do great things. Remember when we were fourteen? What those talent scouts said? *I* was destined to be a star: '*The Irish*

*Kate Winslet,*' they said. '*That Sinéad Delaney—a natural.*' I'd go home, watch *Titanic* for the millionth time, dreaming of my turn in Leo's arms, but *my* turn never came."

"We all slog through tough times—"

She pointed with her dwindling cigarette. "You want *tough*, Mark? Here's tough. My highlight reel, yeah? Until I met Wink, the best of Fallon Delaney boasted two tampon adverts, three low-budget Irish movies where I spent half my time naked on my back, and a few videogame voiceovers. So, unless you can compete with that, Mr. I'm-On-TV-Every-Week, then just shut the fuck up."

"Fal, you've only been at it for what, five years?" His voice softened. "You've only started."

"Yeah, started to lose hope. You have no *idea* what it's like. Stuck in Dublin, barely scraping by with my shit barista job, sleeping on my friend's sofa...I couldn't even afford new headshots."

He shook his head. "I've been there too. It doesn't excuse—"

"No, you haven't been *there*, walking away from the ONLY thing you *ever* wanted to do..." Surging towards the table, her fingers pounded the end of the cigarette into smithereens in an ashtray. "*You* never jacked in your dream. *I* did. Last November, I finally called it a day—it hit me: maybe, they're *right*. Maybe, I'm just not good enough. And there I was, filling out online applications for college nursing courses, when a friend emailed about the audition and chemistry read—with YOU of all people." She flung herself back into the sofa. "So, I went. One last kick at the can, nothing to lose, and I met Wink—"

"Who swooped in and saved the day. Hurrah!" Mark waved his hands sarcastically.

"He offered me a *lifeline*! He said he would go above and beyond to land me auditions, new roles, if I'd only help *him*—help YOU! And he's been good to his word."

"Christ, Fal..."

"It didn't seem like a big deal. After Alex and Duff left the party, Wink asked me to stay close to you, make sure you were drinking—a lot—and take you back to the hotel. No sex, no actual cheating required. We'd snap a few photos at the pub and make it look like something was going on then leave it to your drunken blackout and Alex's imagination to do the rest."

"So, you faked a bunch of photos? Made up shit to hurt a girl you didn't even know?"

"Mark, I'm sorry, okay? I'm *sorry*. I'm not a bad person." She picked at the ends of her hair. "I did what I had to do for my career—and yours. If I'd known Wink wasn't telling the truth, I wouldn't have gone through with it. I'm not that girl, babe. You *know* that. I don't break up couples. I don't do the dirty on other girls, it's not my style."

Mark scoffed. "Well, you did a bang-up job making it look like you did. The condom—"

"Was *Duff's*! We had sex before the party."

"You fucking thought of everything."

"Bollocks! I *really* liked him. I didn't shag him to conveniently plant a used condom for later! Jesus."

"Came in handy for your *improv* though, didn't it?" Mark looked away, shaking his head.

"You passed out on my bed. I took off your clothes and fell asleep beside you. I did what Wink suggested, nothing more."

"You acted your little heart out that morning. Poor Fal. *So* guilty. *So* upset about Duff finding out. *So* many tears…I'm such a MUG. I totally bought it. Maybe you really are the Irish Kate Winslet, after all…"

"Shut up, Mark, and stop playing the victim. You signed with Wink for a reason, too. I know he promised you higher profile roles, a bigger fanbase, right? His ambition matches yours—you're the most *driven* actor I know! It's almost scary."

"This conversation isn't about why *I* signed with Wink. It's about why *you* did, and the deal you made with him. I just never realized Alex was part of it." He scoffed. "That first day on set, you said you were happy for me—and her. Obviously, you didn't mean it."

"I did mean it. I *was* happy for you, and I liked Alex when I met her—I *really* did. I even told Wink early in the evening, she seemed really nice, not like he'd described her…but then she got *so* wasted, and that confirmed what Wink had told me: she was a *train wreck*, a distraction you didn't need."

"Oh, come on! You never cared about what this would do to me—or Alex." He stared her down. "You only cared what it could do for *you*."

"I was just trying to get my foot on the acting ladder—at last, get what I deserved…and maybe you got what you deserved, too. You're not blameless here, Mark. You never told Alex who I was or how long we dated." She sighed. "Not being honest with your girlfriend about what we had…how *good* it was? That's on you, lover."

"I had my reasons." Mark shrugged.

"Moving the honesty goalposts again, eh?"

"You? Lecturing me on *honesty*? That's rich, now that I know our hookup in Manchester—*our relationship…*grew from this lie…" Mark got up, grabbing his jacket.

"Babe, wait." Fallon clasped his hand, her diamond ring glinting in the low light. "Don't leave tonight. Please? It feels like old times, right? Going to bed *angry* with each other…let me try to make it up to you…"

She tugged at the belt of her robe, letting it slip from her shoulders.

"Not this time, Fallon." Mark shook his head, putting on his jacket.

# Forty-Six

*New York City, next morning*

An incoming FaceTime alert woke Alex up. She squinted at the tablet face down in the sheets and flipped it over: ten past eleven…Freddie…

"Hello?" she moaned into a pillow.

"Good morning, Sparkly Girl." Freddie beamed in the July 1st sunshine from the rooftop deck of his Archway flat.

"Eurgh. I'm hardly sparkly. I feel crap. Barely slept."

"Lex, I'm sorry. I held off and held off, but it's almost quarter after four here, and the chippie closes at six."

"That's…two hours away, and it's not like you have far to go—it's downstairs."

"Yeah, but I have lots of juicy goss!" He popped open a bag of cheese and onion crisps.

Simon, a cup of green tea in his hand, pulled up a patio chair beside Freddie. "Hey, gorgeous. Thanks for the kombucha home-brew kit. It's brilliant!"

"Hey, Si. Happy Birthday! I hope Freddie was joking about

fish and chips tonight. A veggie sausage doesn't exactly scream happy thirty-sixth, does it?"

"That's why I made a reservation at the Chiltern Firehouse."

"And that's why I'm eating crisps *now* and chips when I'm done talking to you...grilled cauliflower hearts? Gross!" Freddie took a deep breath. "So...are you sitting comfortably?"

"You can see for yourself, Freds. I'm in bed."

"Start as you mean to go on, lady. Just lie back and think of Keegs."

"If you're going to goof around—"

"Don't pretend you haven't gone there in your head—I saw your face yesterday. You can't pretend with me...actually, you won't have to pretend *at all.* Put away your battery-operated boyfriend, Lex." He stuffed a handful of crisps in his mouth.

"Freddie!" Alex sat up.

He took a deep breath. "So, Mark and I spoke this morning, and he told me *everything...*"

And Freddie told Alex everything...

Simon adjusted his sunglasses. "Wink's plan went off like a well-rehearsed play."

Alex covered her face with a pillow. "Argh! I completely fell for those photos, Mark being upset about the used condom—all of it. Well, at least I know everything..."

"Actually, you don't," said Freddie.

"I don't?" Alex flipped the pillow behind her.

"You don't know about Manchester." Freddie munched his last crisp. "Wink was up to his dirty tricks again during *Constellations*. He told the tabloids about Mark and Fallon's teenage relationship. He also hinted that *maybe* the onstage romance in *Constellations* was becoming hot and heavy backstage, too. Everyone loves a showmance..."

Alex crossed her arms over her t-shirt. *Not everyone!*

"…even better if it's first loves reuniting and falling for each other as adults."

Simon waved away a wasp. "People love that shit, including producers and directors. I bet they'd cast Mark and Fallon more often if they're all over the press and social media, and guess whose agent commission would be quids in? Wanky Winky."

"What a dick. He's such a manipulative asshole." Alex sneered.

"To make his showmance story look real, Wink encouraged Fallon to hang out with Mark in Manchester—go for dinner, drinks. She was up for it." Freddie shrugged. "Why wouldn't she be? Getting noticed by the press, casting agents, directors, and she could do it guilt-free. A week earlier, she'd dumped Duff—get this, she caught *him* cheating!"

Alex smirked. "Karma."

"But Mark was being as sociable as a rock." Freddie tore open a Curly Wurly chocolate bar. "He missed you, Lex, terribly, and I think the emotions portrayed in *Constellations* weren't helping. After each day's rehearsals, he would disappear to his hotel room—alone. I know, 'cause he'd call me, miserable—he'd sad-FaceTime me. I even spotted a framed photo of you two behind him," Freddie mumbled, his mouth full of chocolate-coated caramel.

"Really?" Alex sank back into the pillows.

"Mark told me Wink pulled him aside in early March, said *Constellations* ticket sales were lagging. He found out later that Wink was bloody lying—the play's run was practically sold out! Anyway, Wink said they needed to drum up interest to sell tickets, and if Mark got papped with Fallon, it might do the trick. You know Mark—bloody workaholic—his play *had* to be successful, and he felt like he owed Wink for his damage control on the *Promise* set back in January. So, he went along with it. Mark thought he had nothing to lose because he had already lost you."

Simon jumped in. “And Wink tipped off the paps, so they caught them shopping, getting cosy in bars around Manchester…it looked bloody real, and then one day, it was.”

Alex took a deep breath.

Freddie sighed. “The New Year’s shag never happened but in April—Fallon got her claws in.”

Alex closed her eyes.

Freddie glanced at Simon, who nodded to his fiancé to keep going. “It was a relationship of convenience, Lex—he didn’t love her. He told me that this morning. They were both on the rebound. By mid-April, they were already over, but Wink had them agree to keep up appearances until *after* the January release of *A Promise Unspoken*—to sell tickets, build up tabloid buzz.”

Her eyes popped open. “Hang on…so, the past three months was all a PR stunt?”

“Yep, they were under my nose and even fooled *me*,” said Freddie.

She stared at her tablet. “They were only *really* together for a month?”

“Not even—two weeks, Lex! And all the photos together? All staged.”

“Seriously? Even Florida…the beach?”

“Yep! All for the camera, darling. But Lex, they weren’t even *in* Florida! Mark and Fallon were in LA meeting casting directors, that beach was a short drive away! Wink must’ve *told* Fallon to tag it as Florida, and before you ask, they stayed in separate rooms the entire trip.”

“So, they’re not engaged…”

“Oh, *God,* no!” Freddie swigged from a can of cola. “That gossip piece in the *Mail*—fed to them by Wink.”

“But Fallon has Niamh’s ring…?”

“She does, but it’s not an *engagement* ring! Mark explained everything: it's a bloody Delaney family heirloom. Fallon's mum died five years ago, left Niamh the ring in her will, but Niamh always thought Fallon should have it. She asked Mark to get it repaired and polished last summer so she could send it to Fallon. He was just bringing it back to Dublin for his mum when you found it."

"Oh, God. I got it so wrong." She hid her face in her hands. "So, he wasn't planning to propose to me..."

"Mark wasn't about to propose to *anyone*, not with that ring, anyway." Freddie stretched back in his chair. "He said he's done with Fallon and their fake relationship bullshit, and he's going to read Wink the riot act. So, darling...bloody brilliant, right? No New Year's shag, no engagement—nothing to stop you taking him back!"

"I can't, Freds." Alex sighed. "Mark's married to his *acting*. His life's a whirlwind, and he still works like a madman, all in the public eye. None of that's good for my anxiety."

"But you haven't had a panic attack in months, and you would know how to handle his absences better now—"

"It doesn't matter. Mark's lifestyle is not my idea of a healthy long-term relationship. It just isn't. Besides, the stability I hoped I'd find with Mark, I've found on my own. I don't need a *guy* to save me—I can save myself." She shrugged at her friends on the other side of the ocean. "I'm sorry. I know you were hoping for a different answer—"

"But you love him."

"Sometimes love isn't enough, Freds."

Freddie looked like he had been slapped.

Simon stepped in. "Well, none of us will see Mark for a while. He doesn't have to report to Mexico for *Throttle* until August, so he's staying with his mum. He's on a strict diet and workout regime for the film, said he needs to focus and get his head straight."

"I guess, yeah, if he's going to compete with The Rock," said

Alex.

“Mark’s trainer gave him a new nickname—The Pebble.” Freddie raised an eyebrow.

“Oh, jeez.” Alex winced. “I bet he hates it.”

“Yeah! He does.” Freddie snickered. “So, lady…shifting subjects slightly—when’s the last time you had *two* gorgeous men spend the night?”

“*What*?! Never!”

“Get the groceries in, darling! Si and I are Big Apple-bound. We’re coming over next week for your birthday.”

“Really?” Alex’s first grin of the morning lit up her face. “What about work? Can you afford it?”

“My boss won’t even know I’m missing, so *fuck him.* Si has a trillion air miles from flying to Montréal, and Harry said we can bunk in that loft you’re hogging.”

“Hey, the more, the merrier!” Alex grinned.

“Ah, NYC! For reals.” Freddie kissed Simon’s cheek. “We’re also swinging by Montréal on the way home. Get this, Lex: I’m dragging Si to his first comic con.”

“And I’m dragging Freds to meet my parents—properly—as my fiancé.” Simon nodded.

“I wonder what Simon’s dreading more…” Freddie’s cheeks couldn’t hold back his grin.

# FORTY-SEVEN

The bounce of Alex's knee, hidden underneath the hem of her skirt, was out of sight from Laurel Rodriguez, the artistic director of the 59E59 Theaters. This woman held *Thirteen*'s off-Broadway fate in her hands as she flicked through the manuscript. Laurel paused, reading a scene for a few minutes, and then continued her tour through the pages. *Flip, flip, flip.* Eyes glued to each page turn, Alex's knee bounced faster.

Laurel slapped the manuscript closed and removed her glasses. "Well…"

Holding her breath, Alex met Laurel's eyes.

"*Thirteen* is unlike anything we've staged before…the time travel aspect…"

*And…!* Alex's heartbeat rose to her throat.

"Is it true that your grandmother was the inspiration?"

"Yes!" She exhaled with a shaky grin. "She was a dancer, an actress in Manchester during the fifties. She's quite the character."

Laurel nodded. "I can tell! Well, *Thirteen* is heartbreaking and inspiring, a beautiful story of love and redemption. I have to say, Alex, it's perfect for our 'Brits Off-Broadway' season next year. I think New York audiences will really enjoy it."

Alex's eyes widened, matching her smile.

"So, our Brits season happens April through July. For *Thirteen*, I'd like to propose a run of three weeks—probably late May into June."

*It's all happening!* "Great!" Alex bounced to the edge of her chair.

"We can offer you the going rate for an off-Broadway debut. Peggy's typing up your formal offer now. It will include royalty rates as well as a breakdown of the pre-production payment schedule—our theatre prides itself on paying the playwright for time spent during meetings, design consults, casting sessions, readings, and rehearsals. I'm sure you'll find it fair."

Alex nodded. *Wait till I tell Dad—and Joan!*

"Take a few days to consider our offer. Let me know, say…" Laurel peered through her glasses at her *Hamilton* wall calendar. "…a week from now, Monday, July 9th?"

"That would be perfect. Thank you!" Alex's cheeks ached. *What's to consider? My play performed HERE…in a 195-seat theatre just steps from Central Park!* She wanted to scream *YES* from the top of the Empire State Building but swallowed her excitement. The week would allow her time to meet with an agent and find out whether the theatre's offer accurately compensated her work. *Thirteen* was her baby—there was no way she was going to place it into the bathwater without checking the temperature first.

"Wonderful. Be sure to pick up the envelope from Peggy before you go." Laurel stood up, extending her hand. "Thanks for trusting *Thirteen* to us, Alex. I'll speak to you next week."

"Thanks, Laurel." Alex shook the artistic director's hand and left the office with a grin that shone so bright, only the lights of Times Square could rival it.

# Forty-Eight

*Four days later*

"You sure you can't join us for a birthday bunk off?" Simon pulled several American bills from his wallet to pay the waitress.

"Yeah, c'mon, Lex! Say hi to Lady Liberty with us." Freddie set his fork down on his empty breakfast plate. Just fifteen minutes earlier, it was heaped with heuvos rancheros.

"I wish, but I have to finish edits on *Suffragettes* and send them to the Lyric Hammersmith before noon, so I'm under the gun." She licked maple syrup off her thumb. "Lucy said she'd FaceTime me after that."

"Best leave you to it." Simon paid the bill and stood up from the bench.

They headed outside into the sunny sauna on Gansevoort Street.

"Thanks for breakfast and my present." Alex pointed at her summery dress with its thin straps and star print. "I *love* my Simon Desjardins original!"

Simon beamed. "I just hope the shop on the Bowery likes my

designs as much as you do."

"What time you headed there?" asked Alex.

"Meeting's at four." Simon put on his sunglasses. "I'll pop back and grab my designs around half three."

"Okay." She nodded. "You know where you're headed?"

Simon pointed past Freddie. "Yeah, that way, give or take. It's been ten years since I've been here, but it'll come back to me."

"Well, if you need anything or get lost, text me, okay?"

"Oh, I plan to get *very* lost," said Freddie. "There's no better way to get under the skin of a new city, especially one with mega pretzels beckoning from every corner." He squinted through his camera. "Ooh, and that Shake Shack place. Food hug!"

Alex raised her eyebrows at Si and mouthed, "Good luck."

Simon chuckled, steering a camera-wielding Freddie towards Washington Street. "Cheers, Lex!"

Alex broke out into a light jog back to the loft. With only two and a half hours until her deadline, every minute counted.

A click of her finger—send. The edits on *Suffragettes* zoomed across the Atlantic Ocean with five minutes to spare. Alex pushed her chair back and stretched. If the Lyric Hammersmith approved these rewrites, the play could be in front of London audiences late next year.

A FaceTime trill on her tablet interrupted her reverie. *Right on time, Lucy.* Alex's eyes lazily left her laptop, landing on her iPad.

*Mark Keegan would like to FaceTime.*

*WHAT? Oh, God!* Alex flinched.

She sat up straight, licked her lips, and ran her fingers through her hair. In the five days since Mark's New Year's acquittal, she'd half-expected a text or email from him. Just *something* to soothe the hurt, make amends, but nothing came…until now.

*Breathe, Alex. Breathe!*

She leaned away from her tablet. Time to yank the reins. Her heart was galloping full speed ahead in a direction that felt familiar for all the wrong reasons. She would always love Mark, but she couldn't *be* with him. Their lives were like pieces from different puzzles, impossible to fit together. She knew that; her heart bore the scars.

Ignoring the call wouldn't erase the questions that were gnawing away at her. *Fuck it.* She grabbed the tablet and hit accept.

Niamh popped on screen, sat in her wheelchair in her bungalow's conservatory.

*Oh!* Alex exhaled, disappointment and relief leaving her lungs. Mark's mum smiled, her eyes crinkling in the corners—just like her son's. *Damn.* Had Mark put her up to this? Why else would *she* call—on her son's tablet?

"Alex! Happy twenty-fifth birthday."

"Thanks, Niamh. How are you?"

"I'm good, love. You look well."

Alex's foot jittered. What to say next? *Ugh.* "Yeah…I guess New York City agrees with me."

"Oh, you're not in London?"

*Hmm.* So, maybe Freddie didn't tell Mark she was in New York? Or maybe he did, and Mark just didn't tell his mum? *Wait…Why do I care?* Mark's absolution didn't change why she had left him. *Nothing has changed, Alex! Remember that!*

"No. I'm working here for a few months."

"Are you staying in a safe area?"

"I am. The neighbourhood's nice, lots of cafés, dogs…trees."

"Good. Can't be too careful."

"That's true." Alex nodded, the crumbs of this conversation feeding the butterflies in her stomach. Niamh and Alex may have only known each other for four months before 'the shag that didn't happen', but they had always talked about things that mattered. They didn't 'do' stilted casual chat. It certainly didn't help that two massive questions hung over every word—was Mark listening in? And *why* was she calling? Best to play it safe. "How has your summer been, Niamh?"

"It's been pouring, love, but the sun finally found us five days ago. It's been lovely for Mark."

Alex took a deep breath as her eyebrows tensed along with her shoulders. What to say to that? A soft smile spoke for her while she searched for words. The cars on the street below were the only sounds passing through her tablet's microphone.

Niamh grinned warmly, but her eyes bore through the screen as if she was trying to get a sense of how Alex was really feeling.

"Mark's not here, love. Sorry, I should've said straight away—my tablet broke, so he gave me his." Niamh pulled her cardigan over her shoulders. "He doesn't know I'm calling."

Her words didn't bring relief. They actually made the tumbling in Alex's stomach turn into a full-on gymnastics routine.

"There have been so many times I wanted to reach out to you..." Niamh's smile slipped away. "...but Mark made me swear not to tell you everything that's gone on."

*Everything?* Alex's brows creased. "Sorry?"

"Mark experienced loss at a young age, and there were times when I feared that I had lost my sweet, happy-go-lucky little boy. He would go to a dark place, sometimes...become sullen, angry with everyone. I think part of him to this day blames himself for what happened..." Niamh took a deep breath. "Oh, I've probably said too much."

*Huh?* "Sorry, Niamh, but...I don't understand."

His mum bowed her head, remaining silent. Awkward times a thousand. Alex threw out the first thing that popped into her mind.

"I'm sorry I didn't call to say good-bye."

Niamh looked up, kindness in her eyes. "Oh, love, us Keegans hold on to the hellos, not the good-byes…"

Alex would never forget *their* first hello… The emotions of that day were imprinted on her heart: the panic over losing Niamh's house key, the relief of finding it, the fear of meeting Mark's family and the joy of discovering that—like Mark—his loved ones were friendly, kind, and hospitable.

Despite it being *her* birthday, Niamh had made Alex a chocolate biscuit cake and asked questions about her playwriting, her family in Manchester, and the flat she shared with Mark. She listened intently and praised Alex for her triumphs, both personal and professional, and she wasn't territorial like Devin's mother. When Alex held Mark's hand or met his eyes with a loving smile, Niamh beamed, nodding her approval. During that three-day weekend, Mark's mum showed more interest in Alex than her own mother had done during her three years in London.

But the warmth of Mark's sister did more than put Alex at ease that visit: it changed everything. Grace shared emotional stories about her engagement and wedding, and while Mark and their mum were in the kitchen, Rhys was in the bathroom, she leaned in with a cheeky, conspiratorial smile. "When *your* time comes, Fappy will propose with Mum's ring," she whispered.

*Your time?*

Unlike the rest of the sentence leaving Grace's mouth, those two words lit up Alex's brain like a blinding camera flash, refusing to fade. A gentle nudge of Grace's elbow diffused their brightness, dropping Alex back into the conversation, but she had missed most of the ring's description, her ears only picking up "…Beatles lyrics engraved inside the white gold band."*The ring I just saw in Mark's backpack—MUST be it!*

Back then it had all matched up—or so Alex had thought.

Now, almost a year later, sat here talking through the tablet screen with Niamh, the memory made her feel silly and embarrassed: the ring Grace gushed about wasn't the ring she had found in the backpack after all.

"Since the day we met, you've always felt like part of our family." Niamh's eyes didn't waver. "You know it's not my way to interfere but—"

"Niamh—"

"Mark hasn't been completely honest with you. You two need to talk…if there's any hope of moving on and being friends again. I know my boy owes you that much, love."

*Being friends with Mark.* Alex wasn't sure she could be. Seeing him with whomever he happened to be dating at the time would be a constant reminder of what would never be. Sometimes, the best way to heal and move on was to remain strangers.

"Niamh, I don't mean to be rude, but I *have* moved on. My plays are in demand. I'm working here until the end of summer. And to be fair, Mark's moved on, too. I appreciate what you're saying, but…I think talking will just stir up a lot of stuff that's better left in the past." A pang squeezed her heart. "I'm sorry."

Niamh nodded, resigned. "I understand."

The *Sherlock* theme drowned her out.

"Is that your phone, love? You ought to get that." Niamh smiled. "And Mark will be home from the gym soon."

Alex picked it up off the desk. "Oh, it's London. Sorry, Niamh. I have to go. Thank you for the birthday wishes. It was lovely seeing you again."

"Take care, darling." Niamh waved and the tablet went black.

Alex accepted the call. "Hello?"

"Good afternoon, Alex. It's Sue at the Lyric Hammersmith calling to confirm receipt of the final *Suffragettes* edits. Is now a good time to talk?"

By three-thirty p.m., Alex was nose deep in edits for Lucy's graphic novel. She welcomed the work: it was fun and challenging, and a distraction from Niamh's strange call.

A key clicked the lock. Her eyes didn't leave her laptop screen. "How was the sightsee—"

"SURPRISE!" Freddie and Simon burst into the loft. "The party starts NOW!"

Alex jolted in her chair and spun around so quickly, she almost flew off.

Freddie smirked in the doorway, cradling a large box of Sprinkles cupcakes in his skinny arms. Simon filled the space behind him with a bouquet of twenty-five red balloons bobbing around his head.

"What about your meeting?" Wide-eyed and giggly, Alex leapt out of her chair towards the couple.

Simon shrugged. "I fibbed—it's Monday morning."

"You're sneaky!" Alex laughed. "But I love it!"

"Not so fast…" Freddie shifted the cupcake box out of her reach, tossing his hair from his eyes.

He walked in, and Simon followed, wrestling the rambunctious balloons through the doorway, revealing…Lucy and Harry. Tied to the handle of Lucy's case, a foil Paddington Bear balloon waved in their wake.

"No way!" Alex did a happy dance on the spot and threw her arms wide, gathering Lucy and Harry into a group hug.

Lucy beamed. "Tricked ya!" She squeezed her best friend. "You only turn twenty-five once. There was no fucking way I'd miss it."

"Happy Birthday, Lex." Harry kissed her on the cheek. "We're a week early—"

"I don't mind!" Her eyes strayed to Freddie, lifting the lid to the cupcake box. "I'm happy you're here!" Her smile softened, allowing a shaky laugh to escape.

"You...sure?" Lucy pulled back slightly. "You preoccupied with something? Besides those chocolate cupcakes..."

Alex sunk slightly. "Mark's mum called."

Lucy's face pinched. "Why?"

"What?" Freddie mumbled through a bite of cupcake. "You talked to *Mark*?"

"No, he wasn't there. Was still weird, though. Niamh said something about Mark not being completely honest with me. What's that about?"

"Fuck." Lucy threw her hands in the air. "You don't need that. Not on your birthday."

"Do *you* know?" Alex turned to Freddie, who was licking peanut butter frosting off his fingers.

He shrugged. "Got me. You gonna call him?"

"No. Why would I do that—"

"Here's a little birthday advice, Sparkly Girl." Freddie placed the half-eaten cupcake back in the box. "Stop listening to your head. Listen to your heart."

# FORTY-NINE

*Three days later*

The bronze statue of Prometheus, reclining in the fountains of the sunken plaza of Rockefeller Center, stared over Lucy's shoulder. "It's not every day we get treated to lunch by an off-Broadway playwright. I could get used to this." She grinned into the July sunshine, fanning herself with a Rock Center Cafe menu.

"To Alex's first New York production!" Harry raised his sweaty beer, inviting his friends to join his toast.

"London's loss is New York's gain!" Freddie clinked glasses with Simon, Lucy, and Alex. "I'm gonna miss you, darling." He raised his voice, competing with the strong lungs of a crying baby two tables away.

Alex sipped her cola. "I'm not moving permanently. I'm just staying a bit longer for pre-production. Most stuff will be taken care of during the next two months while I'm here, and then I'll come *back* next year, a month before *Thirteen* is staged, to help with the rest."

Harry leaned across the table. "Lex, Dad says the loft's vacant until November, so don't rush back—"

"Don't say that." Freddie stuck out his bottom lip. "She'll never come home."

"I will." She elbowed Freddie. "London will just have to wait a little longer!" She turned to Harry. "I'll have to find something special for Budgie to thank him." She put on her sunglasses. "So, guys, how did *your* meetings go?"

Simon grinned. "They loved my designs—they ordered two of the five dresses I presented."

"Oh, Si!" Alex squeezed his arm.

"Mine went brilliantly, too," said Harry.

"Sorry—*what*?" Freddie squinted, cocking an ear towards Harry. He side-eyed the baby.

Harry raised his voice. "The property at West 11$^{th}$ and Greenwich has good bones, the potential for a rooftop terrace. I think Bespoke 2.0 has found its American home—"

The table erupted with a chorus of "That's amazing, Si!" "Congrats, Harry!"

Alex smiled, happy that her friends had such amazing news to share, too.

The baby's wailing grew louder. "Please!" Freddie threw his hands in the air. "Would *someone* give that kid a boob…"

"Someone's hangry, and I don't mean *that* table's baby." Lucy snickered.

The exhausted-looking hipster parents paid their bill and whisked away their red-faced infant. They passed two servers, carrying enough food to feed Alex's group twice over.

"These portions!" Freddie's eyes bulged as his meal was placed in front of him. "They're a gift from God—*God bless America*!" Freddie swiveled this plate, stacked high with a Black Angus short rib burger dressed with sharp cheddar and smoked bacon. It was kept company by a silver cup overflowing with golden French fries.

"Thank goodness we're flying to Montréal tomorrow." Simon stared at his fiancé's plate. "Freddie's forgotten what a vegetable looks like." He glanced across the table. "And no, Lucy, ketchup is *not* a vegetable."

She curled her lip, unscrewed the ketchup, and smacked a massive blob on her fries.

Freddie pointed a fry at no one in particular. "I tried being veggie." He looked at Simon. "*I did*—for you, for over a year—but given the choice between meat sweats or veggie shits, I'm picking food with a face every time. I gotta be me, Si." His eyes slid sideways to Alex's plate. "That penne pasta looks amazing, Lex. I'd Instagram it immediately if I were you."

"No, you go for it, Freds. It will look better on your feed."

"So, what happens to your spot in that TV development scheme back home?" asked Harry.

"I had to drop out." She leaned out of Freddie's way so he could photograph her lunch. "It's happening in two weeks."

"Too many writing commitments…nice problem to have." Harry bit into his Italian panino.

"Don't I know it."

"*Suffragettes* back home, *Thirteen* off-Broadway—I told you, didn't I?" Lucy's lips hovered over a forkful of fries. "I knew it would be just a matter of time, and that silly quote, *you can't make a living in the theatre*, or whatever the fuck it was—that Robert whatshisname can bite me. He never met my bezzie mate."

Alex swallowed a mouthful of tomato-y pasta. "I've got a long way to go before I can diss Robert Anderson. Think about it: I'm still bunking at Tom and Naomi's, and relying on Budgie's kindness over here, but yeah, at least people are returning my calls again. It's a good feeling, but you know what I want to do more than anything else?"

Lucy shook her head, her mouth full of ketchup-drenched fries.

Freddie rolled his eyes. "Please don't say a musical."

Alex smiled. "Finish our graphic novel. A few more all-day sessions and I think it will be ready to shop around."

"Watch out, world! Lex and Lucy are takin' over!" Lucy's raised cocktail was met by clinking glasses around the table.

# FIFTY

*Three days later*

"Thank fuck we're not sending it out tomorrow," said Lucy.

"Why?" Alex typed 'Proposal' in the subject line of a new email.

"*Hello*? Friday the 13th? There's no way in hell I'd send our finished masterpiece out into this nasty world on that spooky day."

"I didn't think of that." Alex typed their log line and attached their graphic novel's submissions agreement, synopsis, and story outline to the email. "Are you okay to fly tomorrow, though? Doesn't that go against your superstitious hocus pocus?"

"Majorly, but I have no choice. Harry's mum is throwing a surprise party for Budgie on Sunday."

Alex attached six pages of Lucy's art to the email. "Want to look it over before I hit send?"

She leaned over Alex's shoulder, her fingers sliding over the trackpad. "Yep. Yep. Looks good. Shame we can't send it to Marvel or DC."

"I know, but a smaller publisher might be the perfect fit for us.

With the biggies, we'd be fighting with *Wonder Woman* or *Captain Marvel* to even get noticed." Alex's finger hovered over the send key. "Ready?"

Lucy took a deep breath and crossed her fingers. "Hit it."

Alex's middle finger did the deed, and the familiar *whoosh* erupted from her laptop's speakers. "It's all happening!"

"Too right!" Lucy beamed. "Go on. Send another one."

Alex opened a fresh email and typed in the next address.

"Lex, this has been the best week of my life…"

"Aw, babe! I *knew* you would love it here. It's so loud and busy and brash—remind you of someone?"

"Ha, very funny. Well, that's *part* of it, but I also feel like I walked in Gran's shoes this week."

Alex glanced up from her laptop, puzzled.

"She lived here, when she was twenty-one."

"Seriously? Lucy, *that* is wicked."

"Yeah, it is. When you moved to London…I couldn't help but think of Gran, leaving home alone at the same age, starting over in another country."

"How long did she stay here?" Alex abandoned her typing, turning to her friend.

"Not long, just over a year. It was the late sixties. She rented a room in Brooklyn, and she tried to find work as a secretary, but people weren't exactly open-minded about hiring Jamaican immigrants. She moved to London when she could afford it."

"I had no clue. Wow, she was so brave." Alex's eyes flicked to her inbox and back to Lucy. "Did your gran draw, too?"

"Not even a doodle. She refused to buy me colouring books. She gave me colouring pencils and blank paper instead, saying, '*Draw what your heart sees.*' I was so little, I had no clue what she meant! I scribbled at first, but then I started drawing people with huge heads."

Alex laughed. “Like aliens? Did she watch sci-fi with you?”

“No, not until I was twelve—the *Doctor Who* reboot. Maybe my early art was inspired by my secret alien abduction!”

“Now *that* would explain a lot…” Alex raised an eyebrow.

Lucy smiled. “I drew all the time, and Gran encouraged me, even during uni applications. The careers advisor pushed me towards nursing, but Gran wouldn’t have it. She marched up there, full of piss and vinegar: ‘*My Lucy is an ARTIST. She’s going to art school.*’ She believed in me.”

Tears glistened in her eyes as she spun her ruby and gold ring. “I miss her so much. If I could be even half the woman she was…”

Alex wrapped her arm around her friend’s shoulder. “Lucy, you’re just like her. You’re loyal, encouraging, loving…if I could take all the best qualities and write myself a best friend, she would be you.”

“Lex…” Lucy sniffed.

“Gran would be so proud of you, Lucy, just like I am.”

“I hope so. The novel is for her as much as for me. I just wish I could tell her, ‘*I did it, Gran.*’”

“She knows, Lucy. I swear she does.” Tears began to sting Alex’s eyes. “I wish I had met her.”

“Me, too. She knew about how we met—online. She thought it was so cool, a best friend on the other side of the world. When I met you in person, a part of me believed Gran made it happen. If she couldn’t be here, she did the next best thing—sent you crashing into me.”

“Crash is the right word.”

Lucy chuckled and dabbed her eyes. “Gran would have loved you—and Joan.”

“Oh, my God—Joan would have *adored* your gran. Imagine, those two together?” Alex snickered. “Double trouble. Now *that’s* a story idea we should work on!”

Lucy jolted up in her chair, eyes wide with excitement. "Yeah!"

"They could be a superhero duo in their youth..." Alex squeezed Lucy's arm. "...or best friends in their golden years, side-stepping into a parallel universe, running an undercover superhero academy for *girls*—"

"Fucking hell, we *have* to do it!"

"We will, I promise." Alex resumed typing.

"Harry said I should find a way to celebrate Gran's life, and something arty would be bang on." Lucy piled her hair on top of her head. "You know, yesterday Harry took me to the street in Brooklyn where she lived."

"Aww!" Alex flashed a smile at Lucy. "He's the sweetest. You got the last good one." She sent off another email.

"Lex..." Lucy bit her bottom lip, letting her curls fall to her shoulders. "Harry...asked me to move in!"

"Lucy!" Alex sat back, grinning.

"It was so romantic! He asked while we were watching the sunset from Brooklyn Bridge. I *almost* cried, but I stuck the landing. Fuck, Lex, I am *so* becoming *that* girl!"

"That's not a bad thing. So, *are* you...moving in?"

"Um, not yet. I don't want to jinx it."

Alex laughed. "Typical *you*."

"I love him, but I also love my space and my flat...when Charlie's not home." Lucy shrugged. "I don't think I'm ready to give it up just yet."

"Nothing wrong with being happy with the way things are—"

Lucy's phone danced across the table with a text. "Oh, it's Freddie. About bloody time! Hang on, I'll read it aloud."

*It's done. Simon came out to his parents. He cried. Then he told them about our engagement. They cried. Then they popped open some cut-rate bubbly. I cried. Wait—I cried because I was*

*HAPPY, not because the champers was terrible. I love Si and his parents and you guys and the entire FUCKING world so hard right now. Give Lex a huge kiss from the future Mr. Simon Desjardins. Looks like Freddie Ryan finally gets his happy ever after. x*

"First you and now this?" Alex waved her hands in front of her eyes. "I'm gonna bawl."

Lucy couldn't contain her smile. "Love conquers all."

Seeing her best friend so loved up and happy, Alex didn't have the heart to disagree.

# FIFTY-ONE

*Two weeks later*

Alex hit print on her laptop. “Revisions coming up, Laurel.”

The ancient printer in the 59E59 artistic director’s office creaked, gasping what sounded like its last breath.

“Sorry!” Alex looked over her shoulder. “The printer’s being temperamental again.”

Laurel stood up behind her desk. “Sounds like the perfect time for a Starbucks run. The usual?”

“Please.” Alex pulled out a twenty-dollar bill from her purse. “My shout.”

Laurel accepted the cash and left Alex alone with the stuttering printer.

Thumbing through the revised pages of *Thirteen* collecting in the printer tray, Alex looked across the room, spotting the *Variety* website on Laurel’s open laptop. The photo, half-scrolled up the screen, was unmistakable—Mark. Curious, Alex couldn’t resist a peek.

Her two fingers swept along the laptop’s trackpad, revealing the headline and article dated the day before, July 25.

*Mark Keegan's Agent Coen Winkler Leaves Agency Following Actor's Departure*

Her eyes widened.

*Following Mark Keegan's departure from the Creative Talent agency, Variety has confirmed that his agent, Coen Winkler, has been let go. It's believed that the agent's exit is a result of Keegan firing Winkler and seeking representation elsewhere. Winkler was the agency's second in command in their London office and worked with up-and-coming clients including Keegan's* A Promise Unspoken *co-star, Fallon Delaney. A source at Creative Talent also confirmed that Delaney is no longer represented by the agency. Keegan is currently attached to the latest in the Full Throttle franchise,* Full Throttle 3: Blood Lust, *which also stars Dwayne 'The Rock' Johnson.*

*Neither Keegan nor Winkler could not be reached for comment.*

"Got yours, Wink." Alex scrolled the page to where she had found it and with a contented sigh, removed her *Thirteen* revisions from the printer.

# FIFTY-TWO

*Three weeks later*

Alex stuffed the latest draft of *Thirteen* into her laptop bag and grabbed her sunglasses and phone from the table. "Okay guys, see you Monday. Enjoy the weekend." She waved to Laurel and the set designer.

Her second-last weekend in New York City beckoned, and she couldn't wait for it to start. Late nights spent reviewing *Thirteen* meeting notes and early mornings plotting out the Gran-Joan graphic novel over FaceTime with Lucy had left her exhausted and desperate for some me time.

Rushing down the hall, she checked her texts one last time. Steve, an editor at a New York men's magazine, had been pursuing her via texts since they met at a 59E59 press night two weeks earlier. He was cute and fun, but Alex wasn't keen, politely declining his offers for coffee or drinks. Unfortunately, his latest text proved he had yet to take the hint: *Alex, I'll be in your 'hood this afternoon. Let's get that drink!*

She perched her sunglasses on her nose and rushed through the door, hoping for a quick, anonymous getaway…

*Ugh.* Midtown's August humidity had other ideas, smothering her like a heavy wet blanket. She could get used to the honking taxis and clogged sidewalks, but New York's suffocating summer heat always made her wilt. Turning right on East 59th, she slogged west into the sun, towards Central Park. The subway would be hot and crowded, so an hour or two spent reading under a shady tree was the perfect way to let rush hour simmer down before her underground descent into Columbus Circle Station.

"Alex!"

A male voice fought with the traffic and a helicopter hovering somewhere overhead. She squinted over her shoulder but didn't see Steve in the parade of hurried New Yorkers. *Thank God!* Alex was a common name. She kept going, her phone buzzing in her hand.

"ALEX!"

She ignored the text and turned around, her sudden stop drawing dirty looks from the sidewalk brigade fighting to get past. Rising to his feet, a guy with a scruffy moustache and beard, wearing sunglasses and a ball cap, was brushing the sidewalk off the butt of his jeans. His ratty white t-shirt was weighed down by a backpack. He looked homeless.

She impatiently turned away and glanced at her phone: *Marmalade.*

…*What?* The blaring taxi horns, rumbling car engines, and raised voices pushing past vanished. Alex swung around, her jaw dropping along with her stomach.

"Hello stranger." Mark squeezed the strap of his backpack, a quick smile raising the corners of his mouth. He stuffed his phone into his pocket and moved closer, his body swaying to the left and back again. Nerves? Or was the pavement too hot for his feet? He removed his sunglasses and hung them from his t-shirt's collar. His normally bright eyes were dull and weary, like life had taken a cruel toll since she had last seen him.

Alex laid a shaky hand on her pounding chest, barely able to speak. "Hi…?"

Mark tugged at his beard. "You look well, Lex."

*Jesus—you don't, Mark!* "What are you doing *here*?"

"Simon told me where to find you."

"*Simon*?" Alex backed up towards the building, out of the flow of foot traffic. Mark followed and leaned against the wall. He smelled of sweat, like he had just come from a muscle-blasting boot camp workout. *He flew up from Mexico to see me?*

"I know, right? I couldn't reach Freddie, so Si helped me out, surprisingly." He looked over his shoulder at the people rushing past.

With Mark's attention elsewhere, Alex's gaze fell to his feet and flew upwards: Converse, tear in the knee of his faded jeans, sweat stains on his t-shirt, hair peeking out over his ears…

He turned back, tilting in. "Look, can we go somewhere quiet to talk?"

Alex's eyes got lost in his beard. *Mark with a beard! What?!* Her sunglasses saved the day—Mark couldn't see her wide-eyed stare. His whiskers were dense and in desperate need of a pair of scissors. "I was headed to Central Park."

"Great." He nodded. "That will be great."

They walked along East 59th Street to the park's entrance just off Fifth Avenue, but their conversation didn't progress as far as they did: they talked about the steamy weather and nothing else. Alex took a sharp right, passing a cart selling hot dogs, pretzels, and soft drinks.

Mark fanned his face. "Can I get you water or an ice cream? It's *so* hot…"

"No, I'm okay, thanks," she said with a pinched smile. "But don't let me stop you."

He fished out several American dollars from his jeans pocket and joined the small line looping around the cart. Alex stepped back, her eyes studying every inch of her ex-boyfriend while he busied himself reading the cart's menu. His jeans hugged his ass and his t-shirt, discoloured with perspiration, stuck to shoulder and back muscles Alex hadn't seen before—souvenirs of his 'Rock'-worthy *Full Throttle 3* workout regime, no doubt. His hair crept past the back of his collar, most likely grown for his movie role. It was so odd. He looked *so* different, and yet…the same. She had intentionally stayed away from *Throttle*'s online press, but all clues today pointed to the fact that Mark's character was rough around the edges and frankly, a bit of a mess.

Water purchased, he turned back to Alex. "Christ, I could *never* live here." He cracked open the bottle and took a large satisfying swig. "It's too much. I always thought London was busy, but this is another level of insanity."

"How long have you been here?"

"A few hours."

"You haven't given it a chance." Alex began walking down a winding path, the park's famous pond to their left.

Mark sped up and tucked the water bottle under his arm. He lifted his cap. His hair fell past his eyes, reaching his nose. He swept it back, hiding it away again under his hat.

"So you're saying I didn't see the best of New York, camped out outside that theatre?"

"You camped out waiting for me…on that hot sidewalk?"

"Yeah." He winced. "For two and a half hours. Sorry if that sounds stalky, I didn't want to miss you. Simon was great, but he wouldn't give me the address of where you're staying. *Shit*, listen to me—that sounds even more stalkerish." His ramble took a break for another large gulp of water. "*This* is more like it." His eyebrows lifted approvingly as he took in the mature trees and green grass along the path. “It’s amazing how the street noise is muted. It reminds me of St. Stephen’s Green in Dublin—only *massive*. So…how are you?”

“I’m good. Thanks.”

“Freddie said *Thirteen* is going ahead off-Broadway. Alex, that’s so incredible. I’m so happ—”

“Thanks.” Alex stopped and crossed her arms. “Why *are* you here?”

“I need to talk to you.”

“Mark, I know about New Year’s. Really, you should have just FaceTimed from set—”

“Lex, I *know* you know about New Year’s. That’s not why I’m here, and I wasn’t on set. I came from Dublin.” His hand squeezed the water bottle. “I dropped out of *Full Throttle 3* two weeks back.”

“What?”

“Turns out it was an offer I had to refuse.” He smirked.

“A million-dollar refusal? Must have hurt.”

“You know I don’t care about the money, and you were right…the *Full Throttle* script was absolute fucking shite.”

“I never said it was shite.” She nudged her sunglasses up her nose.

“You didn’t have to—the look on your face at the Court did.”

“So, if you’re not doing *Full Throttle 3*, what *are* you doing?”

“Figuring stuff out.” He swallowed heavily, playing with the sunglasses hanging from his collar. “Look, there’s something I have to tell you…”

Alex inhaled deeply. Was this the truth Niamh said Mark owed her, so they could move on? Knowing Mark, if she sent him away, he would wait patiently for another opportunity. She didn’t want him sitting outside 59E59 again.

“Okay…follow me.”

She led Mark to a secluded bench with a view of Gapstow

Bridge and the pond. Several pairs of Mallard ducks quacked and playfully wiggled their tail feathers in the murky water while tourists sought shade and ice cream.

Mark sat down heavily and rested his backpack on the ground. His left foot stepped on top of his right, which fidgeted underneath. He half-smiled at Alex and looked away, opening and closing the cap on his water bottle several times.

"After the truth about New Year's came out, I needed time to think, somewhere away from London. Staying with Mum made sense. I was still attached to *Throttle*, so I hired a trainer there to continue my prep. I sought proper help for my stomach ulcer, too."

"Stomach ulcer? Since when?"

His eyes found Alex again. "Since October. I was diagnosed in Austria before Tom's wedding."

"*Seriously*? You've had it *that* long?"

"Yeah. It wasn't always bad, but when it flared, I would slink away to the loo, hide in a stall, gritting my teeth until my pain meds kicked in."

*An ulcer, not drugs...an ULCER. Another one of my assumptions—wrong!* "Mark, you should have told me."

"I *had* to hide it." He yanked his ball cap farther down over his eyes. "You would've told me to pull back on work, take a holiday."

Alex pursed her lips.

He looked down. "And you would've been *right*. I just didn't want to hear it—or slow down. Thing is, my body made that decision for me. By mid-June, I could barely climb out of bed."

"You should have listened to your body earlier—"

"I know, but the biggest movie of my career was coming up. I should have been feeling like I was on top of the world, right? Nope. I felt completely numb, detached from everything going on around me. I was in a really dark place but didn't know why. It scared me. I couldn't see a way out. So, six weeks ago—on your birthday, actually—I decided I needed help."

"What kind of help?" Alex lifted her sunglasses, leaving them on top of her head.

"A psychologist. I've been going twice a week." He tossed back the last of his water and took a deep breath. "Lex, I have to tell you something…a secret, one Freddie doesn't even know."

She swallowed. "Okay."

"I know you'll have questions. I promise, I'll answer every one, but…just listen, okay?"

"Okay." Alex wiped her sweaty palms on her skirt.

"In 1990, my uncle died. Dad inherited his pub, called Keegan's…"

Alex nodded. "Yeah…"

Mark looked down at his shoes. "And remember I told you my middle name was Kieran? It's not…I lied."

***MARK***
***Eighteen years earlier***
***Dublin, New Year's Eve 2000***

Keegan's was a popular, family-friendly pub with a pretty back garden boasting three picnic tables and enough room for kids to run around. Mark's earliest memories were of the pub filled with Celtic music, dancing, and raucous laughter. His dad, Finn, played guitar and sang in a band that performed Beatles and Van Morrison covers twice a week. Customers raved about his wonderful voice. When Mark was five and Grace was eight, Niamh became pregnant and had their baby brother, Kieran.

Like his older brother, the littlest Keegan was smiley and wouldn't stay still. Grace gave him the nickname Squig because he was always 'squiggling about', inquisitive and playful. She abandoned all her stuffed animals and colouring books to dote on him, smothering him with kisses. Mark tried to protect Kieran from Grace's overzealous efforts—having experienced them himself as an infant—and would cart him away to his room, showing off his toy cars and football posters. Their male bonding would end, though, when Grace showed up in Mark's doorway, and their loving tug of war over their adorable brother would begin again. A day didn't pass that the pub wasn't filled with the sweet sounds of the three Keegan children laughing.

When Kieran began walking and talking, Mark and Grace would rope him into their adventures, splashing around in their wading pool or hiding in the nooks and crannies of their large flat above the pub, jumping out to surprise him. He would squeal with a hilarious high laugh and beg his siblings to do it over again.

By the time he turned three, Kieran was Mark's constant shadow. He couldn't escape to the bathroom without Kieran banging on the door. Eight-year-old Mark loved him to bits and always made time to watch his silly TV shows, play with his cars, and make him laugh.

New Year's Eve was one of the busiest nights of the year for Keegan's. Before opening for the lunchtime crowd, Finn and his two sons enjoyed the crisp morning sunshine, kicking around a football in the frost-coated garden. Niamh and Grace were out on the hunt for a party dress, so the Keegan boys took full advantage, shouting and getting covered in dirt without female interference.

"Quick, Mark, pass it over!" Finn darted in front of their impromptu goal—two well-spaced flowerpots—but before he could claim the ball from his eldest son, his phone rang. "Oh, slipped my mind. Food delivery's out front." He waved at his boys. "You lads carry on. Kick it like Georgie Best! I'll be but a minute. Mark, look after your brother."

Mark kicked the ball softly to his mini-me.

"Mine, now!" Kieran giggled and ran after the rolling ball.

"Oi, Keegan!" The older boy living next door shouted from his bedroom window. "You're shite! Betcha a Mars bar you can't do ten keepsie upsies."

Mark squinted into the sunlight. The ten-year-old kid always picked him last for neighbourhood footy games and would rag on him non-stop in front of mutual friends: '*What do ice skates and Keegan have in common? They're both useless on a pitch*'...'*I don't know why coach compared you to Roy Keane. Keane's not crap.*'

Mark *had* to show him. He had to wipe that smug grin off his fat, pimply face. "You're on, you tool!"

*If I concentrate enough, I can do it!*

He hopped over to his brother and claimed the football. "Hey,

Kieran, watch this!" Mark went at it, bouncing the ball up in the air from foot to foot, keeping it off the frozen ground. He counted each strike aloud. "One…two…three…four…five…" He didn't take his eyes off the ball. "…eight…nine…TEN…*ELEVEN*…!"

He kicked the ball higher for a header then caught it in his hands. "YES!" He shouted towards the house next door. "See that, ya idiot?!" The mouthy neighbour responded with a sneer and his middle finger then slammed his window closed.

Mark tossed the football in his hands, his smiley eyes looking over his shoulder. "Squig, whatcha think of—"

The garden was empty…and silent.

"Squig?" Mark spun around. "Where'd ya go?" Mark peeked under the picnic tables and glanced over the leaf-filled wading pool. "Are you hiding again, Squig? Okay…this time, you've *really* got me." He opened the small garden shed and looked under the shelf where Kieran would sometimes curl up into a ball, playing hide-and-seek…but he wasn't there. Mark backed up, scratching his mop of black hair.

"Squig? *Okay*, you can come out now. You win!" He chuckled as his eyes swept the garden. "*You* can have that Mars bar…if I *ever* get it…" Mark looked over the back fence into the neighbour's yard. "Kieran…where *are* you?" He dropped the football and jogged around the side of the pub.

Mark's dad wasn't there. He must have gone back inside, putting away the pies that had just been delivered. Maybe Kieran was with him? But Mark didn't dare ask…if his dad found out he wasn't watching his brother like he had asked—no, he would find him, himself and avoid being told off.

Mark swung around, his eyes darting down the street and across the road. "Kieran! *Kieran*! Stop playing hide-and-seek—NOW."

A cheeky giggle rose from…somewhere. Mark leapt towards

the small garden in front of the pub. No sign of Kieran. He turned back to check next door.

*BEEP, BEEP, BEEP.* The delivery truck lurched into reverse in the pub's driveway.

Mark's stomach dropped.

*I wasn't watching Kieran...Keiran wasn't watching me...*

Mark's eyes widened as he froze in horror.

"WAIT! STOP!"

# FIFTY-THREE

Tears tumbled through Mark's dark eyelashes as he looked down at the Central Park bench. "My brother died from his injuries six hours later…on New Year's Eve."

Alex sat still, frozen in shock. She couldn't imagine Mark's grief or how he had bottled it up for so long—*what does something like that do to a person?* She felt her resolve, her determination to keep him at arm's length and out of her heart, melt.

Her tears made him all blurry. "Oh, God! Mark…" She threw her arms around his shoulders, pulling him in. His body shook against hers, lost in unrelenting sobs. She tightened her embrace, desperate to give him the privacy and sympathy he deserved. He hid his face in the nook of her neck. "It's okay. It's okay. God, I'm *so* sorry."

She cradled the back of his head and slowly rubbed his back, wishing more than *anything* that she could take away his pain. They hugged for several minutes with only their tears speaking for them.

Mark pulled away slightly, wiping his nose. Her hand lingered on his arm, hesitant to release him entirely.

"I blamed myself. Kieran wouldn't have wandered away

…wouldn't have *died* if I had just done what Dad asked—"*Look after your brother.*" But no, I had to show off to that stupid kid. Mum told me over and over, it wasn't my fault. Dad said so, too, but only once—at Kieran's funeral. I remember like it was yesterday. He kneeled down, pulled me close, and whispered to me, "*None of this is your fault, lad. None of it.*" But I couldn't see his face during the hug, Lex. How could I believe him if I couldn't see his face?"

Tears swelled in Alex's eyes, imagining eight-year-old Mark, desperate for absolution, for the love of his father to erase the horror and guilt tormenting his young mind. She squeezed his arm and reached in her bag for tissues for both of them. "I'm sure your dad meant it, Mark. It wasn't your fault. You were just a little boy…"

He gently shook his head and accepted a tissue. "Our family fractured, trying to cope. I felt detached from everyone, lost in my own bubble of guilt. Mum would go overboard with hugs, asking if I was all right every ten minutes. I always said yes, so she wouldn't worry. I had flashbacks…nightmares. I regularly mitched off school with stomach upsets. Gracie wouldn't eat and locked herself away in her room, refusing to play or see her friends, but it was always worse at night, when I'd hear Mum sobbing through the wall. Dad became a shell of his old self…didn't sing anymore. Late on weekends when he thought everyone was asleep, he would drink himself into a stupor in front of the telly. All the while, I *knew* it was my fault. He wouldn't have been sobbing if…if I had just watched Kieran."

He wiped the back of his hand across his cheeks as more tears fell, quickly sweeping them away. "Mum decided she couldn't bear to live in the pub anymore. They argued about it for months until we moved to our house. We tried to rebuild our lives, but couldn't catch a break. The jerk who bought the pub for less than it was worth leveled it and built a block of flats. I know Dad was gutted.

Mum got diagnosed with lupus in 2004 and couldn't continue her job mending clothes at the Delaney's dry cleaners…" He leaned his head back, blinked a bunch of times, and inhaled a shuddering breath.

Silent tears rolled down Alex's cheeks.

"Dad died two months later…I was twelve." Mark bit his lip, trying unsuccessfully to stifle his emotions. "I overheard Mum telling Mrs. Delaney once…she said it wasn't a heart attack that took his life, it was a broken heart from losing Kieran."

Alex grasped his hand. "Your poor family. I can't even begin to imagine…" She sniffed back her own tears, but it was no use. They raced down her warm cheeks and fell, seeping into her blouse.

Mark gathered a slow breath. "I don't know how Mum carried on after that. I *really* don't. She thought about taking us to London for the holiday Dad had planned but couldn't face it without him. Mrs. Delaney pitched in: making us meals, cleaning our house. She rehired Mum, giving her the full-time cashier position. That job was a godsend." He dried his eyes with a tissue. "Me, though…I was the *opposite* of helpful. I went right off the rails, drinking, hanging with a bad crowd. I was letting my whole family down, until our Gracie beat some sense into me one day."

Alex grinned through her tears. "*Sounds* like her. You're lucky to have her, Mark."

A faint smile curled his lips. "Yeah, I am, and Mum. She sat me down that night, and I thought, *I'm in for it now.* But she didn't yell—she *hugged* me, and cried. We both did. I hadn't cried since the day she told us Dad had died."

Alex could imagine Niamh: loving, but firm, trying to put herself in Mark's shoes, to understand his torment. "You have such a great mum."

"Yeah. She wasn't a pushover, though. I knew *some* kind of punishment was coming. Pulling me out of football seemed the obvious choice, but she put me in afterschool drama classes."

"Like you said in your email..."

He nodded. "Mum thought drama would help me. At the time, I didn't get it. I thought drama class was just goofing around, but it meant a lot to Mum, so I wanted to really give it a go, for her..."

"And did you take to it, right away?" Alex smiled.

"Ahh, Lex, I *loved* it. I loved being part of a group, a team really, creating something together. I loved playing with accents, getting lost in my imagination—being someone else for a while. Drama became my escape. Plus, I was *good* at it. People I didn't know clapped and cheered. I couldn't get enough. When I was up on that stage, I wasn't that sad little kid anymore, the one who let his family down, the boy everyone felt sorry for—losing his brother and dad. I knew it made Mum happy, seeing me throw my heart into something...positive."

As the tears faded from Mark's eyes, Alex spotted something else: *determination.* She squeezed his hand. He reciprocated by rubbing hers gently with his thumb.

"I'm still that twelve-year-old kid in a lot of ways. I think a part of me will always feel guilty, but the psychologist helped me see that Kieran's death was just a tragic accident—it wasn't my fault. And Dad...he *was* proud of me...I didn't let him down. I'd like to think he *would* be proud of me now, too, you know?"

"Mark, he would be. *He is.*"

"I hope so. I figured speaking to the psychologist might get my stress and ulcer under control, but I had no *idea* he would make me relive my childhood. It's the hardest thing I've ever done, Lex."

"You're strong—stronger than you think. I don't think I've ever been prouder of you."

Mark smiled. "Thanks. I always thought I was working nonstop for noble reasons: to make sure Mum was looked after, to lay a foundation for my life with you...but my therapist blew that theory out of the water."

Alex blinked rapidly. "I don't understand…"

"My guilt about Kieran and Dad's deaths was feeding my need to work *non-stop*. He said I've been using the *adulation* from fans and audiences as a sort of Band-Aid, to feel better about myself and soothe my guilt over losing them. His words bowled me over. They also made me think about when I gave Mum her new house."

"Really…why?"

"That initial happy feeling…being able to do something so BIG for Mum? I think part of me hoped it might dissolve my guilt for good, but it didn't. On some level, I needed another hit of 'Well done, son!' My therapist said that's why I didn't even consider saying no to anything Wink was putting in front of me. I desperately needed the praise that new projects, new press might get me. I'm basically a praise junkie, chasing jobs non-stop to feel better about myself. The bigger the project, the bigger the audience; the bigger the audience, the more approval; the more approval, the easier it is for me to bury my guilt—for a while, anyway…"

Alex sat wide-eyed. "God, Mark…he's *good*."

He nodded. "I'm not trying to make excuses or place the blame on my sub-conscious, but all those weeks spent away from home, looking for approval…" He hesitated, avoiding her eyes. "It was at the expense of what really mattered, the people I cared about, especially you, Lex." He looked up to meet her eyes.

A breath caught in her throat.

"So…" He squeezed her hand. "There you have it: Mark Keegan is damaged goods—but you have to name the problem to make it better, right?" A sheepish grin flashed across his face. "And I *am* making it better. That's why I fired Wink and Chelsey, why I dropped out of *Throttle*. That's why I'm continuing with counselling—to find healthy ways to deal with my guilt and grief. It's also why I'm here…to come clean, and to apologize, and to thank you.

You saw me pushing myself too hard. You *tried* to save me—"

"I was worried you'd work yourself to death. I just wanted a balanced life for us."

"But I wouldn't listen, would I? I was an arse, making *you* feel like you were being difficult. I am so *so* sorry. I was wrong, not you, and I know what I have to do now—what I *want* to do, and it's not working twenty-hour days or a budget-bloated action film with a shite script. I want my privacy back. I want a balance between work and my personal life. From now on, I'm taking time off—*weeks*, not days—between projects. I'll continue with *Lairds* for as long as they'll have me, and supplement that with what I love."

The old Mark, the one Alex had met in the Royal Court lobby…he wasn't gone. He was *here*. Adorable, caring…honest Mark. A smile overtook her freckles. "Theatre, maybe? Like *Constellations*?"

"Yeah, like *Constellations*." Mark smiled back. "I did that one for you, Lex."

"I heard…" She tossed her bangs out of her eyes. "I saw it, you know."

"I know."

"Freddie?"

Mark chuckled. "Yeah."

She glanced at her hand, happily held in his. "I kinda *stumbled* upon it one day."

"I planned to tell you about it on our anniversary. When that didn't happen, I almost told you when you were breaking up with me, but it was already…too late."

Mark shoved up the brim of his ball cap, exposing his eyebrows. Alex realized just how much she had missed them. She nodded, pensively. "You made me cry—I mean, your portrayal of Roland made me cry. You were *him*."

Mark smiled.

Alex looked away. "Did Fallon know…about Kieran?"

He shook his head. "I never told her about letting him out of my sight, no. Nobody knows, outside of my family. As far as the final police reports were concerned, Dad left two kids unattended for a few moments and tragedy struck."

Sitting in silence, their eyes met.

"Fallon never really knew *me*…not like you did, Lex."

*And no one knows me like you do, Mark.* Alex grinned softly into the passing breeze.

Mark let go of her hand and shifted. His knee collided with hers, but instead of moving it away, he kept it there. "I'm sorry it took me so long to introduce you to Mum."

"It's okay." She reached over, squeezing his hand. "I think I understand now…"

"No." He shook his head, rubbing his thumb over hers. "I felt terrible, keeping you apart. Mum's birthday seemed like the perfect opportunity to right a wrong, and the focus would be on the posh new bungalow. Everyone would be happy. I made Mum and Gracie *swear* not to say anything about Kieran, though. I still wasn't ready to tell you what happened…I was still too ashamed, I think. Part of me hated…*erasing him* from the day, but I did it anyway—for self-preservation."

"Then, I spotted his name—"

"Yeah. I didn't think. You were so upset about the key. I had to show it to you, so you would stop blaming yourself, but then you flipped the keychain over. I swear my heart stopped. I panicked—*lied.* I'm so sorry. I should have been honest that day. I hate myself for lying to you about…everything."

Alex exhaled slowly, staring at the light bouncing off the pond. "I can't judge you, Mark, not after what you've been through. I mean, I wish you'd felt like you could trust me with this when we were *together*. I wish you'd just told me and hadn't thought I would judge you, but I understand why you didn't. I'm glad you felt ready to tell me, even if it's later rather than sooner…" She looked into his eyes. "…but why now?"

"August 17$^{th}$" He gazed up into the cloudless sky. "Today would have been Kieran's twenty-first birthday."

Speechless, she laid a hand over her heart.

"I owed you the truth, and I owed it to Kieran, too…in a way. I know we can't go back in time, but I wish to God I could. If I had your beloved TARDIS, just for the day, I'd put the broken pieces back together again. I'd save everyone, save you and me, then be back in time for Kieran's birthday bash tonight…"

He smiled, but the grin didn't linger. "I did the next best thing. Woke up this morning and caught the first flight out of Dublin. I can't bring Kieran back, but I can make amends with you. I'm so sorry for lying, for always putting work first, for listening to fucking Wink…I'm sorry for *everything*, Lex. Wink may have had his own agenda, but I'm the one who allowed all of that to happen. I allowed you to get hurt, and I'm truly sorry. I know it's…" He took a long, deep breath, releasing her hand. "…too late for us, but there's never an expiry date on honesty, is there?"

*Wait…too late…for us?* Alex completely missed the rest of Mark's sentence. Her stomach clenched in sickly waves—Mark had buried the lede. He really *was* here just to tell her about Kieran and make nice, nothing more, mending the past so he could move forward like Niamh said. *Did I misread his body language, his intentions…?*

"Lex?" Mark leaned in. "You disappeared there for a sec. What are you thinking?"

"Sorry…"

"It's never too late to be honest, right?"

"No, you're right…" She lowered her head and fiddled with her skirt. "I'm glad you told me, Mark. I'm really glad you're working through this."

"One step at a time. I know it's a cliché, but it works…*right*?" Mark's kind expression told her that he knew.

"Freddie told you?" she asked.

He nodded. "You weren't posting on social media. I hope you don't mind that I asked him how you were. I felt glad…*relieved* you were having fewer attacks. I'm so proud of you for getting help."

"Thanks." A soft smile reached her eyes. "I'm glad you didn't cheat on me in Dublin, by the way…"

Mark squinted at the pond. "That's one night I'll probably never forgive myself for. New Year's Eve is always a difficult day, but getting wrecked, hitting the booze and drugs to forget about everything that happened…that's no answer." Mark bowed his head. "I'll never allow myself to fall that low again." He pulled out his phone. "…Wanna see pictures of Kieran?"

"I'd love to," she smiled.

Mark scrolled through his phone revealing a giggly infant, toothless with chipmunk cheeks and Michelin Man arms…

*This photo?* Alex remembered it from the family pictures on the wall at Niamh's old house… Her eyes widened. "I thought that was you!"

"Yeah," he chuckled. "We looked identical at that age." He swiped the screen. "And this one, three years later, still my mini-me." A photo of two little boys in pajamas, surrounded by toy cars, football boots, and wrapping paper, grinned back at her. "This was Christmas just days before…" Mark sighed. "if only…"

With a sympathetic nod, she held his gaze and then looked at the pond.

They sat in silence. A refreshing breeze blowing along the path swept Alex's bangs into her eyes, and Mark reached over and brushed them aside. His fingers lingered in her hair and slipped down the side of her face. The searing New York heat was no competition for Mark's touch. Goose bumps prickled her arms and the back of her neck.

Alex swallowed twice to ground herself. *Maybe I didn't misread his body language?* She smiled softly. "When are you headed back?"

"Tomorrow morning." His hand returned to his lap.

*Damn.* Her heart pinched. "What are you doing now?"

"Might take a wander, look around the park, go see the penguins…" He flashed a half-smile. "Then, check into an airport hotel for the night."

A wander on his own…a cheap hotel? Alex shook her head. If Mark had only ten or twelve hours here, he would spend them with her.

"No. Come to mine. Have a shower, a bite to eat. I'll make up the spare room for you."

"Lex, I *really* don't want to impose…"

"You're not. Besides, you look like crap." Alex smiled and grabbed her bag.

# Fifty-Four

Mark had been in the shower for nearly forty-five minutes. Alex tied her hair into a messy ponytail and chuckled—he was going to be so pruned-up when he climbed out of there.

His lengthy disappearance had gifted her the chance to let their conversation sink in while exchanging her scratchy blouse and skirt for a much cooler bra-less slip dress. She also dressed the king-sized mattress in one of the large, unused bedrooms with fresh sheets and laid a spare bathrobe on the end of the bed. In the kitchen, she adjusted the air con temperature, left a jar of Nutella on the counter—ready for Mark's breakfast in the morning—and stuffed Simon's leftover beer in the fridge. She wanted him to relax, feel comfortable. *She* wanted to relax and feel comfortable, too, but her mind—and body—had other ideas.

She couldn't stop hoping: *Does his naked presence in my shower mean he'll end up naked in my bed?* Seeing him—hearing his confession, holding him through his tears—made her want to go much further than just sharing a takeout dinner across the breakfast bar. *But isn't it a cheap play, making a move on him? He was so vulnerable earlier.* Even if he *was* willing to climb into bed, he was probably too tired. With the long flight, New York's heat, and the emotion of the afternoon, it was a miracle Mark was still vertical…

…and *still* lathering up in her shower.

*Oh, God!* She leaned on the bar, her thoughts drifting to visions of water trickling down his chest, down his thighs… She closed her eyes. *Not helping!* Her heart was racing even faster than when she recognized him on the street. The longer he splashed around in there, the greater her desire grew to yank open the shower's glass door and join him…to feel his lips against hers, feel their softness, their intent as they rediscovered all of her… *Lex, just stop!*

Four words flashed in her mind—*too late for us.*

What if the emotional rollercoaster of the past eight months had erased her from his heart, romantically? What if he wanted—needed—to be on his own for a while? *Could I blame him? Not really.* But embracing him, crying with him, she could no longer avoid the truth: she didn't want him to be on his own now, for a while, or *ever*. He said he didn't want the hectic life he had been leading. He said he wanted his privacy back, to make time for his loved ones. Hopefully, he meant it. She had never stopped loving him and maybe, he still loved her, too, but…how would she survive this evening if he only wanted friendship? What to do?

Freddie's words echoed in her head: "*Today isn't a dress rehearsal for tomorrow…live in the moment…there is no time for regrets.*"

She smiled. *Who knew?* Freddie Ryan: YouTuber, cheese and onion obsessive…*life coach*? *Cheers, Freddie.*

Leaving the safety of the breakfast bar, Alex strode over to the bathroom door. She took a deep breath, and her hand lunged for the door handle as the taps abruptly stopped, plunging the loft into silence. She froze. *CRAP!* The metal hinges of the shower's door creaked. Mark was finally on the move.

*No, no, NO!* What if he stepped out into the living room right then looking for more towels? She couldn't be caught lurking *there.*

She tiptoed a few feet away to the bookcase and fumbled with her iPod, sending music to the loft's sound system. Broods, a band from New Zealand she loved, filled the room with their trippy, indie pop. *Make like you're busy.* She ran over to the breakfast bar, and with her back to the bathroom door, started organizing plates and cutlery.

A few minutes later, the door snapped open.

A wave of steam, imbued with the light scent of his cologne, swept into the kitchen. Damp bare feet padded across the hardwood.

*Finally.*

"Lex?"

Alex turned around.

Mark's light purple shirt was half-open, exposing a glimpse of his chest. His messy beard? Gone, along with his moustache and sad brown eyes, which now smiled along with his mouth. A clean pair of jeans hung low from his hips. As his fingers buttoned up his shirt, its hem lifted, showing off the black band of his underwear.

*Fuck...fuck fuck fuck...* Alex caught her breath.

Mark's eyes crinkled in the corners as he took her in. He slicked his damp hair off his forehead. "Different outfit, Lex? You looked pretty before, but *this* dress…I might need another shower."

She blushed, struggling for words. "Thanks."

Mark caught her stare, his grin growing as he finished fastening his shirt.

*The A/C is still on, right?* Despite Alex's slip of a dress, every inch of her was burning up.

"Food should be here any minute." She turned back to the plates. Who was she kidding? Takeout wouldn't satisfy *her* appetite.

Mark strolled over, standing behind her. He was so close. His breath caressed her neck in waves. "Lex…"

She glanced over her shoulder.

*KNOCK, KNOCK, KNOCK!*

They both flinched, but neither looked away.

Alex weaved on the spot, lost in his eyes…his familiar scent. *Stupid food delivery.*

“Be right there,” she hollered as she slipped past Mark, grabbing her purse from the coffee table and disappearing through the door. A minute later, she returned, toting a large paper bag with a menu stapled to its top edge.

“*Thai*?” Scratching his temple, Mark followed her. “Since when?”

“I don’t know, since…May, I guess?” She dropped her purse on the floor near the sofa and set the bag of food on the bar. She tore it open, placing several cartons of noodles, sticky rice, and chicken on the counter. “I’ve grown to like it.”

Mark nudged closer, checking out their food haul. The warmth of his arm pressed against her bare shoulder sparked tingles all down her spine. Spring rolls and chicken satays were the last things on her mind.

“It’s still your fave, isn’t it?” She turned to face him. “Or did your tastes change? Shit, sorry, I should’ve asked…”

He leaned in and swept her bangs to the side of her forehead. “It’s fine, Lex.” His intense gaze left her eyes to savour her mouth. His fingers flirted through her hair, down to her collarbone, towards the dip in her neck.

The gentle sweep of his fingers…she shivered, unable to speak.

His eyes crinkled at the corners again. “I wasn’t sure in the park. You’re still wearing it…”

Her hand grazed the silver chain necklace with its Vespa charm, meeting his fingers. She refused to let go. “I still love it. It means…everything to me.”

Mark licked his lips. “*Hop on, hold tight, and remember to en-*

*joy the ride*." He reached into his jeans' pocket with his free hand, pulling out a slim silver keychain, free of keys.

Alex recognized it immediately and squeezed his hand—his keychain matched the one in her purse: June 5, 2015, their first date on his Vespa, zooming around London, flirting in the summer sunshine.

"I couldn't bring myself to give it back to you, Lex. I always hoped…"

His words weakened her knees and hastened her heart. Enough of this dance, enough skirting around what she really wanted—Alex knew *exactly* what to do.

Abandoning her necklace, she grabbed his neck and pulled him in, covering his lips with hers. All the months of hurt, of pretending she had moved on, faded as she welcomed him in. His tongue was familiar and possessive, owning her mouth and proving that no one else mattered. Going deeper, Mark moaned, stuffing the keychain in his pocket and locking his fingers onto her waist, grasping tighter and tighter as he pressed her against the cold stainless-steel fridge.

Its chill stung Alex's upper back, jolting her forward, firmly against him. She softly whimpered into his mouth, her hands roaming from his jaw into his damp hair and back down again, slipping along his neck and taking possession of his shirt. It didn't stand a chance. Dragging it quickly from his shoulders, buttons popped as she worked it down his arms to his wrists. The shirt's cuffs wouldn't budge. *Can't get the damn thing off!*

Mark laughed into their kiss and left her lips. "Looks like we're gonna need *a lot* of practice, just sayin'." He freed his hands from the cuffs and flung the shirt on the countertop with a knowing wink.

Alex's eyes widened. Mark's already fit body was leaner, more sculpted. All her fears that the crazy *Full Throttle 3* fitness regime would bulk him up like The Rock fell to the floor along with his jeans and her dress, which Mark lifted over her head in one smooth move.

"Oh, Lex…" Dropping her dress, Mark's hands drifted through her hair. He untied the elastic, releasing her soft waves. He sighed, his hands travelling down her curves, his eyes taking all of her in. "You're so beautiful. God, what you're doing to me right now…"

*I'm not doing enough!* Alex slid her fingers down his firm chest towards his stomach, a path she knew so well. Despite his familiarity, her excitement, she hesitated in the trail of dark hair above his boxer briefs, the soft material stretching with his arousal. "All this time, I've missed you…so much…"

"Christ, I've missed *you*." His thumb grazed her hip, stopping to rest just inside the waistband of her panties. "I thought about you…all the time."

She stared into his eyes as her hands skimmed downwards. Through the cotton, she felt him stir—hard and eager.

He gasped, his mouth invading hers without mercy, like her kiss held the secret to his survival. Teasing her, his tongue was warm and confident, coaxing Alex to fully trust him again.

She answered by grabbing his hand and leading him towards her bedroom. Memories rushed through her mind: how his body fit hers perfectly, how incredible he felt…would it be the same now? Different? *Better*? The ache to find out short-circuited all rational thought. *So what if this is just a one-night stand?* Even if they had no future, she wasn't about to spoil the present. Decisions, writing, London—everything could wait. All that mattered was *this* moment, being with the man she loved. She wanted to enjoy Mark now, while he was there, while he was hers.

They barely made it out of the kitchen—it was like Mark read her mind. He swooped her up in his arms, laying her down on the sofa before pressing his whole body against hers. He kissed down her neck to her bare breasts, circling and taunting them with his tongue and fingers while she buried her hands in his hair, pulling, twisting. She inhaled him deeply, dizzy with his scent—with her desire for more. Her moans prompted Mark to break away.

"I love you, Lex," he whispered between heavy breaths. "I never stopped…I never will."

Her heart couldn't soar any higher. It wasn't *too late.* His love and the sincere twinkle in his eyes was all she needed. "Don't fly to Dublin. Stay."

He bit his lower lip like he was preventing words from escaping.

"Don't leave tomorrow, or Sunday—don't go *at all.* I love you, Mark. Stay here with me?"

A wide smile lit up his face. "Yes…the answer's always yes!"

He lowered his mouth to meet her lips, but Alex took control, kissing him hard and deep while tugging his boxer briefs away from his hips. Mark grabbed hold of the material and finished what Alex had started, allowing her to shimmy out of her panties. She pulled him down against her, feeling his warm skin, his hardness against her hip, his thigh muscles tensed in anticipation.

"Lex…" Mark winced like Christmas had been cancelled. "I don't have a condom. We could just—"

A quick kiss on the lips and her hand dove to her purse on the floor. A feverish rustle…and her fingers reappeared with the foil-wrapped prize. She smirked. "Always '*Be Prepared*'—once a Girl Scout…"

Mark grinned and made quick work, putting on the condom and easing himself gently back on top of her. He tenderly traced her lips with his thumb, the want in his eyes matching hers. "Lex, it's always been you…"

Feeling his body weigh her down…wrapped in his warmth,

immersed in his breath, Alex's hands slipped down Mark's back. A trembling breath left her lungs. "Thank you, for finding me…"

A warm tear trickled down her cheek. His finger lovingly swept it away.

Kissing her softly, Mark pushed inside her. Alex inhaled sharply, rocking with him, falling into a rhythm she knew so well and had desperately missed. Eight months of heartache, loneliness, and misunderstanding were released with each caress, each kiss, their movements as one. Alex, The Girl Who Waited…was waiting no more.

# FIFTY-FIVE

Alex typed a text to Lucy. *Hot chocolate. With ALL the marshmallows!*

"Good morning, Mouse." Mark's smiley lilt drifted over her shoulder.

Hitting send, she set her phone on the bedside table and pulled Mark's arms tighter around her chest, inviting his warm body to spoon hers from head to toe. She giggled. "Waking up to your voice…it *is* a good morning."

Kissing her shoulder, Mark curled around her. "What were you doing?"

"Texting Lucy."

He cuddled into Alex's hair and inhaled. "Mouse, can we just lie here and never move?"

"We can lie here, but I'm nixing the *never moving* part. We have eight months to make up for, Keegan."

"It's a good thing I have no work lined up until October…" Mark's fingers traced the delicate *Doctor Who* quote tattooed on the inside of her forearm. "…since I'll be otherwise engaged as an amateur porn star for the next month and a half—in the shower, on the floor, against the wall…"

"Promises, promises. Don't get a poor girl's hopes up." Alex shimmied around to face him, her lips close to his. "Mark…there is something…"

"Yeah?" His eyelids hovered contentedly as he stroked her hip.

"Something you should know…" She bit her cheek. "No more secrets, right?"

"Right."

"Freddie may have said, but…*I* want to explain." She took in a deep breath. "This summer, there was a guy…"

Mark closed his eyes. "The guy from the Court?"

"Yeah." She winced. "I slept with him…but it was over before it really began."

"Lex, I can't lie—I *hate* that guy. I don't like that you were with him, but we both went off the rails, and that's *my* fault—"

"Mark—"

"No. If I had been honest with you, sought help sooner, we wouldn't have split…or slept with other people."

"I thought I'd lost you to Fallon…"

"Fallon was the first girl I slept with, yeah, but what I felt for her as a teenager or for two fucked up weeks this spring doesn't compare to how I've *always* felt about you, Lex. What *we* share—this *no-one-gets-me-like-you* love—is the real deal. You and me, we just make sense. We belong together."

A breath caught in Alex's throat. She swore her heart skipped a beat, hoping he really meant it.

He brushed the hair from her eyes. "I'm so grateful for this second chance. I'll do everything I can *not* to mess it up."

Alex wrapped her arm around him, laying her head on his shoulder. Mark reciprocated with a kiss that he held in her hair.

"I wasn't honest about my anxiety. I hid so much…since April last year."

"April? But...that's when we moved in together."

"*And* I quit the National, and Wink came on the scene and sent you jetting off everywhere..."

"Christ, Lex. Any one of those things is a massive change, but all at once? Fuck! I was such a shit boyfriend, not noticing what was going on with you—"

"You're not a mind reader, Mark. I didn't want you to worry or get distracted at work, so I lied. I would say I was fine on FaceTime and then spent the next half-hour bawling in the shower."

"Oh, Mouse, what are we *both* like?" He caressed her cheek. "Hiding the truth to spare the other..."

"I should've gone to therapy, but I wasn't ready. My doctor prescribed pills I didn't take. Getting help then felt like giving in, admitting I was a loser who couldn't keep it together on her own. Obviously, I know better *now*. There's no shame in getting help. There's no shame in being a work in progress."

"Too right. Seeing my therapist is the smartest thing I've ever done." His brows creased. "I hate that you felt you couldn't tell me..."

"But that's why I'm telling you *now*." Her eyes widened, hoping Mark was on the same page. "Things are different now, right?"

"Things *are* different now. No more secrets, no more hiding the truth. We both have to communicate more, yeah? Be upfront about what's going on with work, what we're feeling, even if it's not all champagne and roses." He kissed her softly. "So, what did you do...about your anxiety?"

"Two weeks before Christmas, everything was piling on top of me...I could barely hold it together. I was selling things to pay rent and buy gifts. Theatres were ignoring my emails..."

"Oh, *babe*..."

"A panic attack started over the stupidest thing—a ribbon I

couldn't curl on Lucy's Christmas present. I couldn't breathe, I was shaking…so, I took a pill and felt…calmer…but also dizzy, and my sight was blurry. I took one every day hoping the side effects would fade, but they didn't. I stopped taking them on Boxing Day. I thought they'd be out of my system by New Year's, and I could have a drink…"

Mark propped himself up on his elbow. "Lex! Is that why—"

"Yeah." Alex nodded sheepishly. "I'd never intentionally get hammered in front of your castmates. I mean, *really*…I picked the lamest drink on the menu."

"I wondered how mojitos could be so deadly!"

"I won't make *that* mistake again! I know I'll never be cured of my anxiety, but at least I've found a way to manage it."

"I'm so proud of you, Lex." Mark smiled kindly. "Okay, here's something else *you* should know…I didn't hurt myself in a snowball fight. I fell from a horse."

Her eyes widened. "I knew it!"

"*And*…I dislocated my shoulder."

"Oh, Mark!" She rubbed his arm. "I *knew* it was something serious."

"I *knew* you did, but that didn't stop me from carrying on the snowball charade! I only did it to keep you from worrying."

Alex frowned. "See? Lying is too much work. It's *exhausting*."

Mark shifted closer, his hand stroking her ass. "I'd rather conserve my energy for more pleasurable pursuits…"

Alex gave him a lingering kiss.

"Christ, eight months…I've missed so much. You've written a graphic novel. You now like Thai food! You jog, have two plays slated for the stage next year…is there anything else I've missed, Miss Overachiever?"

"Well, I quit jogging. Hated it! I fast-walk instead. Oh…I

binge-watched every episode of *Friends*."

"You *didn't*? Well, that's unbelievably hot." He raised an eyebrow. "How *you* doin'?"

Alex giggled. "*You're* the overachiever." Nose to nose, she kissed his lips as her fingers played in his hair. "I can't believe you learned Portuguese."

"Just a little for *Throttle*. I've already forgotten most of it, although this might come in handy: *Você está me deixando excitada*."

She shrugged. "No clue."

"You're making me horny." He grinned mischievously.

"You don't have to say it." Her gaze slid downwards to her thigh. "I can *feel* it."

Mark laughed. "I'm quite relieved I don't have to say that line on film, though. Not exactly Ibsen, is it?"

"Not even close." She looked up through her bangs.

"Speaking of Ibsen…" He weaved his fingers through her hair. "I'm gonna need some help learning lines…"

"*No*…really?!"

Mark couldn't contain his smile. "Yeah! I've been cast in *A Doll's House*."

"That's at the Old Vic!"

"Yep. Performances start in February. I'm the male lead—I'm playing Torvald."

"Mark!"

"I don't know what I'm excited about more…the role, or the fact that I'll get to sleep in my own bed for the foreseeable! I can't remember what that's like."

"But this play…it's a *classic. Wow*!"

"I know! Can you believe it? Me, on stage at the Old Vic. I'm still gobsmacked. This never would've happened if I was still with Wink, you know? My new agent is totally in sync with what I want to do—and when, and the timing is perfect. *Lairds* series four shoots in October, so I can prep for the play from November onwards…so get used to me being around—a lot."

"I think I could get *very* used to that." Alex smiled, hugging him tightly.

# Fifty-Six

*Two weeks later*

"Two weeks here, and only recognized once—at the top of the Empire State Building." Mark rushed into the bedroom, running a hand through his fresh haircut. "Ya know, New York is growing on me."

"Good, because we'll be back soon." Alex smiled, giving her open suitcase a final check. "Last year's Christmas gift will be put to good use! Skating under the Rockefeller Center tree, hot chocolate—"

"Better be marshmallows!" His eyes darted from the dresser to the bookshelves, searching.

"*With* marshmallows!" Her grin grew twice its size. "Everything's so sparkly, so hopeful at Christmas. You'll see. New York's decorations are out of this world."

Mark flipped over the bed's pillows and yanked open the bedside table's drawer. "Better than London?"

"Maybe bigger, but not *better*. Nothing's better than London…hey, what are you doing?"

"Lost something…the toy car I carry 'round."

"I saw it on the breakfast bar a few days ago. Maybe check your backpack again?"

"Yeah, I probably missed it." He walked across the room. "Ready to head home?"

"Yes." Her fingers brushed across the weathered cotton of a rolled-up top in her case. "I missed London, but I missed you more. Wait…" She captured Mark's passing hand and pulled him back, pressing her lips against his. "*There*. I'm making up for lost time."

His smiley eyes fell to her case. "Ah, *Mouse*? Have you turned pack rat? Isn't that my old sweatshirt? I thought you chucked it ages ago."

"I couldn't let it go. It made me feel close to you even when I wasn't." Her free hand brushed his stubbly chin. "I know I made you uncomfortable…before, talking about engagements and weddings—"

He opened his mouth to say something, but Alex laid a finger on his lips.

"All that matters to me *now* is being with you. Marriage doesn't prove your love for me. You coming here, sharing your past, being honest about everything…that's worth more than a wedding ring, and it's enough. Really, it is."

Mark pressed his forehead against Alex's. "But no wedding means no chocolate cupcakes."

"I can bake my own cupcakes, no wedding required."

He kissed her softly and pulled away with a satisfied smile. He kneeled in front of his new duffel bag and rifled through the clothes he had purchased over the past two weeks. "Did you see Freddie's text?"

She grabbed her phone from the bed. "The *Marlex, you better bring back a case full of Sno Balls and Ding Dongs, or don't bother boarding the plane* text?"

"That's the one. Demanding little sod. He should have asked

earlier."

"Nah, we can nip to the deli before we head to the airport." Her eyes travelled across her phone. "Oh!"

Mark stopped his search and looked over his shoulder. "All okay?"

"Text from Dad. Says…can't wait to see us next weekend. Joan's calling dibs on *you* for Sunday…there's some scooter rally she's dragging you to? You already said yes?"

"Yeah. She wants me to help her pick out a Vespa." He zipped the duffel bag and stood up. Scratching his neck, he left the room.

Alex giggled and peeked underneath the bed, looking for his toy car. "Mark, when you've got a minute, I want to show you something."

He rushed back, his hand rooting through his backpack.

"Any luck?" Alex stood up. "I'll check the other bedrooms…"

He froze, his eyes widening. "Oh, thank Christ!" He pulled out a small yellow car.

"I know how much you love that old thing. Kinda like me and Paddington." She sat on the bed and exchanged her phone for her laptop. "Some toys are too special to leave behind."

"This one was Kieran's."

They shared a wistful smile.

Mark returned his treasure to his backpack. "Whatcha want to show me?"

"Your anniversary present—*nine months late*." She opened Final Draft on her laptop. "Ages ago, you said you wanted to do something intimate like Simon Stephens' *Sea Wall*, so…"

He sat down, curling an arm around her waist.

"I wrote you a one-man, one-act play. It's called *Shockwave*."

"My God, Lex…" Mark fell silent, his eyes travelling across the screen, line by line, absorbing his girlfriend's script. Alex chewed her thumbnail, waiting.

After a few minutes and a severely gnawed nail on Alex's thumb, he sat back, eyes all misty. "Lex...what I've read so far, it's incredible, but...when did you do this?"

"I started after the final night of *The Great Gatsby*, just before we moved in together. Remember the after-party?"

A smile flashed across Mark's cheeks. "Jägerbombs and Pulp songs on karaoke!"

"You were wearing Freddie's glasses—"

"Pretending to be Jarvis Cocker! I still can't hear 'Common People' without pissing myself laughing. God, I *loved* Sheffield...the audiences, my castmates."

"Yeah, and you said to me, '*The theatre is my happy place. It's where I belong.*' But when Wink took you on, he only put your name forward for movies and TV. I wanted to give you what your heart desired."

"Mouse, I can't believe you wrote this for me." He shook his head, staring at the screen. "I'm...speechless. Thank you." He pulled her in for a kiss.

"I know there's no guarantee a theatre will pick it up..."

"I can't see it *not* being picked up. It's so emotional. When his boyfriend...turns out to have already died? It'll slay people." Mark smiled at Alex. "It would work really well in a smaller space like the Dorfman or upstairs at the Court. I'm definitely showing it to my agent next week." He continued reading.

Alex picked up her phone, diving into her email...scrolling, scrolling... That one could wait, that one was spam. Another message that could wait, another one...that *couldn't*. She opened it and gasped.

Mark snickered. "What did Freds send you now?"

"It's not Freddie." She swept her hair away from her face, revealing a massive grin. "A publisher wants our graphic novel. Mark, Lucy and I have *done it*!"

# FIFTY-SEVEN

*London, a month later*

"You're going to turn into a crunchy Italian nacho." Mark pulled his baseball cap down over his eyes and swung Alex's hand as they left Jamie Oliver's restaurant on Upper St. Martin's Lane. "I can't believe you got an extra order to go."

"They're not for me." Alex released his hand. "They're for you. I made you a care package for tomorrow morning."

Mark grinned. *Love this girl!*

Alex handed him the Jamie's takeout bag and reached into her oversized carry-all, pulling out a large plastic container. "I snuck out at lunch. I got Jaffa Cakes, Nutella snack pots, water, and now these nacho bites." She popped the lid. "Put them in here, and you're all set for your journey. Oh, I got a football mag, too."

"You thought of everything. Thanks, babe!" Mark wedged the bag into the container and snapped the lid shut. "I better call ahead—warn the *Lairds* costume department." He laughed. "I'm gonna need bigger britches when I get to Aberdeen." *Damn early train.* His smile faded. "I wish I could stay at yours tonight…"

"I know, but you'll be closer to the station. Just make sure you set your alarm…don't rely on Freds, okay?" Alex looped her arm through Mark's. "At least you have something to remember me by—our lie-in this morning *was*…" She raised her eyebrows.

*Remember? I've thought of nothing else all day!* Mark winked. "It *was*!"

"Gotta leave you wanting more…so you'll come back!"

"Deal, but only if you throw in more crispy nachos." Mark hugged his care package and smiled, his eyes not leaving her.

"Who says I'll share next time…*Pebble*?"

"*Christ Almighty*!" Mark jerked his head back. "Did Freddie tell you *that*? The lanky shite—I'll *throttle* him. Actually, scratch that—I'll *Full Throttle* him!"

They both laughed.

"Look, you can sniff Paddington to your heart's content, Insta the hell out of Tower Bridge, and hog all the crispy nachos, but call me *Pebble* again and it's the sofa for you, Sinclair."

Alex stopped walking. "The sofa?"

Mark's heart began to race. Seeking privacy, he pulled her close, behind a telephone box. "Well…yeah." His eyes drifted away for a moment, making sure no one was listening. "We'll have to *buy* one first…"

"Buy one…?" she whispered, raising a brow.

*I think she's ready, but…what if she's not?* Mark breathed deeply, hoping to calm his nerves.

"I miss leaving you love notes on our fridge. I miss making you grilled cheese sandwiches when you're on deadline. I miss holding you when we binge-watch TV—on *our* sofa, not Freddie's or Tom's…and I think *maybe* you might miss those things, too…?" He broke into a grin. "We're better together in our *own* flat…aren't we?"

A smile crept across her face.

"And Harry's old place is up for rent November 1st—"

"So, the London Fields lido, pub quizzes at the Cat and Mutton…" Alex leaned closer. "*Broadway Market*!"

"They're ours, if we want them." Holding his breath, Mark beamed. "Move in with me—*again*."

"You do make a killer grilled cheese, so I *could* be persuaded." Alex bounced on her toes and kissed him.

Mark let out a sigh of relief. *Thank Christ!* "Oh, I can be very persuasive, young lady." He pinched her ass and laughed as they walked towards a taxi rank.

# FIFTY-EIGHT

*London, fourteen months later*

*Join Lucy Hardy and Alex Sinclair signing*
STRANGELY GIFTED
*at Forbidden Planet*
*on Thursday, November 28, 2019 from 6 p.m. to 7 p.m.*

The basement of Forbidden Planet bustled with comic fans, early Christmas shoppers, and curious tourists, snapping up the girls' debut before heading out into November's chill. Freddie weaved between bodies, filming their comings and goings for a fandom feature on his YouTube channel.

"Thanks so much. Lovely to meet you." Alex beamed and handed an autographed copy of *Strangely Gifted* to the last person in line. She glanced at Lucy, sat to her right. "Wow! That hour flew."

"I'm gobsmacked." Lucy checked the time on her phone. "People actually showed up!"

"Isn't it cool?" Alex neatly stacked the remaining books. "I want to hug each person, buy them a drink…'*thank you*' just doesn't cut it!" She flipped her phone over. The screen glowed with texts.

Naomi: *Sorry, babe! Can't get away. Catch up tomorrow? x*

Dad: *Call when you can. Let us know how it all went. x*

Niamh: *So excited for you both, have a wonderful night! Gracie, Rhys & I send our love. x*

"Aw, Niamh." Alex nudged Lucy. "You have to meet her. She's so supportive."

"Like mother, like son." Lucy scrolled through Instagram, stopping on a photo of Mark reading their novel on the Tube. "*This*—fucking genius! It's now got over 8,000 likes. We owe Keegs—majorly—he sure pulled in the punters."

Alex leaned in, smiling. Mark's Instagram photo also signaled his limited return to social media. Long gone were his Wink-era Twitter and Snapchat accounts, and his website had undergone a complete makeover, ditching the brooding Harley shots in favour of professional photos from *Lairds* and his plays. A new category had been added, too—awards—including images of Mark posing with his Olivier for Best Supporting Actor for *A Doll's House*.

Her foot nudged two empty boxes and she glanced down at the floor. On top of her bag sat the latest issue of *Time Out*, opened to an interview with her boyfriend. The piece talked about his latest movie, filmed in Estonia last spring, hitting cinemas that day. He also spoke the previously unspeakable—taking a stand for their relationship. Her eyes caught a paragraph.

*"I don't talk about my personal life in the press, but I'm making an exception. In a few instances—online comments, in restaurants, at stage doors—a line has been crossed. If you're a fan of my work, please show my loved ones respect. They don't deserve to be followed or treated badly because I love them. They didn't sign up for this—I did."*

Alex nodded at Lucy. “I can't thank him enough.”

“You’ll find a way!” Lucy shot a look at Mark, laughing with Harry as Freddie filmed them near a shelf packed with books. “Oi! Keegan!”

Mark sauntered over, followed by their friends. “Hey, comic queens…that was quite the crowd, eh? How many sold?”

“All but three.” Alex put the remaining books into a Forbidden Planet bag. “But we can sell out if you, Harry, and Simon each buy one.”

“I have mine already.” Harry leaned over to kiss Lucy on the forehead.

“Don’t I get a freebie for sleeping with the writer?” Mark cheekily raised his eyebrows.

“You’re cute and all but…” Alex crinkled her nose. “No.”

“Well, it was worth a try.” Mark winked and slipped her a ten-pound note. He squeezed her hand, refusing to let go.

Lucy kneaded her left wrist, her grin slipping into a grimace. “How do you do this all day, Keegs? After thirty minutes, my hand was about to snap off—”

“Hey!” Simon appeared over Mark’s shoulder, wiping perspiration from his brow. “Sorry! Traffic from London Fields…”

Mark nodded. “Tell me about it. The roadworks…let’s just say that Mare Street lives up to its bloody name.”

“You can say that again, mate.” Simon gasped, out of breath, and slapped Mark on the back. “Am I too late?”

Freddie turned off his camera and hugged Simon from behind. “Lex saved you one.”

“Aw, cheers!” Simon slapped ten pounds on the table as Lucy pulled his copy out of the bag. “I didn’t want to miss out.”

“Only one left now!” Lucy signed her name with a flourish and passed the book to Alex. She began writing a heartfelt message.

Simon turned to Freddie. “I’d like to have a browse…”

"Go for it." Freddie backed up and lifted the strap of his messenger bag over his head. "I'm gonna help them pack up."

"For you, Si." Alex smiled and gave him his autographed book.

"Cheers! Won't be long, Freds." Simon flicked through *Strangely Gifted* and walked towards the stairs. Freddie watched him slowly disappear upwards, step by step.

"Si goes to a few cons and now look at him?" he whispered, doing nothing to help Alex and Lucy pack up. "Bandwagon-jumping git."

Mark laughed and grabbed the bag containing his book and the last unsold copy. "Isn't this what you wanted?"

"Well, *yeah*, but he's taking cosplay creation to an insane level. I'm talking designer sketches, expensive fabrics, freeze-framing *Doctor Who*, *Game of Thrones*, and *Lairds* over and over. Every single freakin' detail has to be…" He pinched his fingers together. "…*precise*."

"His twelfth Doctor costume for Halloween was incredible," said Harry, scooping up the Sharpies. "The bespoke red lining in his jacket—looked like he stole it off Capaldi."

"Before it was all Balenciaga this, Tom Ford that…now I get *that*, plus *this*." Freddie shook his hair from his eyes. "I can't escape into my fandoms because Si's already there—and now he's setting up a website to sell bespoke cosplay outfits. He says it will be a *nice little earner*." He elbowed Mark. "He's going to ask for the *Lairds* costume designer's deets—to pick her brain."

Mark buttoned up his coat, smiling at Alex. "Better hers than mine."

"Ah, *shaddup*." Lucy stood up and swatted at Freddie. "You love it."

"Joke all you want, missy," said Freddie. "He's whipping something up for you. I've seen sketches. He's thinking Daenerys

Targaryen."

Lucy's eyes widened.

"Yeah, with dragons and everything."

Alex shrugged on her coat and collected Mark's Vespa helmets from under the table. "Lucy, is it okay that Robbie gets the last copy?"

"Sure! Our first international sale! That will teach Tom not to show up."

"Where *is* Tom?" asked Mark.

"Naomi had a late audition…" Harry helped Lucy with her coat. "…and they've got Rex for the night. Tom's looking after him—solo."

"Ergh, I hope he packed away the sex toys." Freddie cringed. "Rex might confuse a penis ring for a teething ring."

Lucy burst out laughing, leading her friends to the stairs. "Freddie! He's almost four! He's done teething."

"Whatever." Freddie played with this camera. "So, what's everyone doing now?"

"I have a presentation tomorrow." Lucy held hands and shared a smile with her boyfriend. "Harry's prepping with me tonight."

Freddie smirked. "*Prepping*? I've never heard it called *that* before…" He followed Lucy and Harry up the stairs and glanced over his shoulder. "Keegs?"

"Lines to learn—pick-up scenes for *Lairds* next week. Sorry, Freds. Another time?"

"Sparkly Girl?" Freddie turned to Alex.

She shook her head. "I have edits…for this guy." Hands full with Vespa helmets, she bumped Mark with her elbow.

"January can't come soon enough." Freddie smiled. "*Shockwave* is gonna be epic."

"I hope so," said Alex. "The Dorfman run is almost sold out."

"It's only the National. No pressure, then." Harry chuckled.

"I think they're coming for Mark, not my words."

"Ahh, stop being so modest!" Mark kissed his girlfriend's cheek as they continued up the stairs. A playful smile crept across his face. "Did Lex spill about *Thirteen*?"

"No…?" Lucy squinted at her friend.

"I was going to, but the signing got busy—"

Reaching the top step, Mark beamed. "*Thirteen*'s transferring to Broadway next year."

"*Wh-What*?!" Freddie popped the flash on his camera.

"You're headed back to New York?" Lucy stopped dead, yanking Harry back by the hand. Her gasp turned into an exuberant grin.

"Yeah!" Alex laughed. "Laurel messaged me earlier…she's been working on a transfer since the run ended in June. It might happen around Halloween next year—*if* she gets the cast she wants."

"Ooh, the casting game starts now!" Freddie furrowed his brow, concentrating.

"Congrats, Lex." Harry hugged her. "Well deserved."

"So, whatcha reckon? Julie Walters for Joan? Or Dame Judi?" Freddie stashed his camera in his bag. "Ben Whishaw for the male lead…?"

Alex shook her head. "Honestly, I have *no* clue. Before they even think of casting, I have to figure out *my* schedule, see if there's a break during *Shockwave* rehearsals to fly over…"

Mark nodded proudly.

"Laurel wants me to meet some producing partners—"

"Well, honey, you better not be too busy schmoozing with theatre royalty to hang with *me*!" Freddie sighed.

Alex smiled. "Will next Monday or Tuesday night do?"

"Monday? Quiz night at the Cat and Mutton, then?" Freddie's face lit up.

"It's a date." Alex and her friends walked towards the store's entrance.

Freddie hung back. "Well, Simon's buying up the shop, so I better help him with his haul, get in his good books so I unbox it for my YouTube peeps—ha!"

"Okay, have fun, Freds. Tell Si goodnight." Mark followed a waving Alex, Harry, and Lucy outside. A small cluster of fans clutching the *Time Out* magazine waited for him, including Daisy. Alex left him to it, joining her friends by the curb.

"Hey!" Mark smiled. "Sorry, I can't sign tonight, but how 'bout a quick selfie?" He posed politely, the bag of books in his hands.

The fans were understanding and let Mark return to his friends…all except Daisy, who wanted more than selfie #336. The girl couldn't spot a hint if it was piano-sized and fell on her.

"Mark, can you FaceTime with my cousin?"

"Ah, sorry, Daze. I can't. I've gotta go, but have a good night, okay?"

Daisy lingered, watching Mark return to Alex's side. She finally gave up and lumbered away.

"So…" Harry waited until Daisy was out of earshot. "I guess we won't see you until *next* weekend?"

"Yep. Up to Aberdeen on Monday, back down on Thursday as *Shockwave* rehearsals start Friday…" Mark winked at his girlfriend as he stashed her books in the under-seat storage on his scooter. "Lex and I have a shopping date for *three* Christmas trees that night."

"Three?" asked Lucy. "Freddie's more of a bridezilla than Naomi ever was!"

Alex shrugged. "He just wants his Christmas theme done right. He's entitled—"

"Yeah, *entitled* is the word." Mark chuckled. "Just wait until my best man speech…"

Alex handed him a helmet. "I still have to write mine. I'm *excited* to be Si's best woman, and I'm really looking forward to the reception—our place is going to be so Christmassy." She looked at Harry. "Listen to me, *our place*. I still can't believe you sold it to us."

"Ahh, you've always loved that flat more than me…" Harry waved at his Uber SUV pulling up to the curb. "…even when Tom stole your bedroom and left you with that titchy box room!"

Alex giggled. "That closet's home to suitcases and Mark's footy gear, now."

Mark grimaced at Alex. "Wow, yeah. I keep forgetting you used to *sleep* in there."

"Well, don't forget *this*, sieve brain…" Lucy gently flicked Mark on the forehead as Harry opened the SUV's door for her. "A week Saturday, seven p.m., Southwark Playhouse."

"Tom's first preview?" Mark nodded. "Wouldn't miss it."

Lucy leaned out the vehicle's window. "Lex, call me tomorrow—lunchtime? I'll need to vent after my presentation."

"I will—good luck!" Alex watched her friends drive down Shaftsbury Avenue.

"So…" Mark tossed his helmet back and forth in his hands. "It's only quarter past seven, how 'bout we check out the Christmas lights? We might not get another chance with rehearsals, and the wedding, Mum and Gracie's visit. I can have us home by half nine…still plenty of time for writing and line-learning?"

"A Vespa adventure? *Hell yeah*! It's been a while…" Alex smiled, hugging her helmet.

# FIFTY-NINE

Mark straddled his Vespa, parked tightly along the curb of Vere Street, a wide smile permanently etched across his stubble. "What's your favourite so far?"

Alex snapped a burst of photos, capturing the twinkling Christmas lights that stretched high above the Oxford Street intersection. She bounced back to Mark's side, ignoring a honking black cab swerving past.

"I loved the massive reindeer in Covent Garden—oh, and the huge boughs of mistletoe dangling over Apple Market."

"Yeah, I know you liked *that* one. I still can't feel my lips..." Mark swayed to his left, avoiding Alex's swatting hand.

Several feet away to their right, four teenage girls stood near the entrance of a Debenhams store, taking sly photos and considering whether to approach. Alex was so mesmerized with London's festive finery that she didn't clue in.

"I liked Carnaby Street, the disco balls, but way too many people. I thought we were going to get swarmed."

Mark put on his helmet. "Yeah, we escaped just in time."

"The paps caught *you*, though. I bet those photos are online already." She took her helmet from Mark's hands. "Nice getaway-driving skills, babe."

"It's easy on these wheels." He glanced at the girls starting to stir. "Hop on, Lex! Let's get a closer look at the lights up ahead."

Alex climbed behind Mark and put on her helmet. "Ooh, can we head to Trafalgar Square after? I want to see the big Christmas tree."

"Yep, it's easy going from here. Ready?"

Alex squeezed his waist.

Mark revved his scooter and joined the flow of vehicles through the intersection. High-end New Bond Street, with its pricey boutiques and world-famous labels, sailed past as they travelled southwards on their Christmas lights hunt.

Reaching the short, pedestrianized stretch of the street, Mark slowed his Vespa to a stop, allowing Alex to jump off for more photos. Huge sprays of glistening lights, fashioned into peacock feathers, fanned out across the night sky, creating a magical archway over their heads. Still wearing his helmet, Mark walked anonymously alongside his scooter, weaving through upscale Christmas shoppers as Alex flittered back and forth across the pavement, taking photos and babbling excitedly.

"Wow! It's SO beautiful!" She climbed on the Vespa. "This is definitely my new favourite."

Photos happily snapped, they drove past Tiffany and Chanel and down a few side streets until they were zooming up The Mall with Buckingham Palace at their backs and Admiralty Arch and Trafalgar Square beckoning ahead.

Alex fondly remembered this route from their first date: their Vespa ride around London and the two hours they had spent in the sun, lounging on the green and white striped deckchairs in St. James's Park. An excited flutter tickled her stomach, just like it had almost three and a half years ago. She squeezed Mark's waist, prompting him to turn his head slightly, acknowledging the relevance of their whereabouts. That hazy June day they shared stories, '*took the piss*' out of each other, and began a friendship that would blossom into the kind of love Alex had only read about in books.

Cheese sandwiches…rollercoasters…the photos and texts that had followed an hour later—Mark's words: "*London is definitely better with you in it*"…

Passing under Admiralty Arch, the wheels of the Vespa jolted over a pothole, bouncing the happy memories from Alex's mind. Her soft gaze snapped into sharp focus.

Except for a few lights illuminating the fountains, Trafalgar Square and its four bronze lions were plunged into almost complete darkness. A huge Christmas tree stood in the centre of the public space, but no lights dazzled from its boughs. Only a shadow of Alex's smile remained. Mark slowed his bike and parked by the curb.

She laid her chin on his shoulder. "Booo! Didn't Traf Square get the invite? They're totally late to the Christmas party."

Mark turned his head. "Now that I think of it…these lights get switched on after the others. We're probably early by a week. Sorry, Mouse."

"It's okay." She laughed. "Gives me a reason to come back when they're lit." She lightly pressed her lips together. "So…home, then?"

"Tell you what…I know a pretty place you'll like, but it's a bit of a drive." He winked. "Hold tight?"

Alex perked up. "Holding tight!"

Mark retraced their journey, flying through Admiralty Arch and back down The Mall. Passing Buckingham Palace, he veered off in a different direction, joining Park Lane as it stretched north along the east side of Hyde Park.

Alex spotted the Animals in War Memorial, a beautiful bronze sculpture including two mules, a horse, and a dog, but Mark zoomed by so fast, she barely had time to blow the pup a kiss. Watching it disappear over her shoulder, she faced forward for the drive along the north side of Hyde Park. She cuddled into him, clasping his waist tighter as she laid her head on his shoulder.

After a few minutes and several traffic lights, Mark reduced his speed. Alex took it as a hint that they were near his intended destination.

Mark tilted his head back. “Welcome to Notting Hill, Lex!”

Alex knew the name but wasn’t familiar with the area at all, so rolling along its posh streets was a welcome adventure. Twinkling fairy lights blinked from the windows of candy-coloured terrace houses and quaint shops peddling on-trend jewellery and clothes.

As the Vespa slowed, a flapping black and white awning above a large shop window on her right stole her breath—*Biscuiteers!* The café famous for its exquisite hand-iced cookies, like the heart and bird-shaped treats Mark had bought for their second anniversary. *So sweet...he must have remembered me saying I wanted to visit!*

He parked along the curb and pulled off his helmet, his hair pointing in all directions. He peered over his shoulder with a mischievous smile, looking ridiculously adorable.

“You did good, babe! I could murder some cookies.” Alex eased her leg over the scooter and gasped at the festive window display of a gingerbread Santa riding a whimsical cookie train around a colourful—and edible—North Pole.

“It’s *adorable*! The website doesn’t do it justice. Let’s go inside!” She bounced over to the door. “Oh, noooo! It’s closed…shut at six.”

“Yeah, for everyone else. I arranged extended hours—just for us.” He waved at the woman inside, who promptly opened the door. “Hey, Evie, thanks so much.”

The smiley brunette nodded. "Great to meet you, Mark. Please come in."

He gestured for Alex to enter first and followed close behind. The shop manager quickly locked the door, preventing the Frank Sinatra holiday classic crooning through their speakers from escaping on the evening breeze.

Alex's wide eyes darted from the blue and white tissue flowers and snowflakes dangling from the ceiling…to the red bows and fairy lights hanging from the framed mirrors in the seating nook…to the twinkling lights hugging the tree. This café didn't just *do* Christmas; it *was* Christmas. The disappointing dark tree in Trafalgar Square was already forgotten.

"Evie, this is my girlfriend, Alex."

"Welcome to Biscuiteers, Alex." The manager grinned. "Please make yourself at home. We have some treats and hot chocolate with marshmallows prepared for you on the table, and if you need anything, I'll be downstairs. I'll leave you to enjoy."

"Thank you!" Alex's eyes flew around the boutique, its vintage feel welcoming and warm and inviting her to explore. *So much pretty.* "Where to look first?"

Mark laughed and kissed her on the temple. "Take your time."

Phone raised, she left Mark's side and began photographing the beautiful gingerbread houses. Next were the cute snowmen, reindeer, and ice skate biscuits.

She pointed to a familiar blue, green, and pink lovebird anniversary tin. "Mark, maybe we could get this one again? Enjoy them together in front of the TV…?"

"Absolutely." He smiled.

She skipped back to him, her eyes dancing with delight. "*This* place is my new Christmas favourite." She turned away and snapped a few more shots of snowflake biscuits. "It's a dream come true."

Festive Frank gave way to a sweet ballad on the shop's speakers. It wasn't Christmassy, it was old…and familiar…

Alex spun around. "Mark, isn't this that song—"

Mark was down on one knee…arm outstretched…an opened velvet box in his hand with a dazzling diamond ring, sparkling under the shop's vintage chandeliers. His eyes barely blinked, brimming with excitement and hope.

She gasped. *Oh. My. God. He's doing it…!* Her hands rushed to her mouth. "Mark!"

He took a deep breath. "Lex, I'm just an actor who reads other people's words. Most of the time, I don't know what to say without a script…but tonight, the words are all mine."

Tears began to glisten in her eyes.

"I never thought I could love someone as much as I love you, Mouse. No matter where I am, what I do, you're always in my heart." Mark's smile grew. "You're the writer, darling girl. So, I'm hoping you'll help me write a new story—the story of us. Alex Sinclair, will you hop on, hold tight, and enjoy the ride with me…for as long as we both shall live?"

"Yes!" Alex beamed through her tears. "The answer's always yes!"

Mark laughed. "That's my line, Mouse!" Tears shone in his eyes as he stood up, and he barely made it to his feet before Alex lunged to squeeze and kiss him.

"Not so fast." He licked his lips and removed the ring from the box. "May I?"

Alex, face wet with tears of joy, gave Mark her left hand.

"Lex, this is Mum's ring, the one Dad gave her when he proposed…"

He slipped on the white gold band with its pretty half-carat diamond. The brilliant gemstone, along with two delicate Celtic love knots hugging it on either side, caught the Christmas tree's fairy lights and glittered on her finger.

Alex had imagined so many times what this moment might feel like, but nothing had prepared her for this joyous reality. The exquisite ring, the beautiful setting, and Mark's cheeky, committed grin were perfection. *Sometimes real life is even better than your dreams...*

"It's engraved with the title of Dad's favourite song—it's about living in the moment with the girl you love."

Tears cascaded down her cheeks as she stared at her hand…lost for breath, lost for words. She pulled the ring from her finger.

Mark's shoulders deflated slightly. "Or I can get you something bigger, something new…"

Her eyes pored over the dainty engraving—*Here, There and Everywhere*—the Beatles song, the one Mark loved, the one playing *right then.* Alex's heart melted…the classic ballad, adored by his beloved father, would forever be part of their *own* story now. *So romantic, so perfect...so Mark.*

Alex returned the ring to her finger and grabbed his hand in a squeeze. "It's stunning! It's *exactly* what I hoped for. *Thank you!"* She threw her arms around his neck and kissed him.

A relieved laugh broke through Mark's lips. "Really? You love it?"

"I do. I *love* it!" She wiped her eyes. "And I love you!"

"Ah, my darling girl." He picked her up and whirled her around, careful not to topple the Christmas tree. "I could kiss you forever! I'm never gonna let you go."

"Tried that once—*never* again!" Alex held her fiancé tightly.

Mark set her feet back on the floor, but Alex still felt like she was flying. The gorgeous stranger who'd caught her eye over four years ago in the lobby of the Royal Court Theatre was hers. The ups and downs of their flirtation around London, months dating and living together, the separations for work, even their breakup—*all worth it.*

In that moment, Alex knew: the paths they had taken, though heartbreaking at times, had brought them closer than ever before—stood here tonight in Christmas heaven with Niamh's beautiful ring on her finger…

She pressed her mouth to Mark's, gently separating his lips with her tongue, their first proper kiss as an engaged couple. It was loving, tender, unhurried, and—perfect. They had shared thousands of kisses, but this one sealed the promise of a million more to come.

*Here, there and everywhere.*

# ACKNOWLEDGEMENTS

I would never have become a writer if it weren't for my mum. That colouring book story of Lucy's? Yeah, that's really mine. Mum wanted my sister and I to draw and write, to express ourselves without being penned in by lines or perimeters. Mum, I want to make you proud, even if you're not here to hold my books or give me hugs. In every story, there's so much of you that lives on. Love you, always.

To my husband, Darren…you bounce ideas around with me, read hundreds of drafts, and come up with the *best* names for Mark's TV shows and movies. When I'm doubting myself, you never do…you bring me hot chocolate and urge me to keep going. Love you, my BritBoy.

My sister Heather, my bezzie mate and the only person I want dancing by my side at a Duran Duran concert. Plus, she's a kickass artist—I love you!

To Zoey—the best dog ever. She understands the word 'work' and tries to prevent me from doing it every day, but her smiley face and beetle bum own my heart—always.

Big hugs to my family and friends: Bill and Tobey; Dad (miss you); Val, Tony, Jason, and Therasa; Sally, Bruce, Lily and Tiki; Esther and Danielle; Gabrielle; Sheila; Maria; Popie; Susan; Michal; and Helen.

Big love to Emily, Vicki, Charlotte, Renate, and Cristina—friendships that began online across miles, borders, and oceans. You are the Lucys to my Alex, in more ways than one.

Yasmin! Thank you SO much for my *LBTM* collage and your writing feedback.

Special thanks to my beta readers who kicked me in the pants and shook up the *London, Can You Wait?* universe when I needed it most.

Seamus and Paula, cheers for your Dublin help, and for taking me to the Stag's Head after Andrew's play.

Amy! Thanks for answering my questions about your experiences in London theatre and sharing crazy fan stories.

My amazing editor Caitlin (Editing by C. Marie) rocks! Thank you for your detailed eye and expertise in making *LCYW* polished.

Crystal Patriarche and BookSparks, thank you for your expertise promoting the heck out of my books to US and Canadian media.

Don't mind me while I fangirl over my fellow authors: cheers to Andrea Dunlop, the first author to graciously provide me with a fantastic book blurb; big hugs to Kristin Contino and Nicole Trilivas for their friendship and for loving London just as much as I do; and, to Colleen Hoover…thanks to you and Stephanie for featuring *LBTM* on Instagram. There aren't enough heart-eyed emojis in the world to express my gratitude to each of you.

Cheers to Teenage Cancer Trust and Biscuiteers for assistance with story details.

I'm a big nerd, so big love to *La La Land*—for keeping me sane this past winter, and for celebrating dreamers like myself.

To all the bloggers, BookTubers, and Bookstagrammers who championed *LBTM* and *LCYW*…I'm so grateful for your supportive reviews, in-depth videos, and gorgeous book photos.

And most importantly, I must thank all the book lovers who purchased and read *London Belongs to Me* and *London, Can You Wait?* and lovingly took Alex, Mark, and the gang into their hearts. You guys make it all worthwhile—thank you! Keeganites Unite! xoxo

# Glossary

Some people, places, or things mentioned in *London, Can You Wait* might not be familiar to all readers. Here are a few helpful explanations:

Ben Whishaw: BAFTA-winning English actor famous for his roles in the Bond franchise (*Skyfall* and *Spectre*), *Hamlet, London Spy,* and *Paddington* (Ben's the bear's voice). "Whishy" is also Alex Sinclair's favourite thespian—besides Mark Keegan, of course!

Dramaturg: A dramaturg collaborates with a playwright, bringing creative input and an objective eye to their work. Think of how an editor would work with an author, and you've got the idea.

Attachment: An attachment is an invite-only, short-term arrangement (ranging from two weeks to several months) between a playwright and a theatre. An attachment gives the playwright a desk, computer, and phone at the theatre. While there, the playwright writes and explores ideas, builds relationships with theatre colleagues, and takes advantage of the professional support available. The playwright is under no obligation to present a finished play to the theatre after their attachment, and the theatre doesn't have to produce whatever work the writer creates. The playwright usually receives a small fee.

National Theatre: The National Theatre is one of the most respected and popular theatres in the world. Its imposing cement headquarters on the South Bank is home to three theatres: the Olivier, seating

1,100; the Lyttelton, with its 900 seats; and the 450-seat Dorfman. It also offers several bars (including the Long Bar where Mark and Naomi worked in *London Belongs to Me*), restaurants, and a cosy café called Kitchen (Yes, *that one* featured in *LBTM*).

Mitching: Irish slang for skipping class. (Thanks, Seamus!)

Cyberman: A robotic villain in *Doctor Who*. (Lucy's Cyberman tattoo is based on a colourful, real-life design I spotted on a woman's arm at a 2014 con in Chicago. We chatted before John Barrowman's panel, and I'm still kicking myself that I didn't get her contact details!)

Swing: A performer in musical theatre who learns several ensemble roles so they can fill in at a moment's notice when an actor is sick or unavailable.

Time Out magazine: Free, weekly London magazine featuring articles and listings for the best in food and drink, entertainment, movies, and events in the city.

TARDIS: The famous blue phone box featured in *Doctor Who*. The Doctor and his companions use the TARDIS to travel through time. TARDIS stands for Time And Relative Dimension In Space.

Minger: An unattractive (or fugly) person.

Olivier Award: The most prestigious theatre award in the UK. Basically, the British equivalent of a Tony Award. (And yes, Alex is right—it would make a handy weapon!)

ADR: Stands for automated dialogue replacement. Sometimes an actor's dialogue in a TV show or movie has to be rerecorded if the background sounds are too noisy, or the lines cannot be understood on the original recording. The actor gets called into a recording booth to perform the lines, which are then 'looped' to match the movement of his/her lips on the screen.

Burying the lede: Journalism speak for failing to start an article with the most important part of the story first.

Pulp/Jarvis Cocker: Some may argue, but I think Pulp are the best band EVER to come out of Sheffield, England (Apologies to Lucy! As per *LBTM,* she adores the Arctic Monkeys). Jarvis Cocker is their nerdy, charismatic lead singer, famous for his eyeglasses, dry wit, and invading the stage during Michael Jackson's 1996 Brit Awards appearance. (Seriously, YouTube it!)

## MENTAL HEALTH RESOURCES

If you or someone you know suffers from anxiety or panic attacks, help is available:

United States
Anxiety and Depression Association of America - www.adaa.org

Canada
Canadian Mental Health Association - www.cmha.ca

United Kingdom
Anxiety UK - www.anxietyuk.org.uk